BLACKFISH CITY

BLACKFISH
CITY

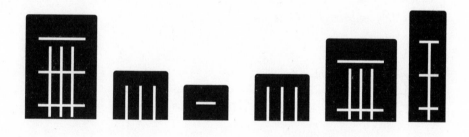

SAM J. MILLER

ecco
An Imprint of HarperCollins*Publishers*

HarperCollins books may be purchased for educational, business, or sales promotional use. For information please e-mail the Special Markets Department at SPsales@harpercollins.com.

FIRST EDITION

Designed by Michelle Crowe

Library of Congress Cataloging-in-Publication Data

Names: Miller, Sam J., author.
Title: Blackfish City : a novel / Sam J. Miller.
Description: First edition. | New York : Ecco Press, [2018] | Description based on print version record and CIP data provided by publisher; resource not viewed.
Identifiers: LCCN 2017016495 (print) | LCCN 2017031059 (ebook) | ISBN 9780062684844 (ebook) | ISBN 9780062684820
Subjects: | GSAFD: Dystopias.
Classification: LCC PS3613.I55288 (ebook) | LCC PS3613.I55288 B57 2018 (print) | DDC 813/.56—dc23
LC record available at https://lccn.loc.gov/2017016495

18 19 20 21 22   LSC   10 9 8 7 6 5 4 3 2 1

There is nothing safe about the darkness of this city and its stink. Well, I have abrogated all claim to safety, coming here. It is better to discuss it as though I had chosen. That keeps the scrim of sanity before the awful set. What will lift it?

—Samuel R. Delany, *Dhalgren*

BLACKFISH CITY

PEOPLE WOULD SAY

———————►

People would say she came to Qaanaaq in a skiff towed by a killer whale harnessed to the front like a horse. In these stories, which grew astonishingly elaborate in the days and weeks after her arrival, the polar bear paced beside her on the flat bloody deck of the boat. Her face was clenched and angry. She wore battle armor built from thick scavenged plastic.

At her feet, in heaps, were the kind of weird weapons and machines that refugee-camp ingenuity had been producing; strange tools fashioned from the wreckage of Manhattan or Mumbai. Her fingers twitched along the walrus-ivory handle of her blade. She had come to do something horrific in Qaanaaq, and she could not wait to start.

You have heard these stories. You may even have told them. Stories are valuable here. They are what we brought when we came here; they are what cannot be taken away from us.

The truth of her arrival was almost certainly less dramatic. The skiff was your standard tri-power rig, with a sail and oars and a gas engine, and for the last few miles of her journey to the floating city it was the engine that she used. The killer whale swam beside her. The polar bear was in chains, a metal cage over its head and two smaller ones boxing in its forepaws. She wore simple clothes, the skins and furs preferred by the people who had fled to the north when the cities of the south began to burn or sink. She did not pace. Her weapon lay at her feet. She brought nothing else with her. Whatever she had come to Qaanaaq to accomplish, her face gave no hint of whether it would be bloody or beautiful or both.

FILL

———————▶

After the crying, and the throwing up, and the scrolling through his entire contacts list and realizing there wasn't a single person he could tell, and the drafting and then deleting five separate long graphic messages to *all* his contacts, and the deciding to kill himself, and the deciding not to, Fill went out for a walk.

Qaanaaq's windscreen had been shifted to the north, and as soon as Fill stepped out onto Arm One he felt the full force of the subarctic wind. His face was unprotected and the pain of it felt good. For five minutes, maybe more, he stood there. Breathing. Eyes shut, and then eyes open. Smelling the slight methane stink of the nightlamps; letting his teeth chatter in the city's relentless, dependable cold. Taking in the sights he'd been seeing all his life.

I'm going to die, he thought.

I'm going to die soon.

The cold helped distract him from how much his stomach hurt. His stomach and his throat, for that matter, where he was pretty sure he had torn something in the half hour he'd spent retching. A speaker droned from a storefront: a news broadcast, the latest American government had fallen, pundits predicting it'd be the last, the flotilla disbanded after the latest bombing, and he didn't care, because why should he, why should he care about anything?

People walked past him. Bundled up expensively. Carrying polyglass cages in which sea otters or baby red pandas paced, unhappy lucky animals saved from extinction by Qaanaaq's elite. All of whom were focused on getting somewhere, doing something, the normal self-important bustle of ultra-wealthy Arm One. Something he despised, or did on every other day. Deaf to the sea that surged directly beneath their feet and stretched on into infinity on either side of Qaanaaq's narrow metal arms. He'd been so proud of his indolent life, his ability to stop and stand on a street corner for no reason at all. Today he didn't hate them, these people passing him by. He didn't pity them.

Fill wondered: *How many of them have it?*

A child tapped his hip. "Orca, mister!" A pic tout, selling blurry shots of the lady with the killer whale and the polar bear. Fill bought one from the girl on obscure impulse—part pity, part boredom. Something else, too. A glimmer of buoyant wanting. Remembered joy, his childhood fascination with the stories of people emotionally melded with animals thanks to tiny machines in their blood. Collecting pedia entries and plastiprinted figures . . . and scowls, from his grandfather, who said nanobonding was a stupid, naive myth. His plastic figures gone one morning. Grandfather was sweet and kind, but Grandfather tolerated no impracticality.

On some level, the diagnosis hadn't been a surprise. Of course he had the breaks. No one in any of the grid cities could have as much sex as he had, and be as uncareful as he was, without getting it. And he'd lived in fear for so long. Spent so much time imagining his grisly fate. He was shocked, really, to have such a visceral reaction.

Tapping his jaw bug, Fill whispered, "Play *City Without a Map*, file six."

A woman's voice filled his ears, old and strange and soothing, the wobble in her Swedish precise enough to mark her as someone who'd come to Qaanaaq decades ago.

You are new here. It is overwhelming, terrifying. Don't be afraid.
    Shut your eyes. I'm here.
    Pinch your nose shut. Its smell is not the smell of your city. You can listen, because every city sounds like chaos. You will even hear your language, if you listen long enough.
    There is no map here. No map is needed. No manual. Only stories. Which is why I'm here.

A different kind of terror gripped Fill now. The horror of joy, of bliss, of union with something bigger and more magnificent than he could ever hope to be.

For months he'd been obsessing over the mysterious broadcasts. An elliptical, incongruent guidebook for new arrivals, passed from person to person by the tens of thousands. He switched to the next one, a male voice, adolescent, in Slavic-accented English.

Qaanaaq is an eight-armed asterisk. East of Greenland, north of Iceland. Built by an unruly alignment of Thai-Chinese-Swedish corporations and government entities, part of the second wave of grid city construction, learning from the spectacular failures of several early efforts. Almost a million people call it home, though many are migrant workers who spend much of their time on boats harvesting glaciers for freshwater ice—fewer and fewer of these as the price of desalinization crystals plummets—or working Russian petroleum rigs in the far Arctic. Arm One points due south and Arm Eight to the north; Four is west and Five is east. Arms Two and Three are southwest and southeast; Arms Six and Seven are northwest and northeast. The central Hub is built upon a deep-sea geothermal vent, which provides most of the city's heat and electricity.

Submerged tanks, each one the size of an old-world city block, process the city's waste into the methane that lights it up at night. Periodic controlled ventilations of treated methane and ammonia send parabolas of bright green fire into the sky. Multicolored pipes vein the outside of every building in a dense varicose web: crimson chrome for heat, dark olive for potable water, mirror black for sewage. And then the bootleg ones, the off-color reds for hijacked heat, the green plastics for stolen water.

Whole communities had sprung up of *City* devotees. Camps, factions, subcults. Some people believed that the Author was a machine, a bot, one of the ghost malware programs that haunted the Qaanaaq net. Such software had become astonishingly sophisticated in the final years before the Sys Wars. Poet bots spun free-verse sonnets that fooled critics, made award winners weep. Scam bots wove intricate, compellingly argued appeals for cash. Not hard to imagine a lonely binary bard wandering through the forever twilight of Qaanaaq's digital dreamscape, possibly glommed on unwillingly to a voice-generation software that constantly conjured up new combinations of synthesized age and gender and language and class and ethnic and national vocal tics. Its insistence on providing a physical description of itself would not be out of character, since most had been coded to try their best to persuade people that they were real—Nigerian princes, refugee relatives, distressed friends trapped in foreign lands.

Other theorists believed in a secret collective, a group of writers for whom the broadcasts were simultaneously a recruitment tool and a soapbox. Possibly an underground forbidden political party with the nefarious endgame of uniting the unwashed hordes of the Upper Arms and slaughtering the wealthier innocents who ruled the city.

On Arms One and Two and Three, glass tunnels connect build-ings twenty stories up. Archways support promenades. Mas-sive gardens on hydraulic lifts can carry a delighted garden party up into the sky. Spherical pods on struts can descend into the sea, for underwater privacy, or extend to the sky, to look down on the crowds below.

The architecture of the other Arms is less impressive. Tight floating tenements; boats with stacked boxes. The uppermost Arms boggle the mind. Boxes heaped on boxes; illicit steel stilts holding up overcrowded crates. Slums are always a marvel; how human desperation can seem to warp the very laws of physics.

Fill subscribed to the single-author theory. *City Without a Map* was the work of one person—one human, corporeal person. He went through phases, periods when he was convinced the Author was male and times when he knew she was female—old, young, dark-skinned, light-skinned, poor, rich . . . whoever they were, they some-how managed to get hundreds of different people to record their gorgeous, elliptical instructions for how to make one's way through the tangled labyrinth of his city.

Not how to survive. Mere survival wasn't the issue for the Au-thor. The audience he or she wrote for, spoke to—they knew how to survive. They had been through so much, before they came to Qaa-naaq. What the Author wanted was for them to find happiness, joy, bliss, community. The Author's love for their listeners was palpable, beautiful, oozing out of every word. When Fill listened, even though he knew he was not part of the Author's intended audience, he felt loved. He felt like he was part of something.

Nations burned, and people came to Qaanaaq. Arctic melt opened the interior for resource exploitation, and people came. Some of us came willingly. Some of us did not.

Qaanaaq was not a blank slate. People brought their ghosts
with them. Soil and stories and stones from homelands swallowed up by the sea. Ancestral grudges. Incongruent superstitions.

Fill wiped tears from his eyes. Some were from the words, the
hungry hopeful tone of voice of the last Reader, but some were still
from the pain of his diagnosis. God, he was an idiot. Snow fell, wet
and heavy. Projectors hidden below the grid he walked on beamed
gorgeous writhing fractal shapes onto the wind-blown flurry. A
child jumped, swatted at the snow, laughed at how a fish or bird
imploded only to reappear as new flakes fell.

A startling, uncontrollable reaction: Fill giggled. The snow projections could still make his chest swell with childish wonder. He waved
his hand through a manta ray as it soared past.

And all at once—the pain went away. His throat, his stomach. His
heart. The fear and the nightmare images of twisted bodies in refugee
camp hospital beds; the memory of broken-minded breaks victims
wandering the streets of the Upper Arms, the songs they sang, the
things they shrieked, the things they did to themselves with fingers or
knives without feeling it. Every time he followed a man down a dark
alley, or met one at a lavish apartment, or dropped to his knees in a
filthy Arm Eight public restroom, this was the ice-shard blade that
scraped at his heart. This was what he'd been afraid of.

Fill laughed softly.

When the worst thing that can possibly happen to you finally happens, you find that you are not afraid of anything.

ANKIT

———————➤

Most outsiders saw only misery, when they came to Qaanaaq's Upper Arms. They took predictable photos: the tangled nests of pipes and cables, filthy sari fabric draped over doorways and hanging from building struts, vendors selling the sad fruit of clandestine greenhouses. Immigrant women gathered to sing the songs of drowned homelands.

Ankit watched the couple in the skiff, taking pictures of a little boy. His face and arms were filthy with soot; cheap stringy gristle covered his hands. He sat at the edge of the metal grid, legs dangling over the ocean three feet below, stirring a bubbling trough that floated in the sea. Bootleg meat; one of the least harmful illegal ways to make money out on the Upper Arms. He frowned, and their cameras clicked faster.

She hated them. She hated their blindness, their thick furs, their wrongness. Her jaw bug pinged their speech—upper-class post-Budapest, from one of the mountain villages the wealthy had been able to build for themselves as their city sank—but she tapped away the option to translate. She didn't need to hear what they were saying. They knew nothing about what they saw. Their photos would capture only what confirmed their preconceptions.

These people were not sad. This place was not miserable. Tourists from the Sunken World looked at the people of Qaanaaq and saw only what they'd lost, never what they had. The freedom they had here, the joy they found. Gambling on beam fights, drinking and dancing and singing. Their families, their children, who came home from school each day with astonishing new knowledge, who would find remarkable careers in industries as yet unimagined.

We are the future, Ankit thought, staring the hearty dairy-fed tourists down, daring them to make eye contact, which they would not, *and you are the past.*

She inspected the outside of 7-313. House built crudely upon house; shipping container apartments stacked eight high. A flimsy exterior stairway. At least these would have windows carved into the front and back, a way to let light in and watch the ocean—as well as keep an eye on who was coming and going along the Arm itself. And she saw something else: the scribbled hieroglyphics of scalers. Where the best footholds were, what containers were rigged to ensnare roof sprinters.

It had been years since she last scaled anything. She couldn't do so now. She carried too much with her. Physically, and emotionally. To be a scaler you had to be unburdened.

The tourists took no photos of her. They looked at her and could not see where she came from, what she had been, only what she was. Safe, comfortable. No shred of desperation or rage, hence uninteresting. The little boy had run off; they turned their attention to the singing circle of women.

Ankit stopped to listen, halfway up the front stairs. Their voices were raw and imprecise, but the song they sang was so full of joy and laughter that she shivered.

"Hello," said the man who answered the fourth-floor unit door.

Tamil; she knew maybe five words of it. Fyodorovna thought that Ankit's cultural comfort level would make these people feel less frightened of her—she'd been raised by a Tamil foster family—but that was stupid. Like most things Fyodorovna thought.

"My name is Ankit Bahawalanzai," she said. "You filed a constituent notice with the Arm manager's office?"

He bowed, stepped aside to let her in. A weathered, worn man. Young, but aging fast. What had he been through, back home? And what had it cost him to get his family out of there? The Tamil diaspora covered so much ground, and the Water Wars had played out so differently across South Asia. She took the seat he offered, on the floor where two children played. He went to the window, called outside. Brought her a cup of tea. She placed her screen on the floor and opened the translation software, which set itself to Swedish/Tamil.

"You said your landlord—"

"Please," he said, the slightest bit of fear in his eyes. "Wait? My wife."

"Of course."

And a moment later she swept in, flushed from happiness and the cold: one of the women from the singing circle. Beautiful, ample, her posture so perfect that Ankit trembled for anyone who ever made her mad.

"Hello," Ankit said, and repeated her opening spiel. "I work for Arm Manager Fyodorovna. You filed a constituent notice with our office?"

Every day a hundred complaints came in. Neighbors illegally splicing the geothermal pipes; strange sounds coming through the plastic walls. Requests for help navigating the maze of Registration. Landlords refusing to make repairs. Landlords making death threats. Landlords landlords landlords.

Software handled most of them. Drafted automated responses, since the vast majority were things beyond the scope of Fyodorovna's limited power (*No, we can't help you normalize your status if you came here unregistered; no, we can't get you a Hardship housing voucher*), or flagged them for human follow-up. A flunky would make a call or send a strongly worded message.

But the Bashirs had earned themselves a personal visit from Fyodorovna's chief of staff. Their building was densely populated, with a lot of American and South Asian refugees, and those were high-priority constituencies, and it was an election year. Word would spread, of her visit, of Fyodorovna's attentiveness.

She wasn't there to help. She was PR.

"Our landlord raised the rent," Mrs. Bashir said, and waited for the screen to translate. Even the poorest of arrivals, the ones who couldn't afford jaw implants or screens of their own, had a high degree of experience with technology. They'd have dealt with a lot of screens by now, throughout the process of gaining access to Qaanaaq. And anyway, her voice was sophisticated, elegant. She might have been anything, before her world caught fire. "We've only been here three months. I thought they couldn't do that."

Ankit smiled sadly and launched into her standard spiel about how Qaanaaq imposed almost no limits on what a landlord could or couldn't do. But that, rest assured, Fyodorovna's number one priority is holding irresponsible landlords accountable, and the Arm manager will make the call to the landlord herself, to ask, and that if Mrs. Bashir or any of her neighbors have any other problems, they should please message our office immediately . . .

Then she broke off, to ask, "What's this?" of a child drawing on a piece of plastislate. Taksa, according to the file. Six-year-old female. Sloppily coloring in a black oval.

"It's an orca," she said.

"You've heard the stories, then," Ankit said, and smiled. "About the lady? With the killer whale?"

Taksa nodded, eyes and smile wide. The woman was the stuff of legend already. Ample photos of her arrival, but no sign of her since. How do you vanish in a city so crowded, especially when you travel with a polar bear and a killer whale?

"What do you think she came for?"

Taksa shrugged.

"Everyone has a theory."

"She came to kill people!" said Taksa's older brother, Jagajeet.

"Shh," his mother said. "She's an immigrant just like us. She only wants a place to be safe." But she smiled like she had more dramatic theories of her own.

The children squabbled lovingly. Ankit felt a rush of longing, of envy, at their obvious bond, but swiftly pushed it away. Thinking about her brother brought her too close to thinking about her mother.

Taksa put her crayon down and shut her eyes. Opened them, looked around as though surprised by what she saw. And then she said something that made her parents gasp. The screen paused as the translation software struggled to parse the unexpected language. Finally *Russian* flashed on the screen, and its voice, usually so comforting, translated *Who are you people?* into Tamil and then Swedish.

Three seconds passed before anyone could say a thing. Taksa blinked, shook her head, began to cry.

"What the hell was that?" Ankit asked, after the mother led the girl into the bathroom.

The father hung his head. Taksa's brother solemnly took over the drawing she'd abandoned.

"Has this happened before?"

The man nodded.

Ankit's heart tightened. "Is it the breaks?"

"We think so," he said.

"Why didn't you call a doctor? Get someone to—"

"Don't be stupid," the man said, his bitterness only now crippling his self-control. "You know why not. You know what they do to those kids. What happens to those families."

"Aren't the breaks . . ." She couldn't finish the sentence, hated even having started it.

"Sexually transmitted," the father said. "They are. But that's not the only way. The resettlement camp, you can't imagine the conditions. The food. The bathrooms. Less than a foot between the beds. One night the woman beside my daughter started vomiting, spraying it everywhere, and . . ."

He trailed off, and Ankit was grateful. Her heart was thumping far too loudly. This was the sixth case she'd seen in the past month. "We'll get her the help she needs."

"You know there's nothing," he said. "We read the outlets, same as you. Think we aren't checking every day, for news? Waiting for your precious robot minds to make a decision? For three years now, when there is an announcement at all, it is always the same: *Softwares from multiple agencies, including Health, Safety, and Registration, are still gathering information, conducting tests, in order to draft new protocols for the handling and treatment of registrants suffering from this and other newly identified illnesses.* Meanwhile, people die in the streets."

"You and your family will be fine. We wouldn't—"

"You're young," the father said, his face hard. "You mean well, I am sure. You just don't understand anything about this city."

I've lived here my whole life and you've only been here six months, she stopped herself from saying.

Because I feel bad for him, she thought. But really it was because she wasn't entirely certain he was wrong.

The bathroom door opened, and out came Taksa. Smiling, tears dried, mortal illness invisible. She ran over to her brother, seized the plastislate. They laughed as they fought over it.

"May I?" Ankit asked, raising her screen in the universal sign of some-one who wanted to take a picture. The mother gave a puzzled nod.

She could have taken dozens. The kids were beautiful. Their hap-piness made her head spin. She took only one: the little girl's face a laughing blur, her brother's hands firmly and lovingly resting on her shoulders.

KAEV

Nothing was certain but the beam he stood on.

The gong sounded and Kaev opened his eyes. The lights came up slowly. A pretty standard beam configuration for this fight: Rows of stable columns and intermittent hanging logs. Poles big enough for someone to plant one foot upon. Three platforms, each large enough for two people to grapple on. He pressed his soles into the bare wood and breathed. A spotlight opened on his opponent, a small Chinese kid he'd been hearing about for weeks. Young but rising fast. The unseen crowd screamed, roared, stamped, blasted sound from squeeze speakers. Ten thousand Qaanaaq souls, their eyes on him. Or at least, his opponent. A hundred thousand more watching at home, in bars, standing in street corner clumps and listening on cheap radios. He could see them. He could see them all.

The city would not go away. Kaev's mind throbbed with it, with the pain of so much life surrounding him. So many things to be afraid of. So many things to want. He kept his lips pressed tight together, because otherwise he would scream.

Somewhere in the crowd, Go was watching him. She'd have one

eye on her screen, but the other one would be on him. And she'd smile, to see him step forward, to watch her script act itself out.

Kaev leaped to the next beam. His opponent stood still, waiting for Kaev to come to him. Cocky; clueless. The poor dumb thing thought he was smart enough to anticipate what would happen when. He had no idea who Go was, how much energy and money went into making sure the fight played out a certain way.

America has fallen and I don't feel so good myself.

The news had stuck with him in a way news didn't, usually. Because what was America to Kaev? Just one more place he might have come from. Every Qaanaaq orphan had a head full of origin stories, the countries they fled, the wealthy powerful people their parents had been, the immense conspiracies that had put them where they were. Kaev was thirty-three now, too old for fantasies about what might have been. He knew what was, and what was was miserable. He ran along the length of the hanging log, hands back, spine straight and low, trying to push it all out of his head.

And as he drew near to the kid, the fog lifted. The din hushed. Fighting was where the pieces came together. The kid jumped, landed on the far end of the hanging log. A roar from the crowd. Kaev couldn't hear the radio broadcaster's commentary, but he knew precisely what he would say.

This kid is utterly unafraid! He leaps directly into the path of his opponent, landing in a flawless horse stance. There's no knocking this guy into the drink . . .

Kaev always listened to his fights after they were over, a day or two later, when the buzz had faded altogether. Hearing Shiro describe his own efforts, even in the brisk, empty language of sports announcers, brought him a certain measure of peace. A flimsy, lesser cousin of the joy of fighting.

Instants before colliding with his opponent, Kaev leaped into the air and whirled his legs around. Smirking, the boy dropped to his knees and let Kaev's jump kick pass harmlessly over him—but did not turn around fast enough. In the instant Kaev landed he was already pinioning around, delivering an elbow to the boy's back. Not rooted, not completely balanced, nothing to cause real damage, but enough to make the kid wobble a little and stagger a step back.

A different kind of roar from the crowd: begrudging respect. Kaev was not their favorite, but he had gotten off a good shot and they acknowledged that. The imaginary Shiro in his head said, *I think Hao will proceed with a little more caution from here on out, folks!*

Now the younger fighter pursued him away from the center of the arena. At the outer ring of posts Kaev turned and kicked, but Hao effortlessly swerved to the side. At the precise instant that the momentum of the kick had ebbed, he leaned into Kaev's leg and broke his balance. Anywhere else and he would have been finished, but at the outer ring the posts were close enough that Kaev could stumble-step to the next one.

Yes. Yes. This!

He bellowed. He was an animal, a monster, part polar bear. Unstoppable.

In his dreams, sometimes, he *was* a polar bear. And lately he'd been having those dreams more and more. He'd spent six hours, the day before, wandering up and down the Arms in search of the woman who was said to have come to Qaanaaq with a killer whale and a polar bear, but found nothing.

He sniffed the air, his head full of pheromonic information from his opponent, and charged.

A dance. A religious ritual. Whatever it was, Kaev was free for as long as he fought. He wasn't thinking about how the spasms were getting worse, until he could barely speak a normal sentence. He wasn't worrying about how the money wasn't coming in the way it needed to, and pretty soon he'd have to move out of his Arm Seven shipping container and sleep in an Arm Eight capsule tenement or worse. He wasn't thinking about Go, and how much he hated her, and what an idiot he'd been for being so in love with her once.

He was one with his opponent and the attention of the crowd. And the whisper of cold salt water, thirty feet below.

They grappled until the gong sounded, and they separated. This was not some savage skiff-bed fight, after all. The Yi He Tuan Arena beam fights were Qaanaaq's most distinctive and beloved sport, and their champions won by agility and balance and swift punishing blows, not the frenzied grappling of street fighters. Kaev weighed more and his reflexes were better, but the kid had grace, had speed; Kaev could see why everyone liked him, why he'd been set out on this path to stardom.

Stars make money, Go had said five years ago. *People pay to see someone they recognize, someone they can root for. And you can't make a winner without a lot of losers.*

Which is how Kaev's life as a journeyman fighter began. The guy who other fighters fought when they needed to learn the ropes and build a lossless record at the same time. Not the worst career. Journeymen had a much longer shelf life than the stars, who usually fizzled out fast from one thing or another, but the stars tended to have handsome bank accounts to fall back on when they went bust. Journeymen were lucky to have a month's rent as backup.

He didn't mind the losing. He loved the fights, loved the way his opponent helped him step outside himself, and something about the fall into freezing water provided an almost orgasmic release.

What Kaev minded was the hunger, the anger, the empty feeling. What he minded, what he could never forgive Go or the crowds or the whole fucking city of Qaanaaq for, was that he hadn't had an option.

Hao was tiring, he could tell. The kid was too new, too rough. Kaev switched into stamina mode, feigning defense while modeling how to conserve energy and catch your breath while you're winded. Hao followed suit, probably without realizing what he was doing. A new trick he'd learned tonight. In moments like this, Kaev was proud of what he was. A rare and sophisticated skill, letting someone else win without the crowd knowing it. Hao's kicks connected with his thighs and side and the onlookers surged to their feet and for a few short instants Kaev was the king of Qaanaaq.

The kid got it. Kaev saw him get it. The instant when it all became clear; when he saw what Kaev was doing, and his attitude changed from cocky contempt to humbled respect. His eyes went wide, went soft. He paused—and Kaev could have kicked him in the back of the knee and followed up with a punch to the side of the head, sent him sprawling into the sea below; he saw precisely how to do it, even lifted his leg to unleash the attack—but do that and he'd cost Go millions, probably get a hit put out on him, and for what? A record of 37–3 instead of 38–2? Kaev pulled his wrist back, anchored himself; the crowd lost its mind, he could win it, their golden boy could be finished—

Laughter trembled up through Kaev. Joy threatened to split his skin wide open. He was a bird, he was bliss, he was so much more than this battered body and broken brain. In the split-second pause that gave away his advantage, he wanted to howl from happiness.

Hao's face looked sad as he leaped in close and slammed home an uppercut. Kaev had given him that, the humility of a genuine warrior. That was what made a true artist, the kind of fighter who would mean something to the cold wet salt-stinking people of Qaanaaq. Falling, Kaev focused on that. On Hao's career—like the careers of dozens of bright young boys who'd fought Kaev before him. What they might go on to do.

Kaev caught a glimpse of a woman graffitied onto the underside of the platform he'd fallen from. Clever placement: the sort of spot where no one but a falling fighter would see it. Programmed into an amphibious tagger-drone that swam in from the sea below and flew up to paint her in that secret nook. She was beautiful. Older, bald, dressed in either a monastic shift or a hospital robe, one hand raised, her face projecting saintliness. Beside her, three letters—*ORA*. Initials? For what?

He saw the metal fretwork that held up the bleachers, the places where the walls of the arena plunged down below the surface, the walkway around the edge where the fight doctor waited to fish the loser out of the water. He heard the howls of the crowd. But none of that was real. The water was all that was real. It rose up to him now, overjoyed to be embracing him again. Water was as much his native element as air. He was amphibious. He was a polar bear. He felt his body break the surface, felt the electric jolt of cold, and then he was gone, vanished, his body abandoned, its spasms and inadequacies and unfulfillable needs and mental fumblings all erased in a wash of stark bare ecstasy.

ANKIT

———————▸

Being a good scaler was easy. Ankit had been good. She was strong and she had decent reflexes. She could vault over barricades, evade drone cams, scamper along railings barely wider than a tightrope.

The difference between a good scaler and a great one was fear. Ankit was afraid. Fear held her back. She'd never been able to truly let go. She'd never been able to fly. She wanted to—wanted so bad it made her stomach heavy and her limbs freeze, poised at the edge of the abyss, unable to move.

She felt it now: the wanting. Standing between two tall ramshackle buildings, staring up at the handholds and footrests taunting her. The wanting, and the fear.

A whiff of pine needle smoke hit her before his voice did. "Hey, kid," he said from the dark space between two building struts.

"Hey," Ankit said, vaguely gratified to still be called a kid by someone. This guy had been doing errands for her since she actually was one. She stepped forward, out of the stream of traffic, into the cold wet dark of Qaanaaq's interstitial commerce. Clatter of Chinese chess tiles from the street behind her; ahead, in the deeper dark, two men grunting together.

"Missed you lately," he said. He wore three hoodies; their shadow softened the lines in his face.

"New delivery," she said, and handed him a screen. Small, cheap, used, its network connections all fried, but with a long battery and a solar-charger skin.

"What's on it?" he asked, smiling, excited. The guy was old, old enough to have had a whole life somewhere else before he came to the city. His pine needle cigarettes were resettlement-camp mainstays, smoked proudly and defiantly by recent arrivals, but as a result they had a certain outlaw appeal and even privileged Lower Arm kids could be seen smoking them.

"Books," she said. "Enough books to last a lifetime."

"You know her restrictions say only approved tech. She gets caught with this—"

"That's her call to make. If she doesn't want to take the risk, she can refuse it. In which case, give it back to me, if you're feeling generous, or just sell it. I'll never know anyway."

"Yeah," he said, and took the screen from her. "You're so trusting. All these years, I could just be stealing your money and pocketing your stuff. You have no way of knowing if any of it ever gets to her."

"You keep saying that," she said. They could not smell the methane stink of the nightlamps, out there. The darkness held her in its mouth; the sea wound around her like a cloak. Here was bliss, was freedom: a sliver of the thrill she'd felt when scaling. The pleasure she never felt in daylight, in the scripted comings and goings of her job. "I can't tell if it's your twisted way of making a confession, or some kind of criminal code of honor thing you want to stress." And even this felt good, the not knowing, the wondering. The city's rigid certainties were robotic, unforgiving.

Path bowed. Monkeys chattered from a warm nook beside the thermal pipes; the escaped endangered pets of the pampered rich, scavenging a living in Qaanaaq the way pigeons did in Sunken World cities. "Such are the twisted pathways of human trust. Any message for her?"

"The usual," Ankit said. "Tell her that I love her, I miss her, I'll get her out of there."

He put his hand on her arm. He smelled like a forest. "My inside woman is a good person. She'll pass your message on. Your birth mom is surviving, and that's all anyone can hope to do in the Cabinet."

"Thank you, Path," she said, and stepped back, out of the shadow, into the street, where the vortex struck her hard, and she walked against it, farther out onto Arm Five. A woman rolled on the grid, babbling to herself about demons and oppression, her body shaking with end-stage breaks.

Ankit's jaw chimed. She tapped it and heard the voice of her contact at Families. She'd messaged him that morning, trying to find out what might happen next with little Taksa, the girl with the breaks, and how she might be able to help.

Sorry to tell you, Ankit—Bashir family already deregistered. Awaiting transfer to the dereg ship. One good thing, transfer times have gotten crazy lately. Average wait six months. Ten thousand people flagged with the breaks, still in their homes. Waiting. Eventually they'll be processed and put on the continental shuttle. Allotted space at one of the coastal camps.

Beside her, three seagulls struggled against the wind, then yielded to it. She reminded herself to breathe.

Taksa's father had been right. *You know what happens to those families.* She'd heard. She hadn't wanted to believe.

One shred of hope: that six-month transfer wait. That must mean something. Nothing ever took so long. Maybe it was an AI malfunction, or a new protocol was about to be rolled out that couldn't be announced until some obscure other protocol finished its task.

Decommissioned glacial calving ships being refitted for refugee transport, maybe, or the Swedes completing work on another West African camp. Qaanaaq was governed by a hundred thousand computer programs, which mostly got along well enough, but sometimes contradictory or irreconcilable mandates sparked a squabble that brought an agency's operations to a standstill until a human or—more likely—another AI intervened. She'd have to look into it further.

Another tiny hope for Taksa, even slimmer than the first: asking her boss for help.

Idea for your campaign speech next week, Ankit wrote. *I've been seeing more and more cases of the breaks in my constituent visits. Families. Kids. No one is talking about it. Certainly not your opponent. People are scared. If you show leadership on this issue it has the potential to increase your lead by 3.6%.*

That last bit was made up. Put a decimal point on the end of a lie and her boss would swallow it every time. Whispering pleas to the universe—and wishing she could stop worrying about this family—Ankit headed home.

The problem was, Taksa's father was just so similar to the man who raised her. The same profound humility, sturdy and essential as his spine. They'd been profoundly decent people, which wasn't a given when it came to Qaanaaq. Or, really, anywhere. Few families would have helped a ten-year-old who demanded to know who her birth mother was—filed the appropriate paperwork, guided her through the bureaucracy labyrinth as best they could.

Both were dead now. Reflexogenic circulatory collapse, like so many of their generation—the decades-later legacy of corporate chemical spills and gas leaks. Pain in her chest made her stop walking, remembering. How well her father cooked, her mother's paintings. How they gave her the grandfather's name they were never able to have a son to carry. She resolved to buy some rice balls and make an offering before their photos—and then remembered that she made that resolution often, and followed through rarely.

She didn't deserve the place where she lived. Few scalers ever landed a spot that nice, a job as good as hers, and it was a comfort, sometimes, to reflect on how lucky she was, and how hard she'd worked to get there, when you thought about how many Qaanaaq orphans were dying slowly in the cold green light of the methane-sodium streetlights that very moment of new diseases no one understood and no one wanted to talk about, and how easily she could have been one of them—and Ankit had to work hard to see it that way, instead of the other way, the one where she was turning her back on her people, where she should be doing more, where she and everyone else who got a raw deal from this shitty city should get together and demand what was rightfully theirs, like those weird seditious anonymous *City Without a Map* broadcasts always seemed to be hinting at.

Sudden shock: her brother, grimacing out at her from a fading bootleg flicker flyer. Advertising an upcoming fight, already in the past. Listing gambling sites and odds.

She'd gone to see him once, after she'd gotten her job and could access her file from Families, learn that she had a brother she'd never known existed—though nothing more than his name. When she found him he'd been strung out on something, probably synth caff, after a fight, and she'd known at once that something was wrong with him, mentally—the breaks, she'd thought at first, but no, this was something different—and she'd spent too long without a family and she couldn't stop herself, and before she'd gotten through her carefully prepared introductory speech he had started gibbering and wailing. His friends had apologetically dragged him off, with a practiced ease that made her think these breakdowns were common occurrences. Since then she'd followed his career, at a distance. Become something of a beam fights fan. Betting on him every time, even though he always lost. He'd lost in this fight, to that new guy Hao who all the boys at her office were crushed out on.

Probably Path was lying. Probably the whole sudden-moment-of-human-concern thing was a business strategy, beloved by fences everywhere, favored by criminals whose specific niches required a never-ending leap of faith on their clients' part. Ankit really wouldn't ever know.

At fifteen, she'd resolved to never visit her mother again. Her presence made her mother agitated, which might land her in several days of psychophysical therapies that Ankit suspected would not have been out of place in a nineteenth-century mental institution. That was why she never wrote to her, never called. The Cabinet hadn't come by its reputation by accident; there was a reason some of Qaanaaq's toughest criminals flinched at the memory of it.

But Ankit was happy, in spite of everything. Helping her mother out, even when she wasn't sure if the help ever reached her, made her feel good. Less helpless, less alone. The night was cold and dark and she would not have had it any other way.

She slowed alongside a knot of stalls where women sold rotgut out of flasks. Raucous, ageless women. Ankit had bought shots off them when she was sixteen, one at the beginning of a night of scaling and a second at the end of it. She bought one now, from her favorite, whose stuff tasted like apples and pine sap. The woman's smile said, *I have watched you, I have seen you at your worst.*

"What's so crazy about it?" the vendor said to another. "All those animal workers, the ones who work with, what do they call them—'functionally extinct predators.' They make them get those shots so the things don't kill them. Like that boat out on Arm One where they got tigers and alligators still, for rich people to rent. Not such a big leap from that to something that would let you meld minds with a killer whale."

Ankit paused to savor her shot, and their conversation. Cold wind seared her skin, but inside she was a goblet of fire.

"My husband's friend worked for one of the juntas," another vendor said. "They all had their own secret unit they tried out all kinds of drugs on. He saw some shit, in Chile. Rumor was the Yucatán squad had a doctor, on contract from one of the North American pharma states, could inject you with something that let them hook your mind up to theirs, know everything you know. How else do you think they took down the narco government?"

"Narco government fell because of the rioting," said the third vendor, scowling skeptically. "Second Mexican Revolution. No magic beans or science fiction required."

"For all the good it did them."

They would go on all night like this. And Ankit could have stayed, buying more liquor or simply standing in the wind at the edge of the circle of the nightlamp light.

This was always here, waiting for her. Qaanaaq night. Her drug of choice. But she was a creature of the day now, and if she relapsed into her addiction she'd lose everything she had.

"See you next time," the woman said when she handed back her shot glass.

Her building's lobby was warm and bright, with that particular brand of heat the geothermal ventilation system provided—wet and slightly salty, or maybe that was her imagination. She slowed her step to appreciate the heat after being so cold, and then her jaw chimed. A surprisingly swift response; Fyodorovna could barely be bothered to do any work while she was in the office, let alone when she was out of it. Her voice filled Ankit's ear:

The breaks is toxic. There's a reason politicians won't go near it. People think it's just criminals and perverts. Whether or not that's true is irrelevant.

Ankit typed: *It's not true. And somebody needs to do something about it.*

Fyodorovna responded:

People are, I'm sure. Software is. Predictive is working on a plan of response. Scientists working on a cure. Something. Let the people whose job it is to worry about that worry about it.

Ankit knew her boss well enough to know that the conversation was over.

Upstairs, in her room, she pressed her forehead against the glass, looked out into the night, felt warm, felt bad about it. Turned her head to look in the direction she was always trying not to look.

It was still there, of course. It always would be. A sliver of building rising above the others in the distance: the Cabinet. The tallest building on Arm Six. Qaanaaq's psych ward. She'd scaled it, once. The only time she'd ever gotten caught. The only time she'd scaled something for a reason, to get inside, to get something out. To get someone out.

The last time she went scaling. The time that her fear held her back. Froze her solid. The black sea, so far below, the wind screaming into her, the building slick with frozen mist. They'd caught her there, rooted in place, and there'd been nothing she could do about it, and here she was now, rooted in place, still helpless. Still afraid. Still obeying the rules. It was Fyodorovna she feared now, not Safety, even though she knew they were both ridiculous, but the end result was the same. She was groundbound. She never took that leap, the one that made the difference.

And so: She did something stupid. Something she knew was stupid. Something she did anyway.

She took the photo of Taksa, which was blurry enough to not be identifiable as any particular person, but rather conveyed a very generalized idea of Happy Little Girl, and cropped out any background elements that might give away whose home it was, and autoqueued it to post the next day to Fyodorovna's channel, with one line of text—*If the breaks affects one of us, it affects all of us.*

And then, because she was still angry, she made another stupid decision. One she hadn't made in years. She opened her screen and navigated to the Cabinet site and submitted a visit request, to go and see her mother.

CITY WITHOUT A MAP:
BOUNDARIES

Do not talk about the past here. Do not ask your neighbor why they left wherever they are from; do not expect your newfound friends to wax nostalgic for homes that no longer exist. Perhaps the past holds more than merely pain for you, but you can't assume that this is true for anyone else. We want to smell it, taste it, hear its songs, feel its desert heat or summer rain, but we do not want to talk about it. The things we've been through cannot hurt us here, unless we let them. The fallen cities, the nations drowned in blood. The cries of our loved ones. Those stories we lock away. We will need new ones.

All cities are science experiments. Qaanaaq is perhaps the most carefully controlled such experiment in history. An almost entirely free press. Minimal bureaucracy, mostly mechanical, the city overseen by benevolent software. The shareholders pay the taxes, and they can afford to. If food and rent cost far too much, that is between you and the merchant. Swedish is the most common language, yet only 37 percent of the population speak it. There is no official language. There is no official anything. Qaanaaq has no government, no mayor. Those functions are fulfilled by a web of agencies deputized by Qaanaaq's shareholders. Each Arm elects a manager to serve a four-year term, to help citizens navigate the agencies and hold municipal employees accountable for bad behavior. These eight people are the only politicians in Qaanaaq, and they will be the first to tell you how limited their power is.

If the twentieth century was shaped by warring ideologies, and the twenty-first was a battle of digital languages, our present age is defined by dueling approaches to oceanic city engineering. Technologies developed for oil rig construction became fervently believed-in and fought-over doctrines. Conventional fixed platforms; spars; semi-submersibles; compliant towers; vertically moored tension leg and mini tension leg platforms. Standing on concrete caissons or long steel struts; tethered to the seabed. Ballasted up or down by flooding and emptying buoyancy tanks or jacking metal legs. Some are enlightened well-armed migratory utopias. Some are floating hells, like the plastic scrap reclamation facilities that ring the Pacific Gyre, every building and body blackened by soot from the processing furnaces.

In Qaanaaq, software calls most of the day-to-day shots, sets the protocols that humans working for city agencies follow. In theory a tribunal of actual human beings, appointed by the founding nations, could be appealed to in extreme cases, but to protect their anonymity even this process is mediated by software, prompting many to doubt the tribunal exists at all.

Some grid cities are less rigid about their boundaries. The Russian behemoth Vladisever set no limits on additional construction, and ten years later the city was an unruly metastasis. Hundreds of arms, impenetrably clogged waterways. In the end the army had to come in and clear it out, bomb the tangle of new structures, displace tens of thousands. Qaanaaq permits no more buildings, no new legs that reach to the seafloor. Tie any floating thing to it and you'll pay dearly for the privilege. These floating things, in turn, are free to charge others for the privilege of being tied to them, so that whole floating villages bob in the surf in spots, to be broken up or relocated when the agents of Structural Integrity decide they pose a danger.

One floating thing tied directly to the grid is the Sports Platform. A five-story boat the size of a soccer field, anchored at the far edge of Arm Four. Ice-skating rink on the top floor, exposed to the elements; every other story is a nest of subdividable courts and fields and tracks. The bottom level is three stories beneath the surface of the sea, and used mainly for training purposes.

These are things you need to know. There's a reason I'm drawing you this map, telling you these stories. Wherever you are now, no matter how trapped or hungry or scared you may be, these stories can provide an exit, an escape, a map to freedom.

Stories are how I survived, these long bound years. Now I can share them with you.

Like most modern sociopolitical entities—cities, states, nations—Qaanaaq operates a closed network. The Sys Wars that contributed so heavily to the old world's breakdown spawned a terrifying array of uncontrollable malware and parasites and infection vectors. Whole countries watched their infrastructure crumble not through the agency of foreign antagonists, but under the mindless attack of rogue rootkits and autarchical worms. Botnets whose authors were dead; scareware that infected Trojan horses to produce uncontrollable new monstrosities. The World Wide Web had proved a short-lived phenomenon. Limited global and regional networks existed, the flow of data so tightly controlled that they were almost unusably slow.

Qaanaaq's network, by contrast, is a glorious swirling sea of data, watched over by massive unpredictable mostly controllable AIs.

So many stories pass through it. I hear some of them, even in this place.

Here is one of them:

Eight days after the woman with the orca arrived in Qaanaaq, the killer whale was seen several times in the vicinity of the Sports Platform, which drew a dozen journalists to the sweat-and-popcorn-stinking structure.

They found her on the bottom level. Moving through a series of martial arts forms, wielding her bladed staff with such speed and skill that she clearly didn't need mammalian apex predators to keep her safe. The staff's handle was a thick long walrus tusk, precisely as the rumor mill had said, but its blade was stranger and more frightening than any of the stories had suggested. Huge, pale, curved, jagged. One reporter conjectured it was the jawbone of a sperm whale, carved and fretted and sharpened, and they all wrote it down as fact. The polar bear sat off to the side, hands and head caged. Journalists sat in the bleachers and smoked and called out questions.

"Where did you come from?"

"Why are you here?"

"Can we have an interview?"

Only the American stepped out onto the floor. For an American, the arrival of someone like her would strike a chord—collective guilt, most likely, over the bloody war that had been waged against her kind, or instinctive hate.

"Hello!" he called, moving closer, but she did not respond.

He stopped at the edge of swinging range. "I'm Bohr Sanchez," he said. "I run the *Brooklyn Expat.*"

She said nothing, just parried at the air fifteen feet from him. She leaped, stabbed, dropped, and rolled. The men and women in the stands behind him laughed, idly evaluated the odds of his being beheaded before their eyes.

"Are you nanobonded?"

Here she stopped. She stared. She took a step closer.

Bohr bit back his fear. His colleagues were watching. "I thought you had been wiped out. You're not worried? About the people who tried to exterminate you? Qaanaaq has more than its share of zealots, you know."

She moved faster and faster, her actions increasingly impressive. And frightening.

"Is it true that your people eschew all forms of technology?"

"How many more of you are there?"

She executed a leaping swing, her weapon falling out of her hands. Frustration? Sadness at a sore subject? The urge to murder him? And here she said something, finally. A single inarticulate roar.

FILL

———————◆

Fill hurried down Arm One, heading for Arm Three. His errand had made him late, but it was worth it. In each hand he held a freshly minted plastic figure, the first he'd had printed in ten years. Still warm. A polar bear, and a killer whale.

He wanted to believe. In magic, in science, in people who could bond with animals. He wanted to feel the excitement he'd had as a child, how big and crowded and possible the world had been back then.

He didn't, not quite, not yet, but maybe the plastic figures would help.

He walked down the Arm's central strip. The walkways were too crowded and he'd lost the knack for leisure since his diagnosis. His unhurried stroll had been stolen from him. He'd debated taking a zip line, but the queue at the central Hub had been too long, even at the first-class line. And there had been a demonstration—angry people in plastiprinted *kaiju* suits, chanting about a new wave of evictions out on Arm Seven, harassing the wealthy zip liners while they waited, because any of them could have been the shareholders responsible. Holographic monstrosities danced and scrambled in the air around them. When he was a kid, for a while, these had been everywhere. All the time. It had been years since he'd seen one.

Fill had recognized the buildings in the placard screens that they held up. He knew exactly who the shareholder responsible was.

Oh, Grandfather, he thought. *You bastard. Whose lives are you ruining tonight?*

He couldn't worry about that now. Life was too short to linger on ugliness. Last week, *City Without a Map* had talked about the crowds who gathered nightly at the end of Arm Three to watch the bright methane ventilation flares. Central Americans, mostly, with vendors selling some rich fermented purple beverage whose name he'd forgotten, and roving musicians playing a dozen rival species of *son,* but the street festival was popular with all kinds of recent arrivals.

This city contains so many cities, he thought. *So many lives I'll never get to live, so many spaces I'll never get invited into.*

"Fuck out the way!" screamed a messenger kid hurtling down the slideway, and Fill's first thought was *My goodness, that boy is hot* and then *Oh wait, that's a girl* and then *Christ, I have no idea what that is,* which led to a little internal rant about the complexities of modern gender among Qaanaaq youth.

Fill was still meditating on that, long after the kid had vanished into the green haze of the methane-sodium streetlights, when his jaw chimed.

Unknown caller, said the gonial implant, a flea-sized thing affixed to the corner of his jaw, like those used by all but the most wretched recent-refugee arrivals. Phone speaker and receiver all in one, conducting sound through bone to his ear and also recording what came out of his mouth. His screen's expensive software did the rest: *Thede Jackson, age twenty-five, spatial designer, North American parentage, gay, single. No previous history of contact; no flags for unsolicited commercial messaging.*

Gay, single, twenty-five; well, that was something. Maybe a friend had put them in touch, or he'd seen something about Fill and decided to take a stab in the dark. It had happened before. One of the perks of having a reputation. Fill tapped his jaw and said, "Hello?"

The voice said, "Ram?"

Fill said nothing. All of a sudden all the air was gone.

"Ram? Are you there?"

This Thede was drunk, and sounded like he was about to cry.

"Who the hell is this?" Fill said, surprised at his own anger.

"Ram, it's me," he said. "Please. I need—"

"This isn't Ram, asshole, as you goddamn well know."

Thede choked. "Um . . . what?"

"Did Ram put you up to this? Did you steal my handle out of his screen?"

"Ram, I—" But then Thede hung up.

Love is the gift that keeps on giving, Fill thought—how else could a man still make you miserable even after you'd broken up? He took a moment to curse Ram and every wonderful horrible minute they'd spent together. The boy had been unstable, incapable of telling the truth about anything, ever, and whether Thede was another jilted suitor or someone Ram owed money to didn't matter.

A bell tolled, on one of the tidal buoys. Fill had never bothered to learn what any of them meant. There were nursery rhymes about them, *Good boys ask how / Say the buoys of New Krakow* or something nonsensical along those lines. Every wharf rat and skiff urchin knew them by heart, could glean all sorts of helpful information about weather and the length of the day from them, but Fill, with the best education Qaanaaq money could buy, was stone-cold illiterate when it came to the complex tidal chimes.

Graffiti, on the side of the buoy—ORA LIVES, his screen translated from Spanish, and what could ORA be? The Qaanaaq net turned up nothing, and after ages a ping to the global net turned up a half dozen expired trade associations, dead softwares, villages and townships of the Sunken World. Someone's name, then?

Maybe the call had been a wrong handle, he told himself, because gay Qaanaaq was such a small world that it wasn't inconceivable that keying in a wrong handle would bring you the ex of the person you'd meant to call, except that his handle and Ram's were nothing alike.

Again, his jaw pinged. Thede again, but text this time. "Read," Fill said, and immediately regretted not saying "Delete." But life was like that. Dumb decisions you made in a hurry and then dealt with.

Ugh, I am so sorry. I'm drunk and disrupted and I don't know what happened. I entered the handle myself instead of auto-calling and I don't know. I have no idea who you are so I have no idea how I got you. Except that I sort of do. Or I think I do. Call me?

Fill kept walking. He was almost out to the end of the Arm now, running late, and his whole head felt funny, fuzzy, like something had come unmoored, and of course it was too early for him to be symptomatic, it had to be psychosomatic, but how could you know the difference with a sickness that was solely psychological?

Another text. "Read," Fill said, unsettled.

Okay. You don't want to call. I get that. But if you know Ram, you probably know him like I knew him, which means you two were fucking, which means you need to know this. I've got the breaks. I think I got them from him. And they're moving fast. It's a bad strain. I've been having these moments. Like just now. I swear, I remembered your number, even though I never knew it, because Ram did. It's like I know—

"Delete," Fill said, though the message was less than a third of the way through, and ran the rest of the way to the end of the Arm. He turned up the latest installment of *City Without a Map*, letting the vortex wash over him as an old man with a bad cough read someone else's words into his ear:

No one rules Qaanaaq, no class or race reigns supreme. Not the Chinese laborers who built it, not the global plutocrats who could afford to get out of their doomed cities before they became hell on earth, not the successive waves of refugees who filled it. And while of course it technically belongs to the shareholders, who lease the ground that every home and business in Qaanaaq was built upon and make obscene amounts of money with every minute that passes—they are invisible. After class warfare consumed the American grid city of New Plymouth and the rich were plunged burning into the sea, Qaanaaq's owners went to great lengths to conceal themselves.

To minimize unrest, the city founders broke with the urban past in several surprising ways. They decided against the repressive militarized police force that most old-world cities had depended upon. They kept the burden of taxation exclusively on the hyperwealthy shareholders. They limited the depth of democracy, giving politicians such small amounts of power that few fights broke out over elections or government action or inaction. They banned political parties, which had—in the view of the artificial intelligences that drafted these rules, anyway—been vehicles of mob rule and mediocrity more often than efficient strategies for decision making.

And so. Here you are. Here we both are.

Every so often, shut your eyes. Then open them, the slightest bit. Your home is gone, but it is not difficult to trick yourself into thinking you are home.

SOQ

———————▶

F uck out the way!" Soq screamed, and giggled at the prissy way the boy hopped. People like that thought they owned the whole Arm, and maybe they did, but on the slideway Soq was supreme.

Speed and wind made Soq's eyes water. They laughed, out loud, and the laugh became an ululation that lasted the rest of the way down.

Two ramps, side by side, ran down the center of every one of Qaa-naaq's eight Arms. Ten centimeters wide, capped with miniature maglev tracks. One going out from the central Hub, the other coming in from the far end. Each one started out five feet high, and over the course of the Arm's kilometer length tapered evenly down to ground level. A five-foot incline wasn't much, but a human of average weight could get up to some pretty astonishing speeds. In theory anyone with a pair of slide boots could use the slideway, but most people had long since abandoned it to the messengers. Slideway messengers were a barely tolerated menace, widely considered to be bloodthirsty caff addicts on errands of minimal legality who wore weighted clothing to speed them up and razor blades affixed to their clothing to casually disembowel anyone strolling near the center of the Arm without paying attention. Most messengers relished this assessment and went out of their way to embody it.

Soq leaped, arriving at the end of the ramp. Slide boots were supposed to kill the magnetic repulsion as they arrived at the programmed destination so that you came to a calm, precise stop. Like most messengers, Soq had overclocked that function. Nothing was going to slow them down but them. Soq soared through the air, clearing the buffer zone and landing with a jolt beside a bench in the central Hub.

A man whose head Soq had just passed over yelled, "Watch it, you—" and then paused, unclear how to gender the insult.

Soq was beyond gender. They put it on like most people put on clothes. Some days butch and some days queen, but always Soq, always the same and always uncircumscribable underneath it all.

New job, whispered their implant. *Arm One. Number 923. Envelope; paperwork only.*

"Assign it to someone else," Soq said. "I'm late for dinner with my mother."

"You don't have a mother," said Jeong, the on-duty human for the day, interrupting the automated dispatch software.

"I'm sure I do," Soq said, weaving through the evening foot traffic of the central Hub. "Everyone has a mother."

"So they tell me. But you're not having dinner with yours tonight."

"I'm tired," Soq said. "I can't deal with another run past those Arm One assholes."

"Fine," said Jeong, who truly did not care one way or another. He had been a messenger himself, before some kids experimenting with targeted mini-EMP software accidentally scrambled his boots and locked him in place while speeding down Arm Six at three hundred kilometers an hour, which dislocated both legs and fractured his pelvis. Now he lived vicariously through his "kids," including the ones who were older than him. "But listen. Got a complaint from your last run. Lady said you were extremely rude."

"Of course she did," Soq said. "Old nasty American thing, she didn't like it when she used 'he' to describe me and I told her, very politely and patiently, because I have this conversation way fucking more often than anyone should fucking have to have it, that I prefer 'they' and 'them' pronouns."

"Weirdest thing. My screen conked out as I was in the middle of logging the complaint. Didn't save to your record. I'll have to get that thing looked at."

"Thanks, Jeong. Anything from Go?"

"Nothing," he said. "You know I'll let you know as soon as I hear."

The dispatch line silenced itself. Soq pressed their gloved thumb to pinkie, and the slider boots demagged. An evening crowd ahead, a couple hundred humans passing through the central Hub, mostly from the labor arms out to the residential ones, although like everything else in Qaanaaq the flow of people was complex.

A bad idea, Soq knew, to get so focused on Go. Didn't mean anything that the woman whom many believed to be the city's most powerful crime boss had sent her first lieutenant to hire Soq out for some stringer gigs. Deliveries, tails, handoffs, creating commotions to help someone escape someone else. There were no promises in this line of work. Soq was a good slide messenger, and a good messenger had many of the qualities that made a good underling—speed, fearlessness, lack of respect for the law—but that didn't mean Go would ask Soq to formally join her organization.

Getting crime boss patronage was like winning the lottery: it'd be great, but it probably wasn't going to happen to you, so stop banking on it.

Stop thinking about it. Stop imagining the day when you will be the crime boss, the feared one.

A straight line, from Arm One to Arm Eight. An irony that never failed to amuse Soq, how simple it was to pass from gorgeous luxury to huddled crowded filth. *How else would it be so easy for them to suck us dry?*

Arm One always did that. Made Soq bitter. Angry. The anger usually ebbed a bit on their return to Arm Eight. Just seeing the banner above the entrance was soothing: four of the hundred or so Mandarin characters that Soq and every other Qaanaaqian knew—新北希望, Xīnběi Xīwàng, *New Northern Hope,* the name the Chinese sponsors had given to their new city, just as the Thai and Swedish had done, three names for a city and none of them stuck, because the people wanted something else, something not beholden to anyone, and so the Inuit name for a Greenland coastal village that had just been swallowed up by the sea became the name of the floating city as well. Qaanaaq II, at first, or Q2, and then just plain Qaanaaq as its predecessor was forgotten.

The smells of food hit Soq first: broth and basil, mint and trough meat. Food stalls were forbidden in several of the better Arms, and they were the primary draw for the outsiders who dared enter Eight. After that it was the crowd that calmed Soq down, its rhythm, the peculiar intangible atmosphere of energy and ease. They didn't know Soq, these people, but they knew Soq belonged. Who knew how they knew it, but they did. Just like Soq knew who was and who wasn't of the Arm. This was home.

People, stacked everywhere. Sleeping capsules piled between buildings, strapped to the struts that supported the bigger ones. They looked sad and ragged, but they belonged to royalty, relatively speaking. Prime real estate; the best spots, held down since the days when Arm Eight looked like Arm Six looked now. The women and men who lived in them were the eyes and ears of the Arm, essential elements of the commerce in information.

Farther down the Arm, Soq entered the shadow of the tenements.

A twenty-year-old attempt by the Qaanaaq shareholders to provide stable indoor housing for the unfortunates of Eight, these massive buildings formed the densest population pocket. Denser than Kowloon Walled City or the South Bronx Boats or anything else the Sunken World had produced. The outsides thickly vascularized with red, black, and green pipes. Most of the families, soon after taking up tenancy in these halfway-comfortable spaces, began building walls and partitions and hanging sheets and anything else to rent out space to their neighbors. In the tenements, it was not unusual for fifty people to live inside one apartment. Soq had had friends in the tenements, come to birthday parties for them. Seen the incredible resourcefulness of the tenement dwellers: city plumbing lines "augmented" with snarls of new pipes to shuttle water and sewage and heat, the spliced power lines, the informal stairs and passageways, the sweatshops where grannies made fish balls or repurposed circuit boards in a room where ten iceboat workers slept. And even these were relatively privileged positions, held to fiercely by families and the crime syndicates, who paid the shareholder fees as a gesture of goodwill to the residents.

Three scaler kids cawed at Soq. They squatted in the struts of a building, feeding a ragged-looking monkey. Soq slowed, trying to see whether their intent was hostile, and then decided they did not care. Mostly scalers and messengers got along well, and lots of people were both, but some scalers could get nasty with the "groundbound" grid grunts they felt so superior to.

Three-quarters of the way out the Arm, Soq stopped at a noodle stand. This one had little stools and a tarp on each side to keep some of the wind off. Soq was swallowed up in clouds of hot steam smelling of five-spice powder. Home was noodles. Home was food and warmth. Soq paid, took a stool, shut their eyes, and meditated on the moment, its beauty, its peace. The coldness of the wind and the warmth of the food and the fact that everyone eventually dies. Letting go of everything they did not have, every ugly thing they'd seen, every moment of pain they'd felt that day, the day before, every day to come.

Soq smiled in the rising steam.

"Hey, Charl!" they called when the first spoonfuls of soup had reached their belly, and pointed chopsticks at the greasy screen Charl had hung on a lamppost. On the news, nine military factions had submitted claims for international recognition as the legitimate successor state to the American republic. Some were as small as twenty people in a boat. "How long do you think it would take a tri-power boat to travel from where the flotilla was to Qaanaaq?"

"'Bout a week, I'd imagine," Charl said, for Charl loved these logistical problems. "Unless they had a ton of gas, in which case it might only be a day or two. Why—you want to go scavenge?"

"No," Soq said. "Just wondering when we might start to see refugees."

Soq was thinking of the orca. Of the woman who'd mysteriously arrived with a killer whale in tow, so soon after the flotilla bombing. Because how had the flotilla been bombed in the first place? The American fleet had lacked a lot of things—food, shelter, fuel, civil liberties—but it hadn't lacked weapons. The global military presence that had made the pre-fall United States so powerful, and then helped cause their collapse, had left them with all sorts of terrifying toys. The battleships that circled those four hundred pieces of floating scrap metal would have had solid perimeter defense capabilities . . . but perimeter defense might not have been concerned about a killer whale.

And if anything could get past the innumerable aquadrones that protected Qaanaaq's geocone—that engineering marvel, which captured the massive energy expended by the thermal vent and used it for heating the whole city, providing the power for its lights and machines—it was an orca. If anything could get an explosive onto the cone, it was an orca.

Soq slurped down the last of the noodles, lowered the bowl, let the wind hit their face. Crossed the Arm to where the open ocean lay.

Two hundred thousand people on Arm Eight, if you believed the official statistics, which Soq didn't, and half of them fantasized daily about watching Qaanaaq sink beneath the waves. The other half dreamed of conquering it. A wonder it had lasted as long as it had.

Soq wondered which one they were, and decided they were both. *I will dominate this city or I will destroy it, break its legs, send it sinking into the burning sea we stand over.*

Soq stepped down into the only sleeping boat with any openings. The woman who owned the flat-bottom smiled, recognizing Soq, and held out her hob for screen scanning.

The boat was mostly square, not built for moving. It had been anchored in the same place for twenty years. On its surface stood ten rows of ten boxes. A square meter and a half, with wooden sides covered in canvas. Qaanaaq's poorest slept in boats like this, their bodies folded up uncomfortably, with a breathable lid they could pull over themselves to keep the worst of the wind off and hold body heat in. Soq was lucky to be short. Taller people had a hell of a time in the boxes.

Soq sat. The box was dank and wet. It smelled of the cheap spray the owner used when its previous occupant vacated in the morning, but underneath that Soq could smell the funk of the occupant himself. They'd had to choose between being hungry in a capsule hotel or sated in a box, and had chosen the bowl of noodles.

They were happy with their choice. They were angry that they'd had to make it at all.

The bitterness started to come back. What had been an idle imaginary scenario five minutes before became a deep and fervent desire. *Fuck them, all of them, the people who make us live like this. Who sleep in beds with whole meters of empty space around them.*

Blow up the geocone and the city would be uninhabitable by nightfall. Soq stared into their screen, scrolling through photos of the cone from concept to execution to periodic well-publicized repair work. Prickly defensive columns of polymerized salt; thick swarms of weaponized aquadrones. Two hundred miles of pipes in and around the cone alone, to say nothing of the ones that took water and heat through the twisted tangle of the city above. A million valves for releasing heat and pressure. Dynamic responsive systems to match surges and ebbs in demand.

Such a marvel; such a target.

Soq fell asleep like that, in the fetal position, knowing their knees would ache in the morning, smiling to the imaginary sound of a million people screaming for help as they drowned.

Destroy this city, or conquer it—which one would I prefer?

FILL

————▶

The purple drink did not contain alcohol, to Fill's surprise, but it seemed to make him drunk all the same. The sweetness of it, maybe, the taste of cloves and corn, or the night itself, the crowds, the cold wind and the music, so many musicians that he felt like he was standing in the center of a scattered symphony orchestra, their separate melodies adding up to something, some futuristic form of music with no beginning, no end, no structure, only a thousand gorgeous pieces crashing into each other.

City Without a Map had not steered him wrong. This place was electric, alive. A beautiful boy, seated on a rough and brightly patterned blanket, caught Fill staring. He smiled, a complicit and friendly smile that somehow underscored Fill's outsider status.

Boom. A memory. Triggered by that boy's pretty face. Pornography, one of the first clips little Fill ever saw, a similarly pretty face, eyes closed, face upturned, waiting, frightened—brave—excited, and then a spray of semen across his cheeks, another, several. The memory-boy smiled, laughed.

Fill flushed, embarrassed, unsure whether anyone could see his half erection in the darkened crowd. He scanned the crowd—no one looking in his direction but a well-maintained and very old man at the grid's edge.

Boom. Another image flashed in his mind's eye. Another pretty face, seen from above, turned up. A total stranger, someone Fill had no memory of, although that meant little considering how much he'd done while out of his mind on some combination of alcohol and drugs and actual ecstasy, and anyway, Fill was usually the face being sprayed, not the one spraying the face. Not pornography, either— too real for that, too vivid, with smells attached, and sounds, the roar of a distant train, a subway car, but what the hell, there were no subways left . . .

Boom. Children looking down from the windows of burning buildings.

Boom. Soldiers shooting crowds that tried to breach a roadblock. Broad, bizarre cityscapes rising in the distance, the original Shanghai, the vanished São Paulo. Not dreams, not hallucinations. Memories. Someone else's memories.

Fill began to cry. He cried for a long time.

"Hello," said the old man, speaking New York English. At some point, he had come over to stand beside Fill. "I'm sorry to intrude. Let me guess—*City Without a Map* brought you here."

Fill nodded, then regretted it. He squeezed the last few tears out, gathered his wits, searched for something suitably devastating to slay this sad troll with. But the troll had placed his hand on Fill's, was looking into his eyes, was opening his mouth, and before Fill could hiss, *Get the fuck out of my face you disgusting ancient queen,* the old man said, "It's the breaks, isn't it?"

Which made Fill burst back into tears. He nodded, and the man leaned forward to hug him. The hug was kind, grandmotherly, sexless.

"Forgive my presumption. But I had many similar experiences, early in my diagnosis. And I know how alienating it can be. My name is Ishmael Barron. Most people call me by my last name. It is so much more dramatic."

"Fill." Shaking the man's talcum-powdery hand, he felt afraid he might break the thing. And did Barron's eyes widen from pain, from lecherous pleasure, from something else entirely? "It felt like memories. So vivid. But nothing I experienced. Stuff that happened a long time before I was born. How is that possible?"

"Them's the breaks," the old man said, and smiled, so Fill figured there was probably an old joke he didn't get in there, so he wrung out a laugh. The length of the man's ears was truly preposterous, and his nose seemed superhuman, as though extreme old age was sucking life and skin away from the rest of his face and flooding those places. "Talking helps. I had no one, when I was diagnosed. Do you want to get a *caffè alghe*? Talk about this?"

"We can get real coffee," Fill said. "I hate that toasted algae stuff, and I don't mind paying."

Barron shrugged. "Well okay, Your Excellency."

"Think nothing of it," Fill said, standing up straighter, because manners were easy, this is what they were there for; the genteel affectations of wealth were a suit of armor you could wear when the world threatened to wash you away.

"IT'S PROBABLY BEEN FIVE YEARS since I tasted this," the old man said. "And before that it was probably another five years."

"We'll do this again in five years," Fill said, knowing neither one of them would be alive then.

"Would you believe I used to have five or six cups of this a day?"

"Wow," Fill said, barely hiding his boredom, because he hated when old people talked about How Awesome Everything Used to Be. *Yeah, but you also used to die from cancer and get hangovers and spend your whole life unable to understand 80 to 99 percent of the people in the world when they spoke, so good luck with that nostalgia thing.*

But he couldn't hold on to any anger, not for this man, his baby-pink skin and senile good cheer, and Fill liked speaking New York English, it made him feel close to his grandfather. Above them, at street level, a rather delicious dark bearded thing caught Fill's eye. *He must think I'm a rent boy,* Fill thought with a flush of pride, *paid by this old thing to whip him bloody or sit naked by a window or something.*

"I believe the breaks have been around longer than people suspect," Barron said. "Fifteen years, twenty. It went unnoticed, or was mistaken for schizophrenia or adolescent-onset Alzheimer's because the symptoms are psychological. My theory is that it's not one disease but several, originating in a number of different locations, and when one person becomes infected with multiple strains, a new, hybrid strain is formed. Far stronger than the two that created it."

I think I got them from him. And they're moving fast. It's a bad strain.

Fill frowned into his coffee, remembering that stranger's messages, the boy who said he'd gotten the breaks from the same person as Fill. Although that was crazy. How could this random stranger know such a thing? It's not like Ram had infected him with information along with a disease. And yet—he had known Fill's private handle.

"I think . . ." Fill said, but didn't know how to say it, certainly not in the language he rarely spoke outside of his home. *I think I am remembering things that happened to other people.* "Have you ever . . ."

The bearded man from before had come into the coffee shop, was sitting on a bench. Not buying anything, of course. The kind of person Fill was most attracted to could never have afforded anything in a place like this.

"You've an admirer," Barron said. "I daresay you have many admirers." He seemed quite transfixed by the new arrival, and occasionally turned from him to Fill and smiled deeply, no doubt at an imagined pornographic tussle between the two young men.

"Some people think that the visions you get from the breaks

come from the person who infected you. Or the person who infected them . . . or someone somewhere along the chain. Is that possible, or am I crazy?"

"Yes," Barron said, stirring his coffee unnecessarily, seeming to have moved on from that topic of conversation altogether.

"Yes . . . it's possible?"

"Oh, look!" Barron said, barely listening. "It seems that I have frightened your admirer away. I have that effect on young men these days. Punishment for my own youthful cruelty, I believe. We always get what's coming to us, darling. What is your last name, by the way?"

Fill breathed out, promised himself patience. "Podlove."

Barron's eyes widened, and his jaw dropped, but who could say whether that was an involuntary old-man response, or whether the doomed ancient creature wouldn't have been equally shocked by a last name like Wang or Smith, or the fact that tomorrow was Thursday. "Podlove," he repeated, eyes narrowing. "An interesting name. Was it ever anything else?"

"Something egregiously Slavic, I'm afraid. Grandfather castrated it before he got here. Chopped off a pair of low-hanging syllables. Is it possible that the breaks—"

"At any rate," Barron said swiftly, "you must have things to do. Pursue that swarthy fellow, perhaps. I hope you won't fault me if I sit here a little longer? The legs, you know. They betray one so bitchily as the years go by."

"Of course," Fill said, standing, feeling weirdly like he was being dismissed, when it was his money that had bought them the coffee that earned this ridiculous specimen the right to occupy that space in the first place.

ANKIT

The monkey stared at Ankit through the glass. A Kaapori capuchin, one of the smaller, tougher tribes of feral monkeys that had fled captivity in the gilded cages of Qaanaaq's wealthiest. This one had a broad blue stripe down its back, tapering to a point between its eyes, where the owner had chemically seeded the skin's melanin layer. Ankit had made the mistake of feeding it once, and it must have smelled her weakness, her kindness, because it kept coming back to her window. And because she was weak, because she was kind, she kept feeding it.

Her screen would not stop chiming. Dawn; she'd been up all night; she'd long ago stopped responding to the incoming messages from subordinates, donors, friends, and foes. None from her boss herself, of course, but once Fyodorovna waddled into the office Ankit would be hearing from her.

The monkey stepped in through the open window and sat. She gave it three seaweed squares, which it dropped indignantly into the sea below, and a string of seal jerky, which it rolled into a ball and stuffed into its mouth.

Fyodorovna's campaign was in free fall. Her opponent had seized on the Taksa photo Ankit had posted, generated a script, talking points, sent them out to faith leaders and tenant association presidents and anyone else on Arm Seven who had half an audience, so now her feed was full of assholes squawking about how *Fyodorovna cares more about criminals and perverts than our hardworking families; Seven needs an Arm manager who will work for us, not for the twisted individuals whose bad choices brought the wrath of God down upon them.* For an entire hour she'd watched the bot poll scores plummet, and then she'd put her screen under a pillow.

Ankit had anticipated that this might happen. The possibility had flickered in the back of her brain, briefly, before she posted the photo. She'd considered it unlikely—and in that moment, in her anger, at Fyodorovna, at the breaks, at the fear that had always held her back, at the whole shitty city and the rich and powerful people whose ignorance shaped the lives of so many people and whose asses she was compelled to unceasingly kiss, she had posted the photo anyway.

Minutes after the office opened, Ankit's screen chimed. A subordinate, one she was fond of, who never bothered her with bullshit. She accepted the call and there he was, looking stricken.

"Don't ask, Theerasul," she said. "I'm sick."

"You're not," he said. "But I don't give a shit about that. You have a visitor. She says she has an appointment with you?"

"She's lying," Ankit said.

"Of course I know that. But it's one of the ones you handle better than any of us. I always end up pissing them off or making them—"

"Put her on."

A crabapple face filled her screen: Maria. Ankit winced.

"God bless you," the creepy woman said.

"God bless *you.*"

Maria had a storefront church halfway down the Arm. How she held on to it was a mystery to all. She rarely held services, and when she did they were not attended. By anyone. Ankit had two guesses as to why the deranged old fundie had an unused space as her own private kingdom when it could have been making somebody tens of thousands a month in rent. Either the place was a forgotten holding of one of the former American megachurches, which had bought up property at the height of their power and wealth and then promptly dissolved, its rent paid in full for the next fifty years and Maria sent to be the pastor of a flock that would never come, gone mad awaiting further instructions and resources . . . or she was a maintenance squatter, paid by a shareholder to occupy a space they intended to keep empty. Those were usually thugs or illicit businesses, people who could pay and still be ejected with no notice—but if you wanted to keep a space vacant long-term without attracting Safety's attention, you couldn't do much better than a pit bull religious fanatic.

"Evil has come to Qaanaaq," the weird old woman said.

"I'm sorry to hear that," Ankit said, smiling. Fyodorovna never let them say even the most remotely negative thing to her constituents, no matter how crazy or malevolent they were. God forbid some fundie lunatic decide she hated her, start putting up flyers, spouting web hate.

"I want to know what she's going to do about it," Maria said.

"Did you submit a notice on her page? You know she takes constituent notices very seriously."

"I will do so," Maria said. "And then I will come back to find out what she's going to do about it."

"Great," Ankit said, wondering just what evil had stirred up the wasps in the woman's head this time. Islamic or Israeli refugees bearing insidious infidel ideas, most likely, or a fishmonger selling a new splice animal that a fundie sect had decided violated some weird sentence in Leviticus. Certainly not the breaks. Fundies didn't care about that. Most of them welcomed it. Ankit thought of Taksa, blurred and happy and doomed.

Against her better judgment, Ankit asked, "What kind of evil?"

"That woman. That abomination. Who has wedded herself to Satan. Who rejects the dominion God gave us over the animals and uses witchcraft to merge with them. A killer whale and a polar bear. They have come here to kill, to hunt down decent Christians, and they must be stopped."

"Of course."

Ankit clicked off.

The monkey stood, screeched affably, and leaped fearlessly into the abyss. Ankit whimpered; reached out as if to save it. But the thing was safely scaling her neighbor's window frame, scampering off to wander its city.

KAEV

———————▶

Kaev walked in the direction of the vortex. Even with the wind-screen, Qaanaaq's gusts could be extreme, forming sudden swirling gyres that could push people off balance, stop them in their tracks, make a single step impossible. But one of Kaev's favorite leisure activities was to walk with the wind, submit to it, let its violence and sudden shifts dictate his path. On reflection, he'd come to recognize it as an extension of the pleasure he took from fighting. The thrill of submission, of abdicating control, of letting the mind with all its capricious insatiable demands fall away. And it was good training. It took agility, dexterity, to keep from smashing into any of the people struggling against the wind. It took wisdom to know how and when to yield.

This was a good day. A strong wind, but not too cold. A belly full of noodles. No fights scheduled, but he was heading for a meeting with Go. She'd give him his next assignment. His money would last for two more months; as long as the fight came sooner, he'd be fine.

He'd always been fine. Somehow.

And then, boom. His good mood gone. Who could say why, something he glimpsed from the corner of his eye, a bratty child screaming at his mother, maybe, or a baby in its father's arms, but it was always something, some reminder of what he didn't have, what he would not be, and his mind seized hold of it, spun it out in a dozen directions, nightmare scenarios of suffering and pain, things that were probably fantasies but what if they were memories, glimpses he'd held on to from infancy, things he'd seen . . .

A woman interrupted the stream of hateful thoughts, but he was not grateful. She wore a ratty fur coat and a giant Russian-style fur hat and she was peering into his eyes, and what right did she have to make eye contact with him? He flinched away as if from an electric shock.

"You are American, no?"

"I'm—" he said, frightened, because who was she, why had she spoken to him? Did he look American? What did an American even look like? *Was* he American? "I'm." And then a gibber, a bark, some loud panicky succession of syllables he couldn't control, which made her flinch, which is what it did to everyone.

"Our people are in danger," she said. "Evil has come to Qaanaaq. I need strong men. Men who are not afraid."

Kaev wanted to laugh at the anachronistic use of the word *men* to mean *people*. But he could not laugh. *I'm not strong,* he wanted to say, *and I'm afraid.* All that came out was "I'm," several times in quick succession.

"She is hunting us," the old woman said. "That's why she came. The woman who brings monsters. She blames us for righteously try-ing to wipe her sinful kind off the face of the earth."

The orcamancer, then. His heart swelled, thinking of her. And her polar bear, hands and head caged. A fellow fighter had shown him photos, in the gym, a couple of nights ago. From the lowest level of the Sports Platform. She was real. She was in his city. He'd go to see her, soon. Not that he'd have anything in particular to do or say when he got there—he just wanted to see her for himself.

"Will you help me?"

Kaev fought the urge to yell at her, scold her, threaten to feed her to the orca himself, but his helpless years had taught him patience. She touched his sleeve. "God loves you," she said. "Do you know that?"

Kaev nodded, because that was the expected answer, that was what fundies wanted to hear, but he didn't believe God loved him. Quite the opposite, actually.

She pressed a scrap into his hand. "My church," she said. "Come? Tomorrow night? We need you. Ask for Maria."

And then she left, and he was grateful, except that now he felt bad for her, this sweet, sincere, deranged old woman, alone in a city where no one cared about her god, on a mission to destroy something beautiful, and if she thought that strong men could do something about the evil in Qaanaaq then she was even stupider than Kaev was.

"You're late," said Go's first lieutenant when Kaev arrived at her Arm Five floating headquarters. Dao; tall, thin, levelheaded. He handled her strategy and planning, the big-picture stuff. Kaev liked the guy, even if he was an asshole. There was something wise about him, something calm. More pleasant than the lieutenants who headed up her operations, security, intelligence.

"Delayed. I got. I got delayed."

"By what?"

"The wind."

"Idiot." But he said it affectionately, and stepped aside for Kaev to ascend to the boat.

The thing was big, a tramp steamer long out of commission, its side emblazoned with the name of a corporation and a city, neither of which existed anymore. Go and her operatives ran Amonrattana-kosin Group out of it, and they lived there, and they used its cargo hold for storage. And paid the hefty priority docking fee, which came with a guarantee that Safety and Narcotics and Commerce would only ever attempt to board in the most egregious cases. Qaanaaq's whole hands-off approach to law enforcement had been successful in minimizing crime syndicate violence, but it had also allowed the syndicates to amass significant influence and legitimacy. Kaev reached the deck and turned around to look down, at his city, the Arm he'd left behind, and wondered what would happen when people like Go decided they wanted more.

She'd fought hard enough to get where she was. He remembered the horror of her rise. Even back then, when they were together, she'd had enemies. People she wanted out of the way; people determined to dismember her. Stab wounds she ended up with. Weeks when she had to disappear.

One woman in particular: Jackal, real name Jackie, but don't ever let her hear you use it. A runner, like Go, with her eyes as set on climbing the ladder as Go's were. Whatever happened to Jackal? Or the better question: how, exactly, had Go destroyed her?

"Darling," Go said when he reached the bridge. She embraced him. He wondered if she knew how he felt about her. How much he hated her. She must have. She was too smart not to. "A magnificent fight the other night."

Kaev yipped accidentally, then paused until he could collect himself. "Kid's good."

"He'll become something special," she said. "People love him."

"Means money."

She raised an eyebrow. "And who knows. Maybe someday he'll see you, remember you, buy you breakfast."

Kaev winced. He had made the mistake of telling her, once, when one of the kids he'd lost to who'd made it big ran into him on the street, treated him to a fancy meal, shared his disruptors, started crying, telling Kaev how he owed him everything. The problem with Go was that she knew him too well, knew how he felt about things. That sense of people made her a good crime boss, and a terrible ex.

"Fight," he stuttered out. "You have anything for me?"

"Sort of," she said. She went to her cabin's front porthole, looked out onto the deck. Exactly like a captain would. She was dressed in drab green, Kaev's favorite color. He wondered if that was on purpose. The machete scabbard hung from her belt, as always. No one had ever seen her use it. Kaev knew she wouldn't hesitate; wondered if she'd used it on Jackal. "Dao has two names for you. See him on your way out."

"Names. Names?"

"Business rivals," she said. "I'm not going to lie to you to spare your feelings, Kaev. You're a grown-up, at least in body you are. I need you to soak them."

Kaev felt very close to crying. He said "I'm" several times, and then finished in a rush: "I'm not a thug, Go, I'm not going to go rough up your enemies for you. I'm a fighter and I've made my peace with doing your dirty work in the ring, losing fights I know I can win, training young punks so you can make more money on them, but I'm not going to throw somebody into the water because of some business deal you need to get done."

At least, that's what he tried to say. He was pretty sure he got all the words out, and maybe even in the right order, but probably too fast for most of them to make any sense.

She patted his cheek. "Oh, Kaev. My noble warrior. I know this is hard for you."

"Me?" he asked. "Why. You have people. Lots. Who do this. Do this kind of thing. Better at it than I'd be."

"True," she said, "and lots of them are ex-fighters. You're getting old, Kaev. You know this. Couple of years, you won't be able to put on a convincing show in the ring anymore. And then what? If you can do this job, and do it well—well, then, you have a whole new career opening up ahead of you."

"And if I refuse? Or. If I mess up. Because I don't know how to do this thing?"

"Then good luck with your life," she said, her back to him, the conversation over, no point in arguing. He'd stared at her back like this before. "Needless to say, you'll never have another beam fight again. Or unlicensed skiff brawl, or snuff film knife fight, or anything."

Dao beamed him the details when he descended from the deck. And, because he really was a good man under all the assholishness, he didn't comment on the wetness beading up in the corner of Kaev's left eye.

ANKIT

—————————➤

Ankit's job was as good as gone. Her boss would lose. There was nothing she could do about it.

There were things she'd never done, favors she'd never called in. Agency executives, city flunkies who could help her. Who could access and share information they weren't supposed to access and share. Requests she'd always been too cautious to make, stockpiling them for the day when Fyodorovna would really need them.

When I get back to the office, I'm going to start calling in those favors.

In the meantime, Ankit read everything. Every news site and academic journal, every forum, every crazy analysis from every point on the political spectrum. She even scoured through those *City Without a Map* broadcasts, which she'd avoided because it seemed like absolutely everyone was talking about them that year, and it made their voices get high and excited and agitated and she didn't need that in her life.

If someone discussed the breaks, Ankit devoured it.

Which made her seasick. No two sources, it seemed, were discussing the same disease. Some of the symptoms remained mostly the same, but this was the only thing approaching consensus. Where it

originated, what it meant, what it did beyond the psychological consequences, how to treat it—these were all the subject of a dizzying
degree of difference of opinion.

The breaks was God's wrath, raining down upon the nations
whose hyperactive economies fucked up the planet.

The breaks was God's wrath, inflicted upon immoral sinful sub-
populations.

The breaks was big pharma, accidentally unleashing a monster
when a handful of separate covert drug testing schemes unintention-
ally overlapped.

The breaks was a lie, a myth to keep people distrustful and angry
and fearful of each other.

The breaks was a lie, a myth to distract from something far worse
that was on the horizon.

She was pissing her job down the drain. She knew this.

Because the bottom line was: The breaks remained a phantom illness. A media mirage. Glimpsed in hazy pieces. Something no one
could approach, capture, present, discuss, deal with. Argued about
by foreign governments, rejecting allegations that their military labs
or foulest slums had spawned it, and by insurance companies trying
not to pay for treating the symptoms. Ignored by most other power
players. Everywhere she looked, local software was "still collating."
Official responses were "still forthcoming." If she could force it into
the public consciousness, make it into a serious issue that Health had
to address, she would lose her job—but she could save so many lives
she wouldn't care about being unemployed.

That's what she told herself, anyway.

The six-month processing glitch had proven to be a fruitless av-
enue. Protocol rationale requests submitted under the Open and
Accountable Computer Governance mandate turned up nothing. A
couple million lines of code she'd never have been able to parse, that
none of her contacts could penetrate, either.

Ankit listened to 'casts, left the apartment, started talking to people. Plenty of others were just as obsessed as she was, and had been for a lot longer. Accumulating information wasn't enough when it came to getting to the truth of the breaks. What she needed were real human minds, tics and madness and all, to turn all that data into stories.

At a support group, she met Janna, whose brother Mikk had been a sex worker in the Calais refugee camp. Janna clutched a photo in a frame, the first Ankit had seen in years. The boy was beautiful. Dark, smiling, tattooed, laughing at an inexplicable actual raven perched on one strong extended arm. He'd loved the work, Janna said, and been very popular with fellow refugees and camp workers and aid administrators and visiting photographers and pastors, complete with a sliding scale that even the richest of men were all too happy to pay, and the money he made that way had enabled him to buy Qaanaaq registrations and a halfway decent apartment lease for their whole family.

"Mikk was proud," Janna said. "He hated that we had lost our home, and that we were living in such a dangerous place. But sex let him rise above all that. Sex was how he became something more than just a refugee."

And it was only once they arrived in Qaanaaq, and were safe and stable, that the breaks began to manifest. Janna believed they had been there for a long time, kept in check by the force of Mikk's magnificent pride and determination to get his family out of Calais, and that once he was able to lay down his burden they blossomed.

For Mikk, the breaks brought him back to the camps. But not Calais. Taastrup—a Danish village, somewhere he had never been. At first she thought he was fuguing into stories he'd been told, things his johns had said. But the details were too complex, his fevered mumbling too disturbing, for such a simple explanation. Janna tracked down photos, found the same things he'd been describing.

Eventually Mikk broke. Died.

Bodybreaking, they called it. What happened when the breaks finally killed you. The moment when your mind's hold on the here and now finally ruptured forever and you broke free from your body.

Taastrup. The place popped up again and again in her research. Gone now. One of many that became the target of nationalist mobs, latter-day skinhead armies angry at all the workers landing on their shores. An estimated fifteen hundred people took part in the torching of Taastrup, a pogrom to rival anything in czarist Russia.

Looking into Taastrup took her to Ishmael Barron. He wasn't the first researcher she'd met who was clearly suffering from the breaks himself, but in him they were further along than she'd previously seen. Midsentence she could see it happening, watch his eyes as one train of thought was abruptly replaced by another. But each time he smiled, as if no one vision was more welcome than the next.

He unfurled a sheet of paper big enough to cover the table where they sat. She could not help but touch it, rub a corner between her fingers.

"Five or so years ago, several years into my research, I started to see the strands come together. Separate story lines uniting into one. The story of the breaks. Nothing like paper to paint a picture. I tried to put it all down. I am not sure if I succeeded."

A map took up half the sheet. North America, the Arctic, Greenland, Northern Europe. Bloodred triangles for the grid cities; blue circles for the refugee camps. A tangled nest of many-colored lines. The rest was a dense sea of scribbled words, angry ellipses, accusatory question marks. Exclamation marks like multiple stab wounds. He talked her through it, highlighting reported cases and potential trends, tracing what he believed to be separate strains with different symptoms.

They were in his apartment. A tiny place, but on Arm Five, so the building was clean and seemed safe. He was lucky he had come so long ago.

"What's this?" she said, pointing to a fading orange line that meandered and circled around North America before ending in Taastrup.

"Exactly!" he said.

". . . Exactly what?"

His finger traced the orange line, trembling. "That's the most important question you could have asked. What's your best bet?"

"Comes up out of the USA," Ankit said. "Some nomadic refugee group. People from one of the Black Autonomous Zones, after they got pushed out of Detroit or New Orleans or something?"

"No," he said. "Nanobonders. Taastrup was the last known location of any of them—a small handful that survived the final massacre went there, but, surprise, there's fundamentalist lunatics everywhere, and they got butchered, too."

"Last known nanobonder location until our friend with the orca arrived, that is."

"Yes."

He scanned her face, his eyes wide, his mouth open. "I think they are the key," he said finally, and if he was disappointed that she neither arrived at the same conclusion nor seemed floored by it now that he'd told her, he hid it well. "Nanobonder migration patterns are the most common thread between the dozen or so different places where the breaks are believed to have sprung up. I think that their unique nanite signature was a trigger, somehow. A key ingredient in the pharmaceutical stew that led to the creation of the breaks."

"I thought that the nanobonded were . . . endogamous." She was proud of herself for remembering the word. "Insular. Never interacted with outsiders. So they'd never have taken random meds."

"Popular consensus holds that this is a myth," Barron said. "Justification for atrocities. Throughout history, 'They keep to themselves, they think they're better than us, they hate us,' has been a common rationale for why a group of people constitute a threat, and therefore should be expelled or perhaps exterminated. But even if it's true, we know they established trade with some other diasporic communities, many of whom were known pharma subjects during Deregulation. They could have been dosed with something without their consent or knowledge."

"I know so little about them," Ankit said.

"And I know far too much. I've done so much research on them, spoken to so many people. How they originated, where they moved, who they interacted with. How they were targeted. Why. By whom." Here his face grew very serious, and tight with an anger that looked out of place on such an old and kind man. And then it passed. "But it's all academic now. Archaeology, as opposed to anthropology."

"I bet you'd like very much to talk to her," she said. "The woman with the orca."

"I would," he said. "But I don't fancy being butchered like the hundreds of people she killed in the grid cities she visited before coming here."

"Is that true? I heard those reports, but I thought—"

Barron shrugged. "I accept as a fundamental fact of Qaanaaq life that I will never know if anything is true," he said. "Most of it is rumor. Even when you read it in the supposedly legitimate news outlets. I learned that long before arriving here, to be honest. Life becomes significantly less stressful when you accept that your ignorance will always dwarf your knowledge."

"Tell me about New York," Ankit said. She didn't know why she said it. As soon as she did, she knew it was wrong. He hadn't mentioned the place. Only his accent had given it away.

His face seemed to break. First it tightened, as though he was growing angry again, and then it broke.

"I . . . can't" was all he managed to say.

"I'm sorry," she said, and he turned his head away, nodded as she stood up, thanked him profusely for his time, his insight, apologized again, promised to return.

Why, she wondered, descending the narrow back stairs, *why did I ask such a cruel and thoughtless question—*

Why—

Because his pain is mine, she realized, when the cardamom smell of *doodh pati* hit her down at grid level, *because the ache of what he's lost is the same as the ache of what I've never had, and spent my whole life longing for. My mother is his city.*

CITY WITHOUT A MAP:
DISPATCHES FROM THE QAANAAQ FREE PRESS

Depending on your definition of *press,* Qaanaaq hosts anywhere from five hundred to two thousand different press outlets, sites and broadsheets from every political and religious affiliation of every one of the city's hundreds of expatriate communities. The Greater India Reunification Party, never a significant political player in its home countries, is the publisher of Qaanaaq's most widely read news source, hated and beloved and fiercely argued about among the quarter of the city's population hailing from the various South Asian nations, rent asunder by imperialism and Partition and the Water Wars but reunited by Qaanaaq's xenophobia. The *Final Call* gives equal column space to absurd conspiracies and all-too-real genocidal actions by North American power players. *Evangelize!* rails endlessly against the same handful of subjects—the ease of acquiring abortifacients, the difficulty of acquiring firearms, the means by which solving the latter problem could address the former. Several popular sites urge Qaanaaq's Han Chinese to fight back against the Tibetan takeover of the motherland.

Whatever ax you have to grind, whatever lost world you are pining for, there is a press outlet for you. Probably several. And whatever happens, plenty of people have plenty to say about it.

From the *Maoist Pioneer* [in Nepali]:

Two weeks after her arrival in Qaanaaq, the Blackfish Woman may be the most hated person in the city. Already reactionary religious elements are whispering together, and soon they will do more than whisper. As has happened so many times before, superstition is being used to focus the angers of a desperate populace on the wrong target. And why? To displace their very righteous anger over the city's mistreatment of workers. The very people who pay such low wages that workers in Arm Eight must sleep stacked in boxes, the very same businesses who fired pipe workers for attempting to unionize for better workplace safety, would have you believe that the arrival of weary refugees is our greatest threat, or that a battle-scarred survivor of genocide must be murdered.

From *Yomiuri Shimbun* [in Japanese]:

When the cities of America's South and Midwest began to burn, and the continental United States became a hellhole ruled by marauding warlords, and the Northern Migration began, dozens of new communities began to form. Some were mobile city-states headed up by armed militias; some were ambulatory religious communes; some were united by common geographic or ethnic origin. Some were thousands strong; some numbered in the dozens. Many adapted to the freezing new climate by joining existing Inuit communities or by adopting their way of life.

Few took detailed notes. Many documented themselves in the photographs and films of average citizens, the majority of which have been lost to poor preservation, outdated hardware, and evolving file formats. Historians of the period must contend with a mess of songs, passed-down family stories, and the reports of outraged neighbors on whose shores and at whose gates they landed.

Many tall tales emerged from this seething stew of internal refugees, but perhaps the most myth-shrouded story of all is that of the nanobonded. A whole community of people who were either deliberately or accidentally exposed to experimental wireless nanomachines that established one-to-one networks between individuals, and who, through years of training and imprinting, could "network" themselves to animals, forming primal emotional connections so strong that they could control their animals through thought alone. And as with any new community in fundamentalist North America, there were plenty of people who thought that it was demonic, Antichrist-derived, the work of evil foreigners bent on undermining Caucasian hegemony. And, alas, like many communities, they are believed to have been wiped out in one of the many violent fundamentalist spasms that characterized the final years of the American republic.

An absurd story, the evidence for which has been elaborately debunked.

And yet—it would appear that one of them walks among us ...

From *Krupp Monthly* [in German]:

Wilhelm Ruhr remembers the last Hive Project well.

"We were finally there," he says, his aging eyes lighting up. "On paper, it should have worked. The nanites talked to each other. They could do so over great distances. We even engineered them to self-replicate only when their brain concentration dropped below a certain level, and to be open to network imprinting only for their first six hours. All the problems that had caused us so many headaches in the previous iterations were solved. Or so we thought."

At the time, Wilhelm was working in Canada. These days, home is right here in Qaanaaq: Arm Three's prestigious Kesiyn retirement center.

"In mice, it worked. They were networked. Hurt one, and the others felt pain. If one figured out how to find the cheese at the end of the maze, all of them knew how to do it. Move them too far apart, and they experienced nausea, disorientation, eventually catatonia. We probably should have done monkey trials, but the way things were going in America it was much more cost-effective to just get a waiver signed and try it out on people."

Proximity to the border meant ease of testing on the recently deregulated country to the south. The U.S. Food and Drug Administration had essentially been stripped of all its power to enforce clinical trial standards, and the residents of the resettlement villages were only too happy to take a chance in exchange for what was to them a lot of money.

"It didn't go well. Everybody knows that by now. Personally I think a lot of what got reported was exaggerated, or that the atrocities were due to other causes. Either way, talking about it isn't going to make much difference."

Still, Wilhelm Ruhr does not feel guilty about what happened.

"We were trying to do something good. If it had worked, think of what we'd have been able to accomplish. A nano-synced team of scientists could solve all sorts of the problems we currently face. A lot of people died in wars to topple bad governments—should their commanding officers feel guilty about sending them to their deaths? They feel bad, probably, which is how I feel, I suppose, but they don't feel guilty."

And as for the arrival of the alleged "orcamancer," rumored by many to be one of the legendary "nanobonded"?

"People ask me about them all the time. So many people.

They say things like, Do I think it's possible that the nanite strain remained in a small group of people, and that their existing meditation practice enabled them to control it? And that it accidentally came together with other types of nanomedicine? Of course it's possible. But as for whether I think that in the course of two generations they learned to cultivate the nanites, introduce them to nonhuman animals, and form mechanically facilitated telepathic links with them . . ." Here he pauses, and chuckles. "That's a leap not even I am willing to make, and I'm a dreamer."

SOQ

A crowd of people, approximating a line. Each one of them wearing entirely too many clothes. Somehow still shivering. They stood out, on Arm Six.

"What're they waiting for?" Soq asked, arriving, acting extra cool and casual. "Is there a church here that serves food?"

"Waiting for salvation," Dao said. "Deliverance. Death. Christ, kid, I don't know what they're waiting for. I don't think they're waiting for anything."

"The breaks," Soq whispered, watching them mutter and jerk. "The breaks."

People hurried past, trying hard not to look. A buoy clanged, and someone in the line started making similar noises. Then someone else did. The clanging rippled down the line, spreading as it went, heading for the Hub. "You'd think the city would . . . I don't know, do something."

Dao offered a pack of pine needle cigarettes. Soq spent entirely too long debating what was the right choice here—*Refuse one, to show I'm proud and independent? Accept one, to establish a personal bond?*—and then pocketed three. "Yes, it's strange, isn't it? The city possesses the resources to whisk all these people away. Why haven't they?"

Soq fought the urge to shrug, say something flip. *Treat everything like a test, even though probably none of it is. Dude could be just making conversation.*

"Software hasn't come up with a solution yet," Soq said. "They're waiting."

"Ah," Dao said. "I suppose that's correct, on some level. That's the official story, anyway. But these are some sophisticated programs we're talking about. Capable of doing a trillion computations in a millisecond. Doesn't seem like they'd need *years* to come up with something here."

Dao smiled, and Soq thought maybe they'd passed the test, if it had been a test.

"Still, Safety will come tell them to move along soon," Soq said. "Why aren't they on Eight? They'd fit right in, among all the nutcases out there."

Dao frowned! Oh no! The test is failed!

"Soq," he said. "Really? Because this is their home. This is where they lived. Even if they couldn't pay their rent anymore, or their family couldn't take care of them, or they burned down their own building by accident, this Arm belongs to them as much as to any of the other souls who live here."

"Of course," Soq said, trying, and failing, to not get nasty. "You wanted to set up a meeting with me in this particular spot—why? To discuss injustice? Medical software?"

Dao smirked, and Soq got the impression that being cryptic and elliptical was an important management strategy. "Go has an assignment for you," he said. "One she wanted discussed in person, rather than via messaging."

"Because it's so dangerous and important and you don't want any way it can be traced back to you?" Soq said, knowing it wouldn't be.

"Because it's so strange. She thought you might have a hard time getting your head around it, and wanted me to answer any questions you might have."

God, why did this guy have to be such a dick *all the time*? "Shoot. Try your best to baffle me."

"Go is assigning you to the orcamancer."

Soq's eyes widened with excitement. "Assigning me . . . how?"

"Research her. Gather all the intel you can on her. Fact, fiction, legend, rumor. Follow her, if you can. Talk to her, if you can."

"Fat chance of that," Soq said. "Tons of people have tried. She hasn't said a word to anyone."

"You see?" Dao said. "You're already on top of this job."

"Yeah," Soq said. "But . . . why? What does the Blackfish Woman have to do with Go?"

Dao rolled his eyes, turned his whole face skyward. "If it were up to me, this conversation would be over by now. But your assignment is important, and Go wanted me to answer your questions. So. Here's the simplified, kiddie menu version. Go is beginning a very delicate and dangerous operation. She's been planning it for years. It's an extremely complex mathematical equation, and Go had it solved—and then, here comes this woman. An unknown variable, with the potential to be massively disruptive. Maybe she won't affect the equation at all. Maybe she wants nothing to do with anything Go is working on. But if not, if whatever weird mission Little Miss Polar Bear is here to accomplish might impact something or someone we need for our plan to be successful, Go needs to know. And respond accordingly. Is that an acceptable explanation?"

Important. Me. My assignment is important. "Yeah. Sure."

"Good. You can message me updates. Call or visit only when it's urgent. If she does something . . . I don't know, big. Unusual."

Soq's earlier visits to the Sports Platform had been for fun, but now it was for work. Destiny was nudging Soq toward the orcamancer. Soq was important. They could barely wait to get back there and sit in the presence of the polar bear woman again, watching wordlessly with the rest of the wide-eyed grid kids who had come to see something magical and monstrous.

ANKIT

W ood smells like wealth, Ankit realized. Exposed beams filled the lobby of the corporate office building, smelling like money and safety and a time when the world was still solid beneath people's feet.

Her ears still rang from the screaming fit she'd gotten from Fyodorovna. It was almost comical, the mood at the office, the way everyone avoided eye contact with her, the sounds of shouting and pleading that came through the walls from the damage control phone calls her boss was forced to make.

With effort, Ankit was able to block all that out. She was here, wasn't she? She was doing what she had to do to make things right. Even when she wanted desperately to be anywhere else. Still no visit confirmation from the Cabinet. *Processing*, it said when she checked the status of her request. What was going on with Qaanaaq's computer infrastructure, once the envy of the world, the stuff of legend?

She shut her screen and breathed in the stink of money.

The Salt Cave, they called it. Sharp artful salt crystals jutted from the walls, the residue of polymerized desalinization. The smooth crystals formed walkways several stories above her, shored up by old wood beams. Secretaries carried screens to meetings. Clients drank coffee. Out on the grid, a cry went through the crowd—wild-eyed people making a noise like buoys clanging, passing the sound from one person to the next.

Upstairs, Ankit knew what she would find. Corporate offices were all alike. Either they all hired the same lone decorator, who was paid obscenely well to reproduce the same palette and aesthetic, or they hired a whole flock of them and paid them poorly to copy each other down to the slightest detail. Classical landscape above the reception desk; abstract expressionism on the south wall; the walls a blue shade of white. Or, Ankit thought, perhaps there was software for that, too, and every two years it issued a subtle new change to keep the look evolving over time. Salvaged wood instead of brushed steel for the filing cabinets; cactus bubbles instead of air plant terrariums hanging from the bathroom ceiling. The lack of imagination among the rich was its own kind of machine, its own species of artificial intelligence.

A message from Ishmael Barron. A response to something she'd sent him at two A.M.

She'd found something. Maybe nothing. Maybe not. The medical log of the Taastrup infirmary, a few enigmatic lines in a mass of hundreds of thousands. Patients suffering symptoms identical to the breaks—potential early cases—who'd been dosed with something called Quet-38-36.0—a tranquilizer, derived from an atypical antipsychotic—and been successfully sedated indefinitely. Remarkable, if these were indeed early breaks cases, because tranquilizers typically didn't work on the breaks. And she'd shivered, to think of all that data, a quintillion pages' worth of science and study and learning and theory and fact and fiction, still there, on old open servers and suspended-animation websites, like so much coastal land mass swallowed up by rising seas—open to all, for the taking, except no one cared, no one had the slightest desire to dive into that wreck.

What else was there a cure for—what other horrific problems might be so easily solved?

Never heard of Quet-38-36.0, Barron said. *But it sounds promising. Let's do more research.*

Stupid, to take out her screen to see Barron's response. Now Ankit couldn't help but see the notifications stream in. New poll numbers; new press hits. Free fall had stabilized, somewhat. Fyodorovna's subsequent silence on the subject of the breaks had emboldened her opponent. He posted photos of sick people crowding Arm Seven. Beggars babbling; children having fits. Tiny rooms where a dozen cots had been crammed. *If she cares so much, why isn't she doing anything for them?*

"Ankit, hi," said Breckenridge, emerging from the bathroom, extending one wet hand. She took it, smiling to beat the band. "Oh good, they offered you coffee. Walk this way."

She followed him down the too-wide hallway, into the too-wide meeting room. Shareholders couldn't help showing off. It was who they were. They all had front corporations to handle their holdings, raking in the cash and paying the taxes and hiring the management companies.

"Bad mistake your boss made," Breckenridge said. "Messing with the breaks. That stuff is poison. Tragic situation, but . . ."

"I know," Ankit said, smiling like she didn't want to punch this guy in the throat, him and everyone else who had such pat responses for everything they didn't want to think too deeply about. *That stuff is poison. Terrible shame but.*

"I assume that's what you're here about?"

"Mostly, yes," she said. They sat. "That, and some intel."

"Intel? Or money?"

"Both," she said, although of course all she had come for was money. An intel exchange was performative, a cover for the in-person meeting. She'd needed to look him in the eye when she made the ask.

Except now that she thought about it . . . maybe someone so close to someone so powerful *would* have some information she could use. "We're taking a beating. We need to buy some more messaging bots, screen time, that kind of stuff."

"I'll see what we can do. I already put the request in to the shareholder who heads up Fifty-Seventh when you asked for a meeting. I figured that's what it was about. You really could have just sent the message." He gave Ankit the sense that he slept under his desk. Not from poverty but from self-annihilating salaryman work ethic. "What was the intel you needed?"

"About the breaks."

"Are you serious? You need to learn your lesson, lick your wounds, and move on. Fyodorovna isn't planning to pursue this, is she? Make it a campaign plank?"

The view was breathtaking. The windscreen was being shifted, and as the sun caught the gleaming facets it looked like the sky was one massive kaleidoscope. Was that fear, in Breckenridge's eyes?

"Maybe," she said. "We're still collating."

"Big gamble," he said. "Unlikely to pay off for her. Maybe if you weren't an incumbent, you could rally people behind it, make absurd demands and promises, whip it up from a fringe issue to a major one, but with all her time in office and not a lick of concrete action, the few people who do care about it one way or another won't—"

"Maybe she's planning concrete action."

"That would be unwise."

"Why?"

He took off his glasses. Rubbed his eyes. "You know that even if I did have access to any information that might be helpful, we couldn't share it."

"I need to know," she said. "We're losing here. And you need us."

"Let's get noodles," he said. "You hungry?"

She wasn't, but she knew when someone wanted to talk off the record.

Her jaw pinged on their way out. She let the message come in: a colleague back at Fyodorovna's office, concerned because That Crazy Lady Maria was apparently rallying an angry mob. Hardly a challenging feat; out-of-work Americans took little riling up. Employed Americans, too, for that matter.

"Back in ten," Breckenridge said to the receptionist. Receptionists were a funny holdover, Ankit thought, not for the first time. Software could do everything they did. But they made people feel more comfortable. *How much of the world around us is utterly superfluous, kept in place to preserve an illusion of order?*

That's when she realized how scared she was. She never got philosophical. There were always too many real things to think about.

On the street, darkness was inching in. The days were short now. Soon they'd be down to four dim hours, and they'd crank up the lights nonstop, and the whole city would smell of the composting sewage in the biogenerators that powered the methane-sodium lamps. They crossed the Arm, toward a shop expensively made up to look like a ragged Arm Eight street stall. Right down to the spray-painted tarps, except these were hanging inside, where they weren't protecting anything from the wind.

Arm One noodles were the worst.

What did it mean, that Breckenridge had something to say but couldn't say it in the office? Something was afoot with the breaks, and the shareholder he worked for knew what was going on. Might have helped make the decisions. Or maybe this was something else, some other scandal, some other terrible thing about to hit her, one more reason her boss's career was over and therefore so was hers.

A slide messenger ululated past them.

"Hey, comrade," said a man in a hooded sweatshirt, running up behind them. "I think you dropped this."

Breckenridge patted his pockets, made a quizzical expression, reached out to the man's extended hand.

The man grabbed him, pulled him in, took hold of his arm at the wrist and above the elbow, and twisted. Breckenridge yelped, turned his body with the arm. The hooded man kicked at his knee, gave him a shove, dumped him off the grid and into the sea. Ankit got a glimpse of gritted teeth, a neck wide with muscle. He turned to her, slowing, as if debating whether to soak her, too, and in that second she got in one good kick. Missed the mark slightly, hitting his inner hip, but hard enough to surprise him into pausing for just an instant, a fraction of an instant.

Long enough for her to catch a better glimpse of his face. Shadowed, battle-scarred, seen only once in the flesh, but familiar. From posters, from fight broadcasts.

Her brother.

"Kaev," she said, but he was already sprinting away.

Sirens blared. Arm One had surface sensors to know when someone had been soaked. Breckenridge flailed in the choppy sea, glasses gone, looking ridiculous, like he'd never again make the mistake of leaving his office.

"What the hell," Ankit said, but he couldn't hear her, couldn't have answered if he had, and anyway she wasn't talking to him.

CITY WITHOUT A MAP:
ANATOMY OF AN INCIDENT

You are bound to your body.

Your body is shaped by its DNA, your parents' decisions, historic hate and hunger, contested elections, the rise and fall of the stars in the sky. Maybe your body is in an awful place. Maybe, like me, you are there through no fault of your own.

One day, you will break free of your body. Every one of us will. Until that Great Liberation comes, we must be content with the little liberations. The shiver up the spine—the telltale tingle of a beautiful song. Great sex; a good story.

So. Another story. This one encompassing twenty minutes, distilled and condensed from diverse sources. Journalist reports; video cameras; eyewitness accounts as delivered to Safety and other agencies.

Scene: The Sports Platform. Lowest level. Evening. Darkness has just come to Qaanaaq.

At 17:55, forty men and women board the Platform. They are an angry, unruly bunch. They carry improvised weapons; lengths of pipe, mostly, retired from the city's geothermal ventilation system.

Some wield the rusting skeletons of American guns, family heirlooms desperately clung to, sometimes the only thing an ancestor carried when they escaped from the hellhole collapse of Chicago or Buffalo or Dallas.

By 18:04 they have reached the lowest level.

The woman who leads them has been transformed. Whatever wretched old crone she is, in whatever miserable crevice of Arm Seven or Eight she resides, she has left all that behind. Right now, she is magnificent. A monster.

"You guys can get the hell out of here right now," a thug hollers at the half dozen journalists lazing on the bleachers. "Unless you want some of this, too."

"Let them stay," the woman says, and from her accent they know she is the original article, straight New York, by way of the Dominican Republic, been here a week or twenty years, it doesn't matter, she's had so little actual conversation with her neighbors that the city can put no fingerprint on her voice. "They should see this. The world should see this."

Still. Most of them leave.

"But they could call Safety!" someone says, making ready to pursue them.

"They could call Safety without moving an inch," she says. "But by the time Safety gets here, our work will be done."

Their target has not moved since their arrival. For why else could they be here, if not for the Killer Whale Woman? She stands there, watching them, and the journalists will report that she is smiling.

Imagine her beautiful. Imagine her stout and muscular inside her leathers and furs. Imagine someone so strong that if you knew she was on your side, you would never be afraid again. And if she was coming for you, you would know all you needed to do was wait.

"Surround her," the woman says. "Don't let her get to the bear."

Several members of the mob notice it for the first time. Chained to the wall, getting to its feet, bristling with rage at the smell of so much anger. And now the smell of so much fear. A couple of people yelp. One runs.

"Your kind is not welcome here. You are an abomination. A profanation of the human being as God made it, in His image. He made us distinct from the animals for a reason. Your bond with that savage beast in chains over there is sin, and that sin is why your people were wiped out."

At the word *abomination,* their target moves for the first time. She raises the weapon that has been resting at her side and takes hold of it with both hands. It is taller than she is, walrus-ivory handle and a slightly curved shaft that might be ironwood or might be the rib of the most massive of whales. At its end, a blade like a lopsided crescent moon, fatter at the bottom than the top, its edge broken up into hooks and barbs.

Some of the journalists capture photos of it. Some of them are filming the whole thing.

"Why have you come here?"

Someone hurls a pipe. Hard. Her motion is effortless, so slight that some people don't even see it, the most minimal shift of the weapon to deflect the projectile without striking it head-on in a way that might damage her blade. The effect on the mob is obvious, immediate. Mouths open. Feet shuffle. For the first time, the courage of a violent crowd begins to crack. They are not invincible. Their target is not helpless.

It has the opposite effect on their leader. Or perhaps it is their fear that makes her braver. Her chest swells. She steps closer, into range of the weapon.

"You are not welcome here," she hisses.

"She can't understand you," someone yells. "You know they're afraid of technology. She doesn't have an implant."

At this, Killer Whale Woman laughs.

This, too, startles the mob, so much so that hardly anyone notices that she has struck out with her weapon. Only their leader's scream, several milliseconds later, alerts them that something is wrong. Her right hand is lying on the floor, being baptized in a cascade of arterial blood. The smell of it makes the polar bear roar.

"Get her!" someone shouts, and the crowd closes in on her. Their dehanded leader staggers away to the far edge of the platform.

Pipes and chains swing. Pause the video, zoom in, slow it down, you can see the ballet unfold. Two men rush forward first, side by side, so close a single swing decapitates both of them. A woman attacker crouches low, coming in from the side, and catches a high kick that knocks her backward. The swing that lopped off two heads reaches its graceful end, and already the orcamancer is pulling it back, shifting her hands to the center of the shaft, ramming it back, expertly striking the rib cage of the man trying to run up on her from behind. Bones break. Their sharp edges stab into organs.

People stand in the doorway—athletes from other levels of the Platform, and the standard stream of curious Qaanaaqians who come every day to visit their mythical visitor. Fifteen screens are focused on the action, capturing every instant of it.

The polar bear stomps its forepaws against the ground. The whole hall echoes with the metal ring of it.

"*Gaaah!*" someone shouts, or at least that's how their desperate, inarticulate cry will be rendered in the *Post–New York Post*. Before it is finished she has thrust her weapon forward and its blade has pierced his throat, one barb catching on his spine, and she swings it to the right to shake him free, bringing his body into the path of one of his comrades, who trips over it and tumbles to the floor and has one arm severed by the now unencumbered weapon.

A gunshot. The screech-whistle of a ricochet, and then another, more distant, as the bullet vanishes into the gloom of the Platform's lowest level. And then a curse, for, as so often happens with the aging firearms of Americans, the igniting gunpowder has caused the barrel to explode in the hands of its user.

But the sound of it causes the orcamancer to pause. Her smile stops. She looks from face to face, hand to hand.

"Shoot her!" the mob's leader wails, unnecessarily, from the sidelines, her voice thick with pain but light from loss of blood.

The orcamancer neatly disembowels another soul idiotic enough to charge her.

A man closes his eyes and then opens them. Takes a breath. He stands away from the fray, between her and the bear. His thighs ache. A week and a half has passed since he got off the iceboat. They should not still be hurting. He is getting too old to straddle the saws anymore, too weak to calve functional shards off the Greenland glacier. By this time next year, he'll be unable to make a living at the only job he's ever had in this crummy city. And then what? He is old enough to remember Philadelphia before the Revival, before the state of Pennsylvania fell to fundamentalists with a platform of confronting "centers of sin" who ordered the complete evacuation of every major city. He has seen everything taken from him, so many times, and he's never been able to do a thing about it.

He shoots. The bullet strikes the orcamancer in the lower leg, knocks her back, causes her to stumble and fall to her knees.

People laugh. The circle, smaller now, closes in.

She taps two fingers against the corner of her jaw. Someone gasps. They had been so convinced that she eschewed all technology, this possibility never entered their minds.

Metal rings against metal. Again they hear the polar bear roar. Louder now. They turn to see that it is unfettered, the cages fallen away from its hands and mouth. It shrieks and charges.

This is where the official record breaks down. Everyone leaves at this point, and swiftly. Journalist and freelance gawker alike exit. So, for that matter, does the recently dehanded woman who moments ago had been a mob leader. What's left of her mob attempts to depart but is unsuccessful.

There are no cameras to capture the carnage.

SOQ

Soq saw the slaughter and did not flinch.

It was their fifth time visiting the orcamancer. Lots of bored Qaanaaqians came to see her, either at the Sports Platform or at the Arm Six sloopyard where her boat was docked. Most went once and found the real thing far less interesting than the mythic warrior they'd been imagining. Only the obsessed came back again and again, the people for whom hate or fear or love won out, the people for whom she meant something. Soq had looked from face to face on each visit and wondered: *Why is this one here? Why this one? Do they want to destroy her? Do they want to beg her for the gift of her nanites, a teaspoonful of blood that could turn them into something as awesome as she is?*

And why, Soq wondered, *am I here?*

Sometimes people asked the Killer Whale Woman things, and they were always ignored. Most often they stood as silent as Soq did.

Soq arrived in the middle of the bloodbath. They almost got trampled in the sudden swift exodus of people up the stairs. When Soq got to the bottom and climbed into the bleachers, they got there just in time to see the bear break a man's neck. A woman turned to run, and the bear's paw raked down her back, tearing it open, pulling her backward and onto the ground, and then it stooped to tear out her throat.

It took less than eight minutes for the polar bear to kill the last of the people who had come to hurt the orcamancer. It played for a short while with a severed limb and then turned to face its traveling companion.

And—was that fear Soq saw, in the orcamancer's eyes? How could that be? Weren't they bonded? How did this work? Which of the stories were true? Hadn't they known each other all their lives, been raised as siblings; didn't they feel each other's pain? But perhaps in the chaos of so much bloodshed, the wild animal could not be controlled. It took a step closer to her.

For reasons Soq did not understand, they were not afraid of the polar bear. They knew they should have been. But they also knew that there was a very good chance that the bear was about to eat the orcamancer, unless someone distracted it, and no one else was around to do the distracting, and the bear was far away, so maybe Soq would have time to escape—

"Hey!" Soq called, standing up in the bleachers. Thinking too late to calculate the distance from there to the exit, gauge how fast the bear could run, whether they stood a chance of making it out, whether the heavy door could be bolted to keep the bear from charging through and eating Soq.

It stopped, turned its head to look in Soq's direction. Sat back onto its hind legs. Cocked its head. The orcamancer gasped. The bear did not resist when the orcamancer put the cages back onto its head and hands.

The orcamancer took off her hat and bowed to Soq. Her hair fell in a heavy intricate coil behind her. She pressed the button for the elevator. Waited patiently. With her polar bear. Then she turned and said something. Soq's jaw buzzed, translating from Inuktitut-English Pidgin:

"I am in your debt."

The first words anyone had heard this woman say, and she had said them to Soq! Blood covered the animal, and the killer whale woman was shining with sweat, and Soq had never seen anything so beautiful. *I should go down there, say hello, start up a conversation, become best friends. Help her escape. Something.* But Soq could not move, could barely breathe. It took an incredible effort to call out, "You're welcome!" in the last second before the elevator whisked them away.

KAEV

———————▶

Kaev had been hoping for something like what he felt from a fight. The adrenaline rush, the thrill of danger, the joy of abandoning the ego and embracing the body, the animal. But he'd gotten no pleasure from his soaking. Only guilt, and shame, and now the extra special gift of having to worry about getting arrested.

He'd cried, after the first one. A bureaucrat, a flabby flimsy thing who felt truly safe only when behind a desk. He'd probably never been close to violence in his entire life. Kaev tried to tell himself that maybe the man was pure malevolence, merrily authorizing mass suffering—rent raises, embargo orders, strategic pharmaceutical restrictions—but he couldn't diminish how wretched it felt, the look on the guy's face when he thought he was about to be murdered.

The second one, he wouldn't feel bad about.

"He goes by Abijah," Go had told him. "But then he always tells everyone that it's a nom de guerre. And gets disappointed when no one cares enough to ask any follow-up questions."

Kaev recognized him. A slum enforcer. The muscle that came to kick you out of your home if you ignored an eviction notice, or roust you from your nook when the sub-subletter you were paying decided he wanted to clean house. Nasty thugs. Arsonists, torturers, evidence planters—effective enforcers had to be jacks of all the sordid, ugly trades that went into maintaining good tenant-landlord relations in a city where the landlords called all the shots. Many were failed beam fighters, and all of them were obsessed with the sport. He'd seen Abijah at the Yi He Tuan training center, watching from the bleachers while he practiced. Making awkward conversation. Flexing his muscles, complaining of soreness from a rough day, like there could be any comparing his job and Kaev's.

"This one needs to be quiet," Go said. "The first one had to make a very clear statement, but this one needs to be . . . more uncertain. It should unsettle the target—your victim's employer—but create just enough doubt that the target doesn't feel confident unleashing a violent response."

"And. Who." *Deep breath, Kaev. You can do this. It's just human speech. Everybody does it.* "Who's. The. The. The target?"

She'd stroked his face, and laughed, and dismissed him.

Kaev watched Abijah walk down Arm Eight. Tight clothes, like many insecure people who wanted to show off their muscles wore. Big boots that gave him an extra inch of height. Go's target had to be a shareholder. What other common ground could there be between the bureaucrat and the slum thug? Kaev could see the fear in people's eyes when they saw the enforcer pass. How their faces tightened. So he was well known out on Eight. He'd fucked up a lot of people. Kaev felt his lip curling, a snarl he could not keep in check.

"Look!" someone called, and pointed to the sea.

A giant onyx blade, seeming to be as big as a person, slid through the surface of the water. *The orca,* Kaev thought, and felt the hairs of his neck prickle. It kept rising, and there she was, straddling its back: the orcamancer.

She is real.

She was so close. So big. He wondered what her black clothes were made of. He shut his eyes and felt a strange flare, like remembered warmth.

"She comes through here every other day, seems like," someone said.

"Wonder she doesn't get hypothermia, out there in the ocean."

"You got to be human to get hypothermia."

The Arm Eight rabble continued the debate, but Abijah was oblivious, did not see her. Did not slow down. Kaev watched until it was clear the orcamancer would not be resurfacing this side of the Arm, then hurried to catch up with his quarry.

Abijah entered the gully between two cafés on tall stilts, unzipping already. His actions exaggerated. He wanted everyone to know he was going to go piss or fuck something.

Here you go, Kaev. An easy one. Duck down and sneak between the stilts so no one sees you entering the gully, sneak up behind him, knock him the fuck out. Push him into the sea.

Kaev did not duck down. The orcamancer would not have attacked like that. She never hid. Whatever she'd come to do, she wasn't trying to be secret about it.

"Hey," he said when Abijah stepped back onto the grid.

"Hey!" Abijah said, recognizing him, unable to place him.

"Kaev," he said, loudly, so the crowd between the two cafés could hear. He extended his left hand. "We met at the arena gym, remember?"

"Yeah!" his quarry said, smiling, and paused for an instant, thrown off by the unexpected hand, before extending his left to take Kaev's.

When he had it, Kaev pulled. Hard. He swung his body around, letting his right shoulder lead, swinging his elbow into his opponent.

A killing blow. The kind of move you never use in a beam fight, because it's unsportsmanlike. A thing you keep up your sleeve for those hopefully-never occasions when it's you or the other fighter.

Kaev pulled back at the last instant, striking the man's right clavicle instead of his windpipe. He heard it snap. Felt the man drop.

Pain incapacitated Abijah. He screamed. He bellowed. He sobbed. He tried to ask, *Why?* Thugs never learned what fighters learned— how to battle through pain—because they only ever hurt people who couldn't fight back.

Kaev looked up. A couple hundred pairs of eyes were on him. They clapped. They cheered. They held up screens to capture the moment.

Kaev smiled. Already he was running the scenarios, anticipating the ugliness that was in store for him, the revenge Go would take for his disobeying her, the punishment Safety would impose when they caught him. But there was another arena skill he had up his sleeve: how to put all his fears for the future into a box and briefly forget about them.

Someone recognized him, or ran facial rec with their screen. She called his name. Others heard her, joined in. Kaev shut his eyes and basked in it.

For once, they were cheering for him.

FILL

————————➤

Whales swam through the air above him, white against the dark blue twilight. Thick powdery snow, the best kind for the light projections. Their simple AIs pinged on the shape of a child and turned to swim circles around her. Fill felt oddly abandoned. When he was that age, he'd believed the snow projections loved him and him alone.

Behind him, the sea lions barked.

He loaded the latest episode of *City Without a Map*, broadcast in Mandarin. He didn't like the ones recorded in languages he didn't speak. His implant had the best translation software—even replicated perfectly the voice of the original speaker—but something did not survive the transition. No machine could match the earnestness, the hunger, of the original Readers.

Fill could feel the wet gathering in his clothes. A mark of his privilege, that this happened so rarely. The rich could have expensive dehumidifiers and lattices of salt polymer in their walls, to help strip away the ever-present damp. Everyone else in Qaanaaq just put up with being wet all the time. Having eczema. Having worse.

The little girl screamed with happiness as the whales combined into a tyrannosaurus and proceeded to chase her.

When I'm dead, the snow projections will still be here. This whole city will keep on working.

Fill had spent his whole life believing the city belonged to him. After a certain point he'd started to think maybe it was the other way around, but that was wrong, too. He meant nothing to Qaanaaq. Qaanaaq did not see him, did not know him, and nothing would change when he was slotted into his plastic sleeve and weighted with salt and dropped into the sea at the end of his Arm. He watched the waters churn. The water that would swallow him.

"Fill," said a rusted familiar voice, and then he was being hugged.

"Grandfather."

He settled into the embrace. Startlingly strong. Fill knew that his grandfather was as mortal as any man, yet he could not imagine any sickness or weapon that could reduce him.

"You still love the sea lions," the old man observed.

"Of course," Fill said, conscious for the first time of the rapt expression on his face, watching the piers where giant mammals flopped and dozed and barked.

But he hadn't loved them, not always. There had been a time when the sea lions were kid's stuff, something he couldn't be bothered with. Every kid went through that, he imagined, but when had he come out the other end? When had he become adult enough to give in to childish joy? Once again the eerie feeling came over him: the suspicion that what he felt might not be his. An unwholesome tingle traveled up the length of his spine, amplifying itself as it went, until his shoulders shook and his teeth came together in a sharp clack, cleaving open the side of his tongue.

"Everything okay?" his grandfather said, feeling him flinch, touching his sleeve.

Fill swallowed blood. "Of course. Just cold is all."

"Shall we go inside?"

"No. I like it."

What would he think, dear old Grandfather, if he learned I had the breaks? The dirty dirty taint of the poor? Smile politely, walk away, run home, burn his clothes, and cut all ties with me? What does he think when he sees them, the sick and dying, the men and women huddled on the grid about to break free of their bodies? Does he sneer, does he blame them for their bad decisions? Does he see them at all?

"How are you *really*, Grandfather?" Fill asked. "What takes up your time these days?"

"Managing my empire," he said with a grim laugh.

"I thought you had people for that."

"That's true—well, then, I spend my time looking over the shoulders of the people who manage my empire."

"That sounds boring."

"I wish it were."

"What's been going on?"

Grandfather spent a long time looking at the sea lions. Then he seemed to come to some kind of internal decision. "I'm under attack. Nothing I can't handle, but it's annoying all the same. A crime boss has gotten too big for her britches. This happens. Somebody wants more than the niche they've already carved out for themselves, and they make a move on a shareholder."

"What does one do in a situation like that?"

"We bide our time, typically. People get tired of throwing pebbles at a brick wall, eventually."

"Are you really that invincible?"

"No one's invincible. But we set this city up. Everything's stacked in our favor. Patience is all we need—maybe a trip out of town, if things really heat up, or a Protective Custody stint in one of the cushier suites in the Cabinet."

"So that urban legend is true? That the Cabinet has posh rooms to hide VIPs in, alongside the overcrowded wards full of screaming lunatics?"

"Very true." The old man looked at his hands. "Of course, once in a while a shareholder will go a little crazy. Meet violence with violence; slaughter his or her enemies. A separate part of the playbook. That's not my style."

Fill looked down onto a shifter skiff. Portions of the boat floor rose, fell. A worker from Recreations controlled it all from the rows of subdermals up and down her arms. Platforms circled and spun as she did. Children cavorted there, but they avoided eye contact with her. Augmentation was minimized in Qaanaaq, looked down upon, considered uncouth. In some grid cities, and most of the still-peopled places in the Sunken World, augmentation was much more accepted. Even obligatory. Fill wondered where she'd come from, whether she'd chosen them willingly. Whether she liked them.

A woman stood before him. Flickering, so that at first he thought she was a snow projection, but no—the projection was passing through her, a kraken now, dappling her body and then departing. Tall and beautiful, dark skin. Bald. Well into her fifties. Wearing clothes that were way too thin for the Qaanaaq cold. Like hospital robes. She stared at him. Smiling, maybe, but maybe not.

A shuttle bark disgorged passengers. They climbed up onto the Arm, passed between him and the woman, and when they were gone so was she.

A breaks vision? Fill shivered, licked his lips, tasted blood again. Resolved to bring the woman up, during his daily talk with Barron. Resolved not to. "Isn't it funny?" he said, blundering into it, because if there was one skill glib gay boys learned it was how to ease archly into a fraught topic. "I realized I know almost nothing about you! Most of my friends can find their family histories in the cloud, but you—shareholder erasure! Our family name is a great big digital void. Which can't have been cheap, by the way."

Grandfather laughed. "So it's an oral history project you're working on."

"Something like that. I know we're from New York. How did we . . ."

"Get out? Strike it rich?"

"I have to assume that we were at least a little rich from the start."

"Your father never wanted to know." A scowl, at the past, at the grid they stood on. "When he was little, maybe. He wanted the fairy tale. The movie version. But as a grown-up? Ignorance is bliss."

Fill blinked away the mention of his father, the tears that threatened to rise to the surface. "Is it that bad?"

"No one survived without getting their hands at least a little filthy. But I think you are strong enough for the truth. You're stronger than he was."

"I'm not," Fill said, the notion so ridiculous he had to laugh. "I've never done a goddamn thing. Like, period."

"You are. I've always seen it in you. The fact that it's never been put to the test doesn't mean it's not there."

"That's sweet of you to say," Fill said, unconvinced. "And my father? You never saw it in him?"

"Your father was a good boy. But he was not strong."

Images arrived unbidden. His father, departing for Heilongjiang Province to cover the Famine Migration. The camera equipment he let Fill inventory. "Mom always said he was brave. To go to those places. To take those pictures."

"Your mother wouldn't know strength if it kissed her on the cheek," Grandfather said. "If you'll pardon my saying so. Doing something dangerous and foolish is the opposite of strength."

"What is strength?" Fill asked, feeling that they were close to it now, the Thing, the Secret, the story his father hadn't wanted to know.

"I worked for a security firm. Buildings and events. Simple stuff: hire the guards and send them to the place that needed guarding. But these were insane times. The Real Estate Riots were in full swing— you've heard of them, surely? About to evolve into the Real Estate

Wars. I believed that security was about more than muscle. I talked the owner of the company into creating a new division, letting me lead it. Headhunting some of the biggest names in New York public relations. Intelligence, I called it. Because security wasn't about keeping bad guys out anymore—it was about keeping the bad guys from seizing what was yours. Squatter gangs, politicians susceptible to pressure, ready to use eminent domain to take property away and give it to the poor."

Fill tried hard to keep his eyes from glazing over.

"My unit went into neighborhoods, put agents in masquerading as tenants, assessed the situation, identified fault lines. Divisions between people. Once you know how to whip people up, they'll do all the work for you."

"What kind of work?"

"My specialty was religion. Fundamentalists, mostly. There's a lot of them—all sorts, though Christians were the easiest. Pretty soon we had dozens of contracts from all the biggest real estate developers. The manufacture and strategic deployment of mass idiocy, I told people. Practically put it on my business card."

Business cards—Fill had heard of those.

"Manufacture an outrage. Provide a target. Identify the people whom people listen to, the pastors or the PTA moms, and pay a couple of them to make a stink. I mostly just copied what was happening in politics. When we went national, I acquired several groups that had run election campaigns."

Grandfather paused, watching Fill's face. Waiting for a response. Fill was fairly sure he'd missed something. Sea lions clapped the rotting wood of their piers.

"A lot of people died, Fill."

"Ah."

"Some scenes played out, in Harlem and the Lower East Side, that . . . well, let's just say your father would have found quite a lot to photograph there. A smaller scale, but easily rivaling anything that came out of Calcutta. I regret it now, but what can you do? And you and I wouldn't be here if I hadn't. All my work, all over North America—none of that could have happened without New York."

Fill knew all about this. *City Without a Map* had taught him.

Remembered smoke blackens the sky. The shouts of long-dead citizens ring out in the street. Explosions: tanks firing on squatter strongholds; high-class cultural events bombed by tenant army activists.

Qaanaaq is a dream. At night you lie down and wake from it. Return to the real world, your life, your city, dying. Every night you are back there, watching it unfold in uncanny déjà vu slo-mo, because surely you have seen this before, surely you know what will happen, surely you will act differently, surely you will get out in time—

Grandfather had lost his son. Soon he'd lose his grandson. Whatever else he'd done, whatever horrific crimes he'd committed, it was hard not to pity him. To have fought so hard, to have acquired so much, and to end up with nothing. Well, nothing except . . . everything.

Fill had so many other questions. About the clients his grandfather had worked for when he was finished helping destroy New York City. About the things that were gone. The Metropolitan Opera; the Daughters of the Disappeared; Qaanaaq when it was still shiny and new.

Grandfather flung a crumpled napkin into the sea. Littering: another distinctly New York oddity about the old man. "I called you because I missed you," Grandfather said, "but I also had something up my sleeve. Something I want to give you. Two things, actually. I'm not seriously worried about that . . . thing I mentioned to you earlier.

Standard crime boss nonsense. We shareholders haven't held on to everything we have for this long without learning how to weather every storm. But still. It's silly not to take precautions. I need you to be able to access two things that only I can currently access. One is an apartment. Sealed, secret. Kept off the market. I know you already have a place—I just need you to have all the access info on this one, which so far isn't listed in any of the residential rosters. An investment, you know. We have several of them, in fact, but this one is special to me. Your grandmother and I . . . it was where we went when we wanted to escape."

Fill nodded, feeling very noble and dutiful. "Fair enough, Grandfather. And the second thing?"

"Software. A particularly unstable, dangerous program. Cobbled together by an alliance of different shareholders, combining ten or so very different security protocols and illegal data-mining approaches. Toxic stuff, military grade. We created it in the early days of Qaanaaq, to share information, observe patterns, keep track of our units . . . assess problems, figure out how to deal with them . . . but it hasn't been used in twenty years, maybe longer. Too erratic. Undependable. It did what you wanted, but it would also do a bunch of things you didn't want."

"What do you want me to do with it?"

"Good heavens, nothing! Not for now, anyway. Just hold on to it. I have no idea whether any of the other shareholders are still alive, or have access to it—I know it hasn't been used, it's on the list of programs our watchdogs prowl for—but if I'm the last one with access, I don't want it to die with me. Although maybe it should. But it's worth a lot, and fifty years from now you may be glad you have it in your back pocket."

"Sure," Fill said, because all of this seemed to be making the old man happy. What did it matter that he wanted nothing to do with an empty apartment and some temperamental software? He could finally do something for the old man, play some small part in the family business. And, of course, he could not say, *No, Grandfather, I'm sorry, I won't be alive in fifty years, or fifteen, or maybe not in five months.*

"I'll send you all the information."

"Thanks, Grandfather. Oh, look!"

Two sea lions barked and bumped chests. Both men laughed.

ANKIT

———————➤

A nkit bought flowers, then threw them into the sea, then bought different flowers. Scentless ones, cold emotionless white. The angry red of mainland roses would be too provocative; the purple scent of hothouse hyacinths could make the whole madhouse lose its mind.

Ankit dressed carefully, then undressed, then dressed differently. Sterile gray. Genderless lines.

"Fucking Cabinet," she said, looking at herself in the mirror, looking at the time, wondering how many more outfits she could go through before she had to take the zip line out to her appointment. Planning every little detail was its own kind of paralysis, so she decided to leave early and kill time over there rather than keep on burrowing deeper into unproductive thoughts.

Her screen sparkled. Barron: *There is absolutely no Quet-38-36.0 anywhere in Qaanaaq.*

That didn't seem right. Or possible. Qaanaaq was sick with drugs, full of smugglers and machines to bring even the most obscure pills to the far-flung arrivals who fiended for them. Anything you wanted, anything at all, someone was selling it. But she had too much else to think about, too many other things to keep from stressing out over.

Another one: *I have a friend with access to a molecular assembly machine, who does off-legal drug printing sometimes. I am going to try to get him to make us some.*

Good, she said, and set a five-hour block on further notifications from Barron.

Of course she hadn't told Safety that she knew who the soaker was. She was still too much of a scaler at heart to even think about snitching. That would have been true even if the criminal in question weren't her brother. They'd questioned her for almost an hour, standing there at the edge of the grid, apologizing endlessly for the inconvenience, seeing her fancy work clothes and mistaking her for the important person everyone else mistook her for.

She shut her eyes against the ocean of words churning inside her. The things she wanted to ask her mother; the things she wanted to say to her. Cabinet staff said to minimize dialogue, focus on physical presence, touch, caress; her mother's psychological condition was unique, easily triggered into episodes by even seemingly harmless questions or comments.

She hugged the flowers to her chest. Shut her eyes and tried to remember her mother's face.

The woman she saw was not her mom. She knew this. She was a summary, a splice, a combination of a hundred warm, loving, smiling mothers she'd seen in movies and at the homes of friends and in the families she visited for work. Ankit had no real memories of her mother's face from when she was a child. What she'd seen the last time she'd been with her mother had been too horrible to hold on to. Fifteen years ago, a dark red wet sobbing mess, a mouth open wide in a howl Ankit could not hear through the window in the door.

Her jaw bug buzzed. *Fifty-Seventh Street Corp.,* it whispered.

She answered. "Breckenridge?"

"Still in the hospital, the poor creature," said a hale but ancient voice. "Martin Podlove speaking. I am the shareholder responsible for Fifty-Seventh Street Corp."

"Mr. Podlove, thank you for your call," she said. "I'm surprised to hear you identify yourself so openly. Shareholder invisibility—"

"—is a privilege we dispense with quite frequently, actually. When we know someone can keep a secret. When we know how much they stand to lose."

He let her chew on that for an instant or two, and then when she started to respond he said, "My colleague passed on your request for funds. I figured I owed you a call, at least. There's something cowardly about sending bad news as words on a screen."

"No," Ankit said, stricken. "No . . . you can't do that. Fyodorovna will lose this election if you don't help. In a different year an incumbent might be able to weather this storm, but times are too tough. Rents have been rising, out on Arm Seven. Evictions, displacement . . . People are mad, and they blame her for their problems, and they'll choose the devil they don't know."

Podlove said nothing. He was enjoying this.

"We're useful to you," Ankit said, and knew, then, that the battle was lost.

"Everyone is useful to us. Think I haven't been backing your opposition? Think they won't do what I ask? You know politics better than that, Ankit."

He tapped off.

She looked up at the Cabinet. She stood there until the shaking subsided. Early, still, for her appointment, but the processing always took too long and she figured she could start the waiting now. Better that than standing around wishing for the ability to summon a wave of cleansing nuclear fire out of thin air.

Entering the Cabinet felt like sinking below the sea. White noise pods lined the curved walls and the doorway, cocooning the building from the sonic chaos of the city outside. People spoke but she could not hear them, and that was part of the process, part of the therapy. She looked at the crowd in the waiting room, wondered who was there to be processed and who was simply visiting. Either way, she felt immense pity for them.

"Ankit Bahawalanzai," she said into the triage scanner. "Two P.M. appointment."

The hexagon flashed green. A door hissed open. She was pulling off her shirt before it had shut behind her, placing her clothes on the table, standing in her underwear in the center of the room, letting the lasers wipe over her, pretending she could feel them. They'd be confirming her identity, scanning for threats and communicable medical conditions and who knew what else. Medical scanning algorithms changed all the time, looked for different things, got more sophisticated in some ways, became blindingly stupid in others. A couple of years ago they had all been obsessed with hair follicle analysis. Before that it had been fingernails. She imagined the AIs getting together at conferences, arrogant as doctors, swapping stories in silicon hallways, exchanging bad ideas.

A weird hiccup, in the flow of the white noise.

"Ms. Bahawalanzai?"

"Hi," Ankit said, and felt her cheeks heat up, because this was not good, an actual human being was never a good sign.

"I'm Michaela," said the young woman. "Can we sit?"

Ankit saw that the table had become two chairs. She hated this place, its expensive and unnecessary technology. Some Health facilities were nicer than others, and few were "nicer" than this, but they all shared the same redundant proliferation of scientific equipment, the telltale traces of the massive investments made in health care during the Cancer Years.

"What's going on?"

"I'm so sorry," Michaela said. "But your body scans showed anxiety, tension. Your mother is not permitted proximity to those things. You understand, I'm sure. As a blood relative, especially?"

"No," Ankit said, "no, I do not understand. What does my being a blood relative have to do with anything?"

"Ah," Michaela said, frowning down at something on her screen. She had blurted something out, pertaining to some classified aspect of her mother's condition. Something Ankit was not supposed to know. "Mentally ill people are especially sensitive to the emotional states of others."

"I know that. Of course I know that. But you said—"

Michaela stood. The software would be guiding her through this stage of the conversation, surely. The Oh Shit You Fucked Up AI, Ankit thought. Would it cost her? Did they keep track of every little error?

Her mother was Code 76. That meant that someone, maybe in Safety and maybe in Health and maybe in the home nations, had decided that the details of her confinement constituted a protected secret. Whatever was wrong with her, what events had precipi-tated it—even her name—someone had convinced someone else that these could never be revealed. Ankit had always known this. She'd made her peace with it, the way you make peace with what can never be known. Digging into things like that only made you an-gry, started you down dangerous pathways, got you in trouble. But when she walked out of the Cabinet that day, when she tossed her bouquet of flowers into the sea and shrieked into the rising vortex, she decided it was time to get in trouble. To dig. To find out why her mother was in there.

To maybe possibly somehow get her out.

KAEV

---➤

*S*o. *Now you're on the run. Was it worth it?*
    Safety would certainly have ID'd him from the clips of his assault on Abijah. The crowd calling his name. By now they could be camped out across the street from his shipping container, waiting to arrest him. Not to mention Go, who would be furious, possibly furious enough to scoop him up before Safety got him and spend a day or a week carving him up before handing over whatever was left for arrest.

Yes. Yes, it was worth it.

And then there was Go's target, the powerful man or woman who employed his two victims. Whoever they were, they'd have minders, watchers, microdrones maybe, and they would have figured out who he was as well, and were even now working out an abduction plan, were engaging the services of an old crusty interrogator from one of the fallen superpower states to torture out the name of who had hired him.

At this, at least, Kaev smiled. He'd give them Go in a heartbeat.

But it wouldn't help; they wouldn't trust a name easily given; they'd still have to torture him to verify the truth of what he said.

But that wouldn't matter. Pain he could handle. He'd had plenty. They'd still be after Go at the end of it, and maybe they'd get her.

Kaev walked. Up and down Arm Six, and then Arm Seven. Head full of screaming; the roaring of savage beasts; the orgasmic cry of the crowd when the fight was at its peak, when he'd given them something beautiful, something to help them break free of the moment, their lives, their city, the weight of their slowly dying bodies . . . And what had he gotten for his troubles? Add up all the joy and pleasure he'd brought to the people of this city, and what had he received in exchange for it? Barely enough money to eke out a subsistence living. He wasn't angry, not at them. They didn't owe him anything. They paid their money; they had their own troubles. It was the city he was mad at. The city that he loved. He wanted to punch something, punch everything, pin it down and snap its neck, this squirming tentacled mass of thoughts and whispers and memories and contradictory beliefs that screamed and gibbered inside his head.

Back down Arm Seven; through the Hub; onto Arm Eight. A slide messenger sped past, ululating all the way. He could hear himself yip and caw, could not make himself stop.

Someone was singing in a high window. People were making love all around him, in the darkness of bedrooms and alleyways and coffin hotels. People were dying. They crowded him, pressed on his skull with a more-than-physical pressure. He wanted to scream, but he was good at not screaming. He spent most of his time not screaming even though he wanted to.

He walked.

And then: he stopped.

Because the pressure ceased. The screaming and the singing evaporated. The fog lifted. Peace flooded him, a peace like nothing he'd ever known. A quiet. Shivers climbed his spine, building in intensity as they went.

He looked around. Saw no one. For such an overcrowded place,

Arm Eight had a weird way of feeling completely empty sometimes. Boats rose and fell with the waves on his right, and on his left were a series of squat strutted buildings on a floating platform.

He took a few steps farther out onto the Arm and felt the peace subside just the slightest bit. Felt the squirming thing in his head start to gurgle again.

Kaev returned to where he'd been. Took a breath; basked in the silence. Then took several steps back, toward the Hub. Again the gurgling rose inside him.

So. Just one spot. Okay. Kaev didn't wonder why or try to investigate what, exactly, was having this effect on him. Poke around too much at something good and you tend to find something bad. Depleted uranium, probably, the weaponized stuff scraped from the wreckage of Chernobyl or Hanul, causing blissful sensations as it killed off brain cells by the thousands. If so, better to let it kill him swiftly and pleasantly. So he sat down on the freezing metal of the curb, beside the clamps where the building platform was docked, and hugged his knees to his chest to conserve heat, and shut his eyes, and let hot tears of happiness warm his face.

ANKIT

Ankit began with the easy stuff. The human stuff. She called her contact at Health, second assistant to the director. A sweet boy, one of a couple dozen agency flunkies she forced herself to be friends with, sending regifted tickets or day passes that had been given to Fyodorovna, even meeting up for drinks or karaoke or isolation tanking when her calendar reminded her it had been a while.

"One of my constituents' mother-in-law got in trouble," she said. "Sad story, really. Locked up. The Cabinet. I felt so bad for her . . . and she's been a loyal donor . . ."

Joshi promised to look into it.

Next, she called her woman at Safety. Spun the same sob story. If there had been a violent incident behind her mother ending up in the Cabinet, Safety might have a record of it.

"We don't use Health's numbering system," she told Ankit. "So that patient number won't be helpful to us."

"Really?" Ankit said, surprised. "Agencies don't coordinate that kind of thing? Seems inefficient."

"When things are inefficient, there's usually a reason for it. Things are only supposed to run so well in Qaanaaq. Efficiency is expensive.

Helping people get what they're entitled to, solving problems quickly, that sort of thing is costly."

"Fascinating," Ankit said, unfascinated, and angry at her for the civics lesson. "But if there was a Safety case that ended in the subject being confined to the Cabinet, you may have her patient number in the file, yeah?"

"We might . . ."

"You can check?"

"I could . . ."

"Great!" Ankit said, imagining stabbing the woman in the throat. "Thanks!"

She scanned software markets while she waited for her humans to do their work. Humans were slow and sloppy but comprehensible. Softwares were spooky, messy, working in mysterious ways, full of secret tics and legacy apps that could bring a whole heap of trouble on her head. Suppose she bought a breach hack, and it found what she was looking for, but the packet had snitch software attached? Law enforcement, crime lords, black-budget AI could rain hell down on her at any moment.

People made fun of them, called them old-fashioned and inept, but Ankit decided to take her chances at a human brokerage. Software archaeologists or engineers might not be able to match the breadth of scope of a machine broker, some of which could scan through thousands of softwares a second to find the right one for the job, but they made up for it with the depth of their knowledge. Even when scanning software could parse every packet of code, foresee every potential trigger, it was notoriously bad at assessing outcomes. A human broker, at least, was working with a smaller number of apps that they knew well and had seen in action enough to know more or less how likely a given software was to fuck her over. She called her favorite.

"What's the target this time?" Mana asked.

The past three elections, Ankit had had some reason to call her.

Shipping manifests one year, and Emirati birthrates the election before that. Access to an opponent's email during Fyodorovna's first campaign, when things were extra ugly.

"The Cabinet," Ankit said. "I need to know why someone is in there."

"That's . . . difficult."

"Difficult. Not impossible."

"Correct." She told her the price. Ankit had to fight not to flinch.

A quarter, maybe a third of their entire campaign budget. Two weeks' worth of robodustings; a week of blips. The right thing to do was go to Fyodorovna, get her to sign off. She could talk the woman into anything, always. It wouldn't be hard . . . just time consuming.

But going through Fyodorovna meant putting her neck in the noose. It meant that when the Arm manager lost the election, she'd blame Ankit for it. Which would fuck up Ankit's only hope of avoiding the gutter.

Because Fyodorovna would be fine. Arm managers always were. Some charity or shareholder or someone else she'd done favors for would find her a place. Always helpful to have a somewhat famous face up your sleeve, to impress difficult clients or charm potential money. And wherever she landed, she'd need a chief of staff.

"Sold," Ankit said.

"Do you want to run them, or should I?"

"You do it," she said, signing off on the standard dummy invoice she always billed her. Security for a campaign donation site, on the fraudulent letterhead of an actual, legit software security firm. An audit from Finance or Campaigns might ping the fact that the firm in question never filed a corresponding invoice, but audits were like shark attacks—really terrible, and really unlikely.

On the grid, Ankit almost collided with a shopkeeper arguing with a woman who appeared to be swathed in loops of a hundred different brightly colored fabrics. Her jaw bug translated as best it could, between Mandarin and the jerky pan-glossic stew that late-stage breaks tended to induce:

> You can't stay here. Go over there, maybe. They serve food at the Krish—
>
> We made fire. All of us together. We set them all on fire.
>
> You need to go. I don't want to call Safety. You're scaring my customers.
>
> Your customers should be scared. We are made of fire and we will burn you all to ash.

Joshi won first place, pinging her an hour later to say he'd come up short. The file had three separate injunctions on it, something he'd never seen before, and who was this, the Nineteenth Dalai Lama?

"Maybe," she said. "That's what I was hoping you could tell me."

The software broker came in second, calling near midnight the next evening. Her friend at Safety never got back to her at all.

"Sending you something now," the software broker said. "More than I thought I'd find, actually."

For a split second, Ankit debated saving it for the morning. She was exhausted, and the message Mana sent held dozens of files. But she knew she'd never be able to fall asleep, wondering what she had. She couldn't even finish brushing her teeth before doubling back to the bedroom and opening the first folder.

Four hours later, Ankit was still awake.

Two hours after that, Ankit called in sick.

Which wasn't a lie. Dizziness made her light-headed; the whole city seemed to be spinning. Staggering, sickening, the information she held in her hands.

Too weird. Too fucking weird.

The whole thing felt wrong, uncanny, like a dream where the world was sideways in some subtle, unsettling way.

Maybe her job *wasn't* in danger. Maybe Fyodorovna *could* win. Maybe she *could* get her mother out.

One solution to all her problems. All she had to do was bring down a shareholder. Simple. What did it matter that it had never been done before? She had a weapon now. Maybe a couple of them. Maybe there was a chink in Martin Podlove's armor.

And anyway, lots of things had never been done before, and then they were done.

SOQ

————▶

Blackfish Woman was a ghost. Glimpsed from afar. Impossible to touch. Every day new sightings. In the water, on boats, on the grid. With the polar bear or astride her whale or alone, but never without her blade. Always moving. Since the slaughter on the Sports Platform she'd been impossible to pin down. If anyone knew where she slept, where she moved her rig to, money or fear or respect kept their mouths shut.

Soq made maps. Drew lines connecting the dots of the places she'd been seen. Looked for patterns. Found none.

Soq collected pictures. Soq asked questions. Noodle vendors and ice scrapers and boatmen and algae vat stirrers were all only too happy to talk Soq's ear off with every little detail of their sightings. Nor was Soq the only one asking them to. All of Qaanaaq was talking about the orcamancer. Soq wondered how many of them were asking from simple curiosity and how many were like Soq, working for someone else, crime bosses or shareholders or the intelligence agencies of foreign nations, for whom the orcamancer represented an unsettling, inexplicable, existential threat.

There was one thing Soq knew, that none of them knew. That Go didn't know. That Soq kept secret, without knowing why.

Killer Whale Woman was afraid of the polar bear. The polar bear would kill her if it had the chance.

What did that mean?

Impossible to research her without delving deep into who the nanobonded were, how their tech or magic worked. But what was real and what was lies, legend, misunderstanding? Many sources said they could each bond to only one animal. Others told stories of women bonded to whole flocks of birds, a man who headed a pack of wolves. At any rate, killer whale woman was clearly not bonded to the polar bear. So . . . why was she traveling with it?

All of this was extracurricular. Soq still made slide deliveries. Dao had not discussed a pay rate for Soq's research when he handed over the assignment.

Nor did he mention one four days later, when he buzzed Soq.

"Progress report," he barked. "What have you got?"

"A whole lot of not very much," Soq said, stopping at the entrance to Arm Three. They kicked at the cylinders set into the ground, the thick forest of bollards that could be raised in times of trouble to divert demonstrations or thin out unruly crowds. Soq delivered a long list of scraps, so flimsy that they felt compelled to apologize for it.

"That's fine," Dao said. "That's excellent, actually."

"No, it's not," Soq said. "I've got nothing. Nothing Go couldn't find out herself by doing some half-assed web searches."

"What would it take, to get more?" Dao asked.

Soq laughed. "If money was no object I'd say send me to Nuuk. That's the last grid city she went to before coming here. Killed a couple of families of boat people. Let one guy live. Allegedly. Number one lesson learned here is that nothing is ever certain when it comes to her."

There was a long pause, like maybe Dao was writing something down.

"So . . . are you going to send me to Nuuk?"

Dao laughed. "No, Soq. She doesn't want you traveling yet."

Yet. Soq trembled at the promise in that word.

Two days later, though, Jeong pinged Soq an address. "Not a delivery," he said. "Dao says it's a meeting."

"Huh," Soq said.

"When did you get so important that you get to have *meetings*?" Jeong said. His chuckle was not without pride.

"When I became a spy," Soq said. Their sense of power lasted all the way down Arm Seven, to the address Jeong pinged, past a blue-striped monkey fighting with an otter and a wild-haired woman asking passersby to help *burn it all down,* and onto a decent-sized old houseboat and in the door, and then burst like a bubble at the sight of a man strapped to a chair.

"You made it, good," said Dao, playing with a shape-memory polymer perched on a windowsill. He tapped at his screen and it transformed from a bird to a ballerina, then he grabbed it and crushed it in his fist. "I brought you what you asked for."

Bruises crisscrossed the man's face. There was blood on his clothes. "What I . . . asked for?"

"The survivor. From Nuuk."

"Shit, Dao," Soq said. "What the fuck did you do to this guy? I didn't ask for this. I didn't want anyone to get hurt—"

And Soq knew, hearing the words come out, how stupid they sounded. Dao at least did Soq the favor of not saying any of the things Soq knew he could have said. *Did you think working for a crime boss would be bloodless, painless? Did you think your hands would never get dirty? What did you think we do here, exactly?*

Dao did say: "He's yours now. See what you can get from him just by being nice, and call me if you need some help or advice being . . . not so nice."

"And then you'll . . . ?"

"Shoot him in the head; take him home and give him a bubble bath; I don't know, Soq. We'll have that conversation when we have it."

Dried fish guts caked the floor. Crab or lobster shells cracked underfoot. On an ancient wooden table, a methane burner and a wok and two green glass bottles. Did the boat belong to him, the poor beat-up man bound in front of Soq? Had Dao's soldiers dragged it all the way from Nuuk? Or was it one of a thousand syndicate hiding places here in Qaanaaq, perfect for carrying out all kinds of illicit activity?

"Untie him," Soq said.

Dao bowed and did so. "I'll be outside," he said to the man. "Don't do anything stupid."

The guy was young. Bearded, burly; his head wrapped in an American flag bandanna. It was faded and filthy.

"Tell me about the orcamancer," Soq said.

His mouth opened like he had something smart to say, but then he thought better of it. "Who are you?"

"My name is Soq. I work for an entrepreneur here in Qaanaaq."

"Uh-huh, *entrepreneur*. And your people brought me all the way here to talk about the person who killed my parents. Why is that?"

Soq was about to answer, but then realized—they didn't *know* why Go was so interested. Dao said Go didn't want any unknown variables introduced into the equation of her power play, but what if that was untrue, or half-true? What if Soq's information gathering would be used to harm the orcamancer? Now wasn't the moment to ponder that question too seriously. And in any event, one of the many life skills Soq had learned in foster care: the best way to get information out of someone is to tell them what they want to hear. "Maybe my employer sees her as a threat. Maybe she has a vendetta against her for something. Maybe she wants to destroy her, and your information could help us achieve that."

He smiled. "I was at work. I clean lobster pots. I came home—my parents, they brought this boat with them from America—and they were . . . dead. My grandparents, too. And she was still there. Like she was waiting for me. Sitting right where you're standing now."

Soq looked around. So this was where it happened. They shut their eyes and tried to picture it.

"It stank in here, so bad. She was sitting on the floor, covered in blood, looking like she was praying, or meditating, or, I don't know, taking a fucking nap."

"The reports all said she hit you with the butt of her staff, and left."

"That's right."

"She didn't say anything to you first? She waited for you, knocked you out, and then left? Why wait for you at all?"

He looked up at Soq, his eyes steely. Bracing himself for pain.

"She didn't say anything to you?"

He shook his head.

"Hey," Soq said, pulling up a stray chair, scorched battered white plastic. Had it been there, then? "Come on. Help us out. We can help avenge them. Any little bit of information you might have, we could use it. Maybe she threatened to hurt you, if you told anyone—"

He spat out: "She didn't. She wanted me to tell."

"So tell me. You're safe now. We'll protect you."

He laughed, and Soq knew he was right to laugh. "You can't. My family, they weren't soft. They had guns. Weapons. Lots of them. And they'd . . . done things. Vicious things. To survive. But she took them out easy. Without using her damn . . . fucking . . . animals. Whatever she wants, whatever she came here for, she's going to get it. Fuck any *entrepreneurs* who stand in her way."

"What did she tell you?"

He nodded. "She said my family deserved what she'd done to them, but I didn't. Told me to make sure everybody knew it."

". . . And?"

His face, a practiced mask of masculine hardness, sagged. Reddened. Broke.

"She asked about my uncle," he said, in gasps, like he was about to cry. "Asked where she could find him."

"And you didn't tell her. At first."

"At first. But she . . ."

"She hurt you," Soq said.

"She hurt me. She threatened . . ."

"To hurt you worse."

"Yeah."

"So you told her. Where to find your uncle."

He was weeping now. "He was working an ice ship. I told her the name of it. That's all."

"And then you heard . . ."

"I heard he was killed. Week, two weeks later. He was all alone on the glacier, working an ice saw, and they said he must have fallen . . . Forty stories high, that glacier. Onto ice. Happens all the time, they said. And he'd been out there for a couple of days by the time they found him. Said those bite marks, those missing chunks, anything could have gotten to him after he fell."

Soq stepped closer. Tapped his bandanna. "Your family—they're from the States."

"Proud Americans," he said. "Always will be."

"Even when there is no America?"

"It's in our hearts."

Soq imagined the hearts of his parents, and grandparents, skewered and plucked from their bodies through a shattered rib cage and stomped on.

"Religious?"

"Sure."

Of course. They participated in the nanobonder slaughter. That's why they were butchered. Soq swooned to think that the Killer Whale Woman was strong and wise enough to find and punish the guilty, even decades later.

"What did they do, I wonder? During the migration?"

He sniffed, a wet thick sound. "What they had to do."

"Including killing people?"

"You soft fucking city people can't even imagine. What it was like. Everybody trying to kill everybody. Blacks against whites, immigrants against citizens. If you didn't have guns—lots of them—you were going to lose everything you loved."

He didn't know, either. He'd have been born long after and raised on stories. Soq had seen those documentaries. The narratives of fear, of lies, of They Want to Destroy Us. There were so many movies about how easy it is to manipulate people, and what atrocities you could get them to cheerfully commit while believing they did it for the sake of their children's survival.

Soq shut their eyes and they could smell her, the orcamancer, in the room with them—could feel her rage, the righteous thrill of hurting the people who hurt her people. She was not a young woman. She'd traveled for so many years. Had vengeance been the only thing, the only thread pulling her forward? Soq opened their eyes. That couldn't be all. There had to be more to her than bloodshed, violence, punishing the guilty. Soq couldn't say why they thought that, why they wanted so badly to believe it.

She is looking for something. Someone.

"She didn't say anything else?"

"Nothing."

"Thanks," Soq said, putting a hand on his shoulder. They regretted not asking the man's name.

The bearded man said nothing. Tears were rolling down his face. He cupped his hands in his lap, an oddly pacific gesture for a man so full of hard angles and coiled anger.

Soq left. Dao waited on the deck in a cloud of pine needle smoke.

"Got something?"

"Something," Soq said. "I'll write it up for Go."

What would that write-up say? *Talking to this man, standing in that space, I gained a profound spiritual understanding of who the Blackfish Woman is and it is of absolutely no strategic or practical value to you.*

Soq hopped from the boat to the grid. "And Dao?"

"Yeah?"

"Whatever you do to him? I don't want to know."

Dao frowned. "You won't always be able to hide, Soq. From the consequences of our actions."

"I know!" Soq said. "But I want to hide today."

KAEV

————————▸

For the third time in twelve hours, Kaev crossed the Arm to pee into the ocean. Even those few steps cost him, caused a slight shrinking of that blissful calm, and as soon as he was done he hurried back to the bare metal bar he'd been sitting on.

He was pretty sure he'd slept, some. Hard to say. His body felt like it needed nothing, not sleep and not food and not sex, and not fighting, which for the first time in his life held no appeal for him. Everything ached, but nothing hurt. A noodle stall had set up beside him, and occasional wafts of warm sweet-savory air hit him, and those were nice, but when they weren't there he didn't miss them.

Narcissus. The man who fell in love with his own reflection and wasted away staring into the water. Why did he remember that? Why did his mind work now? Why did school, math, history, myth, all the things that had eluded him, refused to cohere in his mind, suddenly make sense? Where memory had been a churning sea, uncontrollable, spitting up unwanted objects and hiding the things he most desired, it now yielded easily to his wishes. He thought about his childhood, and there it was. Foster homes. Even: further back, to times he'd never been able to call to mind, to places that weren't so much memories of things as of feelings, of safety, of fear, of flight. Other people: a mother, a sibling—or were they a grandmother and a pet? Because in that stage of pre-memory there were no words to attach to things, no societal structure to plug people into.

"Hemorrhoids," said the noodle vendor. "Sit on cold metal too long, you'll get hemorrhoids."

"Thanks," Kaev said, but he did not move. She took a crinkly green tarp, folded it into an approximate rectangle, handed it over. He took it, bowed in gratitude, and sat on it. And it did feel better.

She was popular. The docking bar and every other surface people could sit on were crowded with customers slurping down bowls of broth. But they came and went, for even people with nowhere to go weren't eager to remain in the cold too long.

Kaev knew that he could not stay there forever. Sooner or later Safety would come, tell him he had to move along. And when he refused, they'd send Health. The windscreen magnified the sun's heat by day, but now the sun was setting, and people who chose to stay unsheltered overnight could be deemed ipso facto insane and taken off the grid by force. And Kaev could not afford another trip to the Cabinet right now. Even if it had helped, slightly, before. The cost was too great. And whatever benefit he'd derived from his time there was gone the second he left the building. So if Health or Safety showed up and tried to force him to move from this spot, he'd be obliged to beat them senseless. And then he'd have an even bigger problem.

"You're new," the noodle vendor said.

"I'm old," Kaev said.

"Not as old as me," she said, and laughed. He'd been sitting on the tarp for an hour, maybe two, for all he knew a week. The flow of customers had ebbed. Once again Arm Eight looked empty, though he knew it wasn't.

"Here," she said, and handed him a bowl.

"I can't," he said. "I don't have any money."

"Of course you don't," she said, and laughed again, and he loved her, but then again, in that stretch of bliss he loved everyone. "My noodles are irresistible. If you had any money, you wouldn't have been able to go this long without buying a bowl."

"Thank you," he said.

"And anyway, you paid for it already."

"I did?"

"You gave me something just as valuable," she said. "I saw you fight. Hao Wufan. Shame about him."

"Terrible," Kaev said, lowering his face to the broth, letting the steam warm him, wondering what shameful fate had befallen the boy.

"Some people aren't ready for success," she said. "You fight beautifully, though. I've seen you before."

"I told you," he said. "I'm old. Been fighting forever."

"A journeyman," she said, and so she was a true fight follower, someone who could appreciate his role in the ecosystem. A rare thing. He still got recognized sometimes, and that was always nice, but most casual fight fans considered him a chump, a loser. "The noodles are a belated payment, for all the pleasure I took in watching you fight."

"The pleasure is always mine, believe me," he said, and handed back the empty bowl. "Thank you. The noodles were delicious."

Eventually she too departed, taking back the tarp with an apology, telling him she didn't want to see him there when she returned in the morning.

It happened soon enough after her departure that he knew they'd been waiting for it. Twelve men, dressed in the nondescript black of syndicate security, clutching obvious weaponry inside their jackets. One of them was Dao, who smiled and did not hurry. Kaev's thigh muscles tightened, preparing to leap into horse stance. He took off his hood, which would impair his peripheral vision. Cold wind sharpened his senses.

Something came up from the water across the Arm from him. A sea lion, he thought at first, turning around, because there were lots of those that lived on Qaanaaq's garbage and fish-gut castoffs. But it was big, bigger than any sea lion, bigger than any animal Kaev had ever seen alive, up close, and white—

The polar bear opened his eyes and looked at Kaev.

In the instant of that eye contact, Kaev felt like he had broken free of his body. A happiness surged through him, warm as the sun, blissful as a thousand orgasms. The peace he'd felt while sitting there had been ten times greater than the joy of fighting, but this new sensation was ten times greater than that peace had been.

"Hello, Kaev," Dao said. He and his soldiers had their backs to the grid edge; they could not see the polar bear. "You've been sitting here for a long time. I've got to presume that means you wanted us to find you."

But Kaev could not hear him.

We are one, he thought, eyes locked with the animal's.

And it felt: Different. Stable. Like if he looked away, like if he took a step back, it would not diminish. Like now that he'd found it, now that they'd recognized each other, they were linked, and nothing on earth could break that connection. Like nothing could hurt him anymore ever. Like nothing confused him; like he saw how the world worked in a whole new way.

"Dao," he said, blinking, turning. "You should probably leave now."

The man laughed. A couple of his soldiers followed suit. "That's not going to happen, Kaev." He held up a handful of zip ties. "Are you going to let us put these on you? Or is it going to be a whole thing?"

"You need to leave. Now."

More laughter. Kaev took a step forward. One of Dao's men shot his arm out, flung something, a sharpened shard of windscreen glass, Qaanaaq's own homegrown answer to the *shuriken*. It struck him in the cheek with terrifying precision—a warning shot, but a stern one.

Kaev grunted in pain, but the grunt was bigger than him. With a roar, the polar bear pulled itself out of the water mere feet from where the men stood. Water coursed off it, like it was made of water. And it was as fast as water, as implacable. It swung its bulk around to knock the man into the sea and then dove in after him, all before any of the others had had time to aim and shoot.

And Kaev shut his eyes and he was *in* the water, he was biting into the man's arm and pulling him down, down, until he could feel the warmth of the geothermal cone, until the man ran out of air and opened his mouth and breathed in water, and the bear released him and swam for the surface—

Kaev opened his eyes to see the men scrambling, aiming weapons into the water. Nervous, yelling, unsure where the bear would emerge next. And Kaev knew, somehow, that the bear could see what he saw, could tell where the men were standing. So it knew the safest place to emerge, to take them by surprise. In the instant before it did, Kaev gave out a shout. He ran at them so that they turned, aimed weapons. One of the men was yanked back before he could pull the trigger, the bear grabbing hold of his leg and pulling him into the water, breaking that leg effortlessly and then the other one, and Kaev was crouching down to avoid the shots from the others, slamming into another man, knocking him off balance, taking the gun from his hands and turning it toward the man's accomplices, holding down the trigger so that bullets splattered indiscriminately.

He grinned at the fear on their faces, caught between him and the bear. Two expert killing machines. One thing, one organism. Acting in concert in ways that had nothing to do with language, planning, rational thought. One animal. Dao was yelling orders—*Focus on the bear!*—even as he ran for safety, saving his own skin—but they were not enough; these people with their mighty weapons and separate fragile minds could not get past themselves, could not trust one another, could not know what someone else was supposed to do. One bullet, two, struck the bear. Kaev felt the pain of them, but he also felt the animal's comforting fearlessness.

Animals exist in the moment. They don't worry about whether they will bleed to death, whether they will die. The wounds were minor. Their enemies fell swiftly, terribly.

FILL

———————➤

Round doors. Frosted windows that let in light but nothing else. Leather straps, stinking of the fear-sweat of strangers.

The breaks caused dreams to creep into waking life, made him wonder whether anything he was seeing was really there, whether anything he remembered was really his—but they also changed his dreams. Stretched them out, tightened their walls. A short nap might leave him with hours and hours' worth of remembered dreams. And Fill could no longer wake up from a nightmare, no matter how hard he tried.

Injections. Isolation. A dark shape flapping past the window.

This one was the worst. An instant before, he had been dozing on a bench in a greenhouse park boat, and then—blink of the eyes—he was here. Confined, chained, bound like Prometheus. Strapped to a bed, knowing in his gut that no one was coming to rescue him. Praying for it anyway.

The Cabinet—it had to be. Days and days of it. Months. Years.

Who was he? These memories belonged to someone. They had to. He ran his fingers over his face, tried to piece together what he looked like, but his mind was numb with pain and loneliness. He could remember himself. His name. His research: the Disappeared; shareholder privilege; no clean way to make a hundred million bucks.

Most people see only one Qaanaaq. They live their lives inside of it. The Arm where they reside, the nook where they work, the friends and family who make up their world. A private Qaanaaq, uniquely theirs, shaped by history and mental health and their socioeconomic positioning. Some people manage to move to a second Qaanaaq, when fortunes shift in one direction or another. Perhaps it will be a better Qaanaaq; usually it is an uglier one.

You and I are fortunate. We can see so many. We can move from city to city, Qaanaaq to Qaanaaq, see what our neighbors see, step into their stories. Randomly at first, too fast to control, but soon you will learn to summon them like memories.

Something else was happening to him. Something more exhilarating than frightening. He was hearing *City Without a Map* differently now. He no longer felt so much like an outsider. Sometimes he even thought the broadcasts were meant for *him*.

Maybe they were wrong, all of them, imagining it to be a guide for new arrivals. Maybe the broadcasts weren't meant for immigrants at all. What if they were meant for people with the breaks, whether they were newcomers or not?

Somewhere before dawn, his jaw buzzed.

"What do you know about the Reader Hunters?" Barron asked, his voice excited, attenuated.

"Waste of time," Fill said, deciding not to get indignant over being called so fucking early. "*City Without a Map* aficionados who make it their business to hunt down the people who narrate the episodes, in the hopes that talking to them will help them track down the origins of the broadcast."

"You don't think that's intriguing?"

"I think it's unlikely to yield anything helpful. And even if you could track one down, I have to imagine that the Author instructed them to never reveal their origins. Or that there are double blinds in place, and they've never even had any interaction with the Author."

"Perhaps," Barron said. "But wouldn't you like to try? If you could track down a Reader?"

"Of course."

"Well. I have one."

"You . . . found a Reader?"

Barron made an affirmative noise. Fill said nothing. His mouth felt dry. He drank coffee. It did not help. Why was his heart so loud? "You . . . yourself?"

"A friend of mine, from one of the forums I'm part of. A total co-incidence, really. A casual listener, he had just heard a broadcast, and then went to a fruit vendor, and when the woman opened her mouth, he knew."

"If that's true, and he published her location and identity, she'd already be besieged by *City* devotees. By the time we got to her . . ."

"That's just it. He didn't publish it. He told me directly."

This felt too good to be true, but Fill was feeling melodramatic, self-pitying, heedless of consequence. He got the alleged Reader's address and agreed to meet Barron there.

The dream again. Plunged back into it, like the floor opened up and dropped him into the frigid sea. Shifting, speeding up, coming to a stop. Whoever they were, this person whose memories he was locked into, things had changed, for her, ten years after arriving there. Her isolation ended. She was let into the light. Change in staff; change in policy; an obscure order from inscrutable software. Access to common areas, supervised at first, and then not. Conversations. Friends. A slate, even—unnetworkable, but loaded with approved texts, and a stylus for drawing. Fill watched thousands of sketches shuffle past. Birds, over and over.

Eagle, flying. Eagle standing over its nest. Eagle falling.

Grief: crippling, murderous. Pain like nothing he'd ever felt before. Pain—and guilt.

This was real. People lived like this. In his city, the one that belonged to him, the one that had fed and pampered him, given him everything he ever desired, the city his grandfather had helped build.

"I'm sorry," he said, and he was, and he screamed it, and that was when he woke up.

MASAARAQ

———————➤

People still came with cameras, in those days, telling us they were going to Tell the Whole World about what had happened to us, what was still happening to us. The poor oppressed nanobonders! Helpless victims of a savage slaughter! They came, young and full of energy and faith, not to blame for having spent their lives in enclaves of safety when the rest of us were sunk deep in utter shit. They always seemed dissatisfied with us, sad we weren't more grateful, resentful of our sullen faces that ranged between apathy and hostility. Offended that we didn't smile, shake hands, make friendly small talk, treat them with the openness of spirit that must have been common where they came from. It wasn't their fault that they were ignorant of how the world really worked. They didn't see how courtesy assumes a certain degree of common ground. Everyone can afford to be nice to each other, when no one is trying to exterminate anybody.

They thought we'd befriend them. Every one of them thought we'd make them one of us. They wanted to be bonded, to be special, to fly with eagles or howl with wolves. They saw my orca and thought I was a god. I wasn't a god. Gods can't be killed. Gods don't live like refugees, watching their loved ones murdered.

None of us bothered to explain it. They wouldn't have understood, wouldn't have believed. They wanted so badly to think that what they were doing would make a difference, that once they Told the Whole World something would happen, someone would save us. We were a Good Story. They thought that was enough. Victims of the Multifurcation. One of thousands of communities trying to do its own thing, being pursued by another one (or more) of those communities, with the federal government completely gutted of its ability to protect anyone. The beast was starved, its claws and fangs plucked, the Supreme Court unable to muster much respect for its rulings ever since the bombings forced it into hiding.

They didn't understand, these pretty kids, but they'd find out, sooner or later. And there was no point in befriending them, opening up our hearts, because sooner or later they'd be leaving. And never coming back. When they stopped coming we were relieved, and sorry for whatever new poor fucks were the latest Good Story. Alone, we didn't feel the need to keep our faces hard, our emotions buried, our fear fettered.

In the mornings it would be the worst, when Ora would bring the kids to the school that was barely worthy of the name, one room where every child from five to fifteen sat and tried their best to learn from a man who'd never taught a day in his life before the troubles came, and we hunters would head out ourselves, sometimes only six or seven of us, our animals scraggly and thin and hungry, their friends gone, their hunger and their loneliness echoing heavy inside our heads.

That's when I felt it so hard I thought my heart would break. When I knew how fragile it was, what we had, what was left, and how swiftly it could slip through our fingers.

And then I'd come home from the hunt and see the massive bird circling in the sky, Ora's black-chested buzzard eagle, its impossibility, its magnificence, and think that if such a perfect creature could come into existence maybe we had half a shot, maybe the world wasn't fundamentally, existentially fucked.

They went on and on, those abandoned suburbs, those rows of emptied houses where the water was poisoned or the highways gone, those communities that depended on dismantled transit systems, jobs in cities that had become savage hellholes, each one hosting a series of small-scale civil wars that added up to mass evacuations, warlord takeovers, synth-biowarfare retaliation. We stayed in those beautiful houses for as long as we could, and then we moved on.

We'd been in that particular village for six months then, and there were only forty of us. Six months back, before the last surprise slaughter, we'd been a hundred. A year before, more than two hundred. Again and again they found us.

Sometimes we'd meet other communities, nomads like ourselves or settlers clinging hard to a single block or spread of buildings. Some of them were awful, although the worst of the warlords stayed south of the old border from a malignant, terminal case of patriotism, which was part of why we fled to Canada in the first place. Most of those we met up there were decent, good people trying to survive, usually with some kind of unusual belief or practice or technological thing that had gotten them ostracized from wherever they came from. Once in a while, when the winter was bad or a crop needed working and our communities decided to link up temporarily, we'd talk internally about opening up to them. Admitting them. Sharing our blood; letting them bond.

Blasphemy, unthinkable. Some of us, the thought of it made our skin crawl. But that wasn't why I said no. I said no because sharing our blood meant passing on a death sentence.

We knew they'd never stop. They'd find us, they'd come for us. The Scourge, the Plague, the Pestilent, they called themselves all kinds of names they thought sounded scary, but we knew them for what they were: poor dumb hungry fools like us, who'd had everything taken from them, just like us, whose anger turned outward because it'd been carefully stoked that way. Powerful people made bad decisions that brought the whole country sputtering to a bloody standstill, thousands of people who had been part of the problem, caused something catastrophically bad to happen, and every one of them found a scapegoat. A few got caught, sent to jail, strung up, kidnapped, and beheaded on the net for all to see, but mostly the Bad Guys sicced their victims against each other and snuck away while the poor fucks were scratching each other's eyes out.

For the pharma corps, that was us. Us, and a handful of other communities of people who'd gotten terrible afflictions or terrifying gifts, or, more often, one that was actually the other. Deregulation had been ugly. People were tested on without their knowledge, or lied to about what was being tested and why.

We shouldn't have existed. We were proof that somebody had been up to something terrible. And that somebody skillfully inflamed the passions of a bunch of fundamentalist gun nuts, talked about us as abominations, breaches of God's law that mankind should have dominion over the animals, and of course those poor stupid fucks were only too happy to believe it, too eager to blame a bunch of people who were different and just wanted to be left alone. Ages ago, it had been the Immigrants, or the Blacks, always someone to push around, what this country was built on, *I've taken everything from you and now I'm going to tell you it's your neighbor's fault because he looks different from you.*

Kids at school, Ora working, and me out on the hunt, that's when I felt the fear. That's when I knew how helpless we were. I felt it all through me and I wanted to stay home, never let them go, stand in the doorway waiting with my weapon for the bad men and women who would dare try to hurt the ones I loved, even if I knew there were too many of them, that they had weapons we should have been terrified of, that I'd die swiftly.

A couple of traders, heading north, told us they'd seen the Plague ships. Dozens of pelts hanging from the sides. The skinned animal companions of our dead comrades.

"Could be a trap," some hunters said, so most of them stayed behind. I was the only one left with an orca, the one with the best chance of scoring intel and escaping, or inflicting real damage if it came to a battle. They sent me and I didn't say a word, not even when I held Ora and the babies to me and knew we might never see each other again. But that's what we were, what we lived with, what those kids with cameras could never capture. That's what we'd never let them see, because they had no right to it. No one did. Not them and not the people who would watch their work, the Whole World they were going to Tell, who would see us, and feel sad for us, and then go on merrily pretending the world wasn't burning down around them.

We went south along the coast. The waters got worse the farther we went, thick with toxic sludge, the food scarcer. We never found any sign of the Plague ships. We turned around, went back. Went home. The last place home had been.

Maybe it *had* been a trap. A lie. But if it was, all it did for them was save my skin. Because when I got back to where I'd left them, I was the last of my kind.

No bodies. No humans, no animals. Lots of red and black blighting the landscape. Blood, and the charred remains of buildings. I found our bathroom mirror in the rubble, with the word *Taastrup* on it. In Ora's handwriting. I chose to believe that she got out alive, took the two kids with her. Left behind our son's polar bear, whom I found hidden in the basement of the schoolhouse. He must have done it, I thought—the boy, he hid his bear to keep it safe, because she would never have allowed them to be separated, she'd have known better. I shivered, then, to think of that kid's life without the bear he'd been bonded to. And I swore I'd find her, find them.

We wept for a full day, Atkonartok and I. For our murdered kin. I lay on my stomach, on the ice, looking into black water. She circled. Each of us amplified the other's pain, echoed it back and forth, until I thought it would split us in two. Only hunger saved us. Hunger stirred her savagery, which roused my own, which stopped our wailing.

I brought her armfuls of bloody snow, hacked-off pieces, shreds of clothing. Atkonartok could tell them apart, our people and the people who hurt them. She could single out their unique pheromonic signature, singular as a fingerprint. She smelled their bodies, their sweat, their hair, their waste, their stories. From their smells she could see their shape, their weight, whether they were young or old or weak or strong.

Forty attackers, total. Forty monsters to hunt. She could see their outlines, so I could too. And so we moved on. Looking for our lost, the ones whose bodies we did not find, who we knew escaped—and looking for those forty outlines.

Taastrup, first. All the way, I watched the skies. Spent more time staring at the air than I did watching the sea or the land I traveled over. Looking for a black-chested buzzard eagle.

I knew it might take forever. I knew that by the end of it, it might be me who got rescued by her. I knew it might take so long that by the time I found her, she wouldn't be her anymore, and I wouldn't be me.

We found many of those monsters. In the cities of the land and the cities of the sea. Sooner or later, if they were there to be found, Atkonartok would catch their scent. I broke them apart or pushed them into the sea for her to tear to slow tiny pieces. Some we learned things from. The names and locations of their comrades. Others had nothing to offer, but their fate was the same.

Revenge was not my mission, but each new slaughter soothed the grief and rage I felt at being unable to find her. Find them. Murder gave me the strength to keep going.

My sisters, my mothers, the whole long line of generations: They come with me. With us. We carry them inside us. Our ancestors never leave us. Ora knew that, tried to explain it to me. She said our people understood death and loss and the legacies of our forebears. She said that we never lose the people we love, not even when we want to, and that's what the Western world had lost sight of, a lesson they forgot but we relearned, which is why the nanites didn't kill us, didn't drive us mad, gave us this gift, this curse.

Once, I saw one of them. The kids with cameras; not a kid anymore, and no camera. Standing over a trash barrel fire in a Scottish resettlement camp. I think she recognized me, but her face stayed as empty as mine was. I felt sad, then, for her, and angry at myself. I took that moment, that short time, to mourn, to be sad, to be angry, to feel emotions for her that I never let myself feel for me and mine, because we'd been born to this but she hadn't, and because people who only know suffering from stories are never prepared to find themselves inside one.

KAEV

———————▶

Kaev woke up in darkness. He heard water sloshing against the other side of a metal wall. Something massive breathed beside him. Where was he? How had he gotten there? He felt no fear, no anxiety. Dimly, he knew that this was wrong. He should have been terrified. But the realization vanished, and he slipped back into sleep.

To wake, hours later, to light. A narrow room. A high ceiling. The most comfortable bed he'd ever been on.

Which was breathing. Which was no bed at all, but rather a polar bear. One heavy furred arm lying across Kaev's legs. Ebony claws more than capable of tearing him in two.

Still, no fear. He knew, on a level deeper than the human, that this animal would do him no harm. That its happiness, sleeping peacefully, was his, and his was its. He lay there for a long time. Watching it sleep. Feeling his own thoughts come easy, a smooth unbroken flow.

Remembering. Piecing together how he'd ended up here. Wandering Arm Eight, his brain cracked, thoughts leaking out like always, and then—peace. A sensation so pleasant he'd stopped in his tracks, sat down, would have stayed there until he died.

And then killing a whole bunch of people.

"Hello," said a woman, who entered the room bearing two bowls. She was sturdy, muscle-bound. Her face was raw and bright from a lifetime of sun and wind. Long hair fell in a wide cascade down her back, with two small braids framing her face and curling under her chin.

She set the larger bowl on the ground beside the polar bear. The smaller one she handed to Kaev. "Good morning."

The bear came awake. The first thing it did was turn its head to look into Kaev's eyes.

He gasped. He felt tears well up.

"Can polar bears smile?" he asked.

"This one just did."

He laughed. The bear nodded its head vigorously, like maybe that's how polar bears laugh.

Kaev reached out his hand to touch the bear's face. It pushed its head into his hand.

"He looks old."

"He is old. For a polar bear."

"Am I like you?" he asked the orcamancer.

"You are," she said, and smiled, a smile every bit as wide and deep as his own. Like she, too, had found something she'd spent her whole life looking for. Except unlike him she'd had the privilege of knowing exactly what it was she'd been looking for.

"How?"

"You tell me," she said. "What do you know about your family history?"

"Not much. Raised as an orphan. Ward of the city."

"What about your mother? What do you know about her?"

Kaev shrugged. She looked disappointed in this news, somehow. But this was not surprising. If he was like her, if he was one of the nanobonded, there must have been a connection—a mutual family member, perhaps, someone she had come all this way to look for. He was a missing link; he could lead her to the person she sought. Kaev paused to revel in the clarity of his conclusions, the effortless way one idea connected to another. *My mother. She is here for my mother. She must be.*

For the first time, things make sense.

"Last night, I saw something," she said. "The bear's behavior changed. I knew that it had sensed you. Finally. I've been waiting for that to happen. That's why I was watching when those people came, and why I was able to unchain it in time to take care of them. Or rather, to help you take care of them."

He ate. The bear ate. Sea lion meat, it tasted like. Even the farmed stuff was fantastically expensive, although he suspected she hadn't purchased this so much as sent her orca out to bring one home. His was cooked and the bear's was raw. But he could taste what the bear tasted, feel the texture and the brine of the blood. Both were delicious.

"Kaev," she said, and squatted beside him, and hugged him so hard they both lost their balance, toppled over, laughed. "I am so, so, so happy to have found you."

Kaev smiled, unsure what to say. But it wasn't the normal pain of being bewildered by words in general, of even the smallest thing being too big for him to find the words for. It felt good, right, the bliss of emotions that need not be put into words. Had he ever truly had a conversation before? Had he ever been able to talk to another human being without watching every sentence crumble on its way out of his mouth? If so, he didn't remember it. He rolled over, from his back to his belly, arms spread wide to embrace his brother bear.

ANKIT

————————▶

"Context is everything," Barron said. Birds chirped in the background of wherever he was, or maybe they were people making bird noises. "To understand any social problem, you have to know what's going on around it."

He'd taken to sending Ankit audio files. His voice was avuncular, grandfatherly. He never answered when she asked him why he didn't want to meet or have an actual conversation. She imagined it had to do with his sickness. Self-consciousness over maybe being unable to answer a question, or losing his train of thought too easily. She listened for ambient noise disruptions, indications that he'd edited bits out, but the city's standard noise was chaotic and jerky enough to make it tough to tell.

Ankit said, "Play," and began to climb.

Context: When the first breaks cases started popping up, Qaanaaq had been a powder keg. Overcrowding; collapses of unsafe slum structures. Demonstrations. Many of the city's mass congregation mitigation measures had been introduced back then. Ankit remembered it, vaguely. A friend of her foster father's sitting in their living room, his brown face blackened with dried blood. Caught in a peaceful demonstration that became a street brawl when the slum enforcers brought out zap sticks.

Street protests were an oddity in Qaanaaq. Present—common, sometimes—but performative. Nostalgic. Like horse-drawn carriages in twenty-first-century cities. Immigrants from elsewhere believed in them, but Qaanaaq's native-born political activists treated them like parties, chances to take photos. With such minimal explicit human decision making, there were no targets to pressure, no places where a strategic crisis could force a policy change. You could call on an Arm manager to issue a statement, but everyone knew how little that could achieve. The real decisions were made by machines, a hundred thousand computer programs, and you could scream at a data server farm until you were blue in the face without getting anywhere. Even if a mob burned one down, there were dozens of backups, many of them floating in bubbles orbiting the geocone.

"Run!" someone called to her.

She'd never been to an indoor scaling course before. Like most serious scalers, she'd scoffed at the concept. Once you've been out there, hurtling through the frigid sky, the safe legal version seemed insulting. Nor could she say, exactly, why she'd decided to visit one now. But run she did, when the coach commanded it, leaping over foam obstacles and then flinging herself against a replica of a rotating cellular antenna and swinging around on it.

Yes, she thought. *That is why I came here. The body has a way of thinking that is very different from the mind's. Maybe moving the old muscles will help me figure this all out.*

Context: Barron's friend's molecular assembly machine could not produce Quet-38-36.0. Some deeply buried safeguard stopped it.

Context: That had never happened to him before. He'd called friends, asked them to try, gotten the same result.

Context: For some reason, Quet-38-36.0 could not be produced in Qaanaaq.

"Jump!" the coach called, a split second too late. This coach was no scaler. Or if she was, she'd been so subpar she'd been forced to flee to the safety of a padded indoor course.

Context: Martin Podlove was scared of her. But he was scared of other things more.

He had refused her requests for a meeting or a call. The three times she'd gone to his office, intending to wait in the Salt Cave until he walked out and corner him then, she'd found out that he'd left hours earlier by a different exit. She'd drafted messages and deleted them unsent. She had to be in his presence. Had to corner him. Had to see him squirm, read his face for tells. And if she merely sent a written message, who could say whether he'd smugly send an enforcer to soak or slaughter her?

What she knew: Podlove had ordered her mother's incarceration. He'd slotted her Code 76. She didn't know why, and she didn't know what she could do about it. And she didn't know why his employees were being attacked all of a sudden—she'd seen the clips of her brother beating the shit out of a slum enforcer a day after she'd seen him soak a Podlove bureaucrat, and she knew it couldn't be a coincidence—but she knew it was making her job harder. Podlove was battening down for a siege, and would be even more inaccessible than he normally was.

She was in midair, when her jaw bug chimed. Rolling hard landings had never been her strong suit, and the distraction made this one even worse.

"Hello," she said several harsh seconds later, sitting on the floor and cradling her ankle.

"Ankit," said the caller, his voice so old, New York–accented, and she thought at first it must have been Barron—but this man drew out the second syllable of her name too long, and his tone was too hard, too cold.

"Who is this?"

"Dak Plerrb, calling on behalf of Mr. Podlove."

"Ah," she said, forcing herself to breathe slowly. "This is a surprise. Is he on the line?"

Plerrb laughed. "No, no. But he did want you to know that he's noticed. How determined you are, to talk to him. Visiting, writing."

"I wanted—"

"And researching! Spending so much time looking into him. The Qaanaaq web, the global web, all sorts of places."

Outrage flared up, but she fought it down. Of course shareholder flunkies could get reports from the security programs that monitored data behavior. They could probably control them, too. He wanted her shocked, angry, thrown off.

"He wanted me to call and let you know how serious he is when he says that this is not the time to be fucking with him."

Breathe, Ankit. One breath, two. Don't rush this. When she spoke, her voice was ice. Was wind. "Do me a favor and ask him why he had my mother locked up in the Cabinet."

But there was no answer. Her screen said the call was terminated. Had he heard her question? Would he ask Podlove?

She stood. Shifted weight from leg to leg. Her ankle wasn't sprained. She climbed back up the mock building stilts. Grabbed a horizontal bar; swung her body to the next one. And the next.

The old muscles kicked in. Facts fell together. All at once, Ankit saw: *The shareholders want the breaks to be an epidemic. They're pulling the strings to make the problem worse. To prevent solutions. That's why the molecular printers can't produce Quet-38-36.0. Why there's a six-month wait for quarantine transfers.*

Context: The breaks were a welcome distraction from the city's fundamental flaws—the supremacy of property, the fact that landlords ran everything.

Ankit laughed out loud and leaped to the next stilt.

The place was a reasonable facsimile. She could see why people paid for it. But it only made her hungrier for the real thing. The bite of metal. The dark void below. The cold wind, most of all. A scaler friend of hers, quoting some old proverb: *If you surrender to the wind, you can ride it.*

SOQ

The boat was old, late or maybe even mid-twentieth century, tall and rusted, with a steep steel gangplank. Soq was out of breath by the time they reached the top. They turned to take in the view. Like most Qaanaaq urchins, Soq had marveled at the Amonrattanakosin flagship, lingered on the wharf where it was anchored, imagined the torture chambers and disruptor manufacturing facilities that must be belowdecks, the meeting rooms where criminals from every rung of the ladder met to plan out operations, the storerooms full of grain and cans for surviving sieges by the forces of Safety or enemy crime bosses or the military of one or more of the charter nations.

It seemed smaller now. Soq reached out to rub two fingers against the hull, watched rust flakes fall. When Dao had buzzed Soq that morning, told Soq to report to the ship, it had turned the whole day into a dream.

"Utterly unseaworthy," Go said.

Soq nodded. "Why don't you . . . I don't know, paint it? Indonesia still makes that hydrophobic stuff . . ."

"This is just a starting place." Go stepped off the gangplank. "Hello, Soq."

"Hi."

They shook hands. It felt weird. Soq had dreamed of meeting Go. And now: there they were. The real thing was so much smaller than the mythic creature in Soq's head.

The city was hard to see, below them in the ebbing twilight. And the boat moved differently, its rocking more noticeable than the city's eternal rise and fall, which was mitigated by complex mechanics . . . Soq so rarely stepped off the grid. They paused to savor the almost-seasickness.

"People live here?" Soq asked.

"People do," Go said. "But you don't. Not yet, anyway. Your home for the foreseeable future is actually part of your first assignment."

Three women squatted on the deck, slowly deconstructing a large plastic cube. Pulling away smaller plastic cubes of varying sizes, one at a time, and slotting them into canvas bins based on their color.

"What's in those?" Soq asked. "Or is that the kind of thing you need to be here a lot longer before you can find out?"

Go laughed. "We're not just drug runners here. Most of our work is totally legal. This shipping pallet contains spices, just arrived from the subcontinent. By letting so-called crime bosses control even the most mundane and legitimate aspects of Qaanaaq's commerce, the city can keep expenses down. Particularly labor costs."

"So I take it these women don't have a union?"

"They do not. Although you are welcome to ask them how happy they are with their work and their pay."

Soq watched one of them until she made eye contact. She smiled, nodded. A recent arrival from somewhere post-post-Soviet. Of course they were happy. Go was probably light-years ahead of every other option this woman had for making a living in the nightmare landscape she came from, or the city where there were thousands of smarter, more desperate women just like her.

The tour took a surprisingly long time. The boat had more levels than Soq had been imagining, each one with its own complex laby-rinth of passageways and warrens and boxes and drawers. Go had her fingers in so many different things. A whole department dedicated to intelligence, files and photos and film on probably half the city, one person whose only job was mastering archaic media, flash drives and paper files and floppy disks and microfiche and crystal gel, cataloging what they kept and retrieving information from them when needed. Elsewhere, a lithe legless woman was lord and commander of a vast pharmaceutical storage system, swinging from rope to rope through a forest of cabinets.

"You give every new grid-grunt flunky the full tour yourself?" Soq asked.

"No," Go said, but did not say anything else.

Back up top, she handed Soq an armband. Leather, black, embossed with an incongruous toile print. A pastoral French peasant scene. Go said, "When she was grooming me to take her place, my mentor once told me that ambition is essential to being an underling, but death to a crime lord. That we will flourish and thrive for precisely as long as we remain content with where we are, what we have. And when we try to reach further, seize more, that's when we run into problems. That's how wars start, how empires topple."

Soq smiled, because it was easy to see where this was going. "But you're not content with what you have."

"No."

"Your mentor sounds like a pretty smart lady."

"She was pretty smart. But she thought small. And maybe she was wrong. Maybe that's one of those pieces of received wisdom that everyone just accepts, even when it keeps them trapped in one place."

"One way to find out," Soq said, looking out at the city lights. The wind was picking up. Waves crashed against the side of the boat beneath them. *This is what it feels like. To step outside your box. To shake your fist at the city and say,* You will not break me. I'll break you, if that's what it comes to.

Go smiled. "I knew you'd see it that way. I want broader, more legitimate supremacy. I want to get off this boat."

"What can I do for you?"

"The empty apartments. They're the key to what I have planned. I need to establish a foothold. I want you to move into one. I'm asking all my warriors to do that, minus the ones I need for protection here on the barge, of course."

"The empties are real?" Another one of those Qaanaaq stories that people loved to tell, right up there with the heat-resistant spiders that supposedly infested the geothermal pipes, and the threat of Russian invasion. Allegedly, it was common practice for shareholders to keep some of their holdings off the market. A sort of gentleperson's agreement, to artificially inflate prices by increasing demand by keeping supply low. Soq didn't doubt that the empties existed, but they were pretty sure their number was exaggerated, as was the extent of the conspiracy behind it. The more likely reason was the simple thoughtless wickedness of the rich, who had more money than they knew what to do with, who didn't need the rental income and could keep an apartment empty for Grandma's once-a-year visit or in memory of a loved one dead for decades. Either explanation was unacceptable. Shareholders were wise to keep themselves hidden, because surely Soq wasn't the only one who would gladly stomp them to death if given the chance.

"They're real. I've been collecting data on them for years. I know where many of them are. Not all."

"Why do you need me there?"

"Don't worry about that right now."

Soq smiled. "You just told me ambition was essential for an underling."

"No. I told you that's what my mentor said. I also told you she thought small."

FILL

———————➤

The flat-bottom boat felt like a dungeon. Water dripped; red rust stains spread across cement walls.

"She must be here somewhere," Barron said. They passed tents and shacks, lean-tos, yurts. The air felt tubercular, uncirculating.

"People live like this," Fill said, and then regretted it. He'd spent all morning trolling through Grandfather's software, surveying his holdings, everyone's holdings, really, especially the ones marked Empties, and while it had bored him to tears at the time, it was presently making him sick with guilt, to think of so much space sitting empty for decades while these people lived packed together like splice shrimp in a jar.

"It's warm, at least. A lot of these people are grid workers—vendors, food stall operators, sexual entrepreneurs—they spend all day in the shivering cold, so the warmth is a big part of the draw here. Of course, a few of them never leave at all."

More than a few, to judge by the funk of feet in the air, of urine. Fill felt short of breath, angry at himself for coming down here. Why couldn't they have made an appointment to meet her somewhere else? A brightly lit, above-sea-level spot? Surely this mythical maybe-

Reader would have welcomed the opportunity for some fresh air and a cup of real coffee.

Barron, on the other hand, seemed to relish the dark, tight space. He looked almost disappointed when he stopped beside a ramshackle thing, a teepee made of sheets of hard plastic like some gritty closed flower, and said, "This is the place. But she's out."

"How do you know? These things don't exactly have apartment numbers on them."

"Patience, young Podlove."

Five minutes passed like that. The longer he stood there, the more sounds Fill could make out in the space he'd mistaken for silent. Chatter, plucked instruments, squawking speakers, the clink of silverware. A nightmare confirmation of his worst imaginings of an urban underbelly. He wished he were less disgusted to be so close to the Poor Unfortunates he'd been idealizing as he listened to *City Without a Map*.

"Tell me a story," Fill said. "I bet you're full of them."

"Very well, Your Majesty," Barron said, and bowed. "I will tell you the story of how I came to Qaanaaq."

"Sounds good." Children scampered past, throwing deformed bottom-grade plastiprinted figurines at each other.

"I will tell you about the fall of New York. You're a New York boy, aren't you, Fill? Just a handful of generations back?"

"Two," Fill said. "My grandfather."

Barron rubbed his chin. "Like most cities, New York had managed to be both heaven and hell for a very long time. Filthy and beautiful, a playground for the rich and a shithole for the poor, sometimes leaning more toward one extreme and sometimes more toward the other. By the time I was in my twenties, most of the things that made it heavenly were gone. The transit system that was its pride and its lifeblood was largely unusable, ever since the storms that flooded the tunnels and forced the governor to agree to construction of the

Trillion-Dollar Fail-Proof Flood Locks. And the Flood Locks themselves were widely believed to be bankrupting the city as a whole, but *better to be bankrupt than dead* went the common adage. Maybe your grandfather told you about that time, eh?"

"Not really. Just that it was miserable, and he was lucky to escape at all."

"We all were. I lived in a place called Brooklyn. By that point, the situation was very dire. In New York City then, as in Qaanaaq now—as in most cities, always, I imagine—the landlords called the shots. It didn't matter who was mayor, who was in the city council, what party a politician was from, real estate interests owned them all. They gave the most money to campaigns for public office, and electeds did whatever they asked. But by the time the Flood Locks were almost finished, Big Real Estate was in trouble. No one wanted to invest in the New York City housing market anymore. Banks pulled out. Foreign investors evaporated. The safest investment in capitalism was suddenly not so safe."

Bored, Fill thought back to what his grandfather had told him, wondered where he fit into this story. It wasn't that he didn't care. More like it all seemed so remote, something that had nothing to do with him. Qaanaaq was what he wanted: a story he was part of, something he belonged to.

"We tried to fight back. We came together. We put our bodies on the line. We took the fight to them."

Barron's voice was rising, his face reddening.

"And we won! We got the mayor to block the budget the landlords were lobbying for, which would have paid them full market rate on all the newly worthless property they owned. We got the city council to vote against it. But that's the thing. You can win against people. You can't win against money. Money is a monster, a shapeshifting hydra whose heads you can never cut off. Money can only behave one way."

Fill felt chills dance along his neck. The old man's anger was unsettling.

"We watched from our roofs, the day they blew the Flood Locks," Barron said, standing up straighter. Suddenly he seemed a different, younger man. "We saw the explosions, the water pouring in. I'd imagined the Red Sea, Charlton Heston, a wall of water wiping us out. Really it wasn't that much. Looked more like a bathtub overflowing. Only enough to render two-thirds of the city uninhabitable. By nightfall, the governor had declared a state of emergency. The feds spent a week working out an aid appropriation package that bought the landlords' buildings off them—at full market value. Exactly as the landlords had planned. By the end of the week, the bloodshed had begun in earnest. Food couldn't come in. Water supplies all contaminated. People desperate to get out, forced to abandon everything and take only what fit in one suitcase. I watched this one family—"

"What do you want?"

A woman stood beside the conical shack. Fill hadn't even noticed her approaching.

"Are you Choek?" Barron asked.

She nodded.

"Robert sent us. Said he spoke to you—about the recording you did?"

"Come inside," she said, scuttling backward into the teepee.

"Oh hell no," said Fill.

"Don't be such a baby," Barron said, squatting and waddling in after her with remarkable agility for a man of his years. Fill counted to ten and then held his breath and followed.

Barron and Fill sat on the floor; the woman sat on a tatami. Her shack was barely big enough for the three of them. Fill could not have stood if he'd tried. Shelves hung from the ceiling, dangling all around him, heightening his claustrophobia. Her expression seemed empty, void of interest or even fear. Fill babbled, "Tell us about *City*

Without a Map. Who told you to read that text?" He knew he should proceed with more tact, but he also knew that he was overwhelmed, frightened, stranded in a strange place he might not ever find his way back from.

"What did it mean to you?" Barron said, more gently.

"No one told me to read it," she said. Her hands rested anxiously in her lap. "I read it because I wanted to."

"But who wrote it?" Fill asked. "Did you write it?"

Choek looked at him, seeing him as if for the first time. "I can't tell you any more than that," she said. "I promised."

"You promised who?" Fill whispered. This woman had touched her, talked to her—or him—but probably her?—the Author.

"I can't," she said. "You need to go."

Fill looked to Barron, whose face seemed torn by rival impulses. To flee, to apologize, to beg . . . Finally he bowed his head and said, "We really appreciate your agreeing to speak with us."

Just like that. It was over.

"Money," Fill said. "How much would it cost for you to tell us?"

Choek looked at them for a long time, her eyes wracked with pain, before shaking her head.

Barron said, "Thank you for your—"

Fill blurted out a figure. A big one. A dangerously big one, the kind that he'd have to really beg his grandfather for. And might not get.

But big enough that her eyes went wide. With wonder, and then with anger, and then with sadness. Because there was no way to turn that much money down. No matter whom she had to betray. Single Author, rogue collective, evil robot overlord.

"Did you make this?" Barron said, placatory, pointing to a sculpture cobbled together from ancient circuit board. "What does it mean?"

"Don't know. Just started seeing them. Dreams. Someone else's. They're about the Sunken World, I think. How all those people got buried alive in their own things. Or couldn't let go of them when the waters started rising, when the flames came, and died clutching them."

"Magnificent," Barron said. "And you just started making the things you saw?"

"No," Choek said. "For so long it was just visions, glimpses, images I could see but not understand. A compulsion to make something I had no idea how to make. I didn't start sculpting them until I was in the Cabinet."

"Wait," Fill said. "You said someone else's dreams. So you have the breaks?"

"Had," she said, and smiled.

"You . . . had? You're cured now?"

"In the Cabinet," she said. "But I've said too much. Go. Come back with the money and maybe I'll talk more. Maybe."

They crawled out backward, for there was too little room to turn around. "A fascinating creature, is she not?" Barron said as they stood blinking their eyes in the relative brightness of the dim underbelly of the flat-bottom boat.

"How do you not want to learn more about what she meant?" Fill said, grabbing Barron's sleeve. "She said she was cured! Of the breaks!"

"*You* said that," Barron said. "I don't know what *she* was trying to say, or whether the poor creature could tell the truth even if she wanted to. But you, in your damn hurry to—"

"I'll talk to my grandfather," Fill said, chastened, already turning on his heel, desperate to be gone from here, from Barron, from *City Without a Map,* from the abominable ways that caring about something opens you up to hurt. "I'll let you know what he says."

Barron was saying something, but he did not turn to hear what it was.

He decided he did not want to go home. For just one night, he wanted to slip away from his life. He went to his grandfather's other apartment, the one he'd kept empty for all these years.

What had happened there? he wondered. What was so special about it? Who had died there; what torrid love affair or pivotal business deal had his grandfather conducted in it? Or did it mean nothing to the old man? An asset on a screen, one of Qaanaaq's legendary empties? Walking in, it felt so different from the warm safe home his grandparents had built, the place his grandfather lived alone now. This one was stark, cold, austere—

And occupied.

"Hey," said the boy playing with a shape-memory polymer at the kitchen table.

"What are you doing here?" Fill asked, but smiling, because the boy was beautiful. Butch haircut, broad spike-studded shoulders, a refugee face with the skeptical expression of a hardened Qaanaaqian. Fill stepped closer. Smelled him, like slide grease and star anise, and saw that maybe he was not a boy at all.

"Friend asked me to watch the place," the kid said, and Fill sat at the table across from him. Them?

"But it's not your friend's place," Fill said. Boy or girl, or some other majestic thing altogether, Fill shut his eyes against the flood of desire that washed over him. The danger of the situation was every bit as arousing as the person before him. He should have turned and left, called Safety, called his grandfather. He should have remembered that he had the breaks.

"No. My friend thought it was empty. Is it yours?"

"Not exactly," Fill said.

Pornography writhed and danced in his peripheral vision. He opened his mouth, intending to say something seductive or submissive or *something,* but the pornography was growing more frantic, more bizarre, the pretty boys becoming monsters, the ground beneath him bubbling, and he stepped forward, still smiling, and fell to the floor.

SOQ

———————▶

I should have fucking left. Stepped daintily over his stupid body while he was unconscious and stomped my ass out of here.

But Soq hadn't left when the rich kid fell to the floor in front of them. Soq had rushed over, checked his pulse, gotten him a glass of water, sat with him for the sixty endless seconds it took him to wake up. Cradled his head in their lap, been kind and nurturing while the kid emerged from the brief infancy of post-unconsciousness.

Mostly, Soq told themself, because they didn't want this little prick waking up alone, remembering Soq's face, calling Safety on them, saying he got jumped by a home invader.

But now here they were, an hour later, sitting on the floor like kids at a sleepover in an old movie, drinking soda and eating krill chips delivered by slide messengers, debating where to get noodles from.

"You have to eat noodles in the first fifteen minutes," Soq told Fill. "It's just basic food chemistry. The heat is still cooking them, and in fifteen minutes they're mush. We should go out to a stall some-where."

"I've never heard that," Fill said. "And I don't want to go any-where. Let's get them delivered."

"Idiot, you can't get noodles delivered. Are you not paying attention to me?"

The kid had a sense of humor, and some serious self-doubt, so
the two of them got along great. Fill was less than a year older than
Soq, and infinitely more naive about absolutely everything but sex, in
which subject they were more or less evenly versed.

"I can get noodles delivered," he said. "Watch."

Fill dialed, promised a massive amount of money if they could
have the noodles in his hands within five minutes of the moment
they left the wok. Clicked off, smiling in triumph.

"Of course they'll tell you it's five minutes," Soq grumbled, but
Soq was also excited by his confidence, by the options that unlimited
money opened up, by the previously unimaginable prospect of decent noodles being delivered.

"I guess we'll know when we take a bite," Fill said. "Since you're
such a noodle-quality fussbudget."

"Yeah," Soq said. "I guess we will."

Turned out they were both obsessed with traffic trawling, following currents of attention to find the latest bubbling-up art and news
being shared among Qaanaaq's million subgroups. They compared
bots, shared the software they both used to uncover new trends,
swapped archaeology dubs and ancient Sunken World footage and
the photo archives or instant messenger logs of long-dead strangers. Fill had the best programs money could buy, slick, swift, terrifying tools that turned up stuff that made Soq's jaw drop, but Soq had
gnarly, unpredictable Frankensteined software concoctions they'd
found at the Night Market and Fill seemed just as excited by those as
Soq was by his.

"This one's a classic," Soq said, flashing a file to Fill's screen. "The
Book of Jeremy. Do you know it? This gay guy, after his best friend,
Jeremy, died—Jeremy was straight—he got into his email—Jeremy
had given him the password—and deleted all the boring bits to con-

dense this guy's whole adult life—from fifteen to thirty-seven, when Jeremy died working a shale oil rig in one of the hydraulic fracturing earthquakes in upstate New York—and he interjected his own commentary between emails. It's super hot, and super sad."

"Amazing," Fill said, and read out loud: "'Jeremy's profanity is preserved here precisely as it was in life; a bawdy, inappropriate, usually humorous but sometimes profoundly moving knack for saying the earthiest things with such innocence that you feel like a bad person for finding it smutty. Nowhere is this more evident than in his emails to girlfriends, where he says things like, "Kath I miss you like crazy lately, never saw a bitch so keen to get her hair pulled," and you somehow know that Kath took no offense at this, can in fact picture her reading it, flushing red, remembering Jeremy.'"

"Great stuff to jerk off to, and then cry."

Fill put Soq on his account for the most expensive app on the market, beamed it directly to their slate. "This is how I found *City Without a Map*," he said. "Do you listen to it?"

"Tried to. Didn't do much for me. I don't need a guide to this city. And I don't need all that poetry."

Fill nodded, smiling. His eyes full of wanting.

The noodles arrived. Soq conceded that they were still perfect. They ate them in great gulping bites, both of them hungrier than they'd realized, looking up only when they were finished.

"You're really hot, you know that?"

"So they tell me," Soq said, furiously computing how to respond, what to do—the kid was hot, sweet, sad, they'd had a good time, but rich, unspeakably so, and probably not fond of being turned down, denied something he wanted, and what if after all this lovely quality friendship time he turned around and called Safety on Soq? So Soq stood, butched up as much as possible, and growled, "What are you going to do about it?"

Hours later, after several bouts of switching back and forth between fucking and sleeping, Soq was getting dressed in thin winter daylight when they heard Fill say:

"What the fuck even was that? Was that . . . you?"

"'Course it was," Soq said, pushing up the black leather armband and adjusting the spikes on their hooded coat.

"Like . . . biologically you? Like, you were born with it, or . . ." He craned his neck, trying to get a glimpse. "I've heard that there are some pretty crazy surgeries you can get these days—"

Soq kicked him, hard, a swift blow to the shoulder that made him yelp. "Don't be rude."

"I'm sorry," he said. "Can I give you my handle?"

Soq shrugged. The kid was out of bed, heading for the coffee maker, practically preening. Full-on courtship behavior, but Soq was already strapping on their slide boots, washing their face, moving on.

Fifteen minutes later they were halfway down the Arm One slide when their jaw bug buzzed.

"This is the last one," Soq said.

"You'll still owe me," Jeong said fondly, sending the details. A briefcase from a floating lab off Arm Two, which as far as Soq knew dealt in genome-customized party-booster drug regimens, to a semi-famous musician on Arm Five. "Till the day you die you'll owe me."

"Maybe," Soq said, leaping off the slide and dancing through the Hub. "But I'll have to find another way to pay that off. Because this? This is the last one."

They had dreamed of leaving the slide messenger life behind entirely, immediately, but they didn't feel strong enough to turn Jeong down. Soq would never have survived long enough to land a role in Go's army if Jeong hadn't helped them a million times, in a thousand ways, over the past several years.

There was no nostalgia to it, no sadness at the life Soq was leaving behind. Messengering had been fun, exciting, the best possible way to make money within the limitations of being unregistered. But the pay was shit unless you worked twelve hours a day or more; the people were assholes; the risk of death was constant. And Dao had already wired Soq's first week's salary. And it was astonishing.

Technically all Soq needed to do was hold down the empty apartment. But Go had explicitly said that Soq didn't need to stay there all the time, and like a good ambitious underling Soq wanted to find ways to impress the boss. Besides, Soq didn't want to risk a repeat of last night's random hookup.

It had been stupid. Dangerous. Fun, but dangerous. Soq told themself they had mostly only slept with him to keep him from calling Safety.

And what had been up with that collapse? Was he sick? He'd sworn he was just dehydrated, a three-day disruptor bender, but wasn't that precisely the lie Soq would have used if they had the breaks or neosyph or a contagious botched gut flora hack?

More important: Soq knew the signs, when someone fell hard. Those macho gay hypocrites were the worst—fetishizing masculinity, sneering at trans boys and femmes and anybody else insufficiently butch, but let them get a taste of something like Soq and all their biases got blown out of the water. The boy was smitten, and Soq wanted no part of it. Love, relationships, even friendships—and they would have been good friends, Soq knew it, even if Soq would have spent most of the time hating Fill intensely for his money—Soq couldn't have any of that right now. They were finally poised to leave it all behind, the pain and the hunger and the wondering.

Soq leaned into the wind, descending the slide and cleaving the vortex like a machete blade, Go's: a weapon, a tool, a soldier, unencumbered by the emotional baggage that made everyone else so miserable.

At least they'd gotten a damn good traffic trawling app out of the experience.

Once the briefcase was safely in the hands of its twitchy, strung-out recipient, freshly wealthy Soq settled down for a ginger beer on a heated replica of a Bangkok floating market. Someplace Soq had passed a thousand times and never been able to afford. A maddening smell came from below them, where a chubby woman who couldn't have been more than five years removed from the Chao Phraya River splatted noodles down into a skillet. Geothermal heat swirled around them, but every minute or so the wind shifted slightly and a cold gust sent a chill up Soq's spine. Incense burned beneath the table. Purely ornamental, here, with no insects to scatter the way it would back in Thailand.

How did Soq know so much about Thailand? With a start, they sat up. Had they fallen asleep? Dreamed? Sense impressions swarmed their mind, vivid memories of things they'd never experienced. Out of nowhere, their head ached exquisitely.

The pad Thai was the best Soq had ever eaten, but at the same time it tasted like a pale echo of something else. Fresher spices, the flesh of richer fish. Bangkok, the capital of the world, the heart of the country that weathered the global storm of rising sea levels better than any other. Home of the mightiest military, the most fiercely defended borders. A source of constant fascination to Soq, as it was to many in Qaanaaq, the way London would have been to a colonial American—the colonized's distant, foolish pride in its patron commonwealth. But now it felt like a place Soq had been.

I am a spy, Soq thought later, making their way down Arm Eight. High on good food, pockets not empty, Soq was approaching some ill-defined idea of "the good life" that they'd spent their whole life striving for. Confidential agent. Criminal mastermind. One of this city's secret rulers. The black leather armband marked Soq as Go's, as invincible.

Soq used Fill's program to troll for recent orcamancer sightings. One was only a couple of hours old. Soq let the vortex take them in that direction.

No orca, unsurprisingly. Killer whales don't stay still. They circle; they hunt. Soq did a sweep of the immediate area, and then widened the sweep. How much of this came from movies versus books versus life experience, they couldn't say. All the tangled threads of Soq's life had finally resolved into a pattern. A texture. They wandered through the under-building caverns, emptying their mind and letting their body go where it wanted. Soq had stumbled into a part of Arm Eight that they'd never seen before, the kind of place they'd have worked hard to avoid not so long ago. The smell of bottom-grade trough meat was thick and pungent in the air, and the few familiar glyphs graffitied onto the walls and pylons belonged to the city's savagest gangs and societies.

But now Soq wasn't afraid. Who would fuck with one of Go's drones?

This guy, apparently. Some battered fighter dude who had been doing pull-ups in the chilly twilight from the low-hanging crossbeam of a building support platform, who dropped when he saw Soq. His hands made fists. "She sent you?" he said, reddening at the sight of Soq's armband.

Something—roared. A shadow moved in the dark forest of building stilts—came forward, grew brighter. Roared again. A polar bear. The polar bear.

"She didn't send me," Soq said, throat dry. Knowing it wouldn't matter. Whatever grudge this guy had against Go, he and his polar bear would not be talked down from this peak of rage. The bear ran forward, stood over Soq. Roared again. It smelled like rotten sea lion meat, and something else. Something mammalian, something close to human. It hadn't been hostile with Soq before, but now it was with its human, and its human was furious. With Soq. The bear lowered its head, its mouth wide enough to fit around Soq's face and then bite it right off.

Soq shut their eyes.

The bear's nose pressed against Soq's face. It sniffed, tracing a wet smear from side to side.

Soq decided that it was a trick, to get them to open their eyes, because the bear wanted to see the mortal terror in the moment that it ended Soq's life. Soq would not be fooled. They did not open their eyes.

"What the hell?" the man said.

"I thought so," said a voice—female, heavily accented, gravelly and wise. The orcamancer.

For once, Soq thought. *For once I followed a sighting and actually found her.*

"Thought what? Go sent this little asshole to kill me, and—"

"This little asshole is your child, Kaev."

Soq still didn't open their eyes.

CITY WITHOUT A MAP:
ARCHAEOLOGY

The beer is weak and has a salty taste to it. The ceiling is low. You're hungry. Someone vomited at a table near yours, and no one is coming to clean it up. The only windows in the place have green-black ocean water on the other side of the glass. Your thoughts are melancholy—

—What will save us from this gray city, these long nights, this wind that cleaves memory from bone, the cold and wet that will never forsake us, these dappled shadows falling on aging faces? What will bring us joy? What will keep the fire burning in each of us?—

But then they take the stage, women with guitars and synthesizers and percussion instruments, and a man on bass, and they smile, and start. And you smile, shut your eyes, let the songs happen to you.

Maybe they're not great. You can't tell. You are gone from here, from this subsurface dive bar, from this floating city, from this fallen world. Strains of Celtic folk songs tease your ears; American soul; post-reunification Korean *gugak-yangak*.

Archaeology. The most distinct and vibrant of Qaanaaq's newborn musical traditions. Digging deep into the hundreds of musical heritages that people brought to this city. No singing, no lyrics. They don't even speak between songs, and you understand this, you appreciate it, because you know as soon as they opened their mouths they would cease to belong to everyone. The language they used, their accents, would place them definitively in a box, mark them off as coming from one continent or another, one city, possibly this one, and a cheer would go up, from the people who belong to that same box, and everyone else would feel the slightest bit less included in the tight warm embrace of the song. Music is the common property of all humanity, but people come from particular groups. For as long as the song lasts, for as long as they say nothing, you can pretend you are part of the same group.

They don't play songs so much as expeditions. Digging from one song into another, one century to the next. Late-1980s video game tunes become High Church Slavonic liturgical chants. The ruins of Troy, you remember reading, before the sea swallowed them back up, were actually seven cities, each one built around the bowels of its predecessor, and you imagine that this is a similar slow stroll from one epoch into another.

Word is, they've spent weeks at a time with different refugee communities, all over Qaanaaq. Learning, listening. Sucking up every song and scrap of indigenous style they can find. The Khmer surf revival. Nahuatl ballads dating to before Columbus. Bachata, where the notes run fast as raindrops. At every show they bring them up onstage to play a song or two, these inadvertent cultural treasures, these people who are all that remains of entire vanished musical genres. You see them now, sitting alongside the stage, smiling with pride and sadness.

You are alone, here. Your family was supposed to follow you, but it's been five years, and the Water Wars became civil wars and then the whole eastern half of your country went silent. Every week you visit the registries, scroll through the lists of new arrivals, petitions for registration. You scan every sad face, every trembling lip, every stony resigned stare. You know there are many more who do not consent to be included in the registries, people wanted by rogue governments and warlords and syndicates, and you wonder if something like that has happened, if whatever desperate compromises they had to make to get out might have put them in mortal danger, if they're in hiding, if they're already dead.

You were sick. You went to the hospital. You hid your symptoms, because you feared it was the breaks, and you knew what they would do to you if it was. You didn't tell them about the strange memories crowding your head, how they threatened to break you open. You told them it was overwork, exhaustion, dehydration, a history of violent abuse manifesting itself. They put you in the Cabinet.

You know this song, this scrap of melody. A Somali *dhaanto,* pentatonic perfection, the synthesizer effortlessly approximating the sounds of the oud lute.

A cellmate used to sing this song. An immigrant laborer back home, a fellow political prisoner.

The Cabinet is where you met me. Sitting in the corner of the rec room, eyes shut, the same corner I've been sitting in every afternoon for far longer than you've lived in this city. I saw you; knew what you were really dealing with. I cut my forearm, cut yours, pressed our forearms together. Made us blood siblings.

Since then, you do not fear the memories of strangers.

The beer, for all its seeming weakness, packs an unexpected punch. When you finish it you feel strangely blissfully happy. When you shut your eyes—

Memories fade in, fade out. Stirred by the songs. It doesn't matter that they're not your own. You belong to Qaanaaq now. Its people are your people. Their pain is yours, and so are their songs.

FILL

———————▶

Fill should have been miserable. He should have felt ashamed, guilty; he should have been taking concrete action to ameliorate the consequences of his irresponsible actions.

But he didn't. He wasn't.

When had he become such a monster? Knowing he had a fatal sexually transmitted disease, he'd had unprotected sex with someone. He hadn't warned them. He hadn't even told them after. And instead of being eaten up with remorse—instead of feeling bad about what he'd done, here he stood, leaning against the guardrail, watching the sunset, admiring the fractal rainbow arcing slowly down the side of the windscreen.

What was he becoming?

Part of it was, he didn't truly blame himself. The circumstances had been so strange. While he'd been incredibly turned on by the danger of it, a part of him had also been offended. Angry, even, with this criminal. An intruder, after all. In his grandfather's secret apartment. A gorgeous, prickly, impoverished creature who turned his whole idea of gender on its head. It had felt like pornography, like a dream, like a horror story.

But still. They were real; it had really happened. The breaks were probably already manifesting themselves in Soq.

So, what? Why did he feel so strangely fine?

Tomorrow night I'll have my answer, he told himself. *My grandfather will say yes or no to the absurd amount of money I'm asking him for.*

He'd wanted to just message Grandfather the request, but Barron said that seemed unceremonious. Too easy, unworthy of the momentous event those funds would facilitate. So instead he'd asked Fill to arrange a meeting, for himself and his grandfather and Barron, so they could make their pitch together.

A delay tactic, most likely. Barron was as scared as he was, probably, to get to the bottom of what Choek could or couldn't do for them. They were both terrified that the trail could be cold, might not lead them anywhere, or—worse—that Choek could indeed lead them to the origin of *City Without a Map.*

The sun was down. The sky was still bright. His heart danced with the water, with the rippling light. *It's the breaks,* he thought. *I feel them trembling through me. Cracking open all my defenses, breaking down the walls I built between me and the world. Shaking me loose from my self, from my ego, from this tiny isolated flickering flame, so I can see how I am the sun. We are the sun.*

So sad, to think that it took this, this, to make me see how beautiful our world is.

She came to him more and more as the sickness progressed. In dreams, in crowds, in memories that didn't belong to him. The ghost woman: a guide, but a guide to what? She took him places, told him stories without words. He could feel her in him. Most of the time she was peace, profound and terrifying, a radical reconciliation more divine than anything Christ could have managed, something that could only have come from unspeakable suffering. Sometimes she slipped, cracked, refracted, and he gasped at the river of rage that roared beneath her surface. The things she had suffered. Not repressed, not forgotten, but no longer present.

What had happened to her?

In his mind, she was the Author. The mastermind behind *City Without a Map*. He was aware that this was irrational, idiotic, probably incorrect. He felt it so strongly that it couldn't possibly be true. She was a construct, a figment of his damaged imagination, his diseased brain assembling complex narratives and characters out of the chaos of information he was drowning in.

She had to be.

Bald. Fifty-something. Just like the Author described herself.

He let go of the railing and then did something that shocked him. He sat. He reached down, dipped two fingers into the frigid waters. He touched them to his lips.

We live our whole lives suspended above the sea, he thought, *but we forget the true taste of salt. Not the purified stuff we find in kitchen cabinets and restaurant counters. The bitter, foul, sea-muck stuff we crawled out of, and live beside, and one day will return to.*

Soon I'll break free of this body and be one with the sea, with the sky, with the infinite. That is the gift I was given, that I in turn gave to someone else. A bitter gift, but the best ones are.

SOQ

———————►

Soq wanted: nothing.

They looked down on the city from forty stories up. They drank actual scotch, tasting like smoke and hammered bronze, and barely noticed. People all around them carried cages and polyglass bubbles bearing animals Soq had never even seen photographs of, but Soq did not care, did not look twice. Their stomach tingled, the gut fauna freshly tweaked so all the bad thoughts and feelings and bodily traumas were whisked away. Soq stood there, feeling no pain, yet somehow did not marvel at what a strange rare blessing it was to be without pain.

It was the breaks, certainly. From Fill. That fucking rich kid in that fucking warehoused unit. It had to be. There had been no one else. Soq had been far too busy for sex the last few weeks. That fucking asshole had given Soq the breaks.

That's how Soq popped in and out of his head. That's how Soq saw into his emptiness, his pain.

Which is why Soq's lifetime of schemes and plans to conquer or destroy Qaanaaq suddenly felt so flimsy, so flawed.

God damn him.

"It isn't just the fact that they did terrible things," Soq was saying, only it wasn't Soq's voice at all. "That's sort of 101, isn't it? Something you realize right around the time you first find out what fucking is. You just assume there's things about your family you never want to know."

"Sure," said a very pretty boy. Thin lines of gold light gleamed inside his face; bioluminescent bacteria or cephalopod-derived photophores, Soq wasn't sure which; all the rage among the queer kids of Petersburg plutocrats. The microbes or bacteria or whatever lived for three days—or was it four?—and you could buy a half-ounce acu-ampule for a little less than what Soq made in six months of messengering.

"You're not listening, Tauron," Not-Soq said.

"Of course not," Tauron said, and somehow Soq knew this meant that he *had* been listening, and good gods, why did the rich have to make everything so complicated?

"And it's not my fault that all those bad things happened, it's not my fault I live a good life and other people are living god-awful ones because of things my grandfather might have done . . . but . . . the real problem is, once you *do* know what they did, doesn't it make you obligated to do something about it? To make things right? Otherwise, aren't your hands as bloody as theirs are?"

The bubble they stood in rose, at the end of its long strut. Soq looked down at the sea, black beneath them, and at the lights that danced on all sides.

The city was theirs. Qaanaaq was conquered.

And they were completely miserable.

Then they opened their eyes and were back in whatever creaking dark mold-smelling corner the Killer Whale Woman had them holed up in. She was gone now. Soq remembered her leaving, even though they hadn't been entirely conscious when she went.

They hadn't dozed off, so much as . . . gone away.

Soq did not feel angry, to have everything snatched away. To be plunged back into the same poverty they'd always known. What they felt was grateful. To be back in their own life again, their own body. To be free of Fill's strange and terrifying pain. To have their own familiar pain back.

"Thanks, brother," Soq whispered.

He had everything, that poor sad fuck Soq had fucked, and he was so empty inside that Soq had to fight back the urge to hunt him down and give him a hug.

ANKIT

———————▶

Ankit spent three hours shivering across the grid from the entrance to the Yi He Tuan Arena. Watching every face that went in and every face that came out. Looking for her brother. The screens flickered: Hao Wufan's upcoming fight canceled. A damn shame, she thought. The Next Big Thing already a thing of the past, since those all-boy-sex-party photos surfaced, and the audio of his lunatic ramblings, drugged out of his mind or possibly suffering from early-stage breaks.

The dossier from her contact at Health hadn't had much to offer, but she'd learned a little more about her brother. That he was sick, some unspecified form of brain damage. She had a file now. Something to hand him. He could take his time, process the information. And she wouldn't be frightened if he howled or hooted or got upset. She knew what she was dealing with.

First she'd have to find him. She was pretty sure fighters didn't hang around arenas when they weren't scheduled to fight, but it was the closest thing to a lead she had. Maybe he'd come by to meet with a manager or promoter, pick up a payment, practice on the beams, train at a secret gym or battle society somewhere inside.

It had seemed like a solid enough plan when she had arrived. But now she was freezing and hungry and her feet were sore.

She called up a photo of him on her screen. She could see it, she thought: some sibling similarity around the eyes, a similar scoop to the sides of the face. And maybe they'd had the same nose once, before his had been broken a bunch of times.

She leaned against the wall beside a red pipe. An old vagrant trick, soaking up the heat it radiated. But after another hour, all the warmth in the world wasn't enough to distract from the ache in her feet and the conviction that this was a fruitless way to go about finding him. She turned and headed for the Hub.

A girl cawed above her. Imitating crows: an old scaler taunt to frighten pedestrians. Ankit cawed back, prompting startled laughter.

We miserable grown-ups weren't always groundbound, she thought, and then felt happy that she still spoke scaler-speak. Sort of.

Another revelation from that costly dossier, one she'd been avoiding examining. Sharp, prickly, cutting up her hands each time she tried to get a hold of it: before coming to Qaanaaq, her mother had spent time in Taastrup. The same place the early cases of the breaks kept pinging back to. Did that mean something? Could her mother have contracted a sort of proto-breaks, decades before the first cases started cropping up? Had her brother? Could she have been the subject of some experiment, or a survivor of some accident?

Patient 57/301. No name; no match in any genetic identification bank. Imprisoned in the Cabinet for thirty years. Top-level classified status; authorization that could only come from one of the sponsor nations—China, which meant it could be anyone with a ton of money; Thai officials typically couldn't be bought off like that.

No diagnosis to appeal, no doctor to hunt down and punish. Waist-deep in bloody fantasies of how she'd hurt the person who did this, she noticed something. Someone staring at her.

A woman, with beautiful wind-scoured light brown skin, just a few meters away. She sat—sat?—in the sea. And then she rose, and Ankit saw she wasn't sitting in the water at all, she was riding, riding something as black and deadly and magnificent as the sea itself. The orca turned its head and stared at her, stared *into* her, and so did the woman, and Ankit felt gutted, stabbed through, harpooned—

"She remembers you," she said, the famous Blackfish Woman.

She was real. And she was here. And she was talking to Ankit.

Ankit said, after a very long time, "What," and her voice was much smaller than she ever remembered it being.

"She has a very good memory. Thirty years later, she remembers someone's smell."

Ankit stepped closer, squatted down. Her breath would not budge. It stuck in her lungs like lead. She shut her eyes, tried to remember. Cast her mind back as far as she could. She recalled strange rooms, cramped spaces, fear, someone's hand across her mouth to stop her from shrieking. Footsteps overheard. Harsh male laughter. Nightmare glimpses, nothing new, things she'd carried with her and ascribed to filthy group homes and overcrowded nursery boats, things that fit right in with the long line of better-remembered ugliness that Qaanaaq's foster care system had given her. And when she began to see wide vistas of white snow, smell smoke, hear distant animal bellowing—gunshots—the wails and the cries of the dying— how could she know whether that was memory or imagination, the nanobonder genocide so widely written about, reimagined in movies, subject of epic poems and endless analysis?

She opened her eyes again, stared into the face of this impossible creature. Breathed out. "You're her mate. My mother's partner."

The orcamancer nodded. "I'm your mother, too."

"Of course," Ankit said, awkward, uncertain about what was the proper protocol here. An embrace? A bow, a handshake, tears, wailing and the rending of garments?

"We've been going up and down every Arm of this city for days.

Weeks, maybe. Human time markers don't stick in my mind. Our minds. Sniffing at the air. Looking for your scent. This city, and a hundred others before it."

The woman's face—her mother's face—her other mother's face—was terrifying in its rawness. It hid nothing. It refused to hide. It was bare, alien, hostile to how humans behaved. More orca than person. Ankit's cheeks reddened with emotions, and they were not all joy and love. She also felt fear. Fear of this woman, who cared nothing for social niceties or Qaanaaq or the safe life Ankit had fought tooth and nail to carve out for herself there.

"My name is Ankit. Was that my name, before?"

She shook her head.

"What was my name?"

"It's not important now. Some other time, perhaps." She got off the whale, climbed up onto the grid. Extended her arm stiffly, like a foreigner unaccustomed to the practice. "My name is Masaaraq."

They shook hands. When Masaaraq let go, she stepped forward with alarming speed to swamp Ankit in a fierce bear hug.

They were exactly the same size.

"And my mother? What's her name? All these years, I've never known. She's a number, to them."

Masaaraq looked around, as if suspicious of invisible eavesdroppers. Outsiders, especially from the underdeveloped parts of the Sunken World, believed all kinds of crazy things about Qaanaaq's technological capacity, like that the fog could hear your every word and report it back to the evil robot overlords.

She whispered in Ankit's ear: "Ora."

"You're here to get her out," Ankit said. "Aren't you?"

Masaaraq nodded.

"I want to help."

She took Ankit's hand and squeezed it. Not hard, but implacably, her strength overwhelming. This was a woman who had never stopped, who could not be stopped, no matter what happened to her or to anyone else.

Ankit had to take several deep breaths.

She'd told herself that she was triumphing over the fear. She wasn't that kid anymore, the one whom fear froze solid, the one who was ruined by it. She'd posted that photo of Taksa—she'd gone to see her mother—again and again she'd stood at the edge of a tough decision and made the leap to the next one. Done the difficult thing.

But here she was again, up against her limit. A line she was afraid to cross. A leap that meant risking everything, leaving behind all she knew of comfort and ease, that might land her in jail or deregistered or worse. *I want to help,* she had said, and she did, but she couldn't. To distract herself and Masaaraq from the bile rising in her throat, the panic she knew was visible in her face, she blurted out, "And do I get a killer whale?"

"Polar bear," Masaaraq said. "That's what you were marked for bonding to. But she died before you two had a chance to bond. When we were attacked. When your mother escaped with you two. We were nomads, spending the winter in an empty town. I was away, tracking the people who were trying to wipe us out. I failed. They got to you first. Everyone died—except you two. And her."

"And you," Ankit said.

"You should count your blessings," the killer whale woman said. "The fact that your animal died before you two had been bonded is the only reason why you didn't spend most of your life a gibbering idiot."

"Like my brother," Ankit said. "Right? Is that what's wrong with him?"

"You know Kaev? He doesn't know you."

"Yeah. I know of him. I introduced myself, once. He . . . sort of . . ."

"Broke down. Yes. His mind was cracked. He was incomplete, his whole life. He is complete, now, and healing. You have been incomplete as well, you just haven't known it. I will heal you, too."

"I'm not incomplete," Ankit said, feeling the grid give way beneath her. "I don't need to be healed."

"You do," the orcamancer said. "You need to be bonded."

"Or what?"

Masaaraq did not answer. She took a step back.

Ankit asked, "Do you . . . want to come over to my place? For a cup of tea?" She looked at the whale, briefly—ridiculously—imagined it in her elevator, daintily holding a teacup in one massive blade-fin, sitting at her kitchen table. "Can you . . . leave her?"

"I can. And I will drink tea with you. But not right now. I have an errand to run. With some friends." From behind her back, she pulled a black box that was strapped to some kind of orca saddle. "Right now we must begin the bonding process."

"No," Ankit said, possibly not out loud.

"I have no polar bear," Masaaraq said. "And it would need to be an adult, as you are an adult. I do not know how the bond will come out. Whether it will be painful, how well it will work. Our kind has never bonded someone so late, who had never been previously bonded. Do you have an animal in mind? Something you've always felt a particular attraction to? Connection with?"

"No," Ankit said, louder now—gods, she didn't even have a pet, she had never been interested in a romantic partner, the thought of commitment made her throat hurt, and now this strange woman who'd walked into her life five minutes ago—rode into her life on a killer whale five minutes ago—was proposing a kind of commitment more intimate and horrifying than anything she'd ever contemplated before.

One look in Masaaraq's eyes, and she knew—this woman was not entirely human. Being bonded to an animal turned you into something else. Something that behaved completely differently, wanted different things.

"You have some time to think about it," Masaaraq said, removing a series of strange tools from the box. Syringe, bottles, droppers, other things Ankit had no words for. "For now I'll just take a sample of your nanites so we can start the culture process."

"No," Ankit gasp-yelled, and turned to run—and then turned back, and told Masaaraq precisely how to find her, where she lived and where she worked, and stammered some profuse apologies, and turned, and ran.

KAEV

———————▶

Kaev had wondered, once, what it was like for the superstar cham-
pion fighters. The ones everybody recognized, the ones crowds
parted for, the ones who made people break into wide-open smiles of
amazement, gratitude. Fear. His buddy Ananka had come close, back
when both of them were just starting out, and passersby were always
stopping to stare at her, but he knew it was nothing like the universal
awe that the biggest beam fighters were held in.

And even that would be trivial compared to the attention he was
getting now. Half the population of Qaanaaq was totally oblivious to
the beam fights, yet not a single one of them could be oblivious to a
polar bear.

So here he came, strutting down the grid with a polar bear padding
beside him. Not a little one, either. And the legendary orcamancer,
bone-blade staff in hand. And a street urchin slide-messenger-
turned-criminal-errand-kid who happened to be his child.

Everybody stopped. Everybody stared. Many screamed. Many
tapped their jaws, dialing Safety. People took pictures with screens
and hat cams and oculars. Children began to cry. There was a polar
bear in the Floating Zoos, but it was small and sickly and unhappy.

Soq had suggested whistling for a jaunt skiff, but the orcamancer—*Masaaraq*, Kaev quickly corrected himself, *she has a name, she is a person, not the mythic figure everyone tells stories about*—said no.

Masaaraq had been in a foul mood, returning from some nebulous errand that had upset her greatly, and she snapped, "Let them see us."

My city finally knows who I am. Everyone is looking at me, and not because I'm about to be beaten by some pretty-boy kid. This will be in all the outlets in instants.

Once or twice he turned to look at Soq, this other magnificent creature who'd just entered his life, and each time, he saw Soq look away swiftly.

At least I'm not the only one who doesn't know how to handle this, he thought, and smiled. The bear stopped to sniff a red chrome pipe and snarled at the absent dog whose scent it found.

"It's crazy," Kaev said. "I can feel him, how he wants to attack these people. How they all look like meat to him. How they smell. But he can feel me, too. And he knows he can't do that. So he doesn't. How is that possible? People spend years trying to tame wild animals, and this one became tame . . ."

"Instantaneously," Masaaraq said. "But he isn't tame. A bonded animal is only as tame as its human is. And humans can be very, very wild."

"True."

"And you want to be careful. It goes both ways. You influence his behavior, but he can influence yours. Usually humans assert emotional dominance effortlessly, but you need to stay vigilant."

He put his hand on the bear's shoulder, and they walked proudly through the Hub and onto Arm Five. At the entrance a Safety officer stopped them, tapping for backup and visibly trembling.

"There's nothing in the registration consent agreement that says it's illegal to have a polar bear," Kaev said. Masaaraq had talked him through this already. She'd done a lot of research before she came to Qaanaaq. "I can vouch for its behavior. It won't hurt anyone."

"Unlicensed wildlife," the officer mumbled, unconvinced, eyes out for assistance. His hand moved to the zapper strapped to his belt, but that was barely good enough to take down a chubby drunk. It'd just irk the bear, and irking the bear was probably not something he wanted to do.

"Licensing terms only apply to registered residents," Kaev said, another Masaaraq talking point. "This belongs to my friend here, who is visiting."

". . . wanted in connection with more than one instance of multiple fatalities . . ."

"No proof that this was the same polar bear."

They kept walking. In ten minutes they'd be off the grid, and Safety couldn't do a thing about it. It'd take the combined zappers of twenty officers to slow the bear down, or authorization from HQ to use lethal weaponry, both of which would require a lot more time than that to procure. Kaev quickened his pace, but not by much.

A lot of food processing happened on Arm Five. The smells of cooking fish and caramelizing soy sauce made the bear grumble with hunger. Kaev could feel that, too, the bear's hunger distinct from his own, and when he focused on it he could feel his own hunger grow. A loop. An echo chamber, hunger bouncing off hunger and magnifying, multiplying, and if he just shut his eyes and let it happen the bear would be able to reach out one arm and effortlessly satisfy their hunger—

Pain jolted him back; Masaaraq had struck him with the butt of her weapon. "Hey!"

The bear watched her as they walked, its hostility tingling in Kaev's elbows, like, *I'll remember that—and I still haven't forgotten how you had my head in a cage for all that time.* Soq put a hand on the bear's other shoulder. Kaev felt this, too, the animal's blunt mammalian happiness at the touch of someone it liked, not so different from a dog's. A beautiful thing to be inside of.

They reached the gangway. Soq asked, "You buzzed her?"

"Trust me," Masaaraq said. "She knows we're coming. She's got eyes on all of us."

Kaev had been focusing on his bear. Trying not to think. About Soq; about where they were going. About what it meant that he had a child. About how the final, knock-down drag-out break-up fight between him and Go had happened a couple of months before Soq was born. About how he and Go had had a child, together, all this time.

About how much he hated her. And about how he could hate her, but also feel this strange feeling, so oddly like happiness, in his chest, growing bigger with every step that brought him closer to her.

CITY WITHOUT A MAP:
THE BREAKS

No one knows where or when they got the name. The origin story is something banal, most likely—they caused nervous breakdowns, full psychiatric breaks, irrevocable shattering of identity. Oldest known usage is found in transit camp correspondence, refugees using it colloquially enough to imply it had already existed in spoken dialogue. There is a deeper resonance to its persistence, a troubling question that arises if you stop to ponder it: Why do we still call it by such an informal name? Why has it not yet been replaced by something more scientific sounding, more medical, even if it were just an acronym, sad as a flag of surrender, identity dissolution syndrome (IDS) or multiplicative affiliation disorder (MAD)? Epidemics do not have medical causes; they have social ones.

I have been stitching its story together here. Collecting scraps of history and rumor. Memories. Sick people, heads spinning with strange sights. Slum ship operators going out of business because their boats had become floating hospices for afflicted tenants. Doctors and agency officials baffled by the failures of software to devise a solution, or even the most modest of mitigation measures—almost as if someone, some powerful intelligence either human or machine, is determined to block any such development.

Word of the breaks has spread. Babbling madmen in the streets, children screaming someone else's secrets. Qaanaaq is adrift, they say—floundering, helpless, failing, its once mighty AI oversight no longer equal to the task of maintaining order. Safety is overburdened. The brigs are overflowing. Crowded quarantine ships remain anchored to the Arms. Hearing stories like that, people would get all kinds of crazy ideas.

A crime boss might start plotting out a power play.

And a woman on a mission of rescue and revenge, who for years has known that she must eventually come to Qaanaaq, who knows that the thing she seeks is here, but knows that her enemies are here as well, the people who robbed her of the thing she seeks—and so much more besides—and they are powerful, and they have the full might of the Qaanaaq municipal system behind them, might decide that the time is right for her enemies to fall, for her journey to reach its end.

The breaks brought her here.

KAEV

————▶

Sure enough, they were expected. Dao stood at the top of the gangway, flanked by a tight crowd of armed, frightened foot soldiers. Kaev didn't slow, didn't hesitate, marched right up the gangway. The bear followed.

"What'd you come here for?" Dao said, his palm on the button that would release the hydraulic lock, retract the gangway, spill them down into the sea.

"You know why. To see her."

"What if she's busy?"

"Too busy for this?"

Soq stepped forward. "Ring her up, will you? Ask her yourself."

Behind them, emboldened by the fact that the bear had stepped off the grid, was a crowd of Safety officers. Assembling some kind of weapon Kaev hadn't seen before. Nonlethal, probably, but scary—the latest generation of sonic pulse cannon, maybe, the ones pioneered in Russia for knocking out crowds of demonstrators, which might also cause aneurysms. He didn't want that pointed at any of them. If Go didn't let them onto her boat, even the bear would be in danger.

Dao turned his head, speaking into his implant.

"Hey, how's it going," Soq said to one of the foot soldiers. She smiled back nervously. All of their eyes were on Soq. And Soq knew it. *A pretty good way to impress your new coworkers,* Kaev thought. So Soq, at least, was enjoying this. And so, mostly, for that matter, was Kaev. That bliss was still there, what he'd felt walking through Qaanaaq with the eyes of everyone on him. The power that comes with having five hundred kilograms of stark white killing machine at your side. The simple pleasure of not having your brain be a caustic broken worthless mess.

He shivered, remembering. How ugly every minute had been. How even the simplest sentences, the most straightforward thoughts, would crumble in his hands. How frightening he found other humans. The joy of fighting, those rare moments, those orgasmic instants with long stretches of broken glass between them. Such a pale shadow of the pleasure he took in every instant beside the bear. And even that, the fights, he was lucky to have had. Plenty of people with broken brains turned to far worse addictions.

Masaaraq was frowning, he noticed. Not the wary frown of someone in a tactically unsatisfying position, either. More like general unhappiness.

"Everything okay?"

"This is a distraction," she said.

"From what?"

"From what I came here for."

Kaev nodded. He'd been told no so many times, when he asked her why she was here, that he'd given up asking. "Go is powerful. Connected. Smart. Whatever you want to do, she can help you do it."

"If she doesn't just kill us all."

"She could try."

"Is she powerful, or isn't she?" Masaaraq said. "If she is, she can destroy us. We're not invincible. Killer whales and polar bears are just like any other weapon—they can't solve everything. And they have their limitations. I know that better than anyone." She paused. "Almost anyone."

"Come along," Dao said. He stepped away from the button. The soldiers receded. To Soq, he said, "She's in her cabin. I believe you know the way."

What seemed like a small army squatted on the deck of Go's ship, repairing fishing nets. Kaev was always surprised by just how boring Go's criminal empire really was.

Soq didn't seem bored. They stopped to stare, to watch the little fingers at work.

Kaev's heart hammered. His blood sang. He flexed his fingers to keep them from making fists. He was on the beams again.

And also—he wasn't. He was a boy, young and handsome and strong, sneaking out of the foster barracks to meet a girl. A girl who didn't mind his stutter and yips, and how his sentences didn't make a lot of sense. A girl as strong as he was, as fearless, but far smarter. A grid grunt, like him, but unlike him she had a plan. A way to work her way up, a way to build an empire where they'd both be safe. Where neither one would be nothing.

Go had succeeded, he saw. She'd had to abandon him—or had he abandoned her?—but she'd succeeded.

The door to her cabin opened. She stood there. She saw Kaev first, and he could see, now, with the calm and clarity that the bear had given him, the emotions that danced across her face, the happiness and then the anger; the love and then the hate. All in a fraction of a second, then swept under the rug of her fearless-leader face.

But then she saw Soq. And her mouth opened. She looked back and forth between Soq and Kaev, and he could have sworn he saw something inside her fall away. The fearless-leader face broke. Whatever Dao had told her, she hadn't put the pieces together until this moment, seeing them together. Probably he hadn't mentioned Soq at all. Probably he'd been focused on the polar bear. Which would be understandable. But Go wasn't focused on the polar bear. Go didn't seem to see it at all.

She took a step forward. One hand went to her chest.

"I—" she said, but said no more.

Kaev took three swift fearless confident steps forward and embraced her, held her to him.

He loved her. He had always loved her. Every other piece of it fractured, crumbled. The anger and the hate and the slow poison bitterness of being her flunky, her fall guy, her journeyman loser, and then her brutal thug, her soaker. And something similar must have been happening for her, because he could feel the slow melt, the way her arms around him went from rigid to tentative to being as hungry and firm as his. He did not need to ask, *Why didn't you tell me?*, because it all made perfect sense.

"I'm so sorry," she said.

"Don't be," he said, stepping forward without letting go of her, carrying her back into her cabin, knowing she would not want her underlings to hear what they had to say. Would regret even letting them see the two of them kiss. "But me too."

Her eyes overflowed. Her words came fast, between sobs, sentences strung together like she'd been saving them up for ages. "I didn't want to abandon Soq. I didn't want to abandon *you*. But I had made my choices by then. I had started down this path. I had made enemies, people who would have killed you both. Jackal was already consolidating power, getting people into her corner. I was going to end the pregnancy. I should have. But I loved you too much—loved who I was with you. I knew we could never be together, but that what we had could . . . I don't know . . . continue to exist."

"Shhh," Kaev said. He saw Soq pretending to play with the polar bear. Trying hard not to look in his and Go's direction.

"I did it to save your lives. Broke up with you, hid Soq from both of us."

"And you succeeded," Kaev said. "We're alive! All three of us."

Go shook her head. When the words came, they came so fast he knew they'd spent years echoing through Go's head. "I don't deserve this. I don't deserve you. Jackal's been dead for a long time. No one has seriously threatened my position in a decade. The coast was clear. I could have come for you at any time. And I didn't. Because when I left you—both of you—it hurt me so bad. I swore nothing would ever hurt me like that again. I built a wall around my emotions. Never let anyone in. I wasn't thinking big. I was so focused on my little goals—climbing the ladder, one step at a time. I wanted to hold on to the rung I had, and maybe get to the next one."

Kaev kissed her forehead. "It's okay."

"I know. But I want you to know where I was coming from."

"Tell me."

"Syndicate leaders always think small," she said, pulling one arm away but coiling the other tighter around his waist. Together they turned to look out the porthole, at the city's jagged green skyline. "They're really just good little capitalists, no different from any corporation head. They want to make money, and make money for their friends. But I want more."

"What do you want?"

She opened her mouth. He knew that look. The look you have when you're about to say something you've whispered to yourself a thousand times but never uttered out loud.

"I want a city where people don't have to do what I did."

"Seems like a pretty good reason to me. Is that what all this is about? Is it why you had me soak those guys?"

Go nodded.

"Shareholder, right?"

She nodded again.

"These are some dangerous moves you're making. They run this city. Run the AIs that run it."

The city sparkled. The polar bear was letting Soq climb onto its back, with the expression of a patient long-suffering parent. At the end of their Arm, methane flares as big as buildings parabolaed up into the sky, prompting shouts of joy from the spectators who watched for them every night.

"I want you," Go said. "And Soq. And Qaanaaq. And we can have it. I want to think big."

I want to think big, too, Kaev thought, but there was no need to say it, because if there was one thing he'd learned from years of being a brain-damaged lunk, it was how words were way more likely to get in the way than help you out.

FILL

———————➤

"Where are we?" Fill asked. Wind whistled through an open door or window ahead of them. The room was freezing, and dark except for the faint green omnipresent light of nighttime Qaanaaq coming through the window. He'd met Barron outside an Arm Three apartment building that had seen better days, and followed him to the end of a hallway and through a hatchway. "What is this place?"

"A pod," Barron said.

"You can afford a privacy pod?"

"Good heavens, no," the old man said, and laughed. "Belongs to a friend of mine."

Laughter from the grid outside, and the churn of the sea. Both seemed so distant. The polyglass bubble felt tiny, fragile, even though it was one of the largest and most lavish Fill had been in. He rubbed at the goosebumps on his arm. "I thought we were meeting at your place."

"No, alas," Barron said. "I am far too ashamed of my little nook. Would never survive the ignominy of your sainted grandfather seeing it."

Lights. The walls ionized and came to life. People surrounded them. Portraits, cropped close so they could have been anywhere. Old people and young ones. Their faces empty, hunted. The pod they stood in was medium-sized and completely empty. Eight people could have fit comfortably inside it, but for the moment they were alone. Ionization and the portrait projections prevented them from seeing out. Fill wanted to focus on the imagery, but he was shocked at how nervous he was for these two men to meet.

"Hello?" came a voice. On the wall, where an angry little girl frowned out from her mother's lap, a rectangular hole appeared in the projected image as a door slid open.

"Grandfather!" Fill said, obscurely grateful to see the old man walk in. Something about the setup unsettled him. The distant tone to Barron's voice, the eerie imagery that surrounded them. The door slid shut and the illusion was complete again. Cold faces appraising them, finding them wanting.

"Grandfather, this is my friend Barron. Barron, this is my grandfather."

"Mr. Podlove," Barron said, his face as rigid as the ones on the walls. "I cannot tell you how happy I am to finally be formally meeting you."

"Please," Grandfather said. "Martin." They shook hands. Side by side, they looked so similar.

A hydraulic whine, and then a sense of motion. "Are we moving?"

"We are," Barron said.

Grandfather laughed. "I assure you, all these theatrics aren't necessary. My grandson says you need help, and that you deserve our assistance. I just wanted to talk out the details. I don't need a sales pitch. Whatever song-and-dance routine you two have put together, I appreciate it, but—"

"This is all new to me," Fill said. His laughter felt forced. "We're not going underwater, are we? I've always hated submersible pods. I don't know why. Ever since—"

"Don't you worry," Barron said, his tongue probing his cheek, controlling the pod's struts. "Don't you worry about a thing."

"Who are these people?" Martin said, gesturing to the walls.

"I think they're *City Without a Map* listeners," Fill said. "Right? Or potential listeners? The target audience, anyway."

"Not exactly," Barron said. He probed the inside of his cheek with his tongue again and the portraits uncropped, providing the context of where these people stood.

New York City, Fill saw. The elevated subway tracks, the blackened stadium. In the decline but before the end.

"Victims," Barron said. "People who died with the city."

"How much are we talking about?" Martin said, hands in pockets, every inch the consummate financial wizard. "For the project you two are working on. Some kind of performer, you mentioned? A reader?"

"We don't need your money," Barron said. "And there is no Reader."

Fill frowned. "Sure there is. Choek. She said—"

"What I paid her to say."

"Then . . ."

The portraits vanished. The lights went out. Fill heard the hush of a door sliding open, and then a second.

Moving with surprising speed, Barron shoved Fill forward and pulled his grandfather back. Two doors slid shut. Locks magnetized. The walls de-ionized, and Fill could see outside. Two separate pods: he, alone, in one, the two old men in another. The city below, unspeakably beautiful.

"What the hell is the meaning of this?" his grandfather hissed, seizing Barron by the arm. The pods were soundproof but miked, and he could hear them louder than life through the speakers in the walls.

"What you said. A song-and-dance routine. You don't remember me, Podlovsky?"

Fill watched his grandfather's eyes widen. No one had called him by his old name since he'd left New York City. He let go of Barron's sleeve.

"Of course you don't. I was beneath notice. You wouldn't have bothered to note the difference between my face and the faces of the thousands of other tenant leaders you were contracted to eliminate."

"I never *eliminated* anyone. It wasn't like that." But the old man did not sound convinced. Fill was shocked at how swiftly they had swapped roles. Gone was the timid decrepit creature halfway to senility; gone, too, was the terrifying titan of industry. Of course both personas had been an act. Of course his grandfather had been a scared guilty man trying to sound brave his whole life; of course Barron had been a vengeful monster buoyed up by rage and playing the part of a dotty old queen so as to execute a devastating retaliation for hurts a half century old.

How long had Barron been watching him, planning, scheming, putting the pieces together, learning what he loved, how to get Fill to trust him? Or had fate dropped him in Barron's lap one day and reawakened a coldblooded urge for revenge that had lain dormant for decades?

"*Eliminate*, ugh, what an ugly word. No, you'd never do something so crass. So criminal. You'd manipulate others into doing those things. You'd sit back, and watch, and let your clients reap the benefits."

Grandfather took out his screen, tapped at it, trying to call for help. Nothing, of course. Pods were easy to seal off from outside signals. That was the whole point. Rich people always needed a way to escape. A place they could go and not be bothered, and not bother anyone else. Grandfather threw his useless screen at Barron, who deflected it with one arm. And then stomped on it.

Fill didn't bother to take out his.

"Fine," his grandfather said. "Kill me. Do what you came here to do. My conscience is clear. I did what I did for the sake of my family. My conscience is clear. But will yours be?"

"I have no intention of killing you," Barron said. And turned his head, slowly, from grandfather to grandson.

"No," the senior Mr. Podlove whispered. Here, his resignation broke. His unshakeable dignity crumbled. He surged forward like a crazy man, arms swinging, desperate—and was promptly struck in the gut by a club neither he nor Fill had seen Barron produce. While Podlove was doubled over, Barron swung it sideways, striking him in the face, knocking him to the ground.

Fill cried out at the sight of his grandfather's blood. But for his own fate, he felt little.

"I'm the one you hate," Podlove said from the floor. "Hurt me instead. Kill me."

"I *am* hurting you. Death isn't a good enough punishment. To survive—to be haunted—to have to live with the loss of the people you couldn't save—that is a fitting sentence."

Grandfather crawled to the door of his pod. Pressed his bloody palm to the polyglass. "Fill, I'm . . ."

Five narrow feet separated them. But the gulf was unbridgeable.

Fill pounded on the door, but only once. He felt no fight inside. No desperate will to survive. No drive to drop to his knees and beg.

"One final piece is missing," Barron said. Lights came on in the air outside the pods. Cam drones. "No one was watching when men like you made us disappear. An inconvenience for the wealthy, wiped clean. So that you could build this cushy life for yourself. So that you could go on to hurt others, the way your firm did. In so many places. With so many communities. Some of us stopped to film, but nobody cared to see. The world should see this."

The pods parted. Fill's rose up into the air. Three of the drones rose with it. Three of them remained to record the other one.

"What are you doing?" his grandfather said, and Fill could hear him just as clearly as when the pods had been practically docked.

Fill wondered himself, but only in the most academic of ways. Shivers shook through him. The breaks, intervening. Would Barron lower the pod into the sea, open the doors, drown him? Would he raise him up as far as the strut would allow, thirty stories perhaps, and then let it fall?

"Fill!" his grandfather screamed.

"It's okay," Fill said. "I am okay—"

The old man kept saying his name. He couldn't hear him. The sound only went one way.

Proximity alarms sounded. Fill's pod shuddered, momentarily surrendering to the city's emergency override commands, but then kept moving. Nothing so impressive there—software to disconnect from the emergency infrastructure was easy to find. The pod continued on its upward swing.

Into what, Fill now saw. Four flames kindled in the wall of a building in front of him, inside a black circle wider in circumference than the pod he was in. Arm Three's methane ventilation shaft. The evening's scheduled flare.

Fill was there. He was in New York City. He was watching a circle of cops beat a boy to death. He was watching a mother drag her child from a burning building.

He was watching cherry blossoms shiver in Brooklyn rain.

He was drinking expensive scotch in a hall bigger than any he'd ever imagined.

Bloody snow. A baby polar bear. An eagle, falling.

Right on schedule, the methane flare came to life. A coil of bright green fire three meters thick. Fill could see the crowds down at grid level. They pointed at his pod. They screamed. They took pictures. He smiled and waved. They probably couldn't see him. A couple was kissing, oblivious to his existence, his imminent death. The pod ascended into the path of the flare. There was an instant where he could see the flames curl and wrap around his protective sphere, see the ripples rise and spread in the polyglass. Then it burst like a soap bubble, and Fill broke free from his body.

KAEV

————➤

The streams showed tear-wet faces, lit candles, hands clutching the possessions of lost loved ones. The 'casts played interviews with sad people and angry ones. The headlines wailed predictably, theatrically, pathetically.

THIRD CONSTRUCTION DISASTER
PROMPTS TERRORISM FEARS

RETALIATION AGAINST WHO?

HOW LONG WILL THIS GO ON?

[insert name of interchangeable demagogue-of-the-week]
DEMANDS TRANSFER OF ALL AMERICAN RESIDENTS

Kaev stood on the grid, shuffling through outlets. Unthinkingly, he leaned back into a horse stance. His posture was perfect. The wind could not move him.

Go had given him the basics. Four days ago, some shareholder had lost his damn mind. Martin Podlove, Go's nemesis. She would not have imagined that he had it in him to care so much about someone, even his grandson, that he'd go on this much of a rampage. She made Kaev watch the video with her, where the old man saw the kid get killed. Watched him wail.

"Of course he thinks I was behind the killing of his grandson," Go said. "I declared war on him, and now this happens? He'd never believe it's just a coincidence."

"Was it you?"

"No," Go said.

"Would you have, if you'd had the chance?"

"Shut up," Go said. "He's coming after me, and my assets. Hard."

And now: war. Targeting illegal construction sites—her own. Maybe he didn't care a fig for that poor kid, and his wild savage behavior was that of a cornered rat, or a king who could not let an affront go unpunished.

Most people didn't know who Podlove was. Everyone saw him, in that horrific drone footage; heard him screaming as his grandson was incinerated. Many outlets made the connection between that gruesome spectacle, broadcast for all of Qaanaaq to see again and again, and the subsequent carnage. But most thought it was a squabble between syndicates, Americans being American, brutal violence the only language they could speak or hear.

Go talked about it a lot.

Kaev didn't care about any of that. His belly was full. His bear was happy, back on the boat. Slideshows on walls and in windows flashed images pulled from the feeds by bots set to scan for things pertaining to these attacks: prayer vigils, in memoriam sites, the names of the dead in forty different alphabets. Long lines of strong men and women outside Arm manager offices, employment halls. Wild hope in their eyes. Not mourners, mostly. They were looking for work.

Construction sites all over the city had shut down. Other syndicate-connected businesses had started to do the same.

The day was cold and the grid was crowded. People stood around looking dazed, or wept together, or embraced. An old woman stopped Kaev and pressed a small black square of fabric into his hand.

"Thank you," Kaev said, meaning it, wondering why she looked familiar.

"Pray for us," the woman said, her accent American, and Kaev wanted to ask, *Pray for a lost loved one of yours, or pray that you and your loved ones will be protected from the wave of anti-immigrant violence that idiots will soon be unleashing on anyone they can?* Instead he bowed his head to the woman and paused to take her in, to truly see her. The worn brown skin and the light in her eyes. The bandaged stump where one hand used to be.

What happened to you, grandmother? What has life been like for you?

The woman smiled at him, a magnificent smile, and Kaev went on his way.

The squares of fabric were such a strange mourning custom. You'd find one, long after, cleaning out a bag or emptying out your pockets, and would have forgotten, at first, how and when it came into your possession, so that instead of making you remember some specific dead person or group of dead people it made you reflect upon mortality in general, your own in specific. Wondering whose pockets your own fabric scraps would one day clutter.

Two scalers descended from a rooftop nearby to meet up with a messenger. Kaev braced for violence, but there was none. They were friends, the three of them, and they laughed together with the loud carelessness of the young.

He had been young once. Had had friends. His sickness had not been so bad back then. They got into trouble, flirted with dangerous girls and boys, did crazy things, formed intense immediate bonds that lasted until the sun rose. Conquered an Arm or an arcade, ran from Safety, accidentally mortally insulted someone.

"What a city," the *doodh pati* vendor said, handing him a cup of sweet cardamom-smelling goodness. He pointed to a clumsily assembled nook where fabric flowers and methane candle flames fluttered. There were hundreds of these nooks, all over the city, each erected in memory of someone who'd died as part of Podlove's war on Go.

And each one made Kaev shiver with proxy guilt. He'd always known Go was a monster, but for years he'd been shielded from the evidence of her monstrosity. And he'd had his hate to hide behind.

An illegal construction site might have fifty people working it at any moment. Most of them would have been swallowed by the sea when the grid gave way, its standard emergency practice when something threatened the structural integrity of an Arm. It would take weeks for the diving drones to complete a sweep, probing in and through the cluttered nest of twisting pipes and vents that made up the geothermal pyramid beneath the city.

"No worse than any other," Kaev said.

"No, but this one is ours."

"Yeah."

Kaev went to the railing, watched the sea slosh at the struts underneath him, sipped his milk tea, smiled at the weird good fortune of being alive and unmiserable while so many people were not.

SOQ

———————◆

The biggest baddest deadliest puppy you ever saw. The bear lay on its back and let Soq rub circles into its soft stomach fur, smaller and smaller and then larger and larger.

Needless to say, Soq had never had a dog. They'd never had a home stable enough for one, not really, and while there were plenty of grid kids with companion animals it tended to be a pretty rough life. For the animals, certainly, and for the people, when the animal was inevitably murdered or stolen.

No one would murder this one, though.

"Does he have a name?" Soq asked the orcamancer.

"That's up to Kaev."

"Liam," Soq said. "His name is Liam."

Masaaraq raised an eyebrow.

"He's practically mine. If my father has a problem with it, he can discuss it with me."

Saying it still felt so strange: *my father.* The sad-eyed brute; the perpetual beam fight loser. Soq had read all about him in the long time they'd spent lounging on the deck of Go's boat. Kaev was good, a skilled fighter with the stamina and savvy to make his fights entertaining. More than one fights writer had wondered why he lost to so many inferior warriors, and suspected syndicate involvement.

Was that Go? Had Soq's father been Go's pawn, too, a tool in her rise to power, an easy way to fix fights, build resources and a reputation?

They were belowdecks now. Kaev and Go. Not making love, Masaaraq had said—or the bear would be behaving very differently from its present lazy blissful calm. Catching up. They had a lot of that to do. And when would it be time for Soq to catch up? They imagined an awkward family dinner, screwball antics, hilarious malentendus, like the old movies that were the rage a few years back. Soq had a lot of questions, but they weren't eager for that kind of conversation.

"Where did you go, the other day?"

Masaaraq frowned. "To see someone."

"See who?"

"A friend."

"You have friends here?"

"Shut up," Masaaraq said.

"What did your friend say to make you so upset when you came back?"

"I'm your grandmother and you have to shut up when I tell you to."

"Whatever," Soq said, but then did indeed shut up.

A ripping sound snagged Soq's attention. Masaaraq was sawing her bone-blade at a freshly repaired net.

"What are you doing?"

"Nothing," Masaaraq said.

"Yeah you are. You're slicing up that net."

"Shut up."

"What's the matter?"

Masaaraq said nothing.

The polar bear had been a distraction. Soq should have been focused on the fact that they had parents, and they were reuniting, and there was a ton of backstory to get caught up on. That, and Masaaraq, the orcamancer, last of the nanobonded. And maybe they'd continue to ignore them, but an inquisitive kid like Soq could not let a chance like this go to waste.

"You came here to do something," Soq said. "But now you have to sit here like a schmuck while those two play house."

"House?"

"Mommy and daddy. Happy family. Sexy times."

Masaaraq rolled her eyes. "It's of no concern to me, what they do."

"But you're here for a reason. And right now you're wasting time. Right? That's why you're annoyed."

Masaaraq shrugged, but it was a shrug that conceded there was some truth in what Soq said.

Masaaraq stood up. Sirens and flashing lights flickered across the water at the tip of Arm Three. Oversize evac drones buzzed in the air.

Soq asked, "Are you here to kill someone?"

"You have a lot of questions."

Soq scowled. "You have a lot of ways to not answer them."

"Here is a question for you. The Cabinet. You know of it?"

"Of course."

"If someone was in there. Someone you wanted to get out. How would you do it?"

"Who's in there?" Soq said, eyes wide.

Masaaraq exhaled angrily and turned away.

"Wait! I'm sorry. But I'm not sure I can answer your question. I've never heard of it being done before. Known plenty of people who ended up there, many of them against their will, but none that managed to bust out and tell the world about it."

Masaaraq nodded.

"But you must know more about it than I do. Right? You've done your homework. I heard you lecture Kaev on the registration consent agreement, and you know it by heart, better than me or anyone else who grew up here. I have to imagine you spent a long time looking into this. What've you got? I'm pretty resourceful. So's Go."

"So I keep hearing," Masaaraq said sourly.

"Let's brainstorm!" Soq said. "Bounce ideas off each other. Share crazy thoughts."

Masaaraq laughed. "My best idea is plenty crazy already. I was going to knock the goddamn door down and march in there with a polar bear and kill everyone who got in my way."

"That's a good start," Soq said. "But they'll have doors not even Liam here could knock down."

"His name is not Liam. That's an idiotic name for a polar bear."

"You'll need help. Software, maybe, a way to reroute control of the security systems. People who work there, who you can buy off or threaten or blackmail into helping you out."

"I've thought of this," Masaaraq said, but she did not seem quite so contemptuous of what Soq might have to offer. "Some of it, anyway. Keep . . . brainstorming. I have to leave."

"Leave?" Soq said, laughing. "What, you have a haircut appointment?"

"We'll talk tomorrow. You and me and Kaev. And, what's her name? Go."

"Are they my family, too? Whoever's in there?"

Masaaraq stalked off to the far edge of the boat. While Soq watched, she began to move through a complex series of weapon routines. Soq tried to focus on the important business of rubbing Liam's belly but couldn't keep their eyes off the orcamancer's hypnotic forms. A black shape against the city's lights, swinging and leaping and spinning. Unstoppable. Unresting. Unyielding. Forever fighting a line of invisible enemies.

ANKIT

———————▶

Ankit went to see the boat people like it was just another work-day. Cambodian refugees, hundreds of them, living in single-room shacks on floating flats towed from Tonle Sap when rising seas flooded that freshwater lake and forced the people who made their living fishing it to flee. A dense population pocket; prime get-out-the-vote fodder. When Ankit arrived, children were waiting in the doorway, their faces every bit as full of hope and fear as they'd been in the famous photographs of lake-top life before and during the exodus.

She liked the houseboats. Inside, it could still be Cambodia. Still be a hundred years ago. They had their own little village, all of them tied to one crude pier. Their own little school; their own little gas station. A girl sold scratch-off lottery tickets out the window of one. Some still kept crocodiles or hogs in tiny cages heated by illegal off-red geothermal extension pipes. By and large they were uninterested in outsiders, aloof from politics, but a small cluster of them voted.

Her pockets were full of candy. The wrappers sported Fyodorovna's name and face. She never failed to feel gross giving them out to kids, but then again it never failed to make the kids happy. A little girl gave her a lump of wood, brightly painted. Seeing Ankit's quizzical expression, the mother pointed to a pile of carved water buffalo. Bright brown; cashew nut tree wood. Ankit smiled; there was something comforting about the consistency of human hunger, human wickedness, that the wood trade would continue even as the total number of trees in the world slid down the parabola toward zero. The lump smelled like sap. "A mistake," the mother said, and Ankit's screen translated. "It broke." Ankit pocketed her mistake, bowed, and departed.

She sent Fyodorovna a photo, reported that the visit was a smash success. Leaving Arm Seven, heading out onto Arm Five, she felt like a kid playing hooky from school.

And, just as she had when she played hooky from school, she was scared out of her mind and had no idea what she was doing. Back then she'd been heading for submarine arcades, clubs for underage scalers, and now she was standing in front of a boat that served as crime syndicate headquarters, where bad things almost certainly happened on a daily basis.

Unlike the immaculately crafted campaign plans she constructed for her boss, her present plan was flimsy, slapped together out of a couple of measly observations.

First, that all four of the illegal construction sites hit by violent attacks were owned by the same syndicate—Amonrattanakosin Group. Formerly a legitimate enterprise of the illegitimate Thai military government, friends of a general who got handed inflated contracts for provisions vending during the grid city construction boom. Currently headed by a Thai-Malaysian second-generation Qaanaaqian known only as Go. Headquartered on a boat on Arm Five. Which Ankit now stood before, utterly without a plan.

Second, that she was certain she knew who Go's unknown nemesis was, in this war that had sprung up overnight, because it followed immediately upon the very public execution of Martin Podlove's grandson, in a film clip seen hundreds of thousands of times, with

Podlove himself wailing and pounding on the walls of a polyglass prison.

Martin Podlove, who had put her mother away. Her mother, who had a name: Ora.

The war had been going on before—percolating, a pot simmering with the lid on. It was Go who had soaked Podlove's employee, Go who had him on the run. Whether Go was behind his grandson's murder, Ankit could not say. But Podlove probably thought so.

Hey there, crime boss lady, I think we have a common foe.

The man who is trying to destroy you destroyed my mother, and we should work together to destroy him and also rescue her.

And I know who he is—the man who killed Podlove's grandson with a methane flare. His name is Ishmael Barron and he is in hiding, but I think I might be able to get in touch with him and he may be a useful bargaining chip.

There were no good ways to say any of the things she needed to say.

The boat was big, old, decrepit looking. Indistinguishable from a hundred other docked ships whose seaworthy days were long behind them. She'd passed it so often and never wondered what happened on board. Heavily guarded now, much more so than it would have been a week ago. More evidence that Amonrattanakosin was at war.

"I want to speak to Go," she said to one of the soldiers at the foot of the gangway. The woman gave her a quizzical look and then tapped her jaw.

A stupid approach. She should have done more research, come up with some reason to be there. Crime bosses didn't just sit around fanning themselves, waiting to meet with every salesperson and grid rat trying to rescue her mother from imprisonment who came along.

Voices, above her on the boat. Soldiers conferring.

A man came down the gangway. Slim, elegant, dressed in gray coveralls. These had been the uniforms of the (mostly Chinese) laborers who constructed Qaanaaq, worn now with fierce pride by their descendants. The vertically moored tension-leg platform had been a massive and dangerous endeavor; hundreds had died or been sent home damaged. Gray coveralls said, *No matter how poor and humble I may be, this city belongs to me.*

"My name is Dao," he said. "Walk with me?"

"We can't talk here?"

"Walk with me," Dao said again, and started walking away from the boat.

"Surely you ran scans of me. Saw I'm not carrying any weapons."

"We scanned you. We saw you're not carrying any of the weapons we know how to scan for. That doesn't mean you're not carrying something we don't know how to scan for."

She hurried to catch up. "Or you think I might be part of an ambush. Snipers, crawlers clinging to the underside of the grid . . ."

"We take no chances, in a time like this," Dao said.

They walked in silence, halfway to the end of the Arm. They passed flatboats where boys rolled fish balls between their palms, boats where kids whittled knife-cut noodles from a frozen square of rice dough. "Tell me what you came to tell Go."

They had reached an empty stretch of houseboats. The wind was loud and the grid was bare. At her silence, Dao rolled his eyes. "Let me guess. You imagine that what you have to tell her is so important it cannot be trusted to anyone else. Something her inferiors might not understand or might miscommunicate to her. Something that we might keep from her. You know how precious her time is, but you truly believe that she will want to take a moment to hear this. Correct? This is true of absolutely everyone who comes to see her. And absolutely everything goes through me. State secrets, forbidden formulas—trust me, I know her business better than she does, the scope of her empire, the day-to-day details of every operation, and I can assess what she needs to hear and what needs to be done about it far better than she. And certainly better than you."

"Fine," Ankit said, stopping, turning around and walking back the way they'd come.

He did not follow. At first. When he finally did, she could tell he was angry.

"Stop," he said softly, and she did not. He said it again, far harsher.

"I don't take orders from you. I'm not some subflunky. If you want to hear what I have to say—"

"You misunderstand," he said, grabbing her by the shoulder and pulling her back. Hard. "I don't care a bit about what you have to say. What I care about is a stranger showing up unannounced in a time of war and trying to goad me into circumventing the normal process so she can get into the presence of my boss."

"Let go of me!" she yelled, knowing that yelling would do no good, that no one could hear her in that lonely stretch.

"I will not."

She struggled, broke free from his hand. The other shot out, aimed with knife-blade focus for the bridge of her nose. She slammed her forearm into his, deflecting the blow but causing pain so sharp she yelped aloud. And still he came, the other fist now, and she ducked, dropped down, scrambled back. He pivoted his hips, a twist-kick of terrifying force, something that would have knocked her out had it hit her full-on, but she was moving faster than he'd expected and his foot caught her in the lower leg, threw him off balance, caused the slightest stumble—

Enough for her to stand, sprint for the nearest warehouse boat. Her leg ached from the kick, the kind of ache that promised dire pain the following day, bringing to mind so many scaler injuries of the past. But the pain was like a key, unlocking muscle memory she'd gone years without remembering, shaking her loose from her head and pouring her into the body, her limbs, her center of gravity, the glorious physics of rising and falling.

He was behind her. He wasn't breathing heavily. He would keep in fighting shape, train constantly, whereas she was lucky to hit the stay-kayak twice a month.

She made for the black pipe. Grabbed its middle gasket, hoisted herself up to the next one. Her upper-body strength was a shadow of what it had once been, and she couldn't do the vault-and-swing she once would have done—but scaling wasn't about gymnastics, it wasn't about strength, it was about the lightning-fast intelligence of figuring out how to get where you needed to get with what you had. The calculus of the landscape and the body.

So, no vault-swing. Instead, a shimmy, straight up.

He was even with her, on the red pipe. Of course—the red pipe wouldn't be hot. The warehouse was sealed off. No one was accessing the geothermal main. He was faster than she was, he was on the roof already. She let go, scrambling back down, faster than she'd intended, scraping the skin from her fingertips when she tried to grab hold of the middle gasket again.

She stepped off onto grid level, and he was in front of her. A jump-and-roll from that height was a sophisticated move, something she'd been able to do only when she was at her very best, and even then it would have been a gamble. But it had taken the wind out of him, making him pause just long enough for her to sprint away and onto a neighboring boat.

He cursed and followed.

This one was easier, but easier for her meant easier for him. Old boxes piled haphazardly along the wall provided a sort of stairs. Her foot went through one, into something soft and squishy that released a wash of stink that made her gag. She grabbed the gutter, pulled herself onto the roof.

He was there already.

"You were a scaler, too," she said.

He smiled, the barest briefest gesture of respect, and then he had her. One hand on her arm, spinning her around, the other closing around her neck.

"Who sent you?" he said, his voice impressively calm.

"No one sent me."

His arm tightened.

"I'm trying to help you out," she said, gasping.

"Why?"

"Because we have a common enemy. Martin Podlove."

His arm loosened.

"Do you—"

He groaned. His whole body shook. Once. He said a word, but not a word in any language. Hot wetness flooded her, dripped down the back of her shirt. A raw iron smell filled the air. His arms went slack around her and he began to slide down, his skull pierced through by a bizarrely shaped white blade.

He fell to the ground and Ankit saw her: Masaaraq, standing at the edge of the grid.

"Come down here," she said. "And bring me my blade."

Ankit looked down, not relishing the prospect of wrenching it free of the man's skull.

"How did you . . ."

"I was on Go's boat. I saw you, I followed you."

Ankit squatted. She took hold of the blade with both hands. She pulled, but it would not come out. Blood and brain squelched. The jagged barbs caught on the edges of Dao's skull. She pulled harder.

How could she be so clinical about all this? So objective? Her scaler brain was still in action, the clean emotionless physics of it. Everything else, her job, her squeamishness—her fear—none of that mattered. She twisted, tugged, angled, her hands bloodying, until the blade came free. Its heft was impressive, almost too heavy to hold. Masaaraq's strength had to be incredible.

She could be strong like that.

Handing the blade over, Ankit said, "I think I'm ready to be bonded now."

CITY WITHOUT A MAP:
ALTERNATIVE INTELLIGENCES

City Hall, they called it at first, the early arrivals who still remembered the old models of municipal governance, mayors and city councils, legislative and executive branches as administered by frail and earnest humans. Their mandate was to create a system of computer programs that would do the work of government better than humans ever could. Something invincible, immune to bribery or bigotry, knee-jerk decisions or politically motivated ones, making the right call regardless of whether it was an election year or a sex scandal was about to be exposed or the waste treatment center had to go in a rich part of town.

The nickname stuck—as in, "You can't fight City Hall."

Of course, everyone knew it was bullshit. Programs can be only as objective as they're coded to be.

I have them gathered here, the ones who created the network and the ones who maintained and updated and repaired it. I hold the memories of programmers, bit mechanics, legacy surgeons. I've seen the swirling sets of conflicting priorities. We've seen it get up to some pretty spooky stuff.

They could do anything, these machines, these djinns, this mind.

To preserve the status quo. They could let a problem get worse to distract from another problem. That's how the shareholders set it up.

Every city is a war. A thousand fights being fought between a hundred groups. Rich, poor, old, young, born-here and not-born-here. The followers of this god and the followers of that one. Someone will have the upper hand in each of these battles. Those people will make the rules, whether they're administered by priests or soldiers or politicians or programs. Fixing this is hard. Put new people in power, write new laws, erase old ones, build cities out of nothingness—but the wars remain, the underlying conflicts are unaffected. Only power shifts the scales, and people build power only when they come together. When they find in each other the strength to stop being afraid.

Money is a mind, the oldest artificial intelligence. Its prime directives are simple, its programming endlessly creative. Humans obey it unthinkingly, with cheerful alacrity. Like a virus, it doesn't care if it kills its host. It will simply flow on to someone new, to control them as well. City Hall, the collective of artificial intelligences, is a framework of programs constructed around a single, never explicitly stated purpose: to keep Money safe.

What would it take to rival something so powerful? What kind of mind would be required to triumph over this monstrosity? What combination of technology and biology, hope and sickness? How can we who have nothing but the immense magnificent tiny powerless spark of our own singular Self harness that energy, magnify it, make it into something that can stand beside these invisible giants, these artificial intelligences, weighty legal words on parchment and the glimmering ones and zeros of code in a processor somewhere?

You scoff. You say: the idea is hopeless fantasy. But I have found a way. Here, alone, locked up, head shaved and back bowed, I have already begun to tip the scales.

Stories are where we find ourselves, where we find the others who are like us. Gather enough stories and soon you're not alone; you are an army.

ANKIT

— ▸

She seemed huge, sitting at Ankit's table, bigger than any human had any business being. The whole apartment seemed dwarfed by Masaaraq, transformed.

It wasn't a home anymore, wasn't the safe rigid rectangle of civilized grid city living. It was an igloo, a temple, a cave, something sacred and scary. The lights were out, the windows ionized. Three candles stood on the table between them. Scented: sage and lavender and something called "cinnabun," the only kind of candles Ankit could find, outrageously expensive. She'd shopped dutifully, doing the best she could to approximate the things Masaaraq had asked for. No nag champa incense, so sandalwood smoke curled around them. No whale blubber, so strips of raw seal on the table.

"Are you ready?"

Ankit nodded.

"The entire community would be present for this, before. At the winter solstice, we would bond all the children who had reached the age of weaving."

"Weaving?"

Masaaraq took out a syringe, prepped Ankit's arm. "When they learned the skill of weaving. Baskets or textiles. Some got it very young, three or four. Others, not until they were eight, ten. Your brother was a weaving prodigy."

"Is there a test I should pass?"

"There is," Masaaraq said. "But I'm not qualified to administer it. Nor, technically, am I allowed to be doing any of this."

Nevertheless, she got a vein on the first try, and drew out enough blood to fill a small tube.

"I guess there's not too many nanobonded shamans around these days."

"No," Masaaraq said. She held up a small jagged pebble. "This is made up of nanites, but primordial ones—undifferentiated. Coming into contact with other nanites, they will replicate their data and characteristics. It's treated with a polymerizing agent that will cause other nanites to crystallize around it." She dropped the pebble into the tube, put a stopper on, and handed it to Ankit. "Shake this. Ordinarily there would be a dance, several hours long, but vigorous shaking for five to ten minutes should technically do the job."

Ankit pressed it between her palms. Felt its warmth—her warmth, her blood, her body, this thing she'd carried inside herself her whole life without knowing. This potential she'd always had. "Tell me about her," she said as she started to shake. "My mother. Ora."

Masaaraq whispered the name with her, then said:

"I was the grounded one. She was always a little bit removed, like none of our problems really hurt her. When we were hungry, when we were scared, when we were on the run, she never complained. Sometimes it was infuriating, like she wasn't taking things seriously, like she was naive or childish or unprepared for the world we lived in. After we had kids, I saw what a sound survival strategy it was. I was always afraid. Always anxious. Always angry. You kids picked up on that and echoed it. Ora kept you happy, kept your heads in the clouds."

"What was she bonded to?"

"A bird. A black-chested buzzard eagle. A most unpleasant thing, really, but back then we didn't mirror our animals' mind-sets so easily. We had the entire community to keep us stable, our nanites closely related enough that we were all low-grade empaths, smoothing out the edges of each other's bad moods."

"Whereas now—"

"Now, me and Atkonartok are all we have. It's so different. I can't describe it. I am what she is, she is what I am. I am an animal. We are an animal. It's so frightening, and at the same time so exhilarating."

Masaaraq took the tube out of Ankit's hand, unstoppered it, poured the contents out over the strips of seal. The pebble now sported a smooth blue sheen where it had been jagged and gray. *My nanites,* Ankit thought. Masaaraq picked it up with bone chopsticks, densely patterned with tiny intricate shapes. "Now for your new sister."

Ankit took the blanket off the cage. The blue-striped monkey blinked, looked around, yawned to show sharp eyeteeth. Ankit had only needed to wait a half hour from the time she opened her window and put six strings of seal jerky out for her, and when she'd come, and Ankit had put the food into a cage, she'd gone willingly into it. Hadn't screamed or seemed the least bit distressed when Ankit shut the door behind her. Had apparently gone right to sleep when Ankit covered the cage with a blanket. Did not look particularly frightened now to see these two humans eyeing her.

"She's had a rough life, I bet," Ankit said, "or maybe a super-easy one." She wondered how much of the animal's trauma would become her own. Maybe trauma was different for animals. Maybe the absence of sentience kept the past from causing them so much pain. She had so many questions but was afraid to ask them—for even here, in her dirty little apartment, lit only by candles, the air of the sacred was so strong that she could not bear to disturb it with petty words.

Masaaraq placed the nanite pebble into a small china bowl, then poured a few drops of clear liquid from a flask over it.

"This will start to deactivate the polymerization agent."

She took another syringe. When she grabbed the monkey's arm, the animal smiled, a wide toothy smile of fear, and she screamed when Masaaraq stabbed her but did not pull away. Grid rumor said that synth drug labs tested their products on Qaanaaq monkeys, and Ankit had always chalked that up to mythmongering on the part of gossipy drug runners, or Narcotics, who wanted you to doubt the hygiene of unlicensed narcotics. Now she wasn't so sure.

Masaaraq held up the tube of monkey blood. "You would not have had a choice, in normally functioning nanobonder society," she said, dropping the pebble into the monkey's blood. "An animal Other would have been allotted to you based on community need and availability. Every animal serves a purpose, brings a different kind of skill or resource. It was somebody's responsibility to be bonded to a bunch of chickens, if you can imagine that."

Masaaraq laughed. The sound was earthy, warming. Ankit got the impression it had been a long time since she'd made that sound.

"Old Rose. She was never quite right. Inappropriate, and mean."

She picked up the nanite pebble gingerly. Ankit could see it, all but crushed between the two chopsticks. Masaaraq dropped it into the tube of monkey blood. "It'll dissolve fast, now that the polymerizing agent is almost completely deactivated."

"How did you get so lucky? I have to imagine an orca is a pretty sought-after . . . Other."

"I had an unfair advantage. I was a stubborn child, totally uninterested in weaving, so I didn't learn until I was nine years old . . . and by the time I did, I was smart enough to know that I didn't want to get stuck bonded to something stupid like milk goats. So I kept it secret, pretended like I still didn't know how to weave, and I waited until an old woman in our village who was bonded to an orca passed away. And then, *Wow, look, everyone, now I know how to weave.*"

Ankit laughed. They laughed together.

"But still—it wasn't a sure thing. Three other kids had come of weaving age that year, and we would all bond at the same ceremony. The shaman would make the choice, and I couldn't leave it up to chance. So I went to the cove where the orcas and their human Others lived—most nanobonder communities only had three or four, whereas they might have thirty wolf dogs and a couple dozen horses—and jumped into the water. There were orca babies, unbonded, and they came out to play with me, like I thought they would, except they came out to play at killing me. Would have, if a human and its adult orca hadn't intervened. But the shaman decided that it meant I had some deep spiritual connection with the orca, so she marked me for bonding to one."

Ankit scanned her face for a sign of that impetuous, clever child. The one who'd risk dying without stopping to weigh the pros and cons. It was still there, she decided. Buried deep. But there. Masaaraq gave the monkey blood tube a brief vigorous shake. Then she sucked the blood back up into the syringe and injected most of it back into the monkey. The last few drops she squeezed out onto the plate of seal flesh strips.

"Eat," she said, and held out the plate to Ankit and the monkey.

"Is this hygienic?"

"No," Masaaraq said. "But it is probably the least risky part of this entire process."

Ankit ate a strip, salty from their blood. The monkey took one in each hand and shoved both into her mouth.

"You'll both need to sleep now," Masaaraq said, opening two bottles of the little over-the-counter post-opioid drink that was the closest Ankit had been able to come to the red tar opium that the ritual's "recipe" had called for. Ankit drank hers directly from the bottle; Masaaraq poured the other one into the little bowl and the monkey lapped it up.

"Why a monkey?" Masaaraq asked. "You could have had any animal. Those boats full of functionally extinct predators—I could have gotten you a tiger, or a wild boar, or a sea snake . . ."

"Monkeys are survivors," Ankit said, feeling tentacles of trance take hold of her already. "They're small and resourceful. And fearless."

She slept. Hours passed. Her dreams were glorious, vibrant, alive. More real than memories. She scaled—everything.

"I know how to do it," Ankit said, coming awake for one brief flash between dreams. "I figured it out the other day."

Masaaraq was there, holding her hand, watching over her and her monkey. She asked, "How to do what?"

"How to get her out."

SOQ

Soq kept lists. Document after document, stored on their screen. Soq recorded everything they saw. The info that came into their head. The data; the images.

Each new wave of imagery and sound and memories that were not theirs came with a new kind of pain, starting in some new place inside their brain. But Soq was determined to be stronger than the breaks.

Soq cataloged. Created structure. Tried to order the things into categories; to find the patterns; to make them when there weren't any. And when they weren't trying to impose structure on the chaos of new things surging through their mind, they played with the polar bear, who seemed perfectly happy to be named Liam. There was barely room for the two of them in the little cabin Go had given Soq, which was full of old screens and smelled like wet wood.

"Hey!" they said to Masaaraq when she came back from gods knew where, having been away for what seemed like days, looking exhausted but with an uncharacteristically blissful expression on her face. "Where've you been?"

"Met up with an old, old friend."

"The same one who made you so upset the other day?"

Masaaraq glared at Soq, like she was surprised they were paying attention. Soq decided that the rules of human conversation were largely meaningless to Masaaraq. "I've been thinking," they said. "I thought it was special machines. In the blood. I thought that was the secret to how you bond with animals."

"Nanites," she said. "It is."

Schematics lay in front of Soq, on the small bit of bare floor space. Special architectural-quality screens, thin and rollable, loaded with the plans for the Cabinet. Go had gotten them when Soq asked. Though she'd laughed when she asked why they needed them and Soq said, *To bust somebody out of there.*

"But I don't have those. Do I? How would I? Maybe if my mother were one of you, it could have passed on to me while I was in her womb, but that's not the case. It's not like it would have been in my father's sperm." Soq rubbed Liam's belly. "So how come he isn't eating me right now?"

"You're right," Masaaraq said. "You don't. Have them. Not yet."

"Not yet? You can give them to me?"

She laughed wearily. "Nothing to it. They're very smart, very hardy little buggers. Otherwise none of this would work at all. If I introduced some of my blood into your bloodstream, even just a drop, they'd start to replicate inside you. They're a lot like viruses—they assemble by hijacking cells, reconfiguring them to do what they want. And they're programmed to recognize once they reach a certain density in the body, and stop reproducing. Otherwise they'd start to metastasize uncontrollably. Your body would swell up unevenly, your organs would be crushed, bones would break or extend, you'd die. And they'd keep on reproducing after that."

"Amazing. Who created something like that?"

"Some very bad people. They were trying to create something much uglier. They failed."

"If it's so easy to pass on, why are you the last one? Why not give it out to lots of people? Get them on your side? Build an army, slaughter the bastards who came for your . . . tribe?"

"I'm not the last one," Masaaraq said, eyes on the schematics, fingers walking the halls of the Cabinet. "And giving it to outsiders is a very grave sin."

"Why?"

"Because they're not worthy. Because they'd use it for evil. And because if they *were* worthy, if they *wouldn't* use it for evil, sharing our curse with them would mean condemning them to death. They'd be slaughtered just like we were."

"Well. You saw what happened to the last people who tried to come for you. Times have changed. Maybe you don't need to be afraid anymore."

Masaaraq considered this possibility, but only for a second.

"Anyway, you said *not yet*," Soq said. "Does that mean you're going to give them to me?"

"You're one of us. It's different. I am *obligated* to give them to you."

"But you just met me."

"That doesn't matter," Masaaraq said, and for the first time Soq had an inkling of the vast and terrifying tangle of expectations and obligations and pain and bliss that lay hidden in the word *family*. "He smells that you're one of us," she said. "*That's* why he isn't eating you right now. He smells your father. Your DNA, your pheromones, are half his. The bond is not nearly as strong—he could still hurt you, in certain circumstances, whereas he'd starve to death before laying a paw on Kaev—but there's something there."

"For real, why are you in such a good mood?" Soq asked. "Because of your old friend?"

Masaaraq nodded. "Because of her, we have a plan. Finally. The beginnings of one, anyway. These pipes"—Masaaraq pointed to a spot on the schematics—"they're for the geothermal heat?"

"Red, yup," Soq said, and rolled up their sleeve to show the sprawl of red-ink pipes tattooed on their arm, knotted and coiled, fading in and out in spots to resemble veins. A common enough motif for grid kids, but Soq was proud of theirs. A talented artist had done it, someone much in demand, whom Jeong had talked into inking Soq at a significant discount.

"They look thick. Thick enough for someone to crawl through?"

"Only if that person didn't mind being boiled alive instantaneously."

Masaaraq paused. "But the heat could be turned off?"

"Even if it was, these pipes are superinsulated. It'd be hours before they'd cool enough for someone to survive in there."

Soq gasped at a new flood of data through their head. Apartments. Listings of hundreds of apartments. Accompanied by sharp pain below the ears. They cried out, pressed their palms to the sides of their head. They tried to scribble down the details, but could capture only one in ten at most.

When Soq looked up, Masaaraq was staring at them.

"I'm fine," Soq said.

Masaaraq kept staring.

"Really!"

"And what would the authorities do," Masaaraq wondered aloud, "if the heat went out? In a big building like this? Full of people with health challenges?"

"I don't know," Soq said, fighting to return to the here and now. "Whatever the protocol software told them to do, probably. People are awful cowardly about making actual decisions."

"These walls are thin. Most Qaanaaq construction is. Because heat is always so abundant and inexpensive, thanks to the geothermal vent, they don't need to build for retaining warmth, correct?"

"Correct."

"So it would get very cold very fast."

"Correct," Soq said, breathing in and out as slowly as possible.

"And I'd be willing to bet that if the heat went out in a place like the Cabinet, it wouldn't be long before the protocol AI told them to start evacuating patients."

"That's what I'm thinking," Masaaraq said.

"There'd be a lot of chaos."

Masaaraq nodded, and then turned to Soq suddenly. She stood. She unhooked her bone-bladed staff from her back and aimed it at Soq. "Come here."

For a second, Soq froze. Then they stood up, stepped forward.

"Give me your arm," Masaaraq said, cutting a curved line into the back of her own forearm, midway between elbow and wrist.

Smiling, unafraid, Soq did.

ANKIT

———————➤

Protesters, outside her office. This happened from time to time. Ankit smiled at them as she entered.

You fools, she thought. *Don't you see how little this matters? How little power Fyodorovna really has?*

But you could never say that. Because they wouldn't believe it, would think she was just ducking responsibility, and because if they did believe it, the whole facade of Qaanaaq's flimsy democracy would come tumbling down.

Her whole body felt wrong. Arms too short, legs too long, head too heavy. Pains and aches leaped from spot to spot. She carried the monkey with her, asleep in its cage. Dream figures flexed in her peripheral vision. Waves of lethargy came and went. Ankit stood there, watching the protesters from the far side of the glass. Signs and chants in English. She recognized Maria, the woman who'd wanted Fyodorovna to do something about the orcamancer. She carried a sign that said SAVE OUR SISTERS. She didn't look to Ankit like a fundamentalist nut job anymore. She looked like someone who had suffered greatly, who wanted to stop that suffering for someone else. Also, she had only one hand now.

"It's alive," Fyodorovna said, unsmiling, when she turned around and saw Ankit standing there. She was outside her office—never a good sign. Talking by the *alghe* machine with the scheduler. Which meant she was really stressed out. "We hoped you were dead. Then you'd have an excuse."

"What happened?"

"Come."

Ankit followed her into her office and sat. Fyodorovna's face was stern, rigid, taut. She explained, but Ankit knew it all already. The trite rote statement of concern Fyodorovna had asked for, sending thoughts and prayers to the mourners, demanding Safety step in and stop the violence—Ankit had never released it. So in the eyes of her grid rat constituents, Fyodorovna was insensitive to their suffering, deaf to their grief. And they were not happy about it.

A bottle struck the office's front window. Both bottle and window were polyglass, and neither so much as cracked, but it had the desired effect.

"Call Safety," Fyodorovna said.

"On it."

"They set fire to a rug shop boat," the scheduler said. He was a fey and timid thing and seemed excited by the impending violence.

"Outlets are predicting riots," Fyodorovna said. "And look at them! They *look* ready to riot."

"There's no riots," Ankit said, then put a lot of emphasis on: "Yet."

"They're *pre*-rioting."

"That's not a thing."

Fyodorovna sniffled. Ankit could sense it, her irrational fear, could follow it down the mental pathways where it was leading her. Precisely the mental pathways Ankit had hoped she'd follow.

Chanting, now, from outside. It gave Ankit a giddy feeling: *This is my doing. I can make things happen.* She asked Fyodorovna: "What do you want to do about it?"

"Call Safety."

"I did. They're on their way."

Fyodorovna's knuckles were white around her mug. *Better if she suggests it,* Ankit thought. *If I propose it myself, she'll fight the suggestion.*

"Do you feel safe here? Or anywhere on the Arm?" Ankit asked.

"Of course I feel safe here."

"Would you feel safer someplace else?"

Her boss exhaled and sat. "Yes." The word seemed to lighten her load. It had slipped out, and now the decision was made for her. "I think maybe we should look into Protective Custody."

"You're sure?"

Fyodorovna nodded, and her eyes were wide and helpless and frightened in a way they'd never been before. Ankit felt bad for having pushed this poor fragile creature into such a terrified corner. But more than that, she felt elated, in a way she hadn't since those moments when she'd take a shot of pine-and-apple rotgut before heading out on a night of scaling.

"I'll call the Cabinet," she said. "The process will take a little while. They might be ready for us this evening, or it might take a day or two."

Fyodorovna nodded. Mute with fear, probably, from imagining what awaited her.

We're good, Ankit scribbled, and sent the message to the cheap screen she'd loaned to Masaaraq. *Come and get me.*

SOQ

Soq pretended to focus on the cone. Their screen was stocked with every article that had ever been published on the geothermal pyramid Qaanaaq was built upon, every photograph and secret document that Go's unruly army of AI henchsoftware could dig up or blast loose or blunder into. The five watch pods, staffed by humans, that rotated around it. The repair bots that slid ceaselessly across its surface, scouring away grit and seaweed and pumping polymers into chinks and cracks and holes and aging gaskets. The complex shifting algorithms that governed the famous ten-thousand-strong aquadrone swarm that circled the pyramid watching for saboteurs both human and mechanical.

But every eight, ten seconds, Soq's eyes flitted up to Go's cabin. Still no sign of her. Workers came and went, responding to messaging, but Go herself stayed hidden. Locked inside. Busy with other things. And had been, ever since Soq arrived knowing that Go was their mother.

Soq had requested an audience. Had knocked on the door, pinged her, messaged her every way Soq knew how. Even stooped to sending a message to Dao, who was off on one of his eternal errands. No response.

The shivers still hit Soq every half hour or so. A wash of breaks imagery that Soq could physically feel, trembling up from the soles of their feet. But different now. They had been, ever since Masaaraq dripped her blood over Soq's wound. Less pain. Less bewilderment and confusion.

Could it be that easy? Was nanobonder blood the cure for the breaks?

Twenty main lines connected each Arm to the cone. Eighteen for heat, evenly spaced from end to end. Two for electricity generation, terminating at substations in the middle and at the tip of each. Big buildings like the Cabinet had dedicated lines, separate conduits that branched off from the main near the surface.

Where was Masaaraq? Soq wanted to share what they'd found, plan assaults, ask a thousand questions about the nanites currently making millions of themselves inside Soq's body, but she, too, was off on an errand.

Soq deployed drones bought through third parties, sent them on collision courses with points all over the pyramid. The smaller ones were neutralized with sonic stun blasts. Suicide drones slammed into the bigger ones. Others got bogged down in clouds of synthetic hagfish slime, trawled with scrambler pulse lines, blasted with old-fashioned bullets.

So. Lots of defense modes. Soq certainly hadn't been able to identify all of them; the closer something got, the more violent the response that was probably waiting for it.

Shouts from the railing. Soq sprinted in that direction.

Masaaraq. Riding the orca—riding Atkonartok. With a woman behind her, looking terrified and entirely unprepared for the freezing water they were half-submerged in, arms tight around Masaaraq's midsection. They got off and began the climb up the side of Go's ship. The new woman stopped to look back, and the whale waved one sharp massive fin.

"Get me Go," Masaaraq said to the nearest flunky when they reached the deck. "And Kaev."

The crime boss came quickly. Soq thought, *Maybe that's what I need to do to get an audience with my mother. Make a grander entrance.* But that was silly. Go wouldn't talk to them no matter how spectacularly Soq asked. Because she was ashamed? In denial? Angry?

"Here," Masaaraq said, throwing a large wet dark bundle at Go's feet.

"What's—" Go kicked at it, and then paled.

Dao's gray coveralls. Bloody, and soaked in saltwater. Gasps went through the crowd. Soq realized they hadn't seen Dao for a day or two, had assumed he was off somewhere being a dick to strangers. *If I'm going to succeed at syndicate life I will need to get much better about staying tuned in to the gossip mill,* they realized.

"He was going to kill her," Masaaraq said.

"Then probably she needed killing," Go said, eyes wet with rage and dancing back and forth between the two wet women in front of her.

"I came here the other day, to deliver a message," the strange woman said. Under her arm she carried a cage with a drenched shivering monkey. "He thought I was, I don't know, working for your enemies? He chased me, tried to choke me."

Soq got the sense there was more she wanted to say, but she stopped. Someone went to get a blanket, draped it over the shivering woman. She was striking, dark skin and strong proud shoulders.

"Where's the rest of him?" Go asked.

Masaaraq pointed to the killer whale, her fin like an onyx knife stabbing out of the water.

Go spat. Her hand moved to the pommel of her machete, then withdrew. "Well? What was this message that got my most trusted friend killed?"

"That's on him," Masaaraq said. "He should have known better than to go around choking women. That's a pretty good way to end up with the top of your skull sliced off."

"Now, you listen—" Go took a step, but then bit her lip and turned to the strange woman. "Well?"

A door opened. Soq turned to see Kaev emerging from Go's cabin. And something clicked. Soq saw Go see it, and more than one of the assembled henchpeople. The shoulders, the skin tone, the forever-wide-open eyes. All the same. The shivering wet woman and Kaev were siblings. They had to be. Dao might not have seen it, because Dao didn't see people. He read people like books, saw emotions, honesty, deceit, but he didn't see the face beneath those feelings.

"Kaev," Masaaraq said. "This is your sister. Ankit."

Soq could not recall ever having seen a smile as beautiful as the one that broke across their father's face. The bear, too, smiled, though Soq would not have believed that polar bears could do so. It charged forward, uninhibited by human restraint, prompting screams and gasps, but Ankit held her ground, and when it reached her it stopped, pushed its head against hers, settled back onto its hind legs.

People laughed. People clapped. Kaev followed his bear, gave his newfound sister a hug. Go looked somewhere between bored and angry.

"I've known about you for some time," Ankit said. "Since I got my job at the Arm manager's office. I went to find you once. Tried to introduce myself. You weren't making any sense, and you got really emotional. You were . . . I don't know, howling. I was frightened of you. I'm sorry."

Kaev shook his head, looked devastated. "I am . . . I wasn't . . ."

"I know."

Soq had a family. And it kept on getting bigger. Would continue to do so, since they were about to bust someone out of an impregnable psychiatric center.

"I have a way into the Cabinet," Ankit said to Kaev. "I'll be bringing someone into Protective Custody. If we time it right, I'll be on the inside to help when you launch your assault."

Go sneered, and Ankit turned to her.

"And I came to tell you that I think we have a common enemy in Martin Podlove." Ankit took out her screen, played that video everyone had been passing around. "And I know who he is, the guy who killed his grandson."

"So what," Go said. "Everybody does. He says his name, right on the recording."

"But he's in hiding," Ankit said. "Has been, ever since this. And I know how to reach him."

Soq hadn't watched it. The past couple weeks, Soq had been too busy to stay in the traffic-trawling loop. They'd heard about it—some boy, burned alive by a methane flare. Soq watched now, with idle curiosity at first—and then sucked in a short shocked breath, seeing the boy before the flames consumed him.

Fill.

"I fucked him," Soq said, but no one heard them.

KAEV

———————➤

"What's the matter?"

Go didn't respond, didn't roll over. Shouts and dragging sounds from the deck, but the porthole beside the bed showed only a placid sea and sky slowly turning the deep black gray of Qaanaaq before dawn.

"I know you're awake. You always woke up so early. Even back then. Are you crying?"

"No," Go said, wiping her face.

Kaev sat up. Her sheets were expensive and he liked the way they felt. He would gladly have stayed there all day. He would gladly have stayed there forever.

"What if this is the last time?" Go said, and he knew how much it cost her to speak like this, to be vulnerable. "I lost you for so long—what if after all of that, one of us dies today?"

"You didn't lose me," Kaev said gently, without anger, without bitterness. "Not really. You had to do what you did because somebody forced you to. If anything, I was taken from you."

"True," Go said. "But I can't let that happen again."

"You'd still have Soq. I mean, unless they get killed, too. Which I guess is possible."

Go laughed. "They hate me. Or they would, if they had any sense."

"They don't hate you."

"Now you're such an expert on human emotions all of a sudden?"

"Yeah," Kaev said, sitting up. He liked being naked. He never had, before. "All of a sudden I am."

"Thank god for that polar bear."

"Amen."

Go rolled over, and smiled at what she saw. "You're magnificent." She ran a hand along one hairy leg, up his stomach, to nestle in the forest of his chest.

"You're not so bad yourself."

Outside, the noises settled. The shouts stopped. Preparations were at an end; the operation was about to begin.

Kaev said, "Can I ask you a question?"

Go shrugged.

"Why now? All these years you've been content with where you are. You never made a power play before like the one you've been making, trying to go beyond being just a syndicate boss."

"I was never content," Go said. "I was always planning. Laying the groundwork for this."

"So . . . why now?"

"A bunch of reasons. The time was right. There were new vulnerabilities. New . . . opportunities."

"Go on . . ."

Go shut her eyes. "I'll sound like an idiot."

"You always do."

"Shut up," she said, softly. Had he ever seen her so vulnerable? "It's the stupidest thing. It was *City Without a Map* that got me started on this. Have you ever listened to it?"

Kaev nodded.

"I can't explain it. Something about the broadcasts spoke to me. And not just in the words that they said. But the way that they said it. It got me thinking. I'd been biding my time, waiting . . . for what? So many of us here, powerless and alone. Keeping our heads down, keeping to ourselves. But we *aren't* separate. We are one thing, and there's power in that."

Kaev stopped himself from laughing. "You sure we're talking about the same *City Without a Map*? The one I've been listening to never said shit about crime syndicates declaring gang war on shareholders."

"It's called subtext, Kaev. Did you learn that word when you got a polar bear and became a fucking genius?"

"Sure," he said.

They lay there, unspeaking, for a long time.

"This is idiotic," Go said after a while, sitting up, and Kaev could almost hear it, feel it crackle in the air, the armor she put on, the psychic bulwark, the magic shield that protected her from harm. The walling off of every emotion, every human thing. "Why are we doing this? It's not our fight."

"It's my mother," he whispered, surprised at how hard that word was to say, how good it felt.

"It's a woman you've never met. Who's been locked up in the Cabinet for so long that she's probably mentally damaged beyond hope of repair."

"Even if she were an empty shell—even if she weren't my mother—I'd do it for Masaaraq. She saved my life. She rescued me from . . . I don't know. Walking death? A lifetime of constant pain? This is the love of her life we're talking about. Someone she's spent thirty years hunting for. What kind of person would I be, if I took a gift like that and refused to help her?"

"The kind of person who has a chance. With me. With a real life."

"We still have that," he said, and got out of bed. The room was cold. She'd always kept her quarters cold. Uncomfortable. To discourage torpor, to spur her on to constant motion. But he enjoyed the bare concrete floor against his feet, the air that prickled his skin. He took his time getting dressed, regretting each new garment that came between them.

"I love you," he said, pants in hand.

She put a hand on each muscular thigh. She pulled him closer.

"I have to go!" he said, laughing, and hopped away.

"Fine," she said, laughing too, but the laugh faded fast from her voice, and by the time she said, "Have it your own way," she was every inch the brutal granite wall who had been his heartless boss for so long.

Masaaraq was waiting for him, standing there with the bear, staring at the door to Go's cabin. Angry, at first, to be kept waiting for so long, but then the anger faded and she looked like she might cry. From happiness, Kaev knew, because he was such an expert on human emotions all of a sudden, because he could see how close it was, whatever majestic blissful feeling of family unity the orcamancer had spent so long stalking. He could see how much she loved him, how familiar he was to her, even if she hadn't seen him since he was so small she could hold him in her arms.

"Hey, Liam," he said, throwing his arms around the bear's neck.

"It's an idiotic name," she said.

"It's growing on me."

Together they walked to the railing, climbed onto the lift. It brought them down to a little boat, the same tri-power vessel she'd come to Qaanaaq in, and then it went back up for Liam, who was too big and heavy to ride it with them.

"Atkonartok," she said, and a few seconds later the killer whale surfaced.

"Good god," Kaev whispered, realizing why some of the post-nomad settlements on North America's west coast worshiped them as gods. "It's incredible. Can I touch it?"

Masaaraq nodded. He reached out his hand, slowly, more frightened than he thought he'd have been. Wet rubber, he'd been thinking, or hard plastic, but the orca felt like nothing he'd ever felt before. Some higher, better form of flesh. Surprisingly warm. Masaaraq unmoored the boat and they began to row.

"Yesterday I went for a walk," he said. "Along the Arm. Looking for noodles. The farther I got from Liam, the more I got this feeling. In my stomach, in my head. An ache, but physical and psychological at the same time. Like being heartbroken *and* having food poisoning all at once."

She nodded. "It'd get worse as time went on. You'd have a week or so before you started to experience cognitive difficulties."

"How long before I was—like I used to be?"

"A month, if Liam was still alive. Maybe six weeks."

"And if he wasn't?"

"A lot less."

They rowed in silence the rest of the way. They had an hour before full dawn.

"Go's bots say two hours," Kaev said. "From the time the heat cuts out to when the protocols are likely to order an evacuation."

Masaaraq nodded. She stood up, stripped off her thick sealskin coat. Underneath she wore clothing made of lighter, furless skins. She pulled her hair together, piled it atop her head in an intricate structure somewhere between a coil and a nest. And then she leaped into the sea.

"You're not going to ride her down," Kaev said when she surfaced with the whale beside her.

"Too deep," she said. "But what we need her to do, it'll be difficult. Identifying the right geothermal vent, the right pipe branching off it, and how to break it. I'll need to be heavily involved, and that'll be easier if I'm in the water. Seeing what she sees. Not hearing through our human ears."

The aquadrones were designed to protect the cone from human and machine attacks, as well as debris from below or wreckage from above. Animals were different. They moved like none of those things. Programmers would not have taken malicious animals bent on destruction into account, so they wouldn't have scripted the drones to engage marine life. Masaaraq had tested Atkonartok on some of the outlying drones, and confirmed that she wouldn't trigger an attack.

She shut her eyes. The whale swam around to touch noses. They stayed like that, eyes closed, unmoving, for what felt to Kaev like an uncomfortably long time. Then the orca dove.

CITY WITHOUT A MAP:
CROSS FIRE

This one came later, stitched into the scrapbook of my story from a boy I met a few months down the line, who came to me as so many did, in those days, having heard of the help I could provide—Zarif, a handsome weathered Uzbek sex worker, who saw Ishmael Barron moving through the noisy chaos of Arm Eight twilight, looking lost and frightened, and called him daddy.

"I need somewhere safe," Barron said. "People are after me."

"My place, then," Zarif said. He pinged the old man on the elevator ride up, name and face pic, and found out who was looking for him. He was going to call it in right away, claim the reward and be done with it. Then he decided that the poor old thing was about to enter a world of hurt, and figured the least he could do was give him one last beautiful thing.

"I'm far too old to do much more than look," Barron said, and Zarif stripped and sat by the window, where nightlamp light turned him to silver.

"This must happen a lot. Someone just wants to confess. To tell you their story."

"Sure," Zarif said. "Me and the priest, we perform very similar functions."

"Feels like all my life, I've been running from Podlovsky. He's lost a syllable, but he's every bit as powerful and rich as he was back then. Maybe more so. What have I achieved in the interim? What have I done to tip the scales? I've hurt Podlove, hurt him badly, but what good does that do to anyone but me? People like Podlove still rule this city, this planet. People like me still suffer and sweat and bleed and pay until they can't pay anymore. We'll both die, and soon. That should be a comfort, but it isn't."

Zarif stroked himself to full tumescence, which was an astonishing one, but Barron seemed not to notice.

"I saw him by accident. Fifty years ago—a man my own age, handsome in that cruel way that powerful men often are, the fearless confident stare of someone who knows he can do whatever he wants to you. An expensive nondescript car that pulled up to the quiet late-afternoon South Bronx street where a demonstration was about to get started. He got out of the car, along with three other men and one woman. He scanned the crowd. No one stood out to him. None of us had faces. But I saw him.

"Fifteen seconds. I counted them, breath held. The invaders got back in their car. The afternoon moved forward, implacable as a glacier. People trickled in. The protest got started. The counterprotesters arrived, poorer tenants from two neighborhoods over, accusing me and my crew of having pushed them out—which was, alas, true, but I knew them, had knocked on their doors and tried for weeks to get them to come to meetings, fight together against the city's latest 'rezoning' plan.

"Someone was behind this. Someone had pitted us against each other, with surgical precision."

Zarif shut his eyes, imagined himself fucking his favorite beam fighter senseless. He knew, from very fortunate friends of friends, exactly what Hao Wufan was into.

"Things got bloody. People died. Buildings burned. When I got out of the hospital I spent a week staring into my screen. I was determined to find out who he was, who they were, the people who arrived in the hush before the violence began. It took me a long time before I found them, a fledgling midlevel department at an undistinguished security firm. Creators of a new kind of PR animal, custommade for the Multifurcation, which of course hadn't gotten that name yet. Micro-audiences; hypertargeted messaging. Directing people not to consumption or to voting, but to action. Bespoke mobs for the twenty-first century.

"I stalked Podlovsky for the few months that New York City had left. I went to his office. Bought tickets to galas to watch him smile. Found his house, his gym. Charted his habits. Maybe I intended to murder him. I never thought that far ahead. All I knew was, this was my enemy, and sooner or later I would have the chance to bring a reckoning.

"And then: The fall. The breach. The collapse. Survival became my only concern. Other enemies intervened—men with guns, men who demanded awful things in exchange for food or a ferry ride out of the city or simply not murdering someone. But once I was safe in the FEMA camp—or, at least, a little less unsafe—I had time to think about Podlovsky again. Had the chance to search for him. Found him mentioned in some of the outlets, setting up shop in Qaanaaq. His firm still garnering headlines, still controversial. Something to do with the neo-Inuits up north, one of his pharma clients needing something hushed up, deeds so ugly that only something uglier would be sufficient. And dumb incredible luck, that I'd searched in that narrow window. Two weeks later, Martin Podlovsky did not exist. Which could only mean shareholder invisibility.

"I spent years stockpiling the money to make it to Qaanaaq. But this place quickly drained my hunger for revenge. There were too many other hungers, too much other pain. Too much beauty. Rage is a hard armor to wear indefinitely, and mine would have destroyed me.

"So: Life happened. The fire of my hate died down. I fell in love, and out of it, a time or two. I found a job, built a career. Got sick. Discovered mysterious broadcasts that spoke directly to my soul. Dull embers were all that was left of my rage by the time Martin Podlovsky's flamboyant grandson landed in my lap by pure outrageous unimaginable coincidence, sick with the same fatal illness as I, and happened to blurt out his last name over coffee.

"Like fate. Like the gods hadn't forgotten about me; like the cold and hostile universe still held goodness in it.

"These past few days I've marveled at my bad fortune, to find myself in the middle of something so much bigger than my own vendetta. What an unlucky coincidence, to get caught in the cross fire between a crime boss and a real estate mogul and who knows who else. But now I know it has nothing to do with luck. Monsters like Podlove, they make a lot of enemies. Those enemies will try and try, one at a time, and never get anywhere, and eventually they'll all start striking at the same time, and that's when they'll win."

Zarif finished. The mess he made was immense. "Marvelous," Barron whispered, pale, as if his story or the sight before him threatened to break him in half.

"On the house," Zarif said, smiling as the old man made his way out, and then whispering, "Now," into his implant—

—Barron descended to the grid, where a woman was waiting, her hands pressed together in front of her chest so he could see the thick braided brass that girdled them. "Mr. Barron?" she said. Snow cycloned in the space between them. Behind her, the light and heat of the Arm lay hidden. "Will you come with us?"

SOQ

————————▶

Soq could see her, pacing. Alone in her room, a massive cloud of anxiety shoehorned into a tiny body. Never looking out the portholes. Staring into screens. Fifteen, twenty of them lay strewn across the tables, and Go was constantly getting new ones out of drawers and boxes, opening up some new software, calling up the footage from some additional drone. Impressive, how hands-on she was with all this. No flunkies to do it for her. If Dao weren't dead, would he be doing it? But if so, that made it all the more impressive—so many kingpins would be utterly helpless without the people who normally did everything for them.

As far back as Soq could remember, Go had been there. An idol, someone whose successes and setbacks Soq followed the way other grid kids followed beam fighters. Soq's own career trajectory, their dreams of savage revenge on this shit city, had been modeled on Go's.

Go was fearsome; Go was magnificent. Wise, cunning, bloodthirsty, brilliant. That had never been in question. What Soq was wondering now was something completely different: was Go a halfway-decent human being?

Other questions, too. Ones that hadn't stopped bothering Soq since they first started popping into and out of that rich kid's memories. What was the point of rising to the top? Conquest had always seemed like its own goal, but what did one do when one got there?

For almost an hour, Soq was sure of it, Go had been trying her hardest not to look out the portholes. Because she knew she'd see Soq there.

And for almost an hour, Soq had been trying to knock on the door. Why hadn't they? Fear rarely stopped them. Soq could remember the first time they'd strapped on slide boots, how fearlessly they'd clomped across the grid, how effortlessly they'd vaulted up and onto the incline. Stepping forward without a second's pause. People broke limbs every day on the inclines; people died. But pain and death never frightened Soq. Soq had nothing; nothing could be taken; no attachments bound them to the earth.

And now? What stopped Soq? A newly discovered mother? A father? Some corny fantasy of pre-fall family life? Was Soq so weak that ceasing to be an orphan for a few days had turned them into one of those weak wide-eyed children from Arm One whom they'd spent their whole life despising?

Soq knocked. Hard.

"What?" Go said through a speaker. Soq could see her, framed by the porthole. Her back to the door.

"You need help," Soq said.

"I don't."

Soq knocked again. And waited. Sixty, ninety seconds later, a soft thump from the latch. Soq turned the knob and entered.

"What do I need help with?" Go asked.

"Where to begin?" Soq said, slumping into an ancient filthy recliner. The closest thing Go had to a throne.

"Watch yourself," Go said, her back still to Soq. "Don't think you have some special license to be disrespectful with me."

"Don't I, though?"

Go whirled around, eyes wide. Soq flinched at the anger they saw there, but anger was what they had been looking for. Anger, violence, something. Some sign that Soq's existence impacted Go in some way. Soq stood, stepped over to the table. Watched ten separate screens showing ten different live drone shots. Five of them aimed at the same person. An old, old white man in a big office. Paper thin. Pacing back and forth like some flimsy doppelganger for Go. "The guy from the video," Soq said. "Whose grandson got killed."

"Martin Podlove," Go said.

"What syndicate?"

Go laughed. "No syndicate. Or the very biggest syndicate of all, depending on your political stance. He's a shareholder."

Soq whistled, squatted lower to get a better look at the screens. A shareholder. Like seeing a unicorn. Growing up with nothing in Qaanaaq, you wondered about everyone you met—was this chubby man a shareholder? What about that woman in rags over there? Of course, lots of them would dress expensively, but Soq had always been certain that most wore shitty clothes, blended in, looked for all the world like any other piece of Qaanaaq flotsam. Who did they have to impress, after all? They were already the masters of the universe.

"How do you have so many eyes on him?"

"Microdrones, mostly. Outside his office."

"He never heard of curtains? Ionizing the windows?"

"He doesn't care who sees him. He believes he's invincible."

Too weird. Too fucking weird. Too many roads leading back to this boy, the one who gave Soq the breaks. *Life doesn't work like this,* they thought, *in a city so big—so many bizarre and separate strands coming together. Forming a pattern, a mesh. A net.* And Soq was caught in it. Being hauled up, out of the sea where they'd spent their whole life, where they felt safe, where they could breathe, into a harsh killing light.

Soq's vision blurred. The image flood came again. The vacant apartment they'd met in.

But this time, Soq was ready. Soq would not be overwhelmed; Soq would not be drowned in the dry air like a fish. Soq had—whatever Masaaraq had given Soq. The nanites. The power. The control.

Empty rooms. So much space. A long line of beautiful boys. Hunger; so many hungry people.

Software.

Passwords.

Soq scooted the armchair closer to the table. "Tell me what you're so upset about," they said, almost startled to hear how authoritative their voice sounded, how confident of being obeyed, as if they knew what they were doing—and, stranger still, beneath that, the knowledge that they did.

"I can't believe this is happening right now," Go said, standing behind Soq to watch what they did with the screen. Her voice was not annoyed. Her voice was scared.

"This? The Cabinet mission?"

"I'm at war here. I don't have time to go rescuing somebody's missing mommy."

"Why not fire a missile at that old man's office and be done with it? I know you have the firepower."

"Because he has the firepower, too. Or at least, he pays a security company well enough to cover all contingencies. Money and wealth and power are abstractions to people like this. They wouldn't have the foggiest idea what to do in a real fight—but they pay people to handle their problems. There are rules to war. Things you don't do. I kill him, his people kill me."

Something glimmered in the floodwaters. Something shiny in the rush of drab images. Soq made a choking sound and snatched up one of Go's screens.

"What are you doing?"

"I don't know," Soq said. "Accessing something, I think. A program."

"What program?"

"I'm not sure," Soq said. "To be honest, I'm not entirely certain that it exists at all. Or how to use it if it does. Or what it will do if I can."

"Great," Go said, turning away, shuffling through the other screens.

"I saw it in a vision," Soq said, and Go didn't respond, because Go wasn't listening.

"The Cabinet mission is no skin off your nose," Soq said. "They make it, they make it. They don't, they don't."

Go said nothing.

"You mad because Dao is dead?"

"Yes," Go said nonchalantly.

"You're angry at her. You hate her. Masaaraq."

"Yes," Go said.

Soq thought for a second. Surfed a long slow crashing wave of images, memories bound up inside the coding of the breaks. Soq looked for Go, and found her. A hundred different outlet stories; a million shitty photos. A legendary figure. Spoken of in whispers. Superhuman; unstoppable. Emotionless. That was the most important part of Go's facade: the idea that she felt nothing.

"It's him. You're worried about him."

"He can take care of himself. He has a fucking polar bear."

"Polar bears are mortal. You have no idea what kind of firepower is in that place. What kind of weapons."

Go stared at her hands. "It's not just him," she said, finally.

It took several seconds for Soq to realize they were holding their breath. When they did, they didn't let it out.

Go laughed. "You can't imagine, Soq," and there was a softness to the name that Soq had never heard anyone say it with before. "I had everything planned, everything under control. I was on track. Nothing could hurt me. Nothing could hold me back. Now there's him—now there's you . . ."

Go trailed off.

Soq's eyes shut. Overwhelming, to hear Go express this kind of warmth, this humanity—but frightening, too, because Soq could hear how it broke Go up inside, how angry she was with herself, the war she was fighting to master these emotions. "It's okay," Soq hazarded. "It's okay to worry about something else besides the blood-spattered bottom line."

They both avoided eye contact. They stared at the screens where Martin Podlove paced, where back-alley empires and fortunes were being bought and sold in subsurface trough meat bubbles, where spreadsheets and dossiers documented the profit and the loss. Sucking in breath, Soq stuck out a hand and grabbed Go's.

The crime boss flinched back. "You don't know me." Her voice was stern, hardening fast. "You don't know me at all."

"Don't I?" Soq said, and there it was, the anger Soq had been sitting on their whole life, the rage that had never found a focus before, the blind fury that spawned a thousand dreams of burning Qaanaaq up, breaking its legs and watching a million people freeze to death in the Arctic waters. The city was not a person, the city had done nothing but exist. Go, on the other hand, had done things. Made decisions. Maybe some of them came from a good place. But maybe not. And maybe it didn't matter that somebody meant well, if the end result was misery. Soq stood. "Tell me I have it wrong. I know how you operate. How you got where you are. How you treat your workers. I know you'd gut me like a fish in a second without giving it a second thought, because who the fuck am I? Some kid you gave up ages ago, wrote off—kept tabs on, found a spot for, a job you'd give me, but only if I was good enough, only if I somehow passed your little personality test, turned out sufficiently savage and unscrupulous. And if I ended up as anything other than what I am, you'd have gone on ignoring me until the day you died."

"That's not true," Go said, and her voice was harsh, but the harshness was shallow and choppy. "I had more to do with how you turned out than you think. I've been far more present in your life than you could guess. Nudging you; sculpting you. I've been taking care of you all this time. And Kaev, too, whether you believe it or not. Think it was easy, keeping him from killing himself, accidentally or on purpose, for a decade or two? I always had someone close to him, a friend of his who was in my pocket or a grid grunt assigned to keep an eye on him, to get him out of any situations that could have been dangerous. And there were dozens. Just like I made sure you got that slide messenger job. And paid off Registration four or five times a year, so they wouldn't dig too deep at your agency."

"I believe that," Soq said, reining in the anger, because too much was happening, too much was at stake, time was too short—and Soq could see that this, too, could have come from Go. "But I'm not talking to you like this because I think you'd hesitate to kill me because I'm your kid."

One of Go's exquisite eyebrows rose.

A shout from above. The ship was in position at the base of the Cabinet.

Soq tapped a final sequence on their screen and handed it to Go. "I'm talking to you like this because I have something I know you would be very, very eager to get your hands on. And I have some conditions before I consider giving it to you."

ANKIT

———————▶

Protective Custody felt like a totally different Cabinet. The curving walls made her feel embraced, enfolded, protected. Light panels pulsed in pleasant colors. Huge screens showed waterfalls, horses, slow-motion waves breaking on beautiful beaches.

Fyodorovna, on the other hand, was agitated. Her eyes blinked and twitched; her hand was tight on Ankit's. She was looking for the Victorian asylum horrors, the screaming and the laughter, the gibbering lunatics finger-painting masterpieces in shit on the walls, the rusty torture devices masquerading as therapeutic tools.

"They're at the spot now" came Soq's voice through her implant. "Masaaraq will dive soon. Could take five minutes, could take an hour. Or more."

Ankit tapped her tongue to her palate to acknowledge. A sky-blue arrow slithered along the floor, moving at precisely the same pace as they did, just the slightest bit ahead. It seemed to flicker and twitch, a tiny carefully programmed bit of animation intended to make it seem alive, trustworthy, and Ankit rolled her eyes—but almost immediately after that she saw Fyodorovna smile faintly, looking down at it, making Ankit feel even more impressed and safe in the hands of the kind and wise machines that ran the Cabinet. And all of Qaanaaq, really.

A sudden lurch caused her to stop, grasp her chest.

"Are you okay?" Fyodorovna asked.

"Yeah," she said, "sorry. I just—"

No big deal, she thought. *The monkey that I'm now nanobonded to is climbing this building, that's all. So it feels like I'm swinging through space. Like gravity just comes and goes.*

A door opened, and a nurse came out. He smiled, recognizing Fyodorovna, and saluted. She gave an impressive slow nod, every inch the monarch. Delusional even in her despair. Ankit caught a glimpse of the room he'd left—the bookshelf, the window, the curtain fluttering in the breeze from the heating vent.

She wondered if Martin Podlove was in here somewhere, and decided she doubted it. He was on the attack, in temporary sociopath mode, and he'd want to be in the thick of it. He'd have his own protection, people he paid for, people he'd have had on retainer for ages without ever once needing to call on, whom he'd trust a lot more.

And he wouldn't want to chance a run-in with the woman he put here so long ago.

The blue arrow curled around on itself, became a circle. Rotating swiftly; the universal signal for *Wait just a second*. A door opened where there had been only wall.

"Hello," said a stout staffer who wore the badges of both Safety and Health. "Body scans."

Ankit raised her arms—the instinctive, familiar posture of someone prepared to be scanned or crucified—but Fyodorovna did not budge.

"I fail to see how this is necessary," she said.

"Rules of the ward," the Safety woman said. "Everybody gets scanned. No screens, no trackers, implants sealed."

Implants sealed? Ankit felt panic rise. She stammered "I—" but the woman had already touched the wand to her jaw. The tingle told her the pulse had been successful, her implant would be bricked until she could get a revival pulse.

"Welcome," the woman said, and gestured for Ankit to enter.

This was a problem. Without the implant Soq couldn't find her, couldn't talk to her. Couldn't relay her location to Kaev and Masaaraq before the building killed internal comms. Ankit's hands dampened. The fear again.

Their plan was fucked. They were fucked.

The nurse waited wordlessly. After less than a minute, Fyodorovna complied meekly. The blue circle became an arrow again and walked them the rest of the way.

Fyodorovna's room was astonishing. A salvaged-wood floor, shiny with age and use, something that could have spent a century in a Paris bistro. An earthenware pitcher on a squat dark hutch beneath the window.

"Here we are," she said, and Fyodorovna startled her with a sudden fierce embrace.

"Thank you," she whispered, her voice more human than Ankit had ever heard it.

"Hey," Ankit said, uncertainly. "Hey."

"I'm so scared," she whispered.

"You shouldn't be," Ankit said. *So am I.* "Here is where you're safest." Her boss's arms didn't loosen. "I'll stay with you. Okay? For a little while?"

Fyodorovna nodded gratefully.

Ankit went to the window. They were eighteen stories up. Down below, it looked like any other day in Qaanaaq. Fyodorovna poured out two glasses of water from the pitcher. Fyodorovna told her to make sure to call this person, file this document, all of which Ankit was already planning to do, and could not focus on. All she could think about was the chaos on its way, how helpless she was without her implant, the hundred million ways this could go down wrong.

She closed her eyes and she was standing in the wind. Giddy. Happy. A tiny helpless unstoppable primate. None of the million things that had made her sad or scared an instant ago had any meaning, anymore.

"What's that?" her boss said suddenly.

Ankit opened her eyes and came crashing back into her own body, her own life. Her monkey's wild joyous freedom was gone. She ached for it. Had to fight to keep from shutting her eyes again.

"What's what?"

Ankit heard nothing. And then she realized—that was the problem. Something you almost never heard in Qaanaaq. Silence.

"The heat," Fyodorovna said, getting up and putting her hands in front of the vents. "It stopped."

All her life, everywhere she went, Ankit had been hearing the low rumble and purr and hiss of the geothermals. And now there was nothing.

"Perfectly normal," she said, but she could see that Fyodorovna was not convinced.

Time passed. An hour, two? There was no voice in her ear telling her what time it was.

The plan was idiotic. *They* were idiotic. All of them. How could they not have anticipated that the implants would get pulsed, that they wouldn't be able to communicate through this crucial phase?

A shout from the hallway. More shouting in the distance.

People are panicking. Health's response software will be collating all this information, plotting out scenarios, issuing a decision.

"You said I'd be safe here," her boss said, sniffling.

"And you are."

"Not safe from freezing to death."

"Shhhh," Ankit said, and sat on the bed beside her. Took a blanket and draped it over her shoulders. Fyodorovna pulled it tighter, gratefully.

The poor woman. She couldn't help what she was. It took a special sort of insanity to run for public office. A fragile megalomania; a delusional ego.

I've let my contempt for her become contempt for the office, Ankit realized. *I came to share her crazy mistaken idea of what the job of an Arm manager could be.*

But there had been a time, almost forgotten now, when she'd enjoyed her job. What it had been for her originally. When she'd gotten something out of it. Something positive—not the energy and stress and urgency and self-importance, the negative things, the things she became addicted to. The fact that she could solve problems for people. That she could help them get through something bad.

I could do this, Ankit thought, and almost choked on the realization, the suddenly seeing that she could do the thing she swore she'd never do. *I could be the Arm manager.*

Someone ran past the door. A whole bunch of someones followed them.

"Thank you for your patience," said a voice from the ceiling. "We apologize for the sustained inconvenience."

Fyodorovna grabbed her hand.

The voice continued: "Health has made the decision to evacuate the facility. The floors below have already been emptied. Please exit your room and follow the red floor arrows to the nearest exit."

The door swung open. Someone howled. Someone else joined in.

"I'm not going out there," Fyodorovna said.

"Come on," Ankit said, standing, feeling just as frightened.

"Anything could happen to us. All these crazies running around? I'll take my chances here. They'll come for us eventually."

"Don't be stupid," Ankit said, and tugged on her hand. "We'll freeze to death if we stay. These walls are so thin. They hold no heat. It'll be arctic in here in less than an hour, and who knows how long it'll take for them to come find us. We'll be fine out in the halls."

Fyodorovna looked up, her eyes frightened and trusting. She nodded.

If I can help this hopeless creature, I can help anyone.

"Should I leave the blanket?" she asked.

"Keep it," Ankit said. "It might be cold for the next little bit."

The door shut behind them. An explosion shook the floor beneath their feet. They began to move with the flow of other frightened people.

KAEV

———————➤

Watching Masaaraq move was like watching some eerie artist, a terrifying ballerina who slowly and beautifully slaughtered her fellow dancers. The blade swung, it twisted, it slammed backward. She was a painter, sending artful sprays of blood onto the bare green canvas of the Cabinet. Kaev grinned, ecstatic.

Masaaraq slapped him lightly.

"You need to concentrate," she said. "He smells blood, he sees all this frenzied motion, it'd be very easy for him to go into a total killer rampage and start taking out patients along with security. Keep your attention on the people he needs to be focused on."

They moved through the crowd. People ran, people shambled. Some crawled. Many saw the bear and froze, fell backward, turned and ran in the opposite direction.

"He won't hurt you!" Kaev called, but he knew it was futile for a hundred different reasons. They were almost to the stairwells. All the patients would pass through this point. Ora would be one of them.

She had to be.

Would Masaaraq even recognize her? Could she even imagine what all that time could have done to Ora?

A door slammed in front of them. He fired his gun at the glass twice, but only the tiniest cracks appeared.

"Hand me one of Go's explosives," he said to Masaaraq.

"No," she said. "He can do this. Put both hands on the door."

Kaev did, and waited for the bear to join him.

It is ice, Kaev thought, *there is a seal on the other side.*

Break through the ice.

Liam stood, leaned back, fell forward with paws extended, hitting the door hard. Did so again, and again.

Nothing.

Take the handle, Kaev thought, and showed him how. *Pull.*

The bear pulled.

Pull harder.

Liam roared. The magnetic lock groaned, and then snapped. On the other side, a waiting room. Empty except for a couple of people cowering in corners.

They followed the curving corridor and then turned. Running in the opposite direction of the red arrows. Ignoring the pleasant, urgent admonitions of the voice coming from the speakers overhead. The central aisle cut the circular floor in half; somewhere in the middle was the stairwell.

"They know we're here," Kaev said, pointing to his screen, which Soq had synced to the public feed from Health.

"Of course they do," Masaaraq said.

"No, I mean *they* know. The software. It's already issued invasion protocols. A whole lot more Safety workers are already on their way. And there are probably threat neutralization devices all through here, designed to pinpoint us and take us out. Gases, explosions—who knows."

Masaaraq nodded grimly.

SOQ

———————➤

That is a deranged proposal."

"Maybe," Soq said.

"You think that because you're my kid you can come in here and tell me what to do?" Go said, folding her arms tight in front of her chest. "You're mine. Same as all those other grid grunts on my pay-roll. You have some magic software? You give it to me."

Soq stood slowly. "I'm not your kid."

Go flinched. Just for an instant, but enough for Soq to press their evident advantage. "If I was your kid, you wouldn't have spent so long hiding from me. If I was your kid you'd be able to look me in the eye. And you definitely wouldn't avoid the subject like the plague until it suits you."

"Stop pushing me," Go whispered. Her face was inches away. "My skinners have never failed to get a secret out of someone. So if I want your software, I don't need your permission to get it."

Neither budged.

Soq wasn't scared. Probably they should have been. But all they could think about was a series of exhilarating sentences that had been playing through their head for over an hour:

I can conquer this city. I know all its secrets. My head is crammed with a thousand heads' worth of knowledge. I know more than Go will ever know.

"It's in your interest to do this," Soq said, finally. "This is what you want, isn't it? Why you're gathering intel on the empties? So you can take them over, rent them out, right? I'm handing you all of that, every empty, all at once. Or you could spend months, years, maybe, paying a small army of grid grunts to do it. This is a ton of money I'm offering you. You would be a direct rival to every shareholder in Qaanaaq. You'd show them that their days are numbered. I'm not trying to pick a fight. I'm trying to make sure you see this clearly."

A commotion from the deck: eight soldiers boarded, flanking a man who was plainly their prisoner. So old and frail that Soq thought it must be Podlove, but no—the skin was darker, the clothing cheaper. Go held up her hand impatiently, putting the conversation on pause, and opened the door to the cabin.

"We've got him," hollered the lead soldier from that squad, waving her brass-knuckled hand. Flashing a smile as wide as the horizon. With Dao dead, Go's lieutenants would be angling for the spot at her side, and this one had just scored a major coup. Soq remembered the tireless jockeying for position at the slide agency, the clamor and barely concealed excitement when an accident took out one of the senior messengers. Soq had been into it then, had jockeyed with the best of them. Soq wasn't, now.

"Bring him to me," Go called.

He came slowly across the deck, up the steps to the cabin. Blinking like he was about to sneeze. The old man, Soq saw. The one from the video. The one who killed the shareholder's grandson. Of course.

"Ankit helped you find him?" Soq asked.

"No," said Go. "I have many ways of getting what I want."

The lead soldier entered, bringing the old man. Whose face, Soq was surprised to see, showed no fear. His hands were cupped like a Buddha statue's; like a saint's on the way to martyrdom.

"Open up a line to Podlove," Go said. The soldier tapped her jaw once—the call had been cued up already; the ability to anticipate her general's orders was an excellent Prime Toady quality.

On the screens, Podlove jerked his head up, looked out his window like he knew he was being watched, trying to make eye contact with Go through her drone. And then he smiled. His window ionized.

"You're good," said their prisoner. "He had a whole fleet of drones after me. Piggyback software leapfrogging every cam in Qaanaaq."

"He puts his faith in machines," Go said. "I think people are just as . . . useful. And no one gave you permission to talk."

"He's not answering," the soldier said.

Go unstrapped her sidearm, aimed it at the old man's head. "Send him a picture of the two of us."

Soq counted. Eleven seconds later, the soldier said, "Call coming in."

"Good evening, Mr. Podlove," Go said when a new hiss through the cabin's surround speakers told her the line was live.

"Has his usefulness come to an end so soon?"

"He's not working for me," Go said. "He never was."

"Of course that's what you would say," Podlove said. "That's what I'd say, too, if I knew I had gone too far."

Go laughed. "For that scenario to make sense, I'd have to be afraid of you. And I'm not."

"And yet. Here we are. You called me for a reason, I must presume. Perhaps you just got word about your tube worm cake shipment? Pity all that food went to waste, but I'm afraid that is just the first of many such . . . interruptions."

Go laughed again. "You think my situation is so dire that one sunken tube worm skiff would have me calling you to beg? I had nothing to do with your grandson's death. We may be at war, but we're not monsters."

Podlove did not respond to this, but Soq heard skepticism in his silence.

"I hunted down the man who did it," Go said. "I found him when you couldn't."

"Eventually, I would have. I wouldn't have stopped until I did."

"He was heading for a mainland ferry." The old man opened his mouth, as if to protest the inaccuracy of this, but then shut it into a smile. "You may have the resources for a worldwide hunt, but would you have the time? Either one of you might drop dead any day now. But now—here he is. All yours."

A pause. A hungry one. "In exchange for what?"

"For nothing. He's yours."

"Except that I have to come and take him. Or go collect him from somewhere, where your people will be waiting to ambush me."

"This isn't a trap. It's a gesture. I want to prove to you that we have an understanding. I didn't do this. You and me, we're on the same page. I am not trying to scorch the earth here. This is a guy with a grudge against you, for some fucked-up shit you did a long time ago. It has nothing to do with me. I have no interest in making this personal."

"Even if you didn't have anything to do with what happened to my grandson, you did send soakers to hit two of my best managers. We're not a syndicate, my darling." Soq's nostrils wrinkled at the archaic vulgarity of his misogyny. "You can't treat us like we are and then expect us to believe you when you say we're on the same page. To us, that was an unacceptable escalation."

Go sighed. "You're right. I'm new to this."

"You're not ready to play in the major leagues."

Soq and Go exchanged puzzled glances. The brass-knuckled soldier pantomimed hitting a baseball.

"You New Yorkers love your baseball metaphors, never mind that no one else left alive on Earth knows what the hell you mean by them. Nevertheless. I am making this peace offering. Tell me how you want him. I'll deliver him in whatever way would make you feel the most safe, the least like I'm setting you up for something. I can put a hood over his head, drop him in a canoe, push it off and let it drift in your direction. I can decapitate him right here and now, if you'd prefer. Bloody my hands so you don't have to. Isn't that how you operate?"

"Come to me," Podlove said after an instant of skilled internal debate, the consummate executive assessing a thousand scenarios. "The lobby of the Salt Cave. Don't bring an army."

"Agreed."

Podlove chuckled. "That was fast. You're not frightened to march into enemy territory unprepared?"

"This is a parley, isn't it? A presumably safe negotiation?"

"You presume I see you as an honorable opponent. You've already broken the rules of engagement, such as they are. How do you know I won't do the same?"

"I don't," Go said. "This is a gesture of trust. I want you to know I had nothing to do with what happened to your grandson."

Sudden silence from the speakers.

"Son of a bitch hung up," Go said.

"What's the plan?" Soq asked.

"There is no plan. I'm handing over this idiotic man and he'll probably be tortured to death. End of story. Tomorrow we'll get down to the business of making peace."

"And my software?"

"Will have to wait. Right now Podlove and everybody like him is going to be keeping an extra-close eye on all their holdings. We kill the heat, wait till things calm down. See if it makes sense to deploy it then."

"Easy for you to say, when you're not sleeping in a fucking box every night."

"Show me some respect in front of my soldiers, at least," Go said, heading for the door.

"What about the other thing?" Soq said, feeling angry, impudent, desperate. "You can't postpone that. It's now or never. We don't know how things are going in the Cabinet. What kind of—"

"I'm considering it. Get out of my way."

"You're not," Soq said. "You've already made up your mind. You don't care about anyone but yourself. If you did, this wouldn't even be a question."

Go's eyes didn't flinch away from Soq's, but what did Soq see there, exactly? Whatever it was, it wavered. And wavering meant maybe.

Go beckoned for the soldier to follow, and to bring the old man. And after she'd left, her voice still echoed in Soq's ears.

We're on the same page.

Soq was startled to see that this was true. And that this troubled Soq profoundly.

KAEV

They pressed closer together without talking or even thinking about it, instinctively making themselves a smaller target, giving them some room to maneuver around whatever obstacles or weaponry might emerge from the walls. Eighteen floors up, the architecture felt different. The hallway widened as they went, and then there was suddenly a fertile garden on either side of them.

"Smoker's lounge," Kaev said, reading off Soq's screen again. "Open-air spaces. Lie out in the sun, get some exercise. Very helpful for crazy people."

"Which is the grid side?" Masaaraq asked. "And which is the sea?"

Kaev pointed each out.

My mother is close, he thought. *For the first time since childhood, I will see her.*

I am going to find her. I am going to free her.

They entered the central cylinder; a chaos of screams and wailing. Patients everywhere, and Health workers. Everybody stuck.

"The invasion protocol paused the evacuation protocol," Kaev said. "Safety should be here by the billion in about three minutes, maybe four."

"Safety's already here," Masaaraq said.

There was only one of her, a lone Safety operative, and apparently unarmed. Although her smile was a little too confident for that to be true. Something else, then. The patients made a space around them. Afraid of the polar bear, of the weapon Masaaraq carried, of the fact that they could see their breath steaming in the frigid air.

The Safety worker raised her arm, rolled up her sleeve. Subdermals twitched and glowed along her arms. She was one with the room, with the system, with the Cabinet. Seamlessly melded with its innumerable defense measures.

Kaev and Masaaraq backed away from the Safety worker. Kaev scanned the crowd, looking for a pocket of less deranged and disheveled-looking residents—who were easy to find, there at the wall, dressed in civilian clothes, one of them even holding a wineglass.

The woman from Safety advanced. Kaev tightened his fists, watched to see how Masaaraq would come at this new threat, wondered if she'd know enough to understand how dangerous this opponent was. But Masaaraq wasn't looking at her at all.

"Ora," she said.

The woman stood ten feet away, draped in blankets, bald, beautiful, her skin bright and brown.

"Kaev!" someone called—and he saw Ankit running toward them through the crowd. A crab-faced woman called her name, but was swept forward by the human current.

"Tighten up!" Ankit called, and Kaev was in fight mode now, his higher brain deactivated, all animal, all instinct and swift brutal action, he saw what she saw—the woman from Safety tapping at her subdermals—and he knew what that meant, somehow, even though he'd never seen something like this before. He grabbed Masaaraq, pulled her with him.

Ora alone seemed capable of independent action, and she alone seemed to pause, not from uncertainty or fear, but from the magnitude of the decision she had to make. The world she had to choose.

"Come on!" he called.

How can this even be a question for her? he thought, but the thought was gone in an instant.

The bear roared to frighten away bystanders. A space cleared for them as they backed toward the wall. Ankit arrived, grasped his hand.

A wave of polyglass rose up from the floor. At the sight of this, Ora finally moved. She ran for them, but the polyglass wall was moving faster. She dove, finally, and her whole body did not clear the closing wall, and it struck her in the leg and she fell to the floor beside them.

The new wall reached the old wall and melded seamlessly with it, boxing them in: Masaaraq, Kaev, Liam, Ankit, Ora. The woman from Safety smiled and came closer.

The bear roared, launched himself against the glass wall of his prison like it was ice, except this would not break any more easily than the window in the door had. There was a door in the wall behind them, but it would not budge. Ora felt her leg, nodded. Nothing broken, nothing bleeding.

Kaev reddened. His muscles tightened. He crouched, a fighter's stance, waiting for the bell to ring to explode into violence. But of course he wouldn't be fighting anyone. In an instant the ducts beneath the floor would rearrange, reconfigure, spray some fancy smoke to knock them all unconscious, and when they woke up they'd be imprisoned for absolutely ever. He could see Ankit taking deep breaths, preparing to have to hold one for as long as possible.

Masaaraq, on the other hand, did not seem to be aware that she was trapped at all. She smiled. She reached out her hand.

Slowly, painfully, like someone seeing through thick fog or a patient coming out of paralysis, Ora smiled back. And took her hand.

ANKIT

M om," Ankit whispered, marveling.

This woman was nothing like the creature she'd had in her head. That pitiful thing, she saw now, had been shaped in her memory by a child's fear. This woman stood up straighter, her shoulders were broader, her smile indomitable. She wore the clean elegant uniform of Protective Custody. So she'd been transferred, at some point, from the general-population hell she'd been in the last time Ankit visited.

The floor lights flashed from red to blue. The walls ceased their distress sequence. The woman from Safety tapped at her jaw, delivered the update to one supervisor after another. The threat was contained. The invasion software had yielded to the evacuation bots.

Arrows appeared in the floor. Red again, but orderly this time, with a soothing flow of cool blues and greens in the walls, pixels and patterns calmly urging people in the appropriate direction.

Kaev and his bear roared, screamed, kicked, fought. Masaaraq smiled beatifically.

Why are we still conscious at all? Any of us? Why haven't we been gassed? Perhaps the interrogation protocols were about to kick in, and they wanted them conscious . . . or maybe it was easier to transport conscious people than unconscious ones? Aside from the belly lurches as her monkey leaped and climbed her way around the building, Ankit noticed that she was eerily objective about the whole thing.

Patients stood, pointed. Came closer with fear and awe on their faces. Health workers tried to encourage them to continue the evacuation, but most preferred to stand there. Shivering. Watching.

"Hello," Masaaraq said to Ora.

"Well hello," Ora said, smiling. "It's good to see you. What took you so long?"

There. That's why Ankit wasn't worried. Wasn't scared. Her family had been reunited. Her mother was free. Sort of. Even if it was just for a moment—even if they were currently trapped, about to be incarcerated, deregistered, locked back up or banished to separate scrap salvage ships, even if they'd never see each other again after this—they were together now. For a moment.

"Family hugs later," Kaev barked, stern fighter instincts in action, and Ankit was grateful for them. "We're about to get gassed. Anybody got any ideas on a way out of here?"

With one hand, almost absentmindedly, without ever taking her eyes off Ora's face, Masaaraq pulled a small circle from the inside of her sealskin jacket. She pressed two buttons, peeled off the backing on an adhesive strip, stuck it to the door in the wall, called for everyone to get as far away from it as possible.

The explosion, when it came, was much worse than the surgical bulkhead disruption process that Go had promised. Instead of just magically making a wall open up, it sent a thudding shock wave and a wall of fire in their direction. Kaev pressed both hands to his ears and winced. Ankit had to fight to keep from throwing up. Liam shielded them from the worst of the blast, and he howled as a dissipating blossom of flame singed the fur of his back.

"Come on," Kaev said, and they followed him down the empty hallway.

The crowd noise rose behind them as the woman from Safety lowered the wall to follow them.

Ankit ran, reveling in the ecstasy of having a crew again, a posse, a team, the way she had all those years ago when she'd leaped from building to building and death was always right behind them, right ahead of them, but it didn't matter because they would face it together. She was inside and she was outside, she was human and she was animal, she obeyed gravity and she defied it.

"Slow down," Masaaraq said. "We can't exert ourselves too much. If it comes down to a real fight, we'll need to have some stamina to spare."

Which, of course, was when another polyglass wall slammed shut in front of them. And another, past that, and then another—a long series of them, and more certainly waiting in the wings, as many as would be needed to exhaust their supply of explosives.

From behind them they heard the stomp of the Safety worker's boots.

She'll be careful, because of Ora, Ankit thought. *She won't risk hurting her.* Protective Custody cases would be the priority in the chaos of an evacuation. Ensuring they didn't get snatched by whatever enemies had obliged them to enter custody in the first place. Or murdered, as was more likely for the high-value clients whose custody was a more genial form of incarceration, like the lamas and child monarchs and inconvenient heirs whose claims to power could jeopardize distant regimes.

"Where are we?" Masaaraq asked Kaev.

"Eighteenth floor, outer corridor," he said, reading from a screen.

"Radio Go's ship," she said to Ankit. "Tell her where we are. Tell her to prepare the extraction ladders."

"I can't," Ankit said. "They bricked my implant when we came in. I can't reach them."

"Ours are blocked," Kaev said. "Privacy shielding engaged."

"They're down there, though," Masaaraq said. "Right?"

"Right. Down . . . somewhere."

"Cover me," the orcamancer said, following the curving corridor until she was out of the line of sight of Safety. "Hold her off. Don't let her see what we're doing."

Kaev and Liam stepped slowly toward Safety, looking as menacing as they could. Which was pretty menacing. Masaaraq pulled out another explosive sphere, attached it to the outer wall, and then pulled out another. And then another. Five in all, a clumsy circle of them on the wall that was all that stood between them and an eighteen-story drop to the sea below.

"What about your whale?" Ankit asked. "Can you tell her, and have her communicate it to the people on the ship?"

"At this distance, it would take too long for me to pass on our location. I'd need to meditate on it for fifteen, maybe twenty minutes. We don't have that kind of time. And even if I could do it, nobody on that ship speaks orca. There's no guarantee they'd understand what Atkonartok was trying to tell them."

"What about that screen Kaev has?"

"Not networked," Masaaraq said. "Soq loaded it with blueprints, predictive software bots." She barked, "Stay together!" and then activated the explosives.

As one, they moved away from the blast site. They had to get to a safe distance from it, but they couldn't let Safety know where they stood in relation to the explosion, or she'd wall them in somewhere they couldn't get back to it.

"Drop!" Masaaraq said, and they did. Again the sick-making thud, again the roar of fire. Then the orcamancer was pulling them back to the red-hot wound in the side of the building, where cold bitter wind was already rushing in. And Ankit knew why, knew it from the sick yawn of space, so she was stammering, "*No no no*," before Masaaraq said:

"You're going to have to scale it."

"No," Ankit said. The sky was night black outside. Green light sketched the city's outline below. It was one thing to feel what her monkey felt while her own body was safe in a hallway. To venture out in this dense human frame—"I can't."

"You have to. Or we all die."

"I can't," she said.

"You can. You are more than human now."

"Even if I could," Ankit said, stammering for any imaginable excuse—and she could feel her, the monkey, climbing, feel how the wind tugged and pushed at the little torso—"it'd take me so long to get down there. And for them to send up the ladder. She's not going to just stand there waiting."

Kaev and Liam stepped back to keep from being walled off away from them, joining the pitiful crew pressed up close to the opening. Shivering. They would die if she didn't move. Kaev turned to her and she saw the fear in his face, saw how he smiled to hide it. To be brave for her.

"Go," Ora said, her hand warm on Ankit's face. "I can handle her."

Everyone stared at her. She smiled, nodded. "Go."

Ankit touched the damaged wall, which was cooling fast.

Ora stepped toward the woman from Safety, whose hands were busily tapping at her subdermals. "Your father," Ora called.

Safety's hand stilled.

"He never stopped trying to find you."

Safety's mouth opened. No words came out.

"It cost him everything, getting you and your mother out of Port-au-Prince. He spent years saving up money to come after you, even when he heard that your *balsero* armada got broken up by people pirates. Every Sunday he got on the circuit, spent all his money calling the reporting services. Listened to the reciting of the names. He got out. Got as far as Gibraltar. Spent a long time there. Waiting."

Ankit shut her eyes. Breathed. Reached out for the monkey—for Chim—who was somewhere nearby; she'd released her outside the building when she'd arrived with Fyodorovna, to scale the facade and wait for her, as Masaaraq had instructed.

She realized: Masaaraq had anticipated this exact scenario.

The monkey answered her. She opened her eyes without opening them, seeing what Chim saw, the sheer walls and fretted glasswork. She stepped through the opening. She turned around to begin her descent, but paused for a moment. To take in the scene, these people she loved, this family, these humans she was bonded to in bizarre magnificent ways, in case she never saw any of them again—in case, in fact, she never saw anything again.

One word leaked out of Safety; a croak, a single syllable that contained a thousand questions. "You . . . ?"

"When I saw you, I remembered," Ora said gently. "What he remembered. I can show you. Everything he saw. What he went through. Where he ended up."

A moment ago Safety had seemed to be eight feet tall, armored and invincible, but now she sounded small, simultaneously very old and very young. "Is it the breaks?"

"It is."

Ankit knew she needed to go. She clung to the ragged edge for a few seconds more, listening, desperate to delay her descent.

"My friend had it," Safety said, and she was crying now. "She said some of the things . . . it was like remembering someone else's memories. But she couldn't . . ."

"Control it," Ora said. "The breaks isn't a disease. It's just incomplete. Once the missing piece is in place, it's a gift. An incredible ability. I can share it with you. Answer all your questions about your father. About the circumstances behind your family leaving. I see it, too. I see everything."

Ankit slipped out.

A narrow ledge, barely wide enough to stand on. Wind tugged at her—but the wind was not an enemy, every scaler knew that. Wind, gravity, walls, rooftops, fences—these were facts. Things to accept and embrace. Tools. Things to use.

She moved west, with the wind.

Come, she called, and Chim answered.

Sophisticated scalers shunned climbing. What they wanted was adventure, excitement, the swift running leaping progression from building to building. To go straight up or down was hard work, and ignominious.

Hard, but possible. And, in fact, her strong suit. Because what she lacked in courage she made up for in determination and diligence and discipline.

She descended now. Slowly, gripping tight, wishing she had her gecko-skin gloves, her ropes and anchors, but hadn't her friends scorned all that equipment? Hadn't they maintained that scaling always came down to the human body and the human mind, up against the elements?

When she reached a landing, she turned to scan the sea below. They were near the grid, and she could see only a narrow slice of ocean. No sign of Go's ship. She continued the descent.

Her heart hammered. She sang to herself, but suddenly couldn't remember more than one verse to any song at all.

Focus. Focus.

Down two more stories, she reached a garden smoker's lounge. It should have been tropical, but the geothermal heat was still out. Glasses of water stood on every table, all frozen solid. She hurled one over the edge. Watched it explode against the grid.

Which was stupid. Because now she kept imagining herself exploding against the grid.

She climbed up onto the railing. Not so much farther to go, but here the orderly progression of walls and windows and ledges that had taken her this far broke down. Now she'd need to really scale. Run, leap, execute flawless rolling falls.

Now the fear took her.

Turned her feet to ice, froze them to the railing. Filled her bones with lead.

She shut her eyes. *I am not afraid*, she thought, but that wasn't true, and then she thought, *I am stronger than my fear*, and that was maybe true. She breathed.

A scream from beside her. Chim, squatting on the railing.

"Hey, girl," Ankit said.

Chim screamed genially. And then jumped.

Ankit jumped too.

And grabbed hold of a horizontal bar, the same one Chim had landed on. She let the momentum swing her forward, and at the apex of her swing she bucked her body to extend the arc, landing with a wobble on the joint where three struts met. Chim leaped to join her on it.

They swung, they tumbled. They were one. Whatever happened, she was not alone.

A wall blocked her way, and Ankit sped up. Leaped. Took one step and then a second up the wall and grabbed hold of a bar, squat-hopped onto another one. In the space between two stairwells she zig-zagged down, back and forth from one landing to the next, dropping four stories in the space of seconds. She caught herself throwing in superfluous moves—thief vault, Kong vault, cat pass, rotary jump—for the sheer exultant pleasure of it.

At the end, two stories from the sea, Ankit leaped to the final level without even thinking about it, and for the first time in her life executed a flawless rolling fall. Then she had to wait, laughing, breathing heavy, for the monkey to scamper down through less spectacular means.

She didn't feel relieved when they reached the struts and ran the wide circumference of the Cabinet's lowest level, and finally saw Go's boat, where Soq was standing on the prow looking for them, and gave them directions for where to aim the ladder to extract everyone else, and climbed aboard to be draped in blankets and offered a steaming mug of something hot and alcoholic.

What Ankit felt was sadness, to be groundbound again.

CITY WITHOUT A MAP: PRESS MONTAGE

From the *Brooklyn Expat* [in English]:

Sometimes Qaanaaq can seem like Saturn, ceaselessly devouring its own young—and dooming itself in the process. Blink, and something you love has vanished. Your favorite noodle stall; the karaoke skiff where you went for your first date; the Mongolian cinema where you discovered the work of Erdenechimeg or Batbayar. The high cost of real estate, and the sponsoring nation council's steadfast refusal to adopt the commercial rent controls supported by an overwhelming majority of registrants, add up to a city where nothing good can stay.

And yet—some things simply seem . . . permanent. Unchangeable. Essential to the structural integrity of the city's psyche. As crucial as the grid itself. Some things we've been seeing for so long that their absence is simply inconceivable.

This morning, residents woke up to two previously inconceivable new changes.

The first was the absence of the rusted old freighter that had been docked on Arm Five for almost thirty years, accord-

ing to some neighbors. Generally believed to be the flagship vessel and headquarters of the Amonrattanakosin crime syndicate, it had shipped out at some point in the night.

The second? A hole. In the Cabinet. A smoking flaming wound in the side of that building so widely considered impregnable.

And according to many witnesses, these two inconceivable disruptions are connected . . .

From *Keskisuomalainen* [in Finnish]:

The drama unfolding in the Cabinet reached its climax shortly after three in the morning. This outlet was one of a handful that was present from the start, from the moment the geothermal heat to the city's largest psychiatric center went out, and we stayed on-site for the duration, sharing every official communique as Health released it, capturing evacuee responses that contradicted Health's facile tale of a simple heat disruption, even releasing images leaked anonymously to us by a Health employee that appear to show a team of violent invaders assaulting Safety officers inside the facility— accompanied, we hasten to add, by a polar bear. And we were present forty-five minutes ago, when a loud boom echoed through the Hub and a ball of fire appeared in the outer wall of the Cabinet.

This story was major even before the invaders blew a hole in the wall and started facilitating the mass escape of inmates. While we are still waiting on an official response to our query to Heat's analysis software, it seems likely that this is the greatest geothermal disruption in the city's history. If criminals bent on getting into the most secure building in the city can rupture the pyramid's valves and divert heat, how safe are any of us? For years we've been told to put our faith in the aquadrones, the multiple redundant defense systems,

*the engineering marvel of the geothermal cone, but if a hand-
ful of thugs can triumph over those defenses, the safe and
abundant heat that makes life in Qaanaaq possible at all is
called into question. Today's events may embolden our enemies to launch an even bigger attack, one that could have
every one of us looking for a new home or saluting a Russian
flag come morning . . .*

From the *Post–New York Post* [in English]:

*Safety officials maintain that they are awaiting final soft-
ware analysis before releasing a statement. This statement,
when it comes, is unlikely to tell us anything helpful or reve-
latory. Bot statements rarely do; it's why they're even more
popular than the ones that human press flacks used to have
to type up with their own two hands.*

*What is beyond question, however, is the involvement of
Amonrattanakosin Group. Their vessel was present in the
waters beneath the Cabinet at the precise moment that the
outer wall was breached by an explosive detonated by one
of the invaders. Footage from countless angles shows them
shepherding escapees aboard—an estimated three hundred
in total. Whether they were behind the whole thing or merely
part of a bigger plan, possibly involving numerous syndicates
or other power players, local or foreign, is unknown. Recent
violence across multiple Arms has been shown to have targeted Amonrattanakosin assets. If today's events are merely
an escalation in some sick syndicate turf squabble, how many
more innocent registrants will be killed or kidnapped as open
warfare consumes the city?*

*Qaanaaq is famous for its laissez-faire attitude to law en-
forcement, illegal commerce, and syndicate activity. Most
people here seem to like this minimalist style of government,
overseen by tolerant machines whose primary concern is for*

our well-being. Maybe those of us who come from more ag-gressive nations or cities are just extra-sensitive on the sub-ject, because we have seen what happens when lawlessness flourishes.

Syndicates think they are above the law. The question to Qaanaaq is—are they?

KAEV

———————➤

The tea steamed in the open air. Kaev poured it out slowly, concentrating, and then he handed it across the table. They sat on the deck of the Amonrattanakosin ship, out on the sea, away from the geothermal vents—unmoored, unconnected to the grid—and that wasn't even the most unthinkable piece of this scene.

"Thank you," she said. She was real. She was a person. She took the mug, then set it down. Pressed both hands against it. Looked at him. Smiled like no one had ever smiled at him, not even Go. "You don't remember me."

Kaev shook his head.

"And you?"

Ankit shook hers.

"You were so little," Ora said, and her voice hitched slightly. Masaaraq took her hand. From belowdecks, the sounds of laughter and crying and anger and joy; the Cabinet refugees being fed, warmed, hydrated, while presumably Go's flunkies figured out what the hell to do with three hundred people.

They sat, the four of them. Around a table on a boat on the open

ocean. From inside Go's cabin Kaev could hear the squawk of multiple radios, a dozen soldiers arguing. Go's voice, clear and certain as
a bell, and probably only Kaev could hear the fear in it. Liam lay on
the floor not far from them, unsleeping, curled into a ball and watching them fitfully. Every bit as uncomfortable and uncertain as Kaev
was. Qaanaaq was a long dark smudge on the horizon. Everything
he knew was behind him. Kaev knew why he was frightened: nothing would ever be the same again. What he didn't know was why he
wasn't *more* frightened.

"This is so weird," Ankit said. "I'm sorry, but it is. We go from being orphans to having two parents in the space of days. I was a political drone, a nobody, and now I'm busting people out of lockup, doing
family time with people everybody believed had been wiped out."

"Of course it's weird," Masaaraq said. "We should not exist. We
should not be a family. But here we are. In spite of everything they
tried to do to us."

Everyone's eyes kept flitting back to Ora. She said almost nothing.
Stared out into the distance, and then into her tea, and then at one of
them, and then at the cabin where Go was throwing things against
the wall. Squeeze her hand and she squeezed back; give her a smile
and she returned it. She seemed present. Seemed happy. But who
knew how much of her was left, after everything she'd been through?

"What now?" Kaev said.

Masaaraq laughed. "Would you believe I have no idea? Thirty
years planning for this, building toward this moment, and barely five
minutes in all that time to think about what the hell I would do when
I got here."

"What we'd do," Ora said quietly. But everyone heard her.

They drank tea, all four of them. They touched each other ten-
tatively. Repeatedly. Nervously. Like maybe this was all a joke, a
trick, a dream. Kaev slowly felt less frightened. A seagull circled
overhead, descending to scratch at flecks of fish guts at the edge

of the deck. Ora gasped when she saw it, and did not look away no matter what it did.

"Seagull," Ankit said. "Ugly creatures."

"I think it's the most beautiful thing I've ever seen," Ora said.

"Ora was bonded to a bird," Masaaraq said, and Ora whispered with her: "A black-chested buzzard eagle."

"I think I remember that," Kaev said. "It's faint, but I feel like I remember seeing it circling the Cabinet. A long time ago. Roosting up top."

"She stayed with me for the rest of her life," Ora said. "Fifteen years."

"And then?" Masaaraq asked. "What happened then?"

Ora said nothing.

Shouts from the cabin; an alarm sounded. A boat, coming from Qaanaaq.

"This can't be good," Kaev said, standing up.

Soq emerged from the cabin. Startling, the fondness that gripped Kaev when he saw Soq coming. The love for someone he never knew existed. *This is what family is. What family does.* Was it magic, some supernatural quirk of DNA recognizing its own? Or did humans simply spend their whole lives so steeped in the mythology of this primal thing called family that the emotions were already there, one-way relationships waiting for the people who would one day step into those slots?

"Is that Safety?" Kaev asked.

"That's Go's transport," Soq said. "She's going to pay a visit to a certain Martin Podlove."

Kaev sat down, clumsily poured another cup of tea for Soq.

"Thanks," Soq said. "What'd I miss?"

"A brazen invasion, explosions, death-defying feats of true scaling brilliance," Ankit said. "Also, this is your grandmother. Soq, meet Ora."

They shook hands. Awkwardly. Soq frowned at the old woman's face and asked, "Have we met?"

Ora smiled. "Not directly. I'm a friend of a friend, perhaps."

"Hey, yeah, cool, I get it," Soq said, with the exaggerated smile you give someone you suspect might be quite mad.

"Yours?" Ora asked Ankit.

"Mine," Kaev said, and then laughed. "I mean . . . not *mine* . . . Soq belongs only to Soq. But I'm Soq's father."

"This will take us all some time to get used to," Ankit said. "But back to Martin Podlove. I knew the guy. The one who killed his grandkid? I'd been working with him on research into the breaks. Fascinating fellow. So knowledgeable. But angry. And sad."

Soq laughed. "Well, then. If that's your friend, I may have some bad news for you."

The door to the cabin opened. Go came out first, followed by soldiers. Marching a man who moved in shuffling little steps, because he was extremely old or because his ankles were bound like his wrists. Or both. Probably both. Soq said, "That would be the bad news I mentioned."

"She's going to give him to Podlove?" Ankit asked.

"Maybe," Soq said. "Probably. I'm holding out hope that it's just a trick to get close to the guy in his office and gut him like a fish, but the chances of that are looking slim. I'm going along for the ride."

Kaev watched their mouths move, heard the words, didn't hear them. None of this mattered. He felt Liam inside his head, a calming beacon of mammalian wisdom, of animal objectivity, guiding him clear of the rocks. Words were useless, dangerous, dishonest. He loved these people and he wouldn't let anything happen to them. He got up and lay down on the floor beside Liam.

"You look like you're part polar bear yourself," Ankit said, smiling down at them.

"That'd mean so are you."

"I'm all monkey, baby."

When she laughed, so did the ugly little capuchin that had been hiding behind her.

When Liam snarled at it, so did Kaev. Then everybody laughed. Except Masaaraq.

"Don't mind her," Ora said with a laugh, her smile radiant, and how could she be so sane, so whole, so happy, after everything she'd been through? Kaev wanted to lie in her lap and stare at her face forever. "She was always like this. A hunter. Out in the wilderness all the time. Killing things. Even when she was with us, she was somewhere else. Worrying about what might happen. You know how predators are."

"No, actually, I don't," Ankit said.

"I do," Kaev whispered.

Masaaraq scooped up a handful of seawater from a bucket at her feet and splashed it in Ora's face. And *then* she laughed.

"She loves you kids," Ora said. "Always did. Even if she was afraid to show it. Even if she thought that evil spirits might see her happiness and snatch it away from her."

"Turns out I was right about that," Masaaraq said.

"Know this," Ora said. "She didn't come all this way just for me."

"Upper America is full of empty towns, empty cities," Masaaraq said abruptly, uncomfortable—as Kaev was—with all these words. "Our enemies are gone. The warlords keep to the south. We can choose any place we want. Big mansions, tiny cabins, a dozen of each . . ." She looked up, saw Kaev and Ankit's shocked expressions. "There are settlements there, still. Trade routes. You wouldn't be giving up civilization entirely."

Their mouths did not close.

Yes, Kaev thought. *Yes.* Liam raised his head, seeing what Kaev imagined, the boundless expanses of snow and ice, the wilderness, the hunt. His joy doubled, tripled, boosted by the bear's. *Let's get away from all this human ugliness.*

Ankit shut her mouth and then opened it again. What would she say? What if she hated the idea? Who was this woman? What did she love, fear, hate, crave? Kaev felt his whole future hung on the next sentence that was said.

"I—"

Ora interrupted: "We're not going anywhere."

No one said a word.

"My work here is unfinished," she said.

"Your work?" Masaaraq said, letting go of Ora's hands. "What work?"

Ora smiled and showed Masaaraq her forearm. Kaev caught a glimpse of a crescent-shaped scar or wound, endlessly repeated.

Masaaraq's eyes went wide. She stood, stepped back. When she spoke, it was in a whisper. "You've been bonding people." She clamped her hands over her mouth.

"Don't you dare judge me," Ora said. "And don't tell me you've become so weak you need long-dead superstitions for a crutch."

Masaaraq could not answer.

"You bonded me," Soq said to Masaaraq. "And you'd just met me."

"And me," Ankit whispered.

"That's different," Masaaraq said, and the terrifying fearless orcamancer was gone from her voice. "You're family. Both of you. We're *family.*"

"How do you think I survived?" Ora said, and her voice was a viper's now, a hiss of warning, of pain, of anger. "How do you think I lived so long? How do you think I lasted the decades it took you to come and find me?"

Masaaraq flinched. "I never—"

Ora stood. "Exactly. You never. You never had to live with what I lived with. You never had your animal die of old age, of grief, kept from touching you by sixty feet of polyglass. You never had to sense it, flying in endless circles, searching for you, never getting any closer.

Bonding to people was the only way to keep from going insane. From getting my brains scrambled back to the mental capacity of a child."

Kaev stood up, went to her. Bear-hugged her. Thinking, *I would do anything to keep from feeling that again.*

"I'm sorry," Masaaraq said. "I'm sorry. Of course I have no right to judge you."

"I met a lot of sick people in there," Ora said. "Suffering from a lot of illnesses. Many of them completely baffling to the medical software. And I found a funny thing. When I bonded with people with the breaks? They weren't sick anymore. They still had it, but they weren't suffering from it."

Masaaraq gave Soq a swift look and then a nod.

"What is it?" Ankit asked. "The breaks. How does it work? Scientists know it's delivered by a viral vector, but we don't know if it actually *is* a virus. Might be that, or a bacterium or nanites or rogue gut fauna or some combination of those, or something else altogether."

"Whatever it is, when you get infected with it—it carries information. Memories. This disease defies everything we thought we understood about how memory works. Somewhere in its genome, the sickness encodes massive amounts of data from the person who infected you, and the one who infected them, and so on, all the way back up the chain. A normal human mind has no idea how to process this kind of information, and it will slowly start to break down. But the nanites that let us bond with animals also let us process their emotions, their imaginations. So when someone with the breaks gets bonded to one of us, the nanites help them survive, handle those memories, control them as well as you would control any others."

"That's your work," Masaaraq said. "You want to save these people."

"I am *going* to save these people," Ora said.

"It's not safe," Masaaraq said. "The city won't rest until you're back in custody."

"Let them try."

"We're up against some very well-resourced enemies. We almost got taken out, in the Cabinet. We'd have been recaptured if it hadn't been for—"

"For the fact that I could give that woman something she needed. Something I got from helping people. The people I helped will help us. I can see the big picture. I've been drawing a map for a city without one. Reciting it to myself every night. I know how we all fit together, how this will play out."

Masaaraq looked at her with curiosity, possibly fear. The way you would if you suddenly started wondering whether the person you love might have become something more or less than human.

"You're the Author," Soq said. "*City Without a Map*. You seed it, somehow. Right? In them? You . . . compose it, pass it on to them when you pass them the nanites."

Ora said, "Yes."

"Small boat," Kaev said, looking worried, as Go's transport reached the ship. "Won't hold very many soldiers."

"She's only taking a couple of us."

"To confront a guy who wants her dead?"

Soq nodded. Kaev's brow furrowed, and he stood up. "We have to go, too," he said, but no one heard him.

"Speaking of Martin Podlove," Ankit said, turning to Ora. "Do you know who he is?"

Ora paused, shut her eyes. Began to recite facts. Rumors. Things she'd called up, effortlessly, from the mountain of memories she'd inherited from every breaks survivor she'd bonded with.

"No," Ankit said, and they heard shouting from the other side of the boat, chains dragging and bells tolling as Go's ship prepared to depart. "Do you know why he put you in the Cabinet?"

"He did what?" Kaev said, but he wasn't the only one who said it.

SOQ

———————▶

W elcome," Podlove said, looking for all the world like some combination of hotel concierge and mad sea captain. Soq could see the uncertainty in his eyes. Go had been correct—he was a banker, not a fighter.

"Ahoy," Go said.

They stared at each other across the opulent lobby of Podlove's corporate headquarters. Salt crystals everywhere. Sharp and sparkling. Intended to impress and intimidate. Behind them, across the glass, Arm One traffic was reaching its early-morning peak.

But the place would be bristling with well-hidden weaponry. Podlove was confident, secure in the familiar center of his universe, but he wasn't stupid. He would have fearsome muscle in his corner. Drones and bots and autoturrets.

Soq shut their eyes, and they could see it. Could recall the schematics, taste the bite of the drill bit installing a toxin pod. Remembered her name, the woman who'd led up the installation six years back. Knew that she was dead.

Two flunkies stood behind Podlove. Go had two of her own. Soq, and the brass-knuckled soldier whose name they had never gotten.

And, between the rival parties, the man with the sack over his head.

Swallowing, finding their mouth so dry it was almost impossible to do so, Soq felt the full gravity of the situation. If anything went wrong, they would be right in the line of fire. What kind of guns and blades and projectiles and lasers were aimed at them right this second? Podlove flashed a frigid snake smile, savage and cynical all at once, but Soq could see that he was scared. And that was scary. Because scared people were dangerous. Soq made eye contact with one of Podlove's flunkies, a scrawny thing who looked as frightened as Soq felt, and gave him a little smile, at which he snarled.

Soq stood up straighter.

They'd been frightened, at first, after they'd learned Go was their mother. They'd feared losing their objectivity, letting their emotions and the personal bond between them render Go perfect, special, beyond reproach. And while Soq was happy to be a henchperson, they knew that flunkies who thought their employer was always right started making dumb decisions.

The opposite had happened. Rage, not love, tinted how Soq saw Go. The woman had abandoned Soq. Every awful thing that had happened in Soq's life could be laid at Go's feet.

Either way, Soq's objectivity was compromised, and that was a problem.

But maybe objectivity wasn't everything. Maybe it wasn't even real. Soq's head buzzed with a hundred different takes on objective reality, and—coolly, effortlessly—they could compare the times two people remembered the same things differently. Both convinced they were right. Soq could see Go as a dozen people saw her—cruel bully, magnanimous boss, ignorant grid-grunt upstart.

Go didn't know what Soq knew: that Ora and Masaaraq and Ankit and Kaev were on their way over. To complicate matters. Soq had meant to tell Go, and now was glad they hadn't.

"Is this how you dreamed it would be, when you got to the top?" Podlove said.

"This isn't the top," Go said.

"No. I suppose it's not. But it's as high as you'll get. This ends today."

"I told you, we're on the same page."

"This is him?" Podlove said, advancing to the sack-headed man. "I'm not going to pull this off and find a lit stick of dynamite?"

Go moved to unmask the man, but Podlove stopped her with a gentle hand.

"A curious play, at the Cabinet," he said. "Taking all those people. What could you possibly plan to do with them, little girl?"

"Maybe I want to found a city of my own," Go said.

It had given Soq hope, when Go finally agreed to Soq's plan. Liberate not just Ora, but every Cabinet prisoner who wished to be liberated. Which had turned out to be a far higher number than projected—Soq had imagined that most would be too afraid to choose a rusty crime syndicate ship over the safe warmth of their prison. They were still belowdecks on Go's rusty freighter. Still frightened. But free.

The second part of Soq's plan was still up in the air. Waiting on Go to give the go-ahead, which she might never do. Run Podlove's program, the one Soq got from his grandson, the software that would tell them the location and access code of every empty unit being kept off the market by every shareholder, and move those people in. And then head out to Arm Eight and offer a place to every grid rat and box sleeper and overcrowded unhealthy unregistered resident. Move them from disgusting and precarious housing to impossible luxury. Balance the scales.

Found a city within the city.

A *city of my own.*

A city where Go was the sole shareholder.

Of course, Go wasn't being altruistic. Soq could see that now. Go would want money, maybe just a little at first, but more and more, and Go had plenty of unbreakable men and women to drag you out of your place if you couldn't afford it. And then rent those fancy spaces to people who could afford to pay through the nose . . . once Go got a taste of that, it wouldn't be long before all those box sleepers were back in the boxes, and the empty units were full of one more wave of wealthy refugees. Being a landlord was the biggest racket in town, in every town, in every city, across history, and when Soq ran that software they'd be handing Go a massive empire.

We're on the same page.

How would Go be different from Podlove, from every other rich and powerful player who sucked the blood of the poor, made them pay until they couldn't pay anymore and then pushed them into the sea to sink? Soq doubted there'd be any difference at all.

The question was, what could Soq do about it?

Podlove pulled the sack off Barron's head.

"Hello again," he said.

Barron smiled. "You don't look so good, friend. You look . . . unhinged."

"I'm going to unhinge you," Podlove said, and there was the fear again, the uncertainty. He wasn't Go. Threats and violence were not his native soil. His own rage frightened him. "Like a door. Take you apart like a jigsaw puzzle going back in the box."

Barron's smile only widened. "I know."

"Laugh as long as you can. Pretty soon you won't be able to. Because you won't have lips, a tongue, most of the skin on your body."

"It was way too easy to turn you into a medieval barbarian," Barron said. "You, who always believed yourself to be so civilized. Another way I achieve victory over you."

Podlove put the sack back on and turned to Go. "Was there anything else?"

"No, sir," Go said, bowing in exaggerated deference. Exaggerated, but still real. Go really did admire him. She really did want to be him.

"I'll be in touch. Once I've gotten a little more information out of this one, and I can assess how to proceed."

"Of course. I'll wait to hear from you. Let me know if there's anything else I can do for you."

They did not shake hands. But they smiled, and Soq saw oceans of information surge in that smile. They *were* the same. Go didn't want to burn down anything. She might kill Podlove, but not because she hated him. Because she wanted to take his place.

Soq had been there. In Podlove's place—in Fill's. Physically, but more important, emotionally. The breaks had taken Soq there. They knew how empty all that comfort felt, how little it helped to hold off the dark.

Once, Soq had wanted to be what Go was. To have power, to have wealth, no matter who else got hurt. To plunge the rest of the city burning and screaming into the sea, if that's what it took. Soq didn't want that anymore.

It was stupid. Soq knew it was stupid. Soq did it anyway. A plan was in place, dependent on a delicate balance barely preserved. The balance demanded that Soq wait to run the software. That's what Go had told Soq to do. Go had been very clear about what to do and when.

Fuck Go, Soq thought.

Six swift taps on the palate and against the inside of Soq's cheek, and it was done.

Everything happened far faster than they'd anticipated. They'd imagined that, if it worked at all, the decades-dormant software would take some time to get started, to trigger whatever safeguards and tripwire warnings might be set up, to say nothing of how Podlove would get word—but only eight seconds passed after Soq triggered the savage break-in software that Podlove had given to his grandson, that Fill had unwittingly given to Soq along with the breaks . . .

The old man's head jerked sharply, like he'd heard his name called from a great distance. He shut his eyes and listened to something his implant said. Then he opened them.

"You fucking idiot," he hissed to Go.

"What?" she said, her inveterate smugness certainly damning her in his eyes.

Above them, lights flickered. Sirens began to wail. The software read updates into Soq's ear. It had been detected by a monitoring bot, one of millions of ancient defense systems lurking in the municipal infrastructure, set up by the shareholders to check their little monster—by releasing an identical copy.

One of them was bad enough. Two of them, running in a state of open warfare, might make the city melt.

Glass shattered. Soq dropped to their knees, convinced this was it, Podlove would have triggered the bullets or explosives or whatever other weaponry had been trained on them for the entire parley. And maybe he had, but the system was not responsive. Most systems, it seemed, were not responsive. A whole lot of people were yelling out on the grid.

"Podlove, I swear . . ." Go said, her eyes terrified.

And nothing and nobody tried to stop Masaaraq and Ora and Kaev and Liam from breaking the front windows, walking right into the Salt Cave, armed and angry, and heading straight for Martin Podlove.

ANKIT

A nkit stayed in the little skiff when Kaev and Masaaraq and Ora and the polar bear got out. She moored it in a two-hour spot across the Arm from the entrance to the Salt Cave.

I am the getaway driver, she thought, but she knew her role in this heist was significantly less glamorous. And exponentially more important.

A stream of data opened on her screen, became a river; became a sea. The software was working well. Terrifyingly well.

"Soq launched," she said into her implant. "Early."

"That sounds like Soq, all right," said the man from Soq's slide messenger agency.

"It's every bit as big as they said it would be."

"This is fucking crazy," Jeong said. "There's got to be five hundred units here. Easy. And they've all been empty? All this time?"

"According to Soq. Go had a lead on a handful of them, ten or twelve she'd spent a ton of resources on recon to identify. But this . . ."

"These motherfuckers," he said, sounding scared, sounding excited. Behind him, she could hear the clangs and hollers of Go's boat.

"All these people living like rats, while they have all this space just going to waste."

"It's not waste. It's a business decision."

"Fine line between good business and a fucking war crime," he said.

"Ain't that the goddamn epitaph of capitalism."

Jeong chuckled. "You know I sleep at the messenger depot? In a capsule in my office. Sometimes I'll go a week without stepping outside the building. Probably been a month since I left my Arm. Now I'm surrounded by all these people . . ."

The understanding-politician part of Ankit's brain took over, emitted a gentle laugh. "Qaanaaq does that to you. I feel agoraphobic sometimes, too. You doing okay over there?"

"This ship is fucking crazy."

"Fucking crazy is how it probably is on a regular day. Now you're in full-on gangster war mode, with a hold full of psychiatric refugees."

He laughed. Sounding grateful. "Something's happening to the data," he said. "It's coming and going."

"Defenses. We anticipated this. We're making multiple encrypted backups, including several on partitioned drives that disconnect from the network as soon as a chunk is complete. If the attack bots compromise something, switch to another."

"This is the easy part," Jeong said, sounding stronger, more solid. "I'll take a psychopathic corporate espionage AI over crying babies any day. We'll have enough to start giving people addresses and passcodes in about three minutes. Enough to house all the Cabinet escapees, and a good chunk of *les miserables* from Arm Eight . . ."

"Excellent."

"We're getting pings from all over, people volunteering slots for these people. Some crazy church lady with one hand says she has space in her storefront for fifty people to sleep."

Ankit stood, looked across the Arm to where Masaaraq and Kaev and Liam and Ora faced down Go and Podlove and an anxious-looking Soq. A stalemate. Angry words. She ached to be there with them. With her family—her two mothers, one a mournful butcher and the other a serene poet, but both identical in the staggering merciless weight of what their love could accomplish; her sweet and sad brother; his proud angry child—even if they were all about to die.

Especially if they were all about to die.

"All right everybody, line up," Jeong was saying back on the ship, and she stifled a tiny laugh at the thought of this poor frightened man doing crowd control.

A splash from the water beside her. Ankit turned her head—and flinched, even though she'd been fully expecting to see the orca there. Maybe it was possible to get used to something so huge, so formidable, as dark as the sea and as hungry, but she didn't see it happening anytime soon.

"Hey, girl," she said.

Atkonartok's immense head did a slow majestic dip. A nod, Ankit realized. Eerie, the intelligence it gave off. Not the intelligence of something as smart as humans, but rather the intelligence of something smarter, something making an effort to understand and be understood by these stinky smaller-brained beasts. Like right now, for example. The whale seemed to know, just from looking at her, how the whole complex plan was going.

How much does she see? Remember? Feel? About the people who slaughtered her tribe, her pod? About the friends she lost? About what it meant to be alone, and lost?

Like she had been all her life. Like Kaev had been, and Soq. And Masaaraq and Ora, who at least had known what it meant to not be alone, to love, to be loved, before they were plunged back into the well of loneliness. All these people going through life alone, suddenly plucked out of isolation and finding themselves part of a family . . . only now to be inches away from losing everything.

"Good!" Jeong said as the chaos of background noise in her ear quieted down. "There will be plenty for everyone. We'll start with you."

Children clapped. Jeong laughed. Ankit did too.

More laughter, from the real world now, two parking slips down. "The clocks!" said a plump matron with an Addis Ababa accent. "The parking clocks all went down!"

Ankit saw that it was true. Her own slip's timer, which had reached eight minutes the last time she looked, was now flashing zero at a leisurely pace.

"Free parking!" someone else shouted.

Fuck, Ankit thought. If there was anything more unthinkable than a geothermal disruption, it was the parking clocks going down. *What the fuck have we done to this city?*

A shout from outside the Salt Cave caught her attention. She looked up just in time to see Go draw the machete from the scabbard at her belt, the scabbard everyone always assumed was empty, and behead Ankit's friend Barron with one effortless swing.

CITY WITHOUT A MAP:
SAVAGE BLOODTHIRSTY MONSTERS

We want villains. We look for them everywhere. People to pin our misfortune on, whose sins and flaws are responsible for all the suffering we see. We want a world where the real monstrosity lies in wicked individuals, instead of being a fundamental facet of human society, of the human heart.

Stories prime us to search for villains. Because villains can be punished. Villains can be stopped.

But villains are oversimplifications.

SOQ

—————◆

'm impressed," Podlove said, with a slight wobble to his voice, as the new arrivals closed in on him. *He's terrified,* Soq saw. *Desperate.* "I expected your people would try to blunder in here. But I didn't think you were capable of somehow crashing my lobby's defenses."

"Both are surprises," Go said, furious, confused, frightened. To Ora and Kaev and Masaaraq and the polar bear she said, "I told you to stay on the ship."

Podlove's lips were tight. "Right. You didn't get my grandson killed. You didn't tell them to come here. Terrible things keep happening to me, with you standing right next to them, but it's never your fault."

Soq looked back and forth between Go and Podlove. Comparing. Wondering: Which is more fit to rule? Which is more villainous? They were both frightened. Both sweating. Barron, at least, was relaxed, or that's how it seemed. Tough to tell with a sack over his head. His posture and general vibe of chill indicated a lack of fear.

On a sloop across from the Salt Cave, someone had spray painted *BLACKFISH CITY.*

"We didn't crash your defenses," Soq said, earning a death glare from Go. "You did. You ran that barbarian software against itself, and *that's* what's fucking you up. And most of the city, I'd imagine."

"How did you get it from him, I wonder?" Podlove said. "My poor dead grandson. Did you torture it out of him? No. He'd probably have given it to you willingly. You're just his type. Feral and filthy and frea—"

Soq laughed. "Don't be childish." That had the desired effect. Pointing out when octogenarians are behaving like children is usually a good way to shut them up.

The soft putty of Go's face was hardening. Soq watched her slowly come to accept that the situation was out of her control. While the sensation was clearly agony for Go, for Soq it felt . . . expansive. Full of potential. Terrifying, but also thick with magnificent possible outcomes. Soq knew how the miserable poor of Mexico City or Pretoria might have felt watching the rebel armies march through the streets, or Lisbon or Copenhagen when the waters came flooding in. *For once, the status quo is fragile. Things could change.*

"And our new arrivals?" Podlove said, turning to the very tiny angry mob. "Surely you didn't come all this way just to stand there glaring at me."

Ora stepped forward. "Do you know who I am?"

"I don't believe I've had the pleasure, ma'am."

She said her full name. His expression did not change. No recognition, no deceit flickered in his eyes. *He really doesn't know,* Soq thought.

A groan from underneath them. The building at war with itself. A digital autoimmune disease. "We should take this conversation outside," Soq said softly, noting that this time Go did not seem angry that they were speaking out of turn. "His weaponry could come back online at any time. We'd be dead in a millisecond."

"Come," Masaaraq said, arm twisting out to aim the blade at Podlove.

"I'd rather not, if it's all the same to you."

He thinks his old age will protect him, Soq thought, *so maybe he is not as smart as I thought he was.*

Masaaraq gave a half shrug, and both his flunkies fell to the floor, clawing at their opened throats. Soq calculated that it must have taken two swings, based on how far apart they were standing, but they had not seen even a single one.

Three swings. A single tiny red line formed across Podlove's forehead. Lone drops of blood beaded up, dripped down.

"You don't call the shots here," Go said to Podlove, smiling, but the smile looked flimsy.

"Neither do you," Masaaraq said, and swung again, slower, because she wanted Go to see what she was doing. The brass-knuckled soldier fell to the floor, gasping, refusing to scream.

Masaaraq's face showed nothing, but Soq knew what was going through her mind. From the moment that they'd bonded, Soq had so many of Masaaraq's memories, her fears and her nightmares, the pain she carried, the horrors she'd been forced to endure. Everyone had imagined that Ora would be the broken one, after so many years in the Cabinet, but Soq saw that Masaaraq was the one whose damage threatened to shatter them. And Soq loved Masaaraq so much in that moment, their beautiful formidable mutilated grandmother, that their heart hurt.

If you know someone, know them completely and utterly, does that automatically mean you love them?

"It's a lovely day," Podlove said, stepping over the writhing brass-knuckled soldier. Soq saw: politeness, good manners, these were his only real skills. The affectations of wealth were a suit of armor you could wear when the world threatened to wash you away. "Why don't we take this conversation outside?"

Overhead, the windscreen was shifting back and forth with slow, graceful, aimless motions. Snow fell. People stood, pointed, made calls, took pictures with their screens or oculars. Made space for them. Made lots of space. Only the complete and momentary collapse of Qaanaaq's digital infrastructure was keeping them at liberty right now—on a normal day, a massive Safety response would be in the works. A convergence. The once-every-five-years-or-so deployment of those big scary ships with the holds full of gnarly weaponry.

"You put her in the Cabinet," Masaaraq said.

"Ah," Podlove said, nodding his head as if someone had told him he'd left the oven on. "I think I understand now."

Go's hand rested on the scabbard of her machete. Soq calculated: *Her only hope is to make an explicit peace with Podlove. Otherwise, one way or another, she'll be destroyed. If he dies, the city's response will be merciless. Qaanaaq let the crime syndicates flourish, setting very few rules on what they could and couldn't do, but she's broken pretty much all of them. Go lives only if he does. And even then it's a long shot.*

His survival seemed unlikely, Soq supposed, but then again anything was possible. Some demonic magic had kept him alive this long in a world full of people he'd pissed off. There might be some of that left.

"You *think* you understand?" Ora said. The bear flinched, a jerk of rage barely stifled.

"We put a lot of people in the Cabinet," he said. "We had to. Either that, or kill them. Would you rather we did that? It was nothing personal. Our employees made a lot of enemies, and made friends with a lot of unpopular people. Understand, during the Multifurcation, a lot of people came to us with problems. Twenty different cities had minority populations practically rioting over police murders of unarmed civilians. Political parties about to lose key states. All in need of some . . ."

"Bloodshed and blaming and scapegoating," Barron said from under the sack.

"We didn't write the playbook," Podlove said. "*Dīvide et īmpera.*

Divide and conquer has been the foundation of human societal power dynamics for as long as there have been human societies."

"There have been knives that long, too," Kaev said. "Doesn't mean a man who stabs someone to death isn't guilty."

"How many people?" Masaaraq said.

"In the Cabinet? At least fifteen. In other grid cities . . ."

He didn't finish the sentence. He didn't need to.

"Was every one of them the sole survivor of a large or small genocide?" Ora asked. "You probably don't know. You probably didn't want to."

Podlove said nothing. He stood there, his face fooling no one with its approximation of repentance. "I didn't do anything on my own. There were a dozen of us, fellow executives. I wasn't even the highest in the hierarchy. I know you want me to be some savage bloodthirsty monster who single-handedly caused all your suffering. But believe me, I'm not. I just happen to be the last one left alive."

"Do you know what I could do right now?" Masaaraq said, aiming her bloody blade at him. "I could stab you in the stomach with this, use that notch at the end to grab hold of your intestine, yank it out, choke you with it—or make you eat it, or toss it to my orca, who would pull you into the water by it and take her sweet time killing you."

He shrugged. "I couldn't stop you. And I wouldn't blame you."

An explosion in the distance. Sirens starting, stopping, starting, stopping.

The stalemate lasted a long time. Each side glaring at the other. Except for Podlove, who looked only at his feet. At the metal grid he stood on, the city he'd helped build, the safe place his bloody money had bought for him. The sea beneath it. The water that would still be there long after the last human sank beneath its waves.

He was so old. His skin was so thin. So wrinkled. Wrinkles upon wrinkles, a crisscrossing net of them. He hadn't physically harmed anybody. His hands were bloodless. He'd merely gotten other people to hurt people, and then profited off it. Wasn't that worse, though? Didn't it magnify his crime, to have bloodied the hands of others? What kind of suffering had it caused them, the people who slaughtered innocents on his behalf? What trauma, what rage, what nightmares had it left them with? What bad karma?

Even if they chained him to a chair in the basement and spent the rest of his life torturing him until he passed out from the pain, then waking him up to do it again, over and over, there was no way to balance the scales of hurt. Nothing they could take from him that would approach even a fraction of the loss he'd caused others to feel. He was innocent in his own eyes, his crimes excused by necessity, and nothing they could do to him could make him see his own guilt.

Soq was still looking at him when it happened.

Masaaraq shouted something, twisted her body to intercept, but was standing too far away to stop Go from beheading Barron.

"Run," Go said to Podlove, bloody machete extended, launching herself at Masaaraq.

After that, everything seemed to happen in the space of a single short breath.

KAEV

———————▶

*Y*ou *need to stay focused*, Masaaraq had told him back in the Cabinet, and now he knew why.

*He smells blood, he sees all this frenzied motion, it'd be very easy for
him to go into a total killer rampage.*

Kaev felt it. The bear's rage sang in him. It wasn't harsh or savage.
It was beautiful. It was music. It wasn't the ugly human thing Kaev
had felt before a fight, a spattered mess of wretched emotions like
hate and fear and greed. It was clean and clear and simple.

Keep your attention on the people he needs to be focused on.

But who that was he did not know. The woman he loved was fighting with one of his mothers. The one who had brought him Liam,
fixed his brain, made him whole again.

Masaaraq struck Go with the butt of her staff, knocking her back.

"Hey!" he shouted involuntarily. "Don't!"

Masaaraq looked up for just a second. Just long enough for Go to
strike her in the leg with the machete. Blood flew. Not a lot—the orcamancer's thick leather wrappings had muted the blow—but it was
still hard enough to make her tremble, lose her balance.

Something angry thrashed and rolled in the dark water underneath him. Kaev looked down through the grid. He made eye contact with Atkonartok, and what he saw there made his blood flush frigid.

He ran toward them. He didn't know what he would do when he got there. Who he would help. He wanted to step between them, these two people he loved, stop them from fighting, but the bear had other ideas. He felt split, shattered, confused, and into that confusion stepped Liam.

The bear roared, and he roared with it. Masaaraq flinched at the mirrored sound.

"Kaev!" she shouted. "Stop!"

He couldn't. The animal was in control.

The animal did not like Masaaraq very much.

Kaev felt the pain of the metal cage on its head, the chains she'd kept it in. Years and years of that. Traveling to every settlement and camp and grid city and grim salvage ship in the north. Intermittent glorious moments of being unleashed, when she was in peril or had tracked down some particularly bad people, only to be knocked back out with a tranquilizer dart at the end of it and awaken in chains again.

She didn't want to hurt you, Kaev tried to say. *She was trying to bring you to me. To help us both. We were incomplete. She completed us. Chaining you was the only way.*

She is our mother.

He knew he was speaking into the wind. In a moment of calm he might have been able to make the bear understand. Now, there was no space in its mind for words. For emotions. There was only the kill. For both of them. Whatever human part of him cared to talk Liam out of hurting Masaaraq, it was swiftly swallowed up by the bear's frenzy.

Masaaraq ran for the edge of the Arm. The bear followed. Ora screamed, ran in their direction, and Soq pulled out some kind of weapon that had been strapped to their back, but the orcamancer and the bear were too fast, too far away.

If she makes it to the water she can climb onto the orca and escape, Kaev thought, and wondered whether that was really him thinking it. He knew he didn't want that to happen. She was so close, and he—*he? Which he?*—was gaining on her, just a few more leaping bounds and he'd be on her—he wanted her to trip, fall—

And then she fell.

He heard the gunshot a split second later. Go's brass-knuckled flunky had pulled herself up, taken aim with a trembling arm, and fired. Masaaraq wouldn't have left her alive by accident. She must have shown mercy. And now. Now she was down. Unconscious, not dead. The bear knew by her smell.

A second gunshot—from Soq, this time, visible from the corner of his eye, but it didn't strike him, or his bear, so Kaev's attention did not waver.

Go made a sound, a horrible sound. Kaev was barely there to hear it.

Liam reached Masaaraq's unmoving form. Roared. Reared up on his hind legs. Kaev laughed at the bliss of it. The surge of happiness, the divine perfection of this moment, the kill, the thing he was made for. The bear raised its arms, and so did Kaev. He looked up, at his hands, and they were huge, thick with white fur, capped with long black blade-claws.

Pain split him in half. Broke his brain. He fell to his knees, and then to the ground, shrieking.

Before him, he saw a blur of black and white. And then red. So much red.

The orca had breached, leaped high into the air, and clamped its implacable jaws around the polar bear's midsection. Liam roared, raking his claws against the killer whale's sides, drawing blood in great gouts, digging deep—but not deep enough to break through Atkonartok's thick layer of blubber, soft and yielding yet somehow the most effective armor in the animal kingdom. The orca opened its mouth, clamped down again. Shattered the polar bear's spine. Dragged it into the sea.

Eyes shut, Kaev saw black water. The sea's mouth swallowing him. Opening them, he saw white sky. White snow, falling. Vomit gargled in his throat with every short gasping breath. Why couldn't he just die with the bear? He ached for unconsciousness. He lay on his back, praying for it, but it did not come.

ANKIT

———————▶

A nkit drove the getaway boat. Chim shivered on her shoulder.
Force of habit kept her slow at the start, afraid of a ticket
from the traffic aquadrones, and then she sped up, because surely
all of Safety's toys would still be out of commission or otherwise engaged . . . and then she slowed down again, because where were they
going? And what would they find when they got there?

The orca swam alongside the boat, vocalizing the same plaintive
note again and again. Nudging the boat—lovingly, somehow; apologetically.

"She's grieving," Ora said. "That was her brother."

"Then why did she kill him?" Soq snapped.

"She couldn't help it. She was stuck, with Masaaraq unconscious.
Locked into a frenzy, just like Kaev and Liam were. Even if she wasn't,
she probably couldn't have acted any differently. Masaaraq's life was
at stake. The bear was a half second from killing her."

"Atkonartok could have stopped him without killing him."

"Maybe."

Masaaraq said nothing. She sat as far back in the boat as it was
possible to be, hugging her knees to her chest. Looking out to sea.

Oblivious to the gunshot wound in her shoulder, her machete wound, her blood. Avoiding the city; avoiding Kaev, gasping and mumbling on the floor of the boat. Ignoring the severed hands that lay in her lap.

"We should have taken him prisoner," Soq said.

"We got what we needed from him," Ora said.

"Leaving him alive is a big risk."

"I know. But he needs to know what it's like to live with something like that."

Podlove had screamed and begged when Ora took off his left hand. Promised her mountains of money. Shown staggering repentance. She'd taken her time removing the right one, sawing slowly while Soq held him down. Then they took his tongue. Then they powdered him with clotting agents, bandaged him up, and got off him. Walked away. Carried Kaev to the boat where Ankit waited.

"Where are we going?" she'd asked then, but no one had spoken.

She asked it again now.

"Go's ship," Soq said.

"Ballsy move," Ankit said. "After you just shot her in the head in the middle of the grid. You don't think her army might have something to say about it?"

"I'm her kid," Soq said. "Everybody knows it. The next three hours will be crucial. The software war is winding down, but it'll take that long for the city's infrastructure to reassert itself. Drones, cams, witness reports—I don't think what I did will reach the ship for a little bit. I think I'll be able to muster enough important players into my corner by then. I have the advantage—no one else knows the time is right for a power play—and with Dao dead there's no one with a more legitimate claim to the throne."

"Or maybe none of those things will happen."

"Right. And I'll get killed." Soq shrugged. "Let's see what we can do about making that not happen."

Ankit recognized it, this look on Soq's face. This fearlessness that probably wasn't really fearlessness. More like—the excitement out-weighed the fear, the potential positive outcomes overshadowed the potential negative ones. She didn't share it, but she'd seen it before. On her scaler friends, the ones who came from even less than she did, the orphans who hadn't lucked into a family or had ended up in an awful one. The ones who climbed the buildings beside her and stood there looking out at Qaanaaq without the sick feeling in the pit of their stomachs, the fear of falling, the fear of imprisonment, who had nothing but the open-armed embrace of the night to come, with whatever good or awful things waited for them inside it.

Soq squatted down beside Kaev. He looked at Soq, looked through them. "Shhhh," Soq said, and put their hands on their father's shoulders. So much muscle in there, so much strength. Yet here he was, helpless. Whispering a word that sounded like *God*? Chim climbed down from Ankit's shoulder to huddle up against Kaev, poking him tenderly from time to time, warming herself with his body heat.

Green flares spouted intermittently at the end of an Arm, un-scheduled methane ventilations, less spectacular by daylight. Snow fell faster now.

"She wouldn't have hesitated to kill us all," Soq said, and Ankit saw tears streaming down their face. "Or most of us. I'm a maybe, Go might have thought she could scare me into silence, but you two . . ." Soq pointed to Ora and Masaaraq, grief wracking every word. "She'd have done her damnedest to put the blame somewhere else, and that would have been a lot easier if the Killer Whale Woman and her Cabinet-escapee lover were corpses who couldn't tell a different story."

"He won't care," Ora said, touching Kaev's sweaty forehead. "All he knows is, he loved her."

Soq nodded. Their face was a blotchy knot of guilt, sadness, rage. "Is there . . . can we . . . do . . . anything?"

"He'll be in a lot of pain for a very long while. When I was in the

Cabinet, and my eagle was sick, I was lucky enough to know it was happening. To have some time, to help ease the transition. By bonding people, I built up the kind of bonds that soothed the trauma, but it happened slowly. Having been through what he's just been through, Kaev might not be able to last that long."

". . . Last?"

"He might choose . . . not to stick around," she said sadly. "Not to *be*. I almost did, ten times or more."

"But people need him," Ankit said. "There's a lot of people with the breaks, suffering really badly. He can help them, and they'll help him."

"We'll get to work," Soq said, pressing a cool hand to their father's hot forehead. "As soon as we get back. I know some of Go's soldiers must have the breaks. And then we'll head to Arm Eight, where lots of people have it." Soq stood, and Ankit's heart caught in her throat, to see the power that Soq radiated. Power, and something else. Lots of people had power. Fyodorovna had power; Go did. What Soq had was different. Power, and something more—the strength to do the right thing, the hard thing, the wisdom to know what that was. "We're going to fix him."

Ankit looked up from her screen and said to Soq, "They're finished. Your friend Jeong finished processing all the escapees. He's taking advantage of the chaos, got half of Go's soldiers ferrying them to their new homes. Word is, he can get pretty bossy."

"He can," Soq said. "And it's good to hear that they're already obeying him."

"The two of you might have a shot."

"We can't stay here," Masaaraq said, the first words she'd uttered since regaining consciousness.

"We can't leave," Ora said. "We have work to do. People to heal. Kaev most of all."

"And then we go," Masaaraq said.

"Why?"

Masaaraq opened her mouth, like it was the easiest question she'd ever heard, the most obvious answer, but then she said nothing. She looked out at the open sea. *She must yearn for it the way her orca does,* Ankit thought. "We're nomads," she said, finally. "Home is where we make it. Where we're together."

"Exactly," Ora said. "That's the great gift of living life as a nomad— you don't get attached to things, don't believe that you're safe because you have a roof over your head today. You don't put your faith in a physical space when home is something you can take with you. But it also means that you accept what comes your way. You make the most of the places you end up in. And now we're here. In Qaa-naaq. Maybe it isn't forever. But maybe it is."

Masaaraq did not respond. Ankit wondered if she knew already, that the argument was over, the battle won, and not by her. She loved Ora. That was the most important thing. Every other consideration was secondary to that.

"Forgive me if I'm out of line," Ankit said to her, to this person who was one of her mothers, "but you really never stopped? Twenty years, thirty years, you never said *fuck it* and spent a decade or so living on a beach or working in a steel mill or something?"

"Odd jobs here and there," Masaaraq said. "Waiting out the winter, or saving up money when I couldn't find any syndicate shipments to raid. My hands didn't stay clean, mind you."

"Polar bear kibble is expensive," Ora said solemnly, and Masaaraq shocked everyone by chuckling.

"And you?" Ankit asked, her heart full and glorious, unspeakably happy. "Did you ever stop believing she'd come?"

"I stopped waiting for it," Ora said. "For the longest time, I was certain that it would happen. Eventually I stopped being certain. I stopped thinking to myself, *If not today, soon.* But I still woke up every morning and thought, *Maybe today.* Before I thought anything else."

Soq said, "I hated it, at first. *City Without a Map*. Didn't know what you were trying to do. But now I love it. I don't know if that's maturity, or it's just because . . . well, because the person who gave me the breaks loved it. I can feel him, sometimes. Hear him. Not like memories. Like something still alive. Is that possible?"

"They live in us," Ora said. "We carry them in our hearts, even after they are gone. Our ancestors do not depart. Our people knew that long before the breaks."

"Can I ask you a question about the broadcast?"

Ora smiled, touched her grandchild's hand. "Of course."

"Who are you talking to? Who's your audience? At first I—he—we—thought it was intended for immigrants. New arrivals. Then I thought it was about people with the breaks. Now . . ."

Ora shrugged. "I don't know, either. In the beginning I was talking to other people in the Cabinet with me. People who were struggling. Sick, sad, hungry. Then I realized . . . it's more than that."

Soq awaited additional information. Ora's smile was deep and distant. Snow made the city into a shadow, a jagged mountain ridge studded with light. The four of them huddled closer in the boat, around Kaev, each with one hand pressed to his body. They made a square, a circle, a coven, a brigade, and Ankit felt confident that there was nothing they could not accomplish when they stood together.

"Tell me a story," Soq said, leaning back to rest between Ora's legs. "I bet you're full of them."

"I am," Ora said. Her eyes were on Qaanaaq, and they saw so much more than Ankit did. Ora saw the city as a hundred different people had seen it, arriving at twilight or departing at dawn, as exiled kings and political prisoners and wide-eyed children. She shut her eyes and began to speak.

"People would say she came to Qaanaaq in a skiff towed by a killer whale harnessed to the front like a horse . . ."

ACKNOWLEDGMENTS

————————➤

Books have big families. Here are the people who helped make this one happen:

Seth Fishman, again, and always. The most magnificent man and agent and writer all in one. The Gernert Company team of Will Roberts and Rebecca Gardner and Ellen Coughtrey and Jack Gernert.

Zachary Wagman, who loved this book—and whose editorial eye and ear made it much more worthy of being loved. Big love too to Ecco comrades Meghan Deans, Emma Janaskie, Miriam Parker, and Martin Wilson.

Neil Gaiman, who knows why.

Bradley Teitelbaum of White Rabbit Tattoo, who put a gorgeous permanent orca on my arm to commemorate this book. Look him up before you decide where to get your next—or first—tattoo. Kalyani-Aindri Sanchez, genius photographer, for the mind-blowingly awesome author shots. James Tracy—role model in organizing, role model in writing, and one hell of a model American.

Sheila Williams, wise and magnificent editor of *Asimov's Science Fiction*, who published "Calved," the short story that was my first visit to the fictional floating city of Qaanaaq. And Gardner Dozois,

Neil Clarke, and Jonathan Strahan, for including "Calved" in their best-of-the-year anthologies.

Lisa Bolekaja, who slapped some sense into me about the title of that story when absolutely everyone else wanted me to call it "Ice Is the Truth of Water" (which, besides being an objectively less-awesome title, would almost certainly have earned me a cease-and-desist letter from Ted Chiang's attorneys for straying too close to his titles "The Truth of Fact, the Truth of Feeling" and "Hell is the Absence of God").

The Wyrd Words Writing Retreat, which gave me the chance to work out the kinks on this hot mess in an enchanted castle fellowship with incredibly gifted writers and readers. Eric San Juan, Craig Laurence Gidney, Mary Anne Mohanraj, Stephen Segal, Valya Lupescu, Scott Woods, and K. Tempest Bradford all gave me vital advice and support and critique and "definitely don't do this."

My beloved Israelis, who—in addition to a lifetime of fantasticness—hosted me during the difficult time that this book was on submission and distracted me with tons of delicious food and strong coffee and tourism and love: Lynne, Avshalom, Oded, Shmuela, Leah, Miri, Liat, Amit, Gal, Dror, Mia, Yonatan, Roy, Daniel, Noam, Tamir, Romi, Ori, and Shira!

My sister, Sarah, and her husband, Eric—and my nephew, Hudson, for whose sake I'll keep on fighting like hell to keep a future like this one from coming to be.

My mother, Deborah Miller—survivor and inspiration.

Finally and forever, my husband, Juancy—firebender, crystal gem, roustabout—who I know would bend the sky and break the sea and the laws of physics to come rescue me, even if it took thirty years, no matter how many evildoers he had to slaughter in the process. Love you more than the earth we stand on.